I SHAVED MY LEGS FOR THIS?!

Theresa Alan
Holly Chamberlin
Marcia Evanick
Lisa Plumbey

KENSINGTON BOOKS
www.kensingtonbooks.com

KENSINGTON BOOKS are published by

Kensington Publishing Corp.
850 Third Avenue
New York, NY 10022

All Kensington titles, imprints, and distributed lines are available at special quantity discounts for bulk purchases for sales promotions, premiums, fundraising, educational, or institutional use.

Special book excerpts or customized printings can also be created to fit specific needs. For details, write or phone the office of the Kensington Special Sales Manager: Attn: Special Sales Department. Kensington Publishing Corp., 850 Third Avenue, New York, NY 10022. Phone: 1-800-221-2647.

Kensington and the K logo Reg. U.S. Pat. & TM Off.

ISBN 0-7582-1085-X

First Kensington Trade Paperback Printing: January 2006
10 9 8 7 6 5 4 3 2 1

Printed in the United States of America

Books by Theresa Alan

WHO YOU KNOW
SPUR OF THE MOMENT
THE GIRLS' GLOBAL GUIDE TO GUYS
GIRLS WHO GOSSIP

Books by Holly Chamberlin

LIVING SINGLE
THE SUMMER OF US
BABYLAND

Books by Marcia Evanick

CATCH OF THE DAY
CHRISTMAS ON CONRAD STREET
BLUEBERRY HILL
A BERRY MERRY CHRISTMAS
HARBOR NIGHTS

Books by Lisa Plumley

MAKING OVER MIKE
FALLING FOR APRIL
RECONSIDERING RILEY
PERFECT TOGETHER
PERFECT SWITCH
JOSIE DAY IS COMING HOME
ONCE UPON A CHRISTMAS

Published by Kensington Publishing Corporation

CONTENTS

Love Is Blind (or At Least Nearsighted)

Theresa Alan

Chapter 1

So here I am, out with my gorgeous date. And his date. A little background:

I'm on a blind date with this cute guy named Craig. He's a friend of a friend of my friend Jenna. He's new to the Chicago area and single and Jenna assured me he was cute. But when she first suggested that I go out on a blind date with him I was hesitant. For one thing, dating is hard enough when you know what you're getting into (or at least think you do). For another thing, well, Jenna's taste in men leaves something to be desired.

I love Jenna more than anything, but she's not exactly normal. She works as a hairdresser at the salon where I work as a makeup artist, and you just have to take one look at her to know that she makes her living in some sort of creative field. She couldn't get away with wearing her long dark hair streaked maroon working at some desk job, that's for sure. She makes her own clothes and beaded jewelry. She covered her red Converse tennis shoes in hundreds of rhinestones to give them a little pizzazz. She's the kind of person who will gladly be the first person out on an empty dance floor despite the fact that she's a spectacularly bad dancer—she jerks her body around paying no attention whatsoever to the actual beat or rhythm of the music, and she flings her elbows about as if she's trying to flee from a burning theater and is attempting to gore the people standing in the way of her escape. And she does this move with her feet that looks like a cat trying to cover up its waste in the kitty litter box. It's not pretty, trust me. Plus, more than once I've seen her go spinning around so fast on the dance floor that she loses her balance and goes flying into a table bordering the dance area, causing drinks to go flying and sending innocent bystanders tumbling to the floor (think of the *Saturday Night Live* character Mary Katherine Gallagher).

Anyway, I love Jenna because she is such a free spirit. I love that she thinks for herself and doesn't worry about what others think of her. However, do I necessarily want to go out with men chosen by a woman who thinks that wearing knee-high orange-striped gym socks with olive shorts is a good idea? Under ordinary circumstances, the answer would be no. But when she told me about Craig, I decided what the hell. I thought, what's the worst that could happen? I'll end up with another funny story to share as I paint the faces of brides on their wedding day and aspiring actresses before they get their headshots taken.

Craig called me a couple days ago and we chatted briefly. He asked me what I wanted to do on our date, and I suggested that we go to the amusement park because it was something we could do outdoors. It's been such a gorgeous summer that it seemed logical for us to be outside enjoying the weather. He was up for the plan but didn't know how to get there so I offered to drive. When I picked him up, I couldn't believe how good-looking he was. I felt momentarily stunned that his DNA could possibly have been assembled into such striking features. His smile was of the megawatt variety that reminded me of cartoon advertisements for toothpaste where the character smiles and a little white star glints off his teeth with a little *ting!* noise. His arms were thick with muscles and I suspected a six-pack lurked beneath his white polo shirt.

I tried not to let myself get too excited, however. Just because I was attracted to him didn't mean he was attracted to me. For all I knew, he thought I looked like a failed science experiment or Mu Shu Pork after it's been in the fridge for three weeks or something.

We drove to the park making polite chitchat.

"Jenna tells me you grew up in Wisconsin," he said.

"Yep, a tiny town about forty minutes from Madison."

"Do you go up there very often?"

"I used to when my parents still lived there, but they retired to Arizona three years ago. Now I don't go back very often, although Jenna and I are going there tomorrow for a wedding. What about you? Where did you grow up?"

"Florida."

"Ooh, winter in Chicago is going to be brutal on you. What brought you here?"

"Job transfer."

"Ah." We drove in silence for a moment before Craig asked me what I like to do for fun. "I read a lot. I love movies."

"I like movies, too," he said. He told me about an art film he saw recently.

"I didn't see that one," I said. As soon as I said it I worried that he would think I was some uncouth simpleton who never saw artsy movies, so I blundered on. "I like movies like that. That's one I'd like to see. Yeah. I like art films, independent films. I have a friend who works at the Telluride Film Festival every summer."

What on *earth* did that have to do with anything? Why did those words come out of my mouth? That was apropos of nothing. *Think,* Heather, *think.* You need a follow-up comment to somehow tie in that non sequitur. "Have you seen any other movies lately?" It was the best I could come up with on short notice.

We talked about movies a little more, but it was a pulling-teeth type conversation. I wasn't too worried—first dates are always a little awkward.

Little did I know how awkward it could get . . .

I parked in the vast parking lot and we paid the extravagant entrance fee. The amusement park was a riot of noise and colors and eye-catching excitement: spinning rides with flashing lights, an endless string of souvenir stands to separate parents from their hard-earned cash, park staff walking around in Bugs Bunny and Daffy Duck costumes pretending to be cheerful when inside they were dying of heatstroke. Screams from the roller coaster riders filled the air and the area thrummed with energy and commerce and squealing children strung out on sugar from ice cream, funnel cake, and colorful lollipops that were bigger than their heads.

For a time, things seemed to be going well for Craig and me. We screamed our heads off on the Demon, the Vertical Velocity, and the Viper; we ate our weight in cotton candy. The only bad thing was that it was hot and humid out, and waiting in the long lines for the rides gave us no protection from the heat. Sticky pools of sweat gathered under my bra and beneath my armpits and across my forehead and upper lip. My deodorant was losing the battle with each passing moment. I knew without having to look in a mirror that my eyeliner was bleeding and clumpy mascara boogers were forming on my eyelashes and that the humidity was electrifying my hair into frizzy lightning bolts jolting out from my skull. Though I suspected that I wasn't looking my best, I wondered if Craig and I might have a future together despite the fact that he looked like a *Baywatch* star whereas if I were cast for TV, it would be as something like "Girl in line at Drugstore Number 4."

I was feeling self-conscious about looking like a "Before" picture with my model-perfect date when we passed by a booth where a radio station was doing this promo for a dating service. It was hosting a contest where a woman chose one of three men from the audience as her date and they would get an evening out paid for by the radio station. It was a *Dating Game* kind of situation: the woman was behind a screen and couldn't see her three choices. She had to ask a series of questions and pick her date based on their answers. Anyway, at the very moment Craig and I were passing by the makeshift stage, the announcer was asking for men to volunteer. Guys were killing themselves to be picked and the moment I saw the girl they'd be going out with I could see why. She was breathtaking. She seemed to me to be about eight feet tall, but then, I'm pretty short so that could skew my perspective. I'm sure she was only about 5'10", but compared to me the girl was a giantess. She looked eerily like Jennifer Connelly, with long dark hair cascading down her back in buoyant waves. The problem was that all the guys trying to rush the stage to get their chance at her were mutts. Mullet-haired, potbellied monsters. Obviously, these cave trolls would not be good for publicity for the dating service. The radio station needed a handsome-prince type and fast.

It was Craig's gleaming smile that did it. One smile from him and the brilliant whiteness of his teeth beamed out like a spotlight and caught the attention of staff people running the *Dating Game* show. In a flash we were accosted by a kid in a KRTG *Rock On!* T-shirt.

"Hey, would you mind coming up onstage? We need another guy up there."

"Oh, thanks, but I'm with someone," Craig pointed to me. I felt a wave of relief. Most guys would have ditched me in a nanosecond for the Jennifer Connelly look-alike goddess. I thought it spoke well of Craig not to abandon me.

"Come on, it'll be fun. Everyone who competes will get a free dinner at Shaw's."

Shaw's Crab House is a pricey seafood restaurant. For a free meal there I might have left even the beautiful Craig behind in my dust. A free lobster dinner is a free lobster dinner, after all.

"Thanks, but really, I can't," Craig said. Even as he protested, the kid in the *Rock On!* T-shirt was essentially pushing him onstage. Craig flashed me a look of "What should I do?" I just shrugged and smiled, thinking it might be fun, and anyway, the chances were only one in three that Jennifer Connelly would choose him.

Jennifer Connelly chose him.

After Jennifer, whose real name was actually Raquel, asked her litany of inane questions (If you could be a kind of tree, what kind of tree would you be? It's a cold day: what sort of hot drink would you prefer to drink to warm up? What is your favorite color underwear?), the announcer asked her to choose Bachelor Number 1, 2, or 3. Craig was Number 3. As I stood there with both my fingers crossed, silently chanting, "Not Number 3. Not Number 3," the traitorous crowd cheated. The audience booed when the announcer said, "Bachelor Number 1?" They hissed when he said, "Bachelor Number 2?" And they whooped and hollered and cheered when he said, "Bachelor Number 3?" Just because Bachelor Number 3 was a Brad Pitt god among men, the crowd chose him.

Shallow bastards.

"We have a winner!" the announcer said. "Raquel, come meet your bachelor!"

Raquel emerged from behind the screen in all her graceful-limbed perfection and squealed when she saw her handsome date. She laughed and got teary-eyed, as if she'd just won the Miss America Pageant, and gave Craig a hug.

In that moment I came to deeply hate her.

"Raquel, meet Craig," the announcer said. "Tonight a limousine will pick you up and take you out to a wonderful meal at Shaw's Crab House, followed by a private boat ride down the Chicago River and an all-expense-paid night in a suite at the Four Seasons Hotel! I want to thank all our bachelors for participating today. To show our appreciation, I have vouchers for a free dinner for two for all our participants. If you don't have a date to accompany you for a romantic dinner, remember single-no-more.com! Just post your profiles and find the right match for you."

The crowd cheered and clapped and the announcer said some other things that I couldn't hear because I was too busy trying to figure out if there was a way I could have Raquel briefly kidnapped by terrorists. Then Craig and Raquel were pulled offstage to a tent. I saw one of the radio station staff people in a *Rock On!* T-shirt talking to them. Craig gestured back in my direction.

That's about the time I started getting a very bad feeling. I stood there melting in the sweltering heat for what felt like an exceptionally long span of time. It was so hot out I thought my brain might just be liquefying, but despite the hardship, I continued mentally plotting Raquel's kidnapping until I finally saw Craig come out of the tent. I was excited for only a moment when, to my dismay, I saw that Raquel was with him.

"Hi, Heather," Craig said to me. "I'm really sorry. I didn't expect that to happen."

I wasn't thrilled that he would be going out for a luxurious night on the town with Raquel tonight, but what was I supposed to do? This was our first date after all. It was a little early to demand that he be exclusive. But why was she with him *now*, while he was supposed to be with *me*, on our *date*?

"Uh-huh," I said, waiting for an explanation.

"I'm really sorry about this," Craig said, "but the radio station asked for Raquel and me to spend some time together this afternoon so they can get some promotional photographs for their Web site."

It wasn't until that moment that I noticed the photographer who had followed them out of the tent.

"All three of us can have fun together!" Raquel said.

And this is how it came to be that I am on a date with a gorgeous man and his gorgeous date.

Chapter 2

For the record, I am not unattractive. I'm pretty, but in a rather unflashy way. For one thing, my nose is not dainty or buttonlike. It's not so atrocious that small children scream and run away in fright, and it's certainly not ghastly enough to warrant the pain and expense of surgery, but every now and then I'll see a picture taken of me from the exact wrong angle and I'll think, "Who is that elephant-trunked girl in this picture? Surely that's not me." The point is, I am no match for an eight-foot tall twin of Jennifer Connelly.

"Hi, I'm Raquel," she says to me. She smiles and shakes my hand.

"It's very nice to meet you," I lie. "I'm Heather."

"This is kind of awkward," Craig says, smiling.

"How long have you known each other?" Raquel asks.

"Actually, this is our first date. We met for the first time just a few hours ago," Craig says.

"A blind date? Aren't blind dates a hoot?" Raquel asks. "What ride should we go on next? Oh! The Viper! Doesn't that look like fun?"

"It is fun, but the line is about forty miles long and we've already gone on it," I say. If I were a better person, I could roll with the punches and pretend this is no big deal. I could act like I'm extremely happy to have someone who looks like a movie star join me on my date when I know that my makeup has melted and my hair is doing its impression of Albert Einstein. But I'm not. A better person, that is.

"Please?"

Craig gives me a "What are you going to do?" look. I want to throw a tantrum that involves kicking Raquel sharply in the shins, and yet somehow I don't think this would give Craig the best impression of me. So instead I smile and say, "Sure."

As we wait in line, the photographer instructs Craig and Raquel to lean in close together and smile and laugh. They both look like models and I feel like the stumpy helper person whose job is to scurry about fetching things for the beautiful people. I'm the nerdy one who is supposed to mop their brow and freshen their drinks and stay the hell out of the picture frame.

The photographer shoots about forty thousand shots of Craig with his arm around Raquel. Raquel's long locks are flowing gently in the breeze while my hair is shellacked to my sweat-soaked forehead. I ask you: where is the justice in this?

There is no escaping the relentless sun as we're herded through the rat maze of a line. Despite the fact we're in a suburb of what's known as the Windy City, today there isn't even the slightest breeze. My clothes are sticking to my skin and I swear it's so hot that my sweat is sizzling on my flesh like oil in a hot pan.

I know I should plaster a smile on my face. My mother spent my entire childhood telling me how pretty I am when I smile. It's true that my smile is probably my best feature. I lucked out by being born with naturally beautiful lips. And thanks to two years of braces and nights spent locked into unseemly metal-mouth scaffolding (i.e., headgear), I have perfectly straight teeth. However, I'm finding it a bit of a challenge to smile just now.

Every few hours, the line moves forward a little and we're able to shuffle forward a few inches. As we wait in the interminably long line, Raquel treats us to her life story.

"I'm a hostess at Uno's? The pizza place?"

Her statements are all questions.

Stop scowling. Smile. You look pretty when you smile and scary when you scowl. The inner voice is part my own conscience and part my mother come to haunt me. I try to smile, but it's a teeth-gritted type of smile that I suspect is even more frightening than my scowl. Anyway, how can I pretend to be happy when my handsome date is viciously being stolen away from me?

If my friend Jenna were here, she'd say something really annoying and upbeat about how I should stay positive and not worry about the future because we never know what might happen. God, I can't *stand* cheerful people. But I'm telling you right now, I'm no psychic, yet I can see Craig's future and I just don't think I'm in it.

Why did I agree to go out with a stranger? I've gone on one other blind date before and it was just as disastrous. About a year ago I decided I would take an active role in kick-starting my love life and I told everyone I knew that I was willing to try anything, I just wanted to get out there and see what happened. One of the customers at the salon where I work told me she had a handsome, wealthy thirty-six-year-old nephew who was straight but had never been married. He sounded too good to be true and, of course, it turned out that he was. But I didn't know that so I said she could give him my number, which she did. He called me and we talked for about half an hour. He seemed confident without being arrogant, nice but not *too* nice, smart but not dauntingly so. We arranged to meet the following weekend.

Just like today, that date started out well. He was decent looking and he seemed normal enough.

Ha!

But that's the tricky thing about dating, isn't it? When they fool you into thinking they're normal and you actually let yourself get a little excited?

He suggested that we meet at an upscale restaurant. I felt

like a princess, drinking from a crystal glass and dining at a table with a rich white linen tablecloth. The waiters wore black suits and white gloves. I sipped my wine and looked across the table at my date and I thought *I could get used to living like this.* I imagined a lifetime of sumptuous meals with him in our future. That's the embarrassing part—admitting to myself how attracted to him I was before I knew about his seamy dark side.

He wasn't shy about letting me know just how extravagantly wealthy he was. I don't want you to think I'm only out to marry a rich guy because that isn't the case. But if I happened to fall in love with a billionaire, well, that wouldn't exactly be a bad thing, now would it?

We shared a delicious appetizer of mussels steamed in a garlic-and-white wine sauce with sun-dried tomatoes. Just as our entrees were being served and I was thinking to myself, *How could this guy possibly be thirty-six and still single? He's so interesting! He's such a catch!* He said, "You are so beautiful, I just came."

I thought he couldn't have possibly said what I thought he just said. I blamed the ambient background noise and decided that surely he must have said something else and I had misunderstood him. When we knew each other better at some point in the future I would ask him to tell me what he had really said, and we would laugh over my mistake.

Over our meal I told him about my job working as a makeup artist. He seemed genuinely interested in my stories about making up the faces of socialites and minor celebrities and brides on their wedding day. And then do you know what he said? He said, "You are so beautiful, I just came again."

That time there was no mistaking it. I stood up, threw my napkin down over my half-finished meal, and said, "That's it. This date is over." And I marched out of the restaurant, outraged and deeply disgusted.

When I told the story later, I turned it into a joke, making my friends and clients laugh. I kidded about how it was no selling point for him to be multiply orgasmic without me even touching him. "Could you imagine if I actually kissed or caressed him? He'd come before I could pucker my lips. Talk about premature!" I kidded. But the truth was, his behavior really creeped me out. He was essentially a verbal flasher. I want to believe in the general goodness of people, but that experience made me wary about getting close to men I don't know.

Yet enough time had elapsed between then and now that I forgot just what a dangerous gamble this whole dating thing is. Now I remember.

At last Craig, Raquel, and I get toward the front of the line. The photographer, a thin, short blond man in his early twenties, tells Raquel and Craig that he'll be waiting on the north side of the ride to get some shots of them coming down the steep drop after the loop-de-loop thing. It's not until he says this that I realize what I should have realized all along: I don't have a partner to go on the roller coaster with. I'm on my own.

Now that we're at the front of the line, things move much more quickly. We're pushed forward by the excitement of the kids in line behind us. Craig and Raquel slide into the front of the car, sitting next to each other. A fourteen-year-old boy in a polyester uniform asks me who I'm with.

"Um, by myself," I say, almost in a whisper.

"Do we have any singles? Any single parties?" he belts out, raising his hand up in the air. Everyone is staring at me, the big loser, who is still all on my own at the age of thirty-three. I don't have a partner for the roller coaster or for my life. I am a freak, and if it wasn't obvious before, it is now, because the entire ride is being held up until we can find me, freak girl, someone to ride with.

At last an enormously fat teenage boy emerges from the throng. His armpit sweat extends all the way down his sides; his face drips with it.

A sweaty fat kid is my partner. That's perfect. Really just perfect.

The moment he slides into the car next to me I realize it's

even worse than I thought. Even though my deodorant is being tested like crazy today, at least I started the day with some, as well as with a shower. I'm fairly certain you'd have to go back a week or two to find the last time this kid showered. And as for deodorant, I don't think he's heard about this handy invention yet.

Kill me now.

The ride takes off and we begin climbing up in preparation for our first plummeting descent. My ears fill with the ominous click-click-click sound of the car being hoisted into the stratosphere. Once I get the hang of only breathing through my mouth, the ride is pretty fun, though the whole thing only seems to last a moment. After all that standing around in line, you'd think the ride would last for longer than a scream or two, but no.

I get off the ride feeling windblown, wobbly kneed, and a little shell-shocked. It takes a moment for my heart to get unstuck from my throat and fall back into place.

"Wasn't that a hoot?" Raquel asks. "So, what do you guys do?" Before either of us can answer, she continues talking. "I'm studying to be an acupuncturist? It can help people with pain, addiction, problems with their marriage? Anything really."

I want to ask her how it can help with a bad marriage. I'm genuinely interested. I've never gone to an acupuncturist, but I definitely believe in homeopathic and other alternative medicine, so I'm curious to learn more, but she won't stop talking long enough for me to ask. I watch Craig watch her as she talks. He clings to her every word with rapt interest. My mood does its impersonation of the Titanic: it just sinks.

The next few hours pass in a whirl of rides, lines, and Raquel's unceasing monologue. At four o'clock, I decide I've logged a sufficient amount of time with my date and his date and I suggest that it's time for me and Craig to go home.

"Um, you know, I sort of lost the girlfriends I came with?" Raquel says. "Do you think maybe I could get a ride home?"

Craig and Raquel look at me. What am I supposed to do? I

can't exactly leave the girl stranded even if I am secretly hoping that she'll accidentally trip and fall off a cliff into a shallow river infested with angry, ravenous piranhas.

"Sure," I say with a smile. I should get an Academy Award for this performance.

We walk out to the parking lot. Craig offers Raquel the front seat and she takes it.

I buckle up and glance at my glasses, which are in their case, sitting on my dashboard. I really should wear my glasses when I drive. I'm not terribly nearsighted, but my vision is poor enough that it's hard for me to see street signs without them, at least until I'm pretty close to them. Unfortunately, I don't like my glasses because I think they make my nose look even more pronounced than it already is, so I often don't wear them when I should. You'd damn well better believe that I'm not going to put them on now.

It turns out that Raquel lives in a suburb that's an hour out of my way. *An hour* I have to drive to get this girl home. Who in the history of the world has had to drive their date's date home? Every second I'm stuck in traffic or stopped at a red light, I wonder what I did to deserve this. Was I a war criminal in a former life? A child abuser? A Republican?

The whole ride there Raquel tells us about being an acupuncture student. She complains about how hard the tests are because she has to learn all about the human anatomy. I want to ask her what exactly she thought she'd learn in acupuncture school if not for a lesson or two on the human body, but again, she doesn't stop talking long enough to let anyone else speak. Until I met Raquel, I would have been open to seeing an acupuncturist, but now I'm skeptical. If a girl this fluff-brained can successfully get through school, I wonder just how safe the art form really is. I'm sure there are lots of non-fluff-brained acupuncturists in the world, but how would you know if you were getting one of the smart variety or one of the fluff-brained sort?

I pull into her driveway, which leads to a huge house. She has to live with her parents because if she can afford such a mansion on the salary of a hostess/acupuncture student, that can only mean she's independently wealthy, and I refuse to believe I live in a world that is so patently unfair.

She hops out of the car. Leaning in the open door she says, "Thank you for the ride! Um, so Craig, I guess I'll see you in a couple hours for the rest of our date?"

"Yep, see you again soon."

"See you then. Heather, it was nice meeting you."

" 'Bye," I say, trying for a smile as I watch her flounce away.

Craig gets out from the backseat and joins me up front.

"I'm sorry things didn't exactly turn out . . . well, I mean, this wasn't your ordinary date," Craig says.

"It's not your fault."

We don't say anything for the entire drive into the city. What is there to say? I can see that Craig is off in his own world, dreaming of Raquel.

Over the course of the afternoon, I've felt Craig's interest in me fade like a colored T-shirt that's been washed a few thousand times. The excitement I felt between us at the beginning of the day is gone. I hate this part of dating: the rejection. Suddenly I start thinking that maybe I'm just not pretty enough or smart enough or witty enough. When I'm not dating, I actually have a decent sense of self-esteem, but one bad date sends me spiraling into a major self-esteem crisis. I know these feelings of self-doubt will pass in a day or two, but right now I'm ready to swear off dating forever. I know that's not a healthy way to think, and after I've had some time to lick my wounds I'll be ready to go out there once again, but not just yet. I'm sure as hell never going on a blind date again. The odds of it working out even when you know something about the guy are pretty low. Your chances of connecting romantically with a stranger are infinitesimal.

I get to Craig's condo in the city and pull into the circular driveway in front of the front door. "Thanks for an *interesting* day," he says with a smile.

"I won't forget it, that's for sure."

"It was very nice meeting you." He gets out of the car.

"It was nice meeting you, too."

He smiles and gives a wave, and then closes the door and walks away. It's the sound of the door swinging shut that slams home this knowledge: he didn't even pretend like he was going to call me. He didn't even give me the "I'll call you" lie.

Ouch. I pause a moment and take a deep breath. Feeling shaky, I put the car into drive. Just as I'm pulling into traffic, Jenna calls me on my cell phone.

"How did it go?" she asks.

"Well, he was gorgeous, just like you said."

"See! I knew it would work out."

"I didn't say it worked out. In fact, it was something of a colossal disaster."

"Oh." She says nothing for a beat. "What happened?"

"How about I tell you in person over drinks and fattening food?"

"Sounds good. I'm just hanging out at home. I'll order a pizza."

"I'll be over in about fifteen minutes."

"See you soon."

Jenna lives in an apartment complex close to Wrigley Field. There is no game today so I am blessed with good parking karma and get a spot on the street only a couple of blocks from where she lives.

Jenna's apartment is like Jenna herself: strange and yet somehow likeable. It's filled with candles and crystals and batik-print fabrics. It's a one-room efficiency so space is at a premium. She has a white wicker daybed that serves as both a bed and a couch. She doesn't have a kitchen table or a desk but she does have a foldable massage table that she bought when she thought she might want to become a massage therapist. Then she realized she had no desire to touch the naked flesh of saggy middle-aged men and she decided to stick to doing hair. She uses the table to store boxes of beads, buttons, threads, and other miscellaneous craftsy stuff.

A half-packed suitcase is open on her daybed.

"I'm almost packed," she assures me. "Are you?"

I nod. "I'm ready. I didn't bring much. Just a dress for the wedding and something to drive home in the next day."

We're going to my hometown for a wedding tomorrow. I went to Wisconsin for a couple days around Christmas to visit my friend Cleo, who was in town visiting her family. When I was there, I ran into another girl I went to high school with, Carmen. Carmen moved to town when her father moved the headquarters of the furniture empire he'd started from the East, where land was expensive, to Wisconsin, where land was cheap. Carmen and I became friends, but our friendship was a volatile one. Carmen is the only child of incredibly wealthy parents, and I'm afraid to say that the spoiled-only-child cliché applied to her in spades. (I'm an only child, too, but my parents didn't have the means to spoil me, much to my regret.) She could be a lot of fun to be around—as long as she got her own way. If I ever dared to suggest that I wasn't on this earth solely to do her bidding, she would stomp off in a huff. We always made up eventually. She had a swimming pool and horses and a pool table at her house; I couldn't resist. I sold my soul for an indoor swimming pool, it's true, but I defy you to find a fifteen-year-old who wouldn't do the same.

When I ran into her at the mall at Christmas, she told me she was getting married. Of course I said all the appropriate things about how happy I was for her. When she invited me to the wedding, I had to admit I was curious to see what sort of ritzy affair would be given for the heir of a hugely successful furniture chain. So I said that it sounded like fun. And I hoped like hell that I would find a boyfriend between then and now. But I didn't. So I'm bringing Jenna as my date instead.

"I'm going to make martinis, 'kay?" Jenna asks.

"Martinis? I'm not sure that's a good idea. Do you have something with a little less octane? A beer or something?"

"You know I don't like beer."

"I know, but some people keep things like that around for guests."

"Not me. You'll drink martinis and you'll like it." The

sound of her buzzer zaps through the air. "That must be the pizza. You get the pizza, I'll get the drinks."

I do as I am told and we meet back at Jenna's daybed. She moves her half-packed suitcase off the bed and hands me a martini. She makes the best martinis in the world. I swear I take one sip and I'm half-snockered.

"Okay, tell me everything," she says. She hands me a paper plate and as I take a cheesy slice of pizza, I tell her my tale of dating woe.

Jenna tries to muster an appropriate expression of sympathy as she says, "I'm so sorry," but before the words are even completely out of her mouth she starts laughing, this wild-hyena kind of cackle that wracks her entire body.

"My ego was so badly bruised today I may never recover. I need sympathy," I say. I try to hide my smile, but the whole thing does seem sort of funny.

"I'm sorry, I'm sorry." She stops laughing for about ten seconds and then erupts into gales of laughter.

"Are you done yet?"

"Sorry. Do you want a DoveBar? Some chocolate might cheer you up." She takes a huge bite of pizza, the cheese dangling between her mouth and the slice of pizza like a fishing line sent out to sea.

"Are you going to have one?"

"I had a DoveBar for breakfast and two for lunch."

"Are you kidding me? You're going to have a heart attack before you're thirty."

"I didn't have the energy for anything else."

"You couldn't pour yourself a bowl of cereal?"

"You have to get a bowl and a spoon, and then you have to *pour* the cereal and *pour* the milk. It's like five steps just to get something to eat."

I extend my empty glass for another martini. "God I freakin' hate dating. I think it's even harder because I'm doing the make-up for brides and bridal parties every other day and it just puts marriage on my brain, you know? If I didn't worry about finding a guy, I'm sure it would just happen."

"I don't know, Heather, I think you have to make things happen. Like take Bruce." Bruce is a hairdresser at the salon where we work. He's an average-looking guy, but he has a date with a new woman practically every night. Jenna and I have often wondered what his secret is. The theory that we've been working with is that women are overcome by his Fabio-style shoulder-length hair. It is good hair, I'll give him that, but I have good hair too and I'm not having guys chase after me with offers of mind-blowing sex every night, damn it.

"Bruce asks lots of women out. Not all of them say yes, but he asks so many that even if only a few agree to go out with him, it still means he's got a date every night of the week."

I pick at my half-eaten slice of pizza. It turns out that pizza doesn't go all that well with martinis, and anyway, since I spent the day eating baked goods the size of hubcaps, my stomach is getting testy. "I guess."

"You have to stay positive."

"I am positive. Why would I put myself through the torture of dating if I didn't cling to a shred of hope that there are a few decent guys left out there for me?" Actually, I'm sort of lying. Secretly part of me believes that the only men who are still single in their thirties are lying sacks of shit. I shouldn't be so negative because I've actually been pretty lucky dating-wise, if you exclude the verbal flasher and my date who began dating another woman halfway through his date with me. I've managed to avoid dating married men, abusive men, and workaholics. I have, however, dated a surprising number of guys who have issues with honesty (the main issue was that they knew nothing about it). They tended to lie about stupid little things, but catching them in those little lies made me lose all trust for them when it came to bigger matters like fidelity. One small lie is a loose thread on a sweater—you start pulling and pulling until you have nothing but a useless pile of thread.

"You know what worries me?" I ask.

"What?"

"I'm worried that I've met the guy of my dreams and I let him go."

"You met the guy of your dreams? Why did you let him go?"

"Because I was fourteen."

"I'm not following."

"His name is Travis. He lived in my neighborhood and we went to grade school together. We were really close friends all through grade school, but then we turned twelve, thirteen, and suddenly hanging out wasn't as simple as it once was. Suddenly I was wearing a bra and getting curves and he was noticing. Things changed between us. This one day at dusk he walked me home from school. We stood in my driveway, and he was looking at the ground kicking stones halfheartedly, looking all nervous. We had been best friends for years, so for him to be nervous around me was just crazy. I knew he was going to ask me out. But I was so shy and stupid then, and I was so scared that if we went out together, our friendship would be ruined forever. So before he could ask me, I said, 'Ihavetogonowbye!' all in one breath, and I ran into the house. We saw each other a few times after that, but things were never the same between us, and a few months later he was sent off to this private school in Pennsylvania. For a long time after that I couldn't stop thinking about him. I kept wondering if I might bump into him over the summer or a holiday when he might be home from school, but I never did."

"So why don't you look him up?"

"I heard through a mutual friend that he got married pretty young. It was a broken condom, shotgun sort of wedding with a baby arriving a few months later."

"You don't know what he's up to now?"

"Not really. But he's been on my mind again. It's so stupid."

"He could be divorced, you know."

"You know what's so awful? I've been thinking that, too. I mean you hear of marriages failing every day, so it's not like it'd be all that hard to imagine a shotgun marriage ending a few decades shy of happily ever after. In fact, it seems pretty likely."

"Why do you think you've been thinking about him?"

"I don't know. I really don't. Desperation maybe."

"Maybe he's the one. Maybe he's your destiny."

"I doubt it. I think I just want to believe there is a guy out there for me, and I know that Travis and I at least connected once upon a time. It's stupid though, for me to fantasize about a guy who lives halfway across the country."

"It's not any different than fantasizing about a movie star or a hero in a novel. It can't hurt."

"Actually, I think maybe it can. I don't think it's a good idea to make some guy you barely know into your dream man. It makes real guys less desirable because there is no way they can measure up." I put my paper plate of pizza beside the bed on an end table that's crowded with candles, a lamp with a beaded lampshade in shocking pink that Jenna made herself, and a thick stack of hair design and craft magazines.

Jenna, who is sprawled on her side, gives me a thoughtful look. "What is your dream guy like?"

This is an easy one. I've had thirty-three years to figure this out. "Well, I like artistic types. Maybe a musician or an artist or something. And I like readers. I read that fewer and fewer Americans are reading than ever before, which I don't think is much of a surprise to anyone, but what interested me about the study was that it said that people who read tend to get more involved in their communities than nonreaders. They volunteer their time at soup kitchens, they join the PTA, they donate to food drives, whatever. I guess what I'm saying is that I'd like a guy who cares about people besides himself and is intellectual enough not to spend all his time in front of the TV."

"Makes sense. What else?"

"The usual stuff. A guy who is thoughtful and kind. A guy I can laugh with. He has to be a good kisser, of course. And he wouldn't have to get drunk to get out on the dance floor. And of course he'd be politically liberal because I wouldn't want to date a guy who canceled out my vote. How about you? Who is your dream guy?"

"Right now, if I could find a guy who had a job and wasn't

a gambling addict or a drug addict, I think I might fly him straight to Vegas for a quickie wedding."

Jenna only falls for bankrupted guys who let her support them for a while until she finally kicks them out, much poorer than she was before she met them. I think it's a good sign for her to say that she wants to find a guy who's employed. It may not sound like much, but for her it would be a major step in the right direction.

"To finding our dream guys," I say, lofting my glass for a toast.

"To finding our dream guys."

When I get home, I want more than anything to simply fall into bed without washing up, but I know my reward for my laziness will be a giant pulsing zit on the middle of my face. I don't have the greatest skin. I'm thirty-three years old and I have to be constantly vigilant or I break out. I spend ridiculous amounts of money on retin-A and other topical drugs.

It wouldn't be quite so bad if I had my mother's skin. She had terrible breakouts when she was young but she looks decades younger than she actually is now that she's older. She suffered when she was young but she's benefiting now that she's aging. Me, on the other hand, I have combination skin, which means that I get a combination of dry, wrinkled skin punctuated with zits so big astronauts could see them from outer space. I think of Carmen's wedding and how I don't want to go to my rich sort-of-friend's wedding with a pimple the size of Mt. Everest on my nose, so I sigh and force myself to the bathroom where I wash my face, apply my retin-A to my zitty areas and antiwrinkle cream to my wrinkly areas.

I don't know why it's important for me to look good in front of someone I have barely spoken to in years, but for some reason it is. Although actually, the thing I really need to worry about isn't renegade zits but whether Jenna will do something crazy. The term "loose cannon" is a good one to describe her. More than once Jenna has gotten so drunk at a party I've had to pry her lips off unsuspecting men (sometimes married men who are within yards of their wives). Jenna also has occasional bouts with kleptomania, although she doesn't call it that. She thinks taking a valuable statue from someone's home is no different than taking a shell from the beach—it's just a keepsake to her. Maybe it wasn't a good idea to invite her, but I didn't want to go alone, and my other friends, while more predictable, just aren't quite as fun.

I climb into bed and images of my day flash through my head. When you think of blind dates, you think of nerdy guys who bore you with tales of their rock collections or something, not gorgeous guys who start dating other women halfway through their date with you. Why couldn't we have been on the other side of the park when the dating game thing was going on? Although, if I'm honest with myself, we really didn't have that much in common. Our conversation was always a little stilted. Still, it hurts to be rejected.

I don't want to stew in feelings of loserness, so I try to think of something happy. Instantly a picture of Travis comes to mind. It's asinine to have fantasies about a guy I haven't seen since I was a teenager. Don't think I don't know that. It's possible— no, it's *likely*—that I'm making him out to be more of a Prince Charming than he actually is. But I know he *is* good-looking, for one thing. At least he was back when we were young. Maybe he's lost his trim physique and all his hair and has developed huge bags under his eyes, but somehow I doubt it. He's an artist, and as I said, I have a weakness for artists. Also, he's the kind of person who can create an astonishing drawing in seconds. In just a few strokes he can capture a scene's essence in such a way that the picture seems more real than the reality because he can convey a feeling that goes beyond what the eye can see.

I always wanted to be an artist. I wished I could do what he could do, but I didn't have his talent. I had some talent— enough to become a make-up artist who brings in a decent salary—but I was never anywhere close to his league.

Despite his gift, he doesn't make his living as a painter but as a real estate developer. I imagine he makes a great living yet still paints and sketches in his free time, which means he has the benefits of being an artist without the drawbacks of crushing poverty. I just wonder if he's still married and what he's up to.

The school I went to for kindergarten through sixth grade was tiny. In my class, there were three other girls and three boys. Travis lived three houses down from me and we walked to school together most mornings. To get to school, we had to walk through the woods, and then past a small lake. As a little girl I had dubbed the woods Fairy Forest. When you live in a small town, there aren't always other kids around to play with, so I spent a lot of time alone playing in those woods with only my imagination for company. The fairies lived beneath the thatches of mushrooms that formed their own miniature murky-white forest, spongy and soft to the touch. There was a green hill covered in ankle-high perennials where rabbits could often be seen darting to and fro.

Travis and I would come home from school and we'd kill time by drawing or painting. It wasn't yet the era of Gameboys or computer games, although I did have an Atari, but Frogger and Ms. Pac-Man got pretty old pretty fast. For a long time, drawing and playing Atari was all Travis and I wanted to do. But when I turned thirteen, things changed. I remember being in the same room as Travis and imagining kissing his lips. The image of kissing him was so intensely real, it terrified me. After that day I started worrying about him asking me out. Maybe when I ran into my house that evening when I thought he was going to ask me on a date, he thought I didn't want him to ask me out because he thought I didn't like him, when in fact I was just young and scared. Over the years, whenever I broke up with a guy, I'd start wondering what Travis was up to and whether things might have been different between us if our timing had been different.

He's the last thing I think about before I drift off into sleep . . .

Chapter 3

So here I am driving up to Wisconsin for a wedding of a friend I don't much like with my whacky friend Jenna who thinks eating DoveBars for breakfast is a good idea. Have you ever had a friend like that, a friend who just makes one bad decision after the other? Someone who makes the wrong choices again and again? Jenna always chooses the wrong guy and is up to her eyeballs in debt. She treats money as if were something radioactive that should be gotten rid of as soon as possible. She would sooner attempt to fly to the moon on a skateboard than open a savings account. But she makes me laugh and she never judges me when I say or do something stupid or when my make-up or hair doesn't look just right. That might not sound like a big deal, but in my line of work, I'm always being monitored by my coworkers and customers to see whether I've put on weight or if my outfit is cute or if my shoes are fashionable. It's exhausting. Jenna likes me just as I am, so when I'm with her I can relax. There are so many people in this world who drain you emotionally. Jenna doesn't drain me; she makes me feel renewed.

It's weird how decisions you make on the spur of the moment can radically alter your life forever. If I hadn't gone to beauty school, for example, I never would have met Jenna. I can't really imagine a Jenna-free life. But I only went to beauty school because I could get through the full-time program in about ten weeks. Ten weeks of school costs a lot less than a four-year degree, let me tell you. It was never my life's goal to work at a salon, though as a little girl I spent hours in front of the mirror playing with cheap make-up I bought in bulk. I had a huge palette of eye shadows and a wide selection of lipsticks in a rainbow of colors from bruise-purple to pale pink to dried-blood red. I liked how different colors could transform my features and even my mood. Today I've put on bright colors in hopes that it'll help me get into a more cheerful frame of mind.

"Where are we staying at again?" Jenna asks me, interrupting my thoughts.

"It's the only hotel in town."

"Why don't we stay with your parents?"

"They retired to Arizona three years ago."

"Right, right. Sorry, I forgot." She says nothing for a beat, then, "Why aren't we staying with one of your friends?"

"The people I was good friends with in high school moved away as soon as they could. We wanted lives that we couldn't have if we stayed here. The people who stayed were the ones who couldn't get married and have kids fast enough. They started popping out babies when they were twenty or twenty-one. They were thinking about protecting and nurturing a child when the biggest responsibility in my life was deciding whether to get drunk off beer or hard liquor."

I left the small town where I grew up precisely because I was petrified of getting married and having kids right away. I wanted adventure and excitement and a career. And *then* I wanted to get married. I've had the adventure and excitement and career. I spent my twenties going to rock concerts and doing make-up for photo shoots and TV shows. I've traveled. I've gone to parties with actors, singers, and rock stars. It's been great, but it's also kind of exhausting. These days I could go for a little less excitement and a little more stability. Of course now that I'm ready for the marriage part, I can't find anyone I'd like to be married to. I figure that there is something like three billion men on this planet. I bet I can find at least one sucker out there to marry me.

When we pull into town, I take my glasses off just in case we run into someone I know. Anyway, I know this town well enough to drive blindfolded.

"Is this it?" Jenna asks.

"Small town, Wisconsin. It's a party a minute here. The wedding isn't for a few hours. How do you want to kill some time?"

"What is there to do?"

"The most exciting thing to do here is to get ice cream."

"I don't want to ruin my appetite. If we're going to a rich person's wedding, there is going to be some good grub there, and I want to eat as much as I can. Why don't we just crash at the hotel?"

"Sure thing." We drive in silence for a minute or two when I see him. "Oh my God," I say, looking out the rearview mirror.

"What?"

"Nothing."

"Come on. What is it? Tell me."

"I'm sure I'm just seeing things, but I think that might be Travis."

"Oh my God! It's fate! Which one is he?"

"I'm sure it's not him."

"If it was him . . . ohhh, the guy in the Audi? He's cute!"

"It's not him. It can't be. What would he be doing here?"

"He could be here for the wedding."

I shake my head. "Carmen didn't move here until high school. Travis had already moved out East by then."

"Maybe he's here visiting family. Maybe it's someone's birthday or anniversary or something. You said his family still lived here, right?"

"As far as I know."

"So it's possible."

"I guess."

"Heather, you have to stop the car. You have to talk to him."

"What am I going to do, pull the car over and flag him down?"

"Yes, that's exactly what you should do."

"Jenna, you are being ridiculous."

"He might be the guy you're destined for. If you blow this chance to talk to him, you'll never forgive yourself for not giving things a chance. I can't let you do that. I insist that you stop the car."

"No! Absolutely not! If we're supposed to be together, fate will bring us together."

"Fate has brought you together, and you're going to throw it all away! Fate can only do so much. You have to do the rest! Stop the car!"

"No!"

"Well then, at the next stoplight, I'm jumping out."

"What are you talking about?"

"You can leave me stranded if you want to, but I won't let you let this chance pass you by. What? Why are you smiling?"

"No reason."

We continue driving along for a couple minutes when Jenna finally realizes what I already know. "Are there any stoplights in this town?"

I laugh. "Not many."

"Are you going to stop the car and talk to him?" Jenna looks back. The guy in the Audi is still behind us, just two cars back, which isn't a huge surprise since this is the main street through town.

"No, I'm not going to stop the car."

"Then I'm getting out." Jenna opens the door while we're moving.

"What are you doing?" I scream.

"I'm jumping out."

"Of a moving vehicle? Are you insane? Close the door!"

She closes the door. "Are you going to stop the car?"

"No. I already said that." My heart is hammering ferociously out of fear that my crazy friend's craziness is going to cost her her life. Also, I know the odds are good that Travis saw Jenna's attempt to leap out of my car. What must he think of me that my companion wants to get away from me so badly that she's willing to risk life and limb to do so?

Jenna opens the car door again. We aren't going all that fast, but it seems pretty damn speedy when you're talking about someone jumping out of a moving vehicle onto the pavement. We are definitely going fast enough for her to get hurt, but I can't slow down much because there is traffic behind me.

"Close the damn door!"

"I'm jumping!"

"You're going to kill yourself!"

"You're going to thank me for this later!"

As I scream and try to yank her back into the car, I swerve all over the road. So as if having my passenger opening and closing the door as we speed along isn't strange enough, now I am weaving like a drunk.

"Close the damn door!"

Jenna closes the door again.

"Oh thank God." I take a deep breath and glance into the rearview mirror quickly. Travis is right behind us now.

"I swear to God, Heather, if you don't stop this car, I'm jumping."

"Jenna, please, be responsible."

"I'm giving you to the count of three."

"The count of three! Are you my mother?"

"One."

Fortunately there isn't much in the way of oncoming traffic for me to crash into because this isn't my finest hour of driving.

"Two."

"Don't you dare. Don't you—"

"Three." Before I can even curse her soul to hell, she opens the door and leaps out of my car, landing on her feet on the bank of the road before falling onto the grassy land and tumbling like a runaway basketball.

"Shit!" I don't want to run my friend (former friend, I

should say) over or get rear-ended, so I drive several more feet and abruptly pull off the road, tires screeching and rocks flying. "Are you okay? Are you okay, you stupid idiot?" I cry, jumping out of the car and running after her.

The land flattens out and she finally stops rolling. She is lying on her back coughing up a storm from the rocks and dust. "I'm okay!" she croaks between coughs.

I hear a car skid off the road and come to a stop at the same time I help Jenna to her feet. Jenna is bent over coughing her lungs out as she staggers back to my car with my help. I desperately hope that whoever stopped is not Travis and that somehow Jenna and I can get back into my car without being seen.

Unfortunately, my attempts to skulk off unnoticed don't quite work out. Just before we can reach my car, I find myself face-to-face with him.

And it isn't Travis.

He does look vaguely like Travis, but only by the wildest stretch of the imagination. Clearly my daydreams of my adolescent friend fogged my thinking and made me see things that weren't there. Especially since, as usual, I'm not wearing my glasses. Like Travis, he's incredibly cute and he has dark hair, but that's where the resemblance ends.

I want to die.

As if the situation weren't quite excruciatingly embarrassing enough, this is what I say: "You're not Travis."

"No," he says, "I'm not."

I could have made up any lie on earth. I could have said that Jenna has some condition where she has the occasional convulsive fit and that's why she'd sprung from my car like an overwrought Jack-in-the-Box. I could have said she had some sort of mental disorder—in fact, she probably *does* have some mental disorder that has so far gone undiagnosed. I could have said she was high on drugs and we were on our way to the rehab clinic. That would have been a perfect cover! But no.

I look at him for only a second more before humiliation spurs me into action. I practically hurl Jenna into the car and—I swear to God—I leap over the hood of the car and jump into the open window of the driver's side door as if I am one of the goddamn Dukes of Hazard. I tear out of there so fast that the tires skid several feet across the pavement. The smell of burnt rubber and the sound of squealing tires fill the air.

"I hate you!" I hiss. "I'm never speaking to you again!"

"I was trying to help!"

"Jenna, tossing yourself out of a moving vehicle isn't the best way to woo a man. Not only is it *not* the best way, it's not even a *good* way!"

"I thought you weren't talking to me."

"I'm not!"

"Anyway, it wasn't Travis."

"Thank God. Thank God. Thank God. If it was Travis . . . well, not only would I be too humiliated to ever see or speak to him again, but what if he'd told one of my old classmates? It would be all over town and I'd never be able to show my face here again."

"Heather?"

"What?" I snap.

"You're still talking to me, you know."

I stay angry with her for the rest of the ride to the hotel. If it had been Travis back there, I may well have never spoken to her again. But by the time we've checked into our room, the whole thing seems kind of funny. After all, it was just some random guy who I'll never have to see again. We get to our room and both stretch out on our beds.

"I thought you were going to kill yourself out there," I say.

"You should have seen the expression on your face. It was *classic*."

"You're sure you're okay?"

"I didn't hurt myself too badly. Nothing several years of physical therapy won't fix."

This cracks me up and the two of us laugh until my cell phone interrupts our revelry. It takes a moment to compose myself before I answer.

"Hello?"

"Heather?"

"Yes?"

"This is Carmen."

"Carmen. I can't believe you're calling me on your wedding day! You must be frantic."

"Not really. I'm kind of bored actually. I have a top-notch wedding planner, of course. Everything has been all arranged. Now there is nothing left for me to do but look pretty and show up. Listen, the reason I'm calling is this: Anthony has a childhood friend whose girlfriend dumped him rather abruptly and he had to come to the wedding alone. Which, I mean, doesn't the bitch know that that's going to cost us sixty bucks because she RSVP'd, and then so tactlessly decides at the last minute not to show up? How rude. Honestly. Anyway, I was hoping you could sort of look out for him."

"Look out for him?"

"I already had the wedding planner change the seating arrangement to put the two of you together. His name is John."

"Carmen, Carmen, wait a second, you're not setting me up, are you? Because I do not do blind dates. No way. Never again."

"It's not a blind date, Heather. It's just that he doesn't know anyone here except Anthony, and of course Anthony is going to be busy tonight. I'm worried that John won't have fun. What kind of hostess would I be if one of my guests didn't enjoy himself? I already told him all about you."

"Carmen, you didn't." I don't believe this. "What did you tell him?"

"I told him what a riot you are and how much fun you are to be with and that you're pretty and smart. What else is there to know?"

"Well what about him? What's he like? What does he look like?"

"Um, well, he's very nice. *You* might think he's attractive."

"What is that supposed to mean?"

"You always went for guys who were kind of artsy, you know. Not your classic Tommy Hilfiger-model type."

I can only deduce that what she means is that he has facial features that look like they were designed by a three-year-old with finger paints. "Carmen, the thing is . . ."

"Heather, this is my wedding day," she says in a whiny tone. "Please do this. For me?"

I know that some brides get a little egocentric on their wedding day (okay, ego-psychotic), but the thing is, Carmen has been commanding me to do her will since the day we met. But it is her wedding after all, and after today, I don't need to ever see her again if I don't want to.

"Okay," I say.

"Great. I have to run. I'll see you in a bit."

I click off the phone.

"What's wrong?" Jenna asks.

"Carmen wants me to chaperone some swamp monster named John tonight. Why do these things always happen to me? Tonight is going to be a disaster. Why did I agree to come to this stupid wedding? Is a little free food and champagne worth all these trials and humiliations?

"I'm sure everything will be fine."

"No, it won't. I'll have some hideous letch stalking me all night. I won't be able to have any fun at all."

"He might be cute. He might be nice. Why do you always assume the worst?"

Jenna and I have talked about this before. Jenna lives in the moment and doesn't worry about what the future will bring. I do my best to anticipate everything that might go wrong. In real life, I'm nearsighted, but in my imagination, not only do I have 20/20 vision but I can see into the future—at least that's what I'd like to think. I like to plan in advance and be prepared for what's coming. I like to foresee any potential pitfalls I could be heading for. That's not pessimism, that's pragmatism.

"Forget it, you're right. I'm not going to worry about it." I will, of course, but I'll do it mentally so Jenna won't give me a hard time about it. "I'm tired. I wouldn't mind taking a quick nap," I say.

"Good plan."

Jenna is out in about four seconds flat. I lie on my bed, thinking about the guy I embarrassed myself in front of. He can't live around here. Nobody in this town drives an Audi. Carmen's family is wealthy, but they're the only ones. People here drive pickup trucks and ten-year-old Ford stationwagons. I wonder where he lives. He was so cute. Way cuter than Travis. Although, to be fair, I shouldn't really compare a flesh-and-blood male to a memory of a fourteen-year-old boy I haven't seen in nearly twenty years.

Eventually I fall asleep too. I wake first and hop in the shower.

I bought a new dress for the wedding and new shoes. The clingy fabric of my dress is pale pink and fitted around my bust and waist and has a skirt that swirls around when I spin. My heels are pale pink as well. Strappy and open-toed, they show off my French-manicured toes.

Jenna looks great. I admit that I was a little worried that she might wear some monstrosity. You can never tell with Jenna. She's a little like Carrie Bradshaw in that way. Sometimes her fashion risks are adorable and trendsetting, and other times you wonder if she dressed herself while blindfolded in the middle of a tropical storm while high on hallucinogenic drugs.

Tonight Jenna is wearing a burgundy dress that flatters her full figure (and matches her hair perfectly) and classy black high-heeled shoes. She sewed the dress herself. Jenna is an amazing seamstress. When I try to sew, the result is decidedly homemade looking. Jenna's work looks like a high-end gown from Paris or Milan.

We drive the few minutes over to Carmen's family estate. A valet takes my car and we are directed to go to the backyard, which is decked out like a fairy kingdom.

It's an outdoor wedding and a tent covers part of the lawn. Beneath the tent are several tables with crisp white linens. The roof of the tent is lined with tiny strings of white lights that shimmer like stars. Flowers are absolutely everywhere—they must have spent a fortune because it feels like we're walking through a botanical garden. The perfumed fragrance of the flowers fills the air. Jenna and I walk past the wedding cake, which is one of the most artistic I've ever seen. It's white and has five tiers. Each tier is designed like a floor in a dollhouse with little pieces of dollhouse furniture instead of frosted flowers. No detail was ignored. There are mini-throw rugs, mini-TVs, mini-telephones. There is a man's blue shirt draped over a tiny chair. The sheets on the unmade bed are rumpled. There's a beautiful armoire and a stylish sofa.

As we walk to our seats, my eyes greedily drink in the sights. The lawn is a photograph from *Better Homes and Gardens* brought to life. There is a waterfall and a large pond with fish. It goes without saying that the landscaping is breathtaking—lush and green with spectacular flowers in shades of deep violet, red velvet, and lush pink.

There is a part of me that is jealous of this enormous house and its manicured lawns, but another part of me thinks about how, now that Carmen has left home, only two people live here. Two. Why on earth would two people need such a huge house and so many acres of land? It seems kind of silly. The property does, however, provide the perfect setting for a wedding.

Dozens of white folding chairs are set up in the backyard with a gorgeous white gazebo decorated in creamy gardenias. Jenna and I take our seats and people-watch for several minutes until the ceremony begins. To my surprise, the wedding isn't a huge one. I'd thought that with Carmen's father being a bigwig businessman, they'd have every businessperson he'd ever crossed paths with at the wedding. But that doesn't appear to be the case. Instead it looks like they stuck to inviting family and close friends. How I managed to swing an invitation I'll never know.

Finally, the music begins and the first of five groomsmen in tuxes and bridesmaids in floor-length strapless red silk walk out and fan out on either side of the gazebo. An adorable flower girl tosses red rose petals. She is so cute I want to rent her to be my flower girl if I should ever get married. Since I'm an only child, I don't have any siblings popping out young kids that I can include in my wedding plans. I'm going to either have to temporarily kidnap a youngster or lease one for the night.

The groom is a handsome man with thick wheat-colored hair and caramel-colored eyes. The music gets louder and everyone stands and turns to watch the bride walk down the aisle with her father. She looks stunning. Her hair is a perfect up-do. Jenna has told me just how annoying it is to style hair like that—it takes forever and she never makes enough money to make it worth the time. But for bridal photos, damn, it sure looks beautiful.

The music stops and we all take our seats again. The minister is a youngish bald man. He's a good public speaker, unlike some of the mumbling officiates I've seen at weddings. He talks about how Carmen and Anthony began this evening as two individuals but they will leave as one. Their individuality will be intact, but they will be a unit, a team. Two people who can no longer just think about their own needs but have to consider the needs of their partner as well. He talks about how they will face good times and bad times and how their love will see them through it all. I cry through the whole thing. Fucking weddings. I can't get away from them. I need to get in a new line of work. Maybe I'll become a divorce lawyer. Then I'll be reminded that love doesn't always equal happily ever after. Love doesn't always conquer all.

But I tell you what: I'd do anything to give love a shot at lasting through the good times and the bad. You'd think that by the time I was thirty-three, I would have been close to getting hitched at least a couple times, but I haven't. I've dated some wonderful guys, but none of them were men I wanted to spend my life with. In my early twenties, I tended to date guys who couldn't commit to a decision on what to have for dinner, let alone to a woman. And at the time, that suited me just fine. I wasn't looking for anything serious. Then as I hit thirty, I was ready for something long-term, but I couldn't find it.

I want my chance to find a guy I want to spend my life with. That's all I want—my chance.

Chapter 4

When Carmen and I were in high school, whenever we got together we got together at her estate because, well, it was an *estate*. There was no way in hell I was going to let someone who lived on acres of land with horses ambling freely about see the tiny little two-bedroom dump I grew up in. She had me over for sleepovers all the time, and I loved being able to spend the night in her big house, pretending like it was all mine. Then I'd go home and feel like my life could never measure up.

That same feeling of inadequacy bubbles in my chest now as we line up to hug the bride and groom, and I'm furious with myself for feeling this way. So what if Carmen is wealthy and gorgeous and her husband is a babe? She must have some sort of hardship in life, right?

Who am I kidding? She lives an enchanted life. She never goes on dates where her date ends up with another woman. That would simply never happen to Carmen.

"It was a beautiful ceremony," I say as I hug her. The beadwork on her dress is stunningly intricate; it's truly breathtaking. "You look gorgeous."

"Thank you. Thank you for coming."

"I really liked your minister. Did he replace Reverend Michaels?"

"No, Reverend Michaels is still there."

By "there" she means the one church in town. Reverend Michaels is a sweet old guy, but he's got to be pushing one hundred. His sermons long ago ceased being lucid. These days he's as likely to stand at the pulpit rambling on about the importance of good dental hygiene as why you shouldn't covet thy neighbor's wife or whatever a more traditional sermon topic might be.

"We got our minister on rent-a-rev dot com," she says.

"Ha! You're kidding me!"

"We told Reverend Michaels we wanted him as our guest since he was so close to us. Fortunately he's pretty much off his rocker so he bought it."

"Well, it was a beautiful ceremony. Congratulations. I'm happy for you."

When Jenna and I are done with the receiving line, we make a beeline for the bar and each get a glass of wine.

"This house is spectacular," Jenna says. "Is everyone around here this wealthy?"

"No one is. This used to be farmland. Carmen's father knocked down the barns and the farmhouse and built this palace," I say.

"The bride's hair is perfect. I don't know if I could have done better myself."

I nod and take a sip of my wine, and then I squint. I can't possibly be seeing what I think I'm seeing. I *am* seeing what I think I'm seeing. "Oh shit!"

"Oh shit what?"

"That's the guy who isn't Travis!"

"Huh?"

"The guy you nearly sent me into a cement bank over when you leapt out of my car like you were Evel fucking Knievel."

"Oh." Jenna flinches. "Sorry about that."

"What the hell is he doing here?"

"Heather, this isn't a huge town. It's not like Chicago. Here you are more or less bound to run into people all the time."

My eyes grow wide when I realize that he's seen us and is

coming our way. I turn away from him and look at Jenna. "Oh, shit, shit, shit! He's coming this way. Shit!" My heart begins racing at a speed worthy of the autobahn and it's not just from embarrassment, I realize, but excitement. I turn back and smile at him.

"Fancy meeting you here," he says.

"Hello, Not Travis." I do my best to pretend like I'm calm and collected. "It's good to see you again. I'm Heather. This is my friend Jenna."

"Jenna, hello. You look different when you're not spiraling across the asphalt." He extends his hand and she shakes it.

"I'm charmed to meet you," she says, regally and with utmost decorum as if she has magically transformed into some high-society heiress. I give her a look. Even when she tries to be normal she is weird about it.

"Heather, it's nice to meet you," he says.

We shake hands. "It's nice to meet you again, too."

"You know, I'm supposed to meet a Heather tonight."

"Oh no. You're John?"

"I am." He laughs. "What a coincidence."

This simply cannot be happening to me. As if it weren't bad enough that Jenna and I humiliated ourselves in front of a stranger, it turns out we have to spend the evening with him?

"Do you often go vaulting out of moving vehicles?" John asks Jenna.

"That was actually my first time."

"What happened was, we thought you were this guy I used to know," I say. "I had something of a crush on him a long time ago in junior high. She wanted me to stop the car and flag you—him—down, but I wouldn't do it, so she took matters into her own hands. It's really silly. I haven't seen this guy in years and I've heard he's married."

John smiles. "You're a good friend."

"I know." Jenna nods.

I realize that I'm staring at John. I tear my eyes away and glance around the yard and my gaze fixes on a familiar face.

"What? Why are you looking at that lady like that?" Jenna asks.

"I think I know her and I'm trying to figure out from where. Oh my goodness! That's Carol Ladler. We went to grade school together. We still send each other Christmas cards every year but I haven't seen her since graduation."

Carol sees me and starts walking our way. It's weird to see how little time has changed her. She has a few more wrinkles and a few more pounds around her waist and her thick auburn hair has been cut short, but basically, she looks exactly like the Carol I went to school with. "Heather? Heather Stanton?" she asks, her eyes bright with excitement.

"Carol! How are you? How are the kids?"

"I'm good. The kids are growing up faster than you would believe. How are you? You look fabulous!"

"Thanks."

"Are you going to introduce me to your boyfriend?"

"This is John, but he's not my boyfriend. We just met tonight."

"It's nice to meet you." He extends his hand for her to shake.

"It's nice to meet you, too. You look like a guy I went to school with. Don't you think he looks like Travis Churchill?"

I laugh. "Maybe a little. You haven't heard from Travis, have you?"

"I sure have! I saw him when he came out to visit his family over Christmas."

"Is he still married to what's-her-face?"

Carol nods. "They have two adorable children. They're very happy. His business is just booming. It's a fairy tale sort of thing."

"Wow, a shotgun wedding that actually worked out. You don't hear of that often."

"Crazier things have happened I guess. Travis is doing very well for himself. You never know, he might end up in the White House. He's running for office. He's a very important man in the Republican party in Pennsylvania."

"Travis is a Republican?" I ask, unable to believe my ears. All these years I've been fantasizing about a guy who votes *Republican*?

"Yep. Well, I'd better get going. Wade is giving me the evil eye. He never was good in social situations. I'm his security blanket!"

"Same old Wade, huh? It was good to see you."

"Maybe I'll look you up if we're ever in the city," she says.

"Do that!" I give a little wave and watch her go. I can feel John's eyes on me and my heart thumps like gym shoes tumbling around a drier.

"So, this Travis. Is that the Travis you thought I was?" John asks.

"Uh-huh."

"Tell me about him."

"Why?"

"I just want to know if I was mistaken for the class nerd or something," he says in a teasing voice.

"He was an artist. He was cute."

"But he must be a little crazy to be a Republican."

I laugh. "Sometimes these things don't show up until you're older, like schizophrenia."

His smile is sexy. I would almost think he was flirting with me, except I know he just got dumped by his girlfriend. He probably hates all women. I'll be his transition woman he uses just for sex. Or one of many of his transition women—I know a lot of guys who feel compelled to go all Hugh Hefner for a while after their heart has been crushed.

"Should we take our seats? We're at table seven," John says. "I checked."

"Sure," I say.

As we walk over to our table, Jenna says to John, "So, this girl who dumped you, were you guys serious? Is your heart broken or what?"

Five-alarm flames of embarrassment burn my cheeks. Why do I forget that no matter how much I love Jenna, she shouldn't be allowed in public?

"You don't have to answer that," I say.

"It's okay. We weren't dating that long. It wasn't serious. But when Carmen found out that we broke up, she freaked out. Apparently Miss Manners doesn't allow single men to attend weddings without a chaperone. Not that I mind." He flashes me that smile of his again.

We sit down at the table and stare at the strangers across from us. There is a frumpy middle-aged woman sitting with (presumably) her husband and their two sullen teenage boys, who both have messy hair that looks like it was taken from the bushy pelt of a buffalo.

"I'm Jenna. This is Heather. Heather is an old friend of Carmen's. Who are you?" Jenna asks our tablemates.

The mom tells us that they are Anthony's father's cousins. All of us nod.

"Where are you from?" Jenna asks.

"Ohio."

All of us nod.

"It's such a beautiful wedding, don't you think?" Jenna tries again.

"Yes."

All of us nod. We can't think of anything to say so we just keep nodding until John says, "Would any of you like some bread?" He extends the basket of bread to one of the teenagers. I know that Carmen and I weren't close, but somehow I'm still offended about getting banished to a table a thousand miles away from the bridal-party table with distant cousins who have as much personality as a laundry basket full of dirty socks. Although Carmen did sit me next to a gorgeous single man, so really, how upset can I be? I like that he offered the bread to others before taking some himself. It's a small thing, I know, but it speaks of good manners and a general concern for others. When you've been dating as long as I have, you start noticing little things. Too often I've invested months in a relationship, and it's not till it's over that I think of all the little flags that should have signaled the problems that would plague us later, but I somehow managed not to notice until our relationship was exploding in a giant ball of flames. Now I try to pay more attention.

By the time the basket gets around to me, there's only one roll left.

"Do you want to split it?" I ask John.

"No, take it. It's yours."

"Are you doing that Atkins thing or something?"

"No." He laughs. "God no. I'm a huge fan of bread and pasta and French fries and baked potatoes. All of it. I've never met a carbohydrate I didn't like."

"Then let me split the roll with you."

"All right."

Our salads are brought out first. It's a gourmet sort of situation—small on portion, big on presentation. It takes me about two bites to finish it off. It's a tasty two bites, admittedly, but I'm going to need more substantial fare soon or the wine is going to make me loopy.

"So, how do you know Anthony?" I ask John.

"We grew up together in California. We used to be close friends in high school, but you know how it goes. I stayed in California and he went to Boston for college. We got new friends . . . new jobs . . . we grew apart. I think he invited me more out of nostalgia than anything."

California. He lives in California. I shouldn't be disappointed by this. What did I think, I was going to meet the guy of my dreams at a wedding in Wisconsin and we'd somehow live happily ever after? It's ridiculous.

A waiter takes our salad plates and replaces them with en trees of salmon, wild rice, and mixed vegetables.

"This is delicious," Jenna says.

"It's better for you than DoveBars for breakfast," I tease.

"I don't *always* have DoveBars for breakfast."

"Personally, I'm always insanely healthy at breakfast because every day I wake up vowing to eat healthily and work out," I say to John. "I start losing my willpower around ten each morning, then I skip my workout and vacuum up a lunch full of as much fat and cholesterol as I can get my hands on. But at breakfast I'm always virtuous. Oh wait, I take that back. Once when I was in Montreal I had this crepe that was as big as a bicycle tire wrapped around a couple pounds worth of fresh strawberries and topped with an obscene amount of fresh home-made whipped cream. That probably wasn't all that healthy, but damn it was tasty."

"It's important to have large quantities of whipped cream for meals occasionally," John says. "Personally I find that there are just not enough whipped food products for my taste."

"That's so true," I say. As we talk, I see that Jenna keeps looking over to where two guys are sitting at a nearby table. As we're finishing up our meals, Jenna says, "Don't you think that guy is cute?"

One guy looks like a banker. The other looks like a bankrupt guitar player in an unsuccessful band. There is no doubt in my mind which guy she is attracted to. (Hint: it's not the banker.)

"The long-haired guy?" I ask, already knowing the answer.

"Hmm-mmm." She nods. "I think I'm going to go talk to him. Do you mind if I leave you?"

"Go for it."

"Do you want to take a walk around the property?" John asks me.

"Sure," I say. "I used to hang out here when I was younger so I can give you a tour."

"Sounds good."

We take our wine glasses. Ordinarily I might be shy around a gorgeous guy I was attracted to. But since I know John lives halfway across the country and things could never work out between us, I know I don't have to worry about trying to impress him.

"I can show you the stables," I suggest.

"I'll follow your lead."

"What do you do for a living?" I ask him as we walk out from the tent-covered section of the grounds onto the lawn.

"I'm an illustrator."

"What do you illustrate?"

"Cartoons. I sometimes do commercials for kids' cereals, things like that, but the main thing I do is a cartoon for Nickelodeon." He tells me the name of it. I explain that I don't have any cousins or nieces or nephews, so I'm completely out of touch with anything targeted to the under-ten crowd and I've never heard of it.

"It's a pretty cute show about a little boy and a little girl and their dog, Riley. They have a magic closet and when they go in it and close the door, they are able to go anywhere in the world. They'll take a trip to Russia or China or South America, for example," John says. "It's a way for kids to learn about different cultures. Remember back in the days when you watched *Sesame Street* how they'd teach you a word in Spanish every now and then? We do the same thing, only we have the characters learn a few phrases of whatever country they're visiting."

"How cool. That sounds like a lot of fun."

"It is."

I can't believe I have been thrown together with a sexy artist and the stupid jerk lives on the opposite coast.

"Do you draw the stuff on paper or is it mostly all done on the computer?"

"It's a little bit of both, actually. Hey! Watch your step!"

He grabs my arm and pulls me back just before I step into a giant oozing pile of horseshit in my open-toed heels.

"Thank you. You are my hero. That would not have been pretty. Somehow I didn't think about how it might not be a good idea to traipse around in the dark in a field where horses hang out all day. Maybe I should show you the creek that runs through the property instead?"

"I'm all yours."

I wish.

I turn and start walking left instead of straight back out to where the stables are. It's a perfect evening. It's warm enough not to need a sweater without being too hot. The fresh air brings me back to when I was a kid and I spent every free second running around in the woods or riding my bike or playing by the lake. I wanted to be outside all the time when I was little. I love my cosmopolitan life in the city, but I spend all my time inside these days. If I do have to go outside to walk a few blocks, I never breathe in deeply because I'd inhale a lungful of exhaust and pollution instead of fresh air.

"How about you, what do you do?" he asks.

"I'm a make-up artist. It's fun most of the time. I like working with women and talking all day. A lot of the time my job feels like a giant slumber party. I just get to laugh and dish with women, and I like that a lot. A few weeks ago I did the makeup for a fashion show. That was a trip. I don't want to seem like I'm pandering to stereotypes, but the truth is, the models were total prima donnas, having hissy fits about whether their wigs were big enough and whether their make-up was overdone enough to make an impression from the stage. It was total pandemonium backstage. One of the models was a guy in drag and I had to fashion breasts for him in two minutes flat using electrical tape. I was like the MacGyver of cleavage."

John laughs. He has a nice laugh. It's warm and inviting. It's warm and low and melodic. I want to find out whatever is wrong with him so I don't have to feel bad about the fact that I finally met a guy who is cute and seems nice but I can't have him because he lives in California. I know that some people do the long-distance thing, but I don't want that sort of relationship. I've done the long-distance thing before, and romantic weekends filled with sex are great, but I don't just want romance and sex. I want it all. I want lazy nights snuggling with a guy watching a video. I want a guy to wake up to and go to movies with. I've had enough nights alone in my bed, enough nights of bringing a book as my companion to a restaurant for dinner, enough nights of having no one to bring as my date to parties. I want someone who is there for me night after night, day after day.

Of course, one night of passionate sex with John wouldn't be terrible. It's been eight months since I've had sex, and there is a part of me that just wants to take him back to my hotel and have my way with him for the rest of the night. The only problem is that I don't believe in one-night stands. I admire women who say they use men just for sex, honestly I do, but I'm afraid I'm not one of them.

"My job can also be fun when I help a woman feel a little better about herself," I say. "I think that people too often feel bad on the inside when they don't look good. Sometimes just a little touch can make a big difference. I think it's more fun to transform regular people into beauties than beauties into knock-outs."

We walk through a stand of trees and come upon the creek. I love the sound of flowing water burbling over rocks and plants and fallen logs.

"Isn't this nice?" I ask.

"It's beautiful."

We walk alongside the creek a little ways until we get to a bench. I sit down and he sits next to me, so close our thighs almost touch.

"So," I say, "tell me about yourself."

"What do you want to know?"

What I'd really like to know is whether he'd like to marry me and have babies together, but that seems a little forward. "I don't know. What do you like to do for fun? What are your favorite TV shows?"

"I don't actually watch any TV. I have a television, but I just watch DVDs on it. I do a lot of reading."

A reader. My God. He *is* my dream man. Why does he live in California? Why? Why, cruel fate, why?

"I like reading too. I also like going to concerts and listening to live music," he says.

"Me too."

"I think it's so important to support local bands."

"Exactly! Not enough people realize how important it is to

support real talent. I think it's so sad that the people who are all over MTV and the radio aren't there because they are talented musicians but because they look good in jeans and can sell products. They are pretty faces with teams of marketers behind them telling them how to look and what to say."

"I couldn't agree more. If you don't support local bands, you lose new voices and talent and ideas. You get McMusic. Everything on the radio sounds exactly alike."

We talk for a while more about the music industry, and then we move on to books. He tells me about a book he just read by Dennis Lehane, and I say that I love Dennis Lehane. We talk about other authors and books we like. It turns out we were both royally pissed at Stephen King for *Dreamcatcher*.

"It started off so promisingly," John says, "and then he goes veering off into this whole new tangent halfway through the book. I thought, Stevie man, where are you going? Come back! Come back!"

I laugh. "That's exactly what I thought!"

In the distance, we can hear the music starting up. "Sounds like the band is starting," he says. "Do you want to dance?"

My heart is already doing the conga. A reader *and* a dancer? Maybe I could move to California. I can't let my dream guy go. "Yeah, I'd love to."

We head back to the party. The band is playing a West Coast swing number.

"You don't know how to swing dance, do you?" I ask.

"Not well, but yes, I do."

"Wow, really? I don't know that I've ever met a guy who could swing dance before."

"When swing dancing became popular for a while a few years back," he says as we walk through the yard, "I would go every week with a friend of mine to this club. We were trying to meet women, of course."

"Did it work?"

"Well, sort of. I met a woman who, on our third date, I discovered was married . . . when her husband confronted me on their porch when I dropped her off."

"You're kidding!"

"No. The crazier thing was, she called me the next day to see if I still wanted to 'see' her."

"Ick."

"That's what I thought. If some guys want to have affairs with married women, that's their business. But that's way too messed up for my taste. I couldn't help thinking it would end up in some kind of reverse *Fatal Attraction* situation or something. Another woman I asked out seemed nice when I danced with her at the club, but on our first date I asked her what she did for a living. She told me she sold some line of vitamins. It was like a Mary Kay version of vitamins, where you sell them to individual people, not grocery stores. For an entire hour she gave me a sales pitch trying to sell me the complete line."

"She gave you a sales pitch on your first date?"

"Our first and last date."

"That's rough."

"Tell me about it. Anyway, I didn't get a girlfriend out of it, but I learned a few dance moves, so it wasn't a total waste."

As we approach the dance floor, John gestures for me to follow him back to our table. He takes off his suit coat and drapes it over his chair, then he takes my hand and pulls me out to the dance floor.

"It's been a while since I've been dancing, so I'm going to be a little rusty," he says.

"It's been a while for me too, don't worry."

We stumble a lot at first, trying to remember how the steps go, but by the third song, I can read his leads and we're literally getting into the swing of things. The dancing makes a light sheen of sweat break out over my face, neck, and arms, and my throat gets dry from all the exercise.

"I'm a little thirsty," I say. "Do you mind if we take a quick break?"

"Sure. I'll get us some wine."

"That would be nice. I'll wait for you at the table."

"I'll be right there."

I'm walking to our table, which is now empty of people,

when Jenna tackles me. She runs at me and dives on me with this sort of bear-hug move and we stumble several steps together. I pray that John didn't see us.

"What?" I ask, irritated. She is twenty-six years old. Shouldn't she grow up sometime soon? Honestly.

"I'm in love."

"Oh?" Pardon my incredulity, but I've heard this before.

"He's got a job."

"Really?" Now I'm interested.

"He's a reporter for the *Chicago Reader*. He covers the music scene."

The *Chicago Reader* is an alternative newspaper that Jenna and I both love.

"That's so incredibly cool!"

"I know. He's name is David Starr, two R's."

"Is he single?"

"Yes."

"Does he do drugs?"

"He used to smoke pot but he quit three years ago."

"Does he have commitment issues?"

"I don't think so. His last relationship lasted two years but they broke up six months ago when she got transferred to Florida for her job."

"Why is he here at this wedding? Does he know the bride or groom?"

"Neither. He's friends with the drummer and thought it might be fun to eat rich people's food and drink rich people's wine."

"Just like us."

"What about you? How's John?"

"Jenna. He is perfect. He's an artist. He reads. He's into music. He dances. He's polite. He kept me from stepping in a pile of horseshit—"

"That's so sweet!"

"And he lives in California."

"No!"

"I know. It's completely heartbreaking. Shhh-shhh, here he comes. I don't want him to know we were talking about him."

"Hi, John! It's good to see you."

"Hey, Jen."

"I'm actually leaving again. I have to go make David fall madly in love with me. I don't have a moment to waste," Jenna says. "I'll see you guys around."

John hands me a glass of wine. He sets his own glass down on the table. "I guess she's hitting it off with that guy."

"It would seem so."

"That's great."

John sits down and rolls up the sleeves of his white button-up shirt and loosens his tie a little. That's when I see it. I see what's wrong with him! He's not a catch! He's a drug addict! This is fabulous!

He sees that I noticed the needle mark in the crook of his arm. "I gave blood a few days ago."

Gave blood, yeah right, a likely story.

"I'm O negative. That's the universal donor type. So I give blood every six weeks. It's a small way to give back to the community." He shrugs.

Could he possibly be for real? He said it so matter-of-factly. Not like he was bragging or lying. It was just a statement.

"That's cool," I say. I think I actually believe him. Which sucks. Because that means that he's still a catch, damn it. "I'm A negative. I give blood often, but not every six weeks. I'm ashamed to admit that I usually don't think about it unless I hear about some terrible tragedy. Then I'm like, 'Oh man! I have to donate blood!' Even if the tragedy is far away, giving blood makes me feel like I'm doing *something*."

"Yep." He nods. "I know what you mean."

We drink our wine and talk about books and music some more. The music stops and everyone is cleared off the dance floor so Carmen can throw her bouquet. I try to become invisible, but it doesn't work. The wedding isn't big enough for us single women to go unnoticed. Carmen's emissaries have been sent to round us up, and I'm accosted by a plump older woman with white hair whipped up like the frothy top of a lemon meringue.

"She is going to throw the bouquet. We need you out on the floor," the woman tells me.

"Oh, thanks, but I'd really rather not . . ."

The woman leans in close to me and hisses, "This is Carmen's big day. She wants you out on the floor."

I think I could be one hundred years old and if someone who was one hundred and one forcefully told me what to do, I would have no choice but to acquiesce. I've spent too many years being trained to respect my elders.

"Okay," I nod and scurry out onto the floor as I have been told to.

There are only about ten of us women on the floor. There are a few older women who I suspect are widows or divorcees, one young girl who is about twelve, and one other woman about my age. Jenna somehow managed not to get roped into doing this.

When I was in my twenties and not in any rush to wed, the tradition of throwing the bouquet didn't bother me. But now that I'm ready to get hitched, the custom seems to rub in the fact I'm a spinster. I stand off to the side as far as I can be from the center of the action.

Carmen smiles at all of us, and then turns around and tosses the bouquet backwards. It's not windy out, so it's not the wind's fault that the bouquet gets lopped back off to an angle. Her toss reminds me of my attempts to bowl. I always aim for the center of the aisle and my ball always veers off into the gutter.

The bouquet is coming right at me. For a second, I want to run away from it as if it were a hand grenade she'd chucked at me and not a beautiful bouquet of gardenias. But it happens so fast I don't get my feet off the ground quickly enough. I'm either going to be pelted in the head with a small garden's worth of flowers or I'm going to have to block the incoming flower missile with my hands, so that's what I do. It's not until I hear everyone cheering that I realize, *Shit, I caught the bouquet.*

The photographer snaps a dozen pictures of me—my own personal traveling paparazzi—before I return to John. "Congratulations," he says with a teasing smile.

"I wouldn't look so smug if I were you, mister. You're going to be next."

We watch Anthony pretend to crawl up Carmen's floor-length gown and retrieve the garter. A white-haired male comes around collecting the bachelors, including John. Anthony throws the garter directly at him. I suspect he and Carmen were in cahoots and this was all a giant plot. Still, if I'm going to have to dance with someone, I'm happy it's John. Also, even if it was rigged, the symbolism isn't lost on me: according to tradition, John will be the next single guy here to take the big plunge and I'll be the next woman to say good-bye to single living.

John and I dance the traditional dance together. His strong arm gently rests on my lower back and his warm hand is in mine as we float along the dance floor.

When the song is over and the dance floor fills up with other people, Jenna approaches us, clutching David's hand.

"Where are the bathrooms?" she asks.

"You know, that's a good question," I say. "They must be inside." Turning to the guys I say, "Do you want to come?"

"Sure," John says. David nods.

We walk across the huge lawn into the side entrance of the house, which leads us to the game room downstairs. There is a pool table, a full bar with a refrigerator, a TV as big as a wall with several plush leather chairs lined up like a movie theater, an air hockey table, and two full-size pinball machines. The bathroom downstairs is currently occupied, so the four of us stand around to wait for whoever is using it to finish up.

"This house is incredible," David says.

"I wouldn't mind a tour. I've never been in a house like this before," John says.

"Do you think they'd mind?" I ask.

"You know Carmen's parents better than we do," Jenna says.

"I barely know them," I say. I only met Carmen's father a couple of times. He was rarely around when Carmen and I were growing up. He traveled constantly and worked a lot. And Carmen's mom always did her own thing and we did ours. It wasn't like I hung out chatting with her. I think a moment, then decide. "They probably wouldn't mind. Maybe we can find a bathroom that isn't being used."

We walk up a flight of stairs to where the living room, kitchen, and dining room are. The kitchen is buzzing with hired help wearing black-and-white uniforms. Since I'm not technically sure we're allowed to go trouping all over the house, I'm nervous, as if one of the waiters or bartenders is going to arrest us for unlawful trespassing. I know it's ridiculous, but I can't help myself.

The four of us go up to the next level. Upstairs it seems that we are completely alone. From the upstairs hallway we can look out over the banister and see much of the house. I point to another staircase and explain that that is where the guest wing is.

"There are six bedrooms in that wing," I say. "Each one has its own bathroom. You can't see the other wing from here, but that's where Carmen's bedroom suite is."

I show them Carmen's father's study, Carmen's mother's study, and then I bring them to the master bedroom. We could fit the house I grew up in inside this room. In addition to the gigantic canopy bed, there is a white marble fireplace. The walls are sponge painted with various lighter and darker shades of green, which gives one the impression the walls are made of marble. They have a couch and a loveseat and a beautifully carved armoire in the corner.

The his-and-her walk-in closets are each the size of my condo. It's like walking into a major department store there are so many clothes and shoes and accessories, all neatly lined up on the white shelves or hanging in perfect rows on hangers.

There are also separate his-and-her bathrooms. When I take a step into Carmen's mother's bathroom, the second my foot hits the marble tile, an alarm goes off. The four of us freeze. I stop breathing for a moment as I wait for a SWAT team to cart us away in shackles or something for sneaking around. The alarm stops as quickly as it started. I hear a door close downstairs and realize that that door is what set off the alarm, not me. I exhale, relieved, and continue walking.

"This is beautiful," John says. "I feel like I'm in an episode of *Lifestyles of the Rich and Famous.*"

Jenna starts going through Carmen's mother's medicine cabinets and the drawers in her vanity.

"Jenna, what are you doing? Cut it out," I say.

"What?"

"It's one thing to take a look around. It's another thing entirely to go digging around in their personal things."

Jenna takes a bottle of prescription drugs out of the medicine cabinet and shakes it. "Valium," she says with a wicked glint in her eye.

This is awful, but I actually feel pleased by the discovery of this weakness of Carmen's mother. She might be rich, but her life isn't perfect. She has some sort of stress in her life that she finds necessary to medicate herself through. I find it ridiculously comforting to know that her life isn't all fur coats and days at the country club and trips to Europe. I'm a terrible person.

"I'm going to use Carmen's dad's bathroom," Jenna announces. "Wait for me. I'll never find my way back to the party without you."

"We'll be here," I assure her.

She runs off and David says, "I've been to some swanky places in my time, but this is the swankiest." He really is cute if you go for long-haired bad-boy types. His hair is dark and curly and reaches his shoulders. It would be great hair for a rock star to whip around as he wailed on the drums or the guitar. "How do you know Carmen?"

"We went to high school together. Her family owns Regal Furniture."

"No shit?"

"No shit."

Jenna returns from the bathroom and asks me what else the house has to offer.

"Well, the coolest thing about this house is the indoor pool," I say.

"Ooh! Show us!" Jenna says.

"Follow me."

We tiptoe back downstairs past the waiters and caterers working in the kitchen. We walk down the corridor to another set of stairs. There are paintings everywhere and large-scale statues. I try not to be jealous of people who have more money than I do, but I have to say that I am a little envious of all the original art they have. At home I have two framed lithographs, a cool black-and-white photograph of young lovers embracing on the bank of the Seine in Paris that I bought at the Taste of Chicago a few summers back, and a sketch I bought off a street artist working on Navy Pier, and that's all the art I own. I would love to be able to plop down a few thousand bucks to support an emerging artist, but I'm afraid I may never make enough money to do that.

We walk down the back stairs and emerge into the pool room. It's dark in the room, with only the moonlight streaming in from the windows to light our way. The moonlight shimmers off the water, which looks almost black in this dim light.

I squint and feel along the walls for a light switch, but I can't find it. Then I decide it's probably better not to turn the light on anyway in case it alerts someone to the fact that we're here.

"This is huge!" John says. He looks around, shaking his head in amazement.

"Let's go skinny-dipping!" Jenna says.

"Okay," David agrees without hesitation.

"Are you guys crazy?" I ask. "What if we get caught? It's bad enough that we're sneaking around as it is."

I do think it would be incredibly rude to go for a dip with a wedding going on outside, but what is really making my heart pound is the idea of taking my clothes off in front of two men I barely know.

"Oh come on, Heather, live a little. It'll be fun!" Jenna is already taking her clothes off. David starts tugging at his tie.

"I don't believe this!" I say to John.

"A dip might be kind of nice," he says. "It was pretty hot out there with all that dancing."

"What? You want to do this too? Am I the only sane person around here?"

"Come on. You only live once, right?" John begins taking off his clothes. "Have you ever gone skinny-dipping before?" he asks, pulling his shirt off.

Oh my lord, look at those pectoral muscles.

Did he ask me a question?

I swallow and peel my eyes away from his chest.

I don't want him to think I'm some stick-in-the-mud who can't have fun. Why didn't I lose those eight pounds I meant to lose before the wedding? Damn!

"No. Have you?"

"This will be my first time. Come on, we'll lose our skinny-dipping virginity together."

Jenna and David are already splashing around making so much noise I know we're going to get caught at any moment. I'll be the one Carmen hates forever because I'm the one who was stupid enough to let Jenna know about the pool in the first place. I'll have to leave Wisconsin in shame. In a small town, a scandal like this will get talked about for years, and of course in the retelling of this event the gossipers will turn it into some raging orgy and not a simple swim. So if we get caught I'll have to live down the embarrassment for *years*.

Also, I don't have an exhibitionist bone in my body. If I didn't have to get naked to shower or have sex, I would happily wear at least some form of clothing at all times.

Although really, what's the big deal, right? We're all naked beneath our clothes. It's not like I'll be showing off something John has never seen before. Anyway, he'll go home to California and I'll never see him again.

"All right," I relent. "But turn around. I'm not giving you a free striptease. This isn't a burlesque show, you know."

My hands are trembling a little as I pull my delicate pink dress over my head. I gently lay it across one of the chairs that surround a patio table. I kick off my shoes, and then stand immobilized, wondering if I have the guts to take off my bra and underwear. They are both a sheer pink fabric. The second they got wet it would be like I was naked anyway. I don't want to have to put my dress back on over wet underwear, so I decide to just go for it.

"Is it safe for me to turn around?" John asks.

"Give me a second." I snap my bra off and pull my underwear off and fling them on the chair with my dress as quickly as I can. Then I jump in the water with a big splash.

"Okay, you can come in now."

I turn away from John so he can get in the pool without me ogling him. He might not mind, but I figure since I didn't want him to ogle me, it's only fair.

The water is the perfect temperature. It's refreshing without being cold. I paddle over to David and Jenna, who are splashing each other and laughing. Jenna shrieks when David tries to grab her and pull her under.

John swims over to me. "God this feels good. I can't remember the last time I went swimming."

Jenna shrieks again and breaks away from David. The four of us all bob around in the water in a square-shaped configuration.

"I've got an idea," David says. "We can play tag. Whoever is 'it' has to keep their eyes closed."

"So we can't get mad at him when he feels us up?" I ask.

"Damn!" He laughs. "You saw through my full-proof plan. That's the problem with hanging out with smart women. I can't get away with *anything*."

"But you forget that there is another man playing. If you had your eyes closed, you could get a handful of something you'd rather not get a handful of," I point out.

David's eyes grow round. "I hadn't thought of that."

"Remember when you were a kid and you spent all day every day in the pool?" John asks.

"What *did* we do in the pool all that time?" I ask. "We'd be in there all day and never get bored. Now, if I'm in the pool, I swim a couple laps, and that's it, I'm out of ideas, so I get out. When I was young, you couldn't drag me out of the pool for anything."

"And when they called the ten-minute break, it was like your entire world crumbled. Nothing was more tragic," Jenna says.

"The adult swim: a few old ladies in their bathing caps doggie paddling so as not to get their hair wet," David says, paddling himself in imitation, his eyebrows raised in an "I'm really too refined to be swimming in a public pool" sort of expression.

"It was like, 'Ten minutes! Not ten whole minutes!' " I say. "I bet they only called the ten minutes to get kids to buy snacks. I mean would a kid really just like, stop swimming and drown because he didn't take a ten-minute rest? It's all a marketing ploy to get you to buy their popcorn and ice cream sandwiches."

Abruptly Jenna yells, "You're it!" at the same time she lightly taps David on the shoulder. Jenna takes off down the pool and David speeds after her, leaving John and me alone together in the dark room.

He smiles at me. "I think this is the most fun I've had at a wedding . . . maybe ever."

"Me too," I say quietly.

I stop swimming in place and put my feet on the ground. We're only in about four feet of water so I don't straighten up completely—I keep my breasts hidden beneath the surface of the water. I extend my arms and run my fingers gently across the surface of the pool. John reaches out his hand and runs his fingers along the inside of my arm. It's a small, simple gesture, but it sends shivers through me. I feel like I've just been injected with a thousand grams of caffeine. I have all the energy in the world. I tap John on the shoulder and declare that he's it, then, in a burst of speed, I swim down the length of the pool with John chasing after me. I suspect he could catch me without a problem if he really wanted to, but he lets me stay a few feet out of reach.

When I hit the end of the pool, I stop and turn. John stops inches away from me. Because we are naked and only inches apart, and because the sexual tension between us is hot enough to set the house on fire, my entire body pulses with desire.

"You're it," he says, touching me gently. He doesn't race away. Maybe I could do a one-night stand with John. Maybe the evening will evolve in such a way that Jenna and David go off on their own and John and I have some privacy to see where our attraction takes us. But if he does try to have sex with me on the first night we've met each other, that can only mean it's the kind of thing he'd do with other women as well, and that's no good. Shit. I don't know what I want. Yes I do. I want John, but not just for one night.

Jenna and David swim back over to us.

"That felt good to get a little exercise," Jenna says. "We spent all day cooped up in the car driving."

"Well, not all day," John says. John lets David in on the story of the first time he met us earlier today. David thinks the story is hilarious.

"You're crazy!" he tells Jenna.

"I am not!" Jenna goes diving on top of him, sinking him beneath the surface of the water. She goes under with him. In that moment they are under, there is complete silence in the room, and I hear a door opening and the distinct sound of footsteps clicking against the floor.

John and I exchange terrified looks. "Somebody is coming!" I whisper-shout.

Jenna and David come up yelling and splashing.

"Shhh!" I hiss. "Somebody is coming!"

We all pause a moment and hear the footsteps approaching us.

"Follow me!" As quietly as we can we swim to the edge of the pool and walk up the steps. I cover my breasts with my arms as I run. My wet feet slap against the blue tiled flooring of the swimming area as I dash over to the sauna with my three accomplices' footsteps padding quickly after me. I can't believe I'm going to get carted out of this wedding naked, dripping wet, and dying of shame. I had wanted Carmen to think I had my shit together, not that I was some crazed, pool-crashing, party-leaving, nudist orgy-lover. Why did I agree to go skinny-dipping? Why?

I open the door to the sauna and the other three nearly crash into me, such is our haste. The sauna isn't running right now so it isn't warm. "Shit, do you think they'll see our clothes? Our wet footsteps?" I whisper.

"I don't know, it's pretty dark," John says.

Jenna giggles. How can she think this is funny? I'm thirty-three years old and I feel like a naughty teenager.

I open the door just enough that I can peer out. I see the door to the pool room open and a figure looking around. It looks like a man, but I'm not wearing my glasses so it's hard to be sure.

Oh God, what if it's Carmen's father and he's decided to take a swim to get a break from the party? I squint as hard as I can, but I can't see who the person is.

"You have a nice ass," John whispers into my ear.

"What? You're not supposed to be looking at my ass!" I whisper back. "We're about to be caught and escorted out of here humiliated. Focus on what's important here."

"I'm sorry. You were running in front on me. I looked up just for a moment, just to see where I was going. It was an accident."

"Yeah, right." Then, studying the figure in the doorway I say, "Why won't that person go away?"

"Heather, relax. It's not like we're going to get thrown in jail or something," John says.

"Oh shit! He's coming this way!" I close the sauna door and take a step back. I run right into John. His hands touch the front of my waist. My ass brushes against his flaccid penis for just a moment before I take a step forward a few inches.

My heart is pounding both because of the proximity of John's naked body and the knowledge we're about to get busted. I know that at worst we'll get yelled at and have to skulk out of the wedding in shame, but still, it's not an outcome I'm looking forward to. I can already hear the gossip hounds in town repeating this story.

I take a deep breath and open the door just an inch again. My heart stops. I don't recognize the man but he's wearing a suit so I assume he's a guest, perhaps a family member. It might be Carmen's father, but my vision is too blurry to be sure.

Despite my imperfect sight, I swear I think I see the man smile at me.

"Why won't he go away? John, I don't have my glasses on, does he look familiar to you? Does he look like the father of the bride?"

John peers out the door. "It's just some middle-aged guy in a shirt and tie. I couldn't tell you who the father of the bride was if you paid me."

It was true for me too: even though he had walked down the aisle with Carmen, nobody was paying any attention to the father of the bride since we were all distracted by the bride herself in all her white silk and gauzy white-veiled glory. I think back to one of the few times I'd met her father in person when I was young. All I remember was the time he drove Carmen and me to the mall. He combed one side of his hair over and as he drove with the sunroof open, his long thatch of hair stood straight up, blowing in the breeze like a very thin Mohawk.

"Does he have white hair combed over his bald spot?" I ask.

"He's just starting to go gray. There is no comb-over action going on."

Okay, so it's not her father. But who is this man and why won't he leave? Could he be a security guard of some sort? If so, why hasn't he run off to fetch a goon squad to have us arrested?

"What is he doing? Why isn't he going away?"

"It looks like he's just watching the moonlight reflecting off the water."

"Why can't he gaze at the water on his own damn time? What are we supposed to do? We're just going to be trapped here naked all night?"

"I can think of worse fates," John says with a smile.

"We could play a game," Jenna offers.

I turn to face her, my eyes wide with horror. A game? Coming from Jenna this could mean something truly whacky. Orgy comes to mind. As much as I'd like a nice sweaty romp with John, I'd like to do it by ourselves in a private and highly secluded area. I am simply not an orgy kind of girl. Jenna, on the other hand, well, nothing she could do would surprise me.

"A game?" I squeak in a Chipmunk's voice. "What sort of game?"

"Like twenty questions or something."

Oh. How do you like that? Jenna went and surprised me.

"So we can get to know each other better," she said. "Isn't that the game where you ask twenty questions about a person? I don't actually remember the rules."

"Twenty questions is where one person thinks of an object and you get to ask twenty questions to figure out what it is," I say. I sit down on the wood bench and tuck my knees into my chest. Everyone has already had a free show by this point, but I have to cling to whatever shreds of dignity I can hold on to. "I think you're thinking of something called 'conversation.' "

Jenna sticks her tongue out at me.

"I'm game," John says. "What's the first question?"

"Um, how about, What is something that you are afraid

of?" Jenna asks. "Who wants to go first? Heather, how about you?"

"Me?" I think a moment. "One thing I'm afraid of is fish. I've been afraid of them all my life. It's really irrational. Like I wouldn't drink orange juice with pulp as a kid because I thought the pulp was fish or, as I called it, 'fishies.' I saw the commercial for *Jaws* when I was a kid and couldn't sleep for weeks. I did finally see the actual movie when I was an adult, and the nightmares returned in full force for weeks after I saw it. Even seeing an unexpected picture of a shark in a magazine can make me scream."

"I take it you avoid oceans?" John asks.

"I have only been to the ocean once, and I swear I'll never go again. I went with a girlfriend of mine to Mexico and she wanted to go snorkeling. We rented scuba gear and she just took off into the water while I stood about ankle-deep and watched her go farther and farther out. Finally I took a deep breath and went into the water to about midcalf, and then I bent down from the waist to take a peek, and there, inches away from my eyeballs, was a weird-looking fish staring at me with this threatening look in his eyes. It wasn't a huge fish, but just being eye to eye with the strange little creature was so surprising that I leapt back out of the water, hurling myself backwards at tremendous velocity, landing on my ass on the sand. I heard roaring laughter all around me and looked around to see the man who rented us the gear slapping his knee and whooping, and all behind me beach-goers loudly hooted with laughter. It was humiliating and it reinforced my belief that the ocean is a dangerous place."

"Did you try again?"

"No, I'm done with the ocean. I'll go swimming in lakes. It's ocean creatures that do me in. Hey, it's not like my phobia keeps me locked in my house all day or causes me to wash my hands a thousand times an hour. It's a manageable neurosis."

After just a few minutes of sitting on the hard wood bench with my knees tucked up against me, my butt is already getting sore. It reminds me of the time Jenna dragged me to this yoga-and-meditation retreat where we sat cross-legged for hours at a time while some yogi guru guy with long white hair tied up in a bun (a guy with a bun!) talked to us about finding inner peace. After a while, I was far too busy willing my legs not to fall asleep to be able to transcend to a higher plane of existence. Who'd have thought that the toughest part of reaching enlightenment was being able to sit for several hours on end?

"Okay, so I've told all. What are you guys afraid of? John?"

John chews on his lip for a moment. "Heights."

"What kind of heights? Are you not able to cross bridges? Ski? What sort of phobia are we talking here?"

"I'll go hiking, but whenever there is some kind of drop without a fence, no matter how far I am from the ledge, I just can't stop thinking that I'm going to trip or some powerful gust of wind is going to come along and just knock me down the mountain."

"All right. You don't get any points for originality, but that was a solid, honest answer. Jenna, how about you?"

"This is going to sound strange." There's a surprise. "But I'm terrified of knitting needles."

"Come again?"

"I know. I've always been the creative type," she explains to John and David. "I was always painting and sewing and doing all these kind of crafts. One of the things I used to do when I was much younger was knit. But I started getting these really powerful images flashing through my mind when I was in class or on the school bus of taking my eye out with a knitting needle. I had to stop."

"Interesting. I've known you for five years and I never knew this about you," I say. "Are you scared of sweaters too?"

She makes a face at me. "Ha ha. No, just needles."

"All right, David, it's your turn. What scares you?"

David exhales. He pushes his hair behind his ears. Looking at the floor rather than any of us, he says, "I'm afraid I might die without ever knowing what it feels like to be truly in love."

I blink. His answer was so completely not what I was expecting.

"You've never been in love?" Jenna asks in a quiet voice.

He shakes his head. "I've been in like, but not love. Not real love."

"Actually, that's a good one," I say. "That's my biggest fear, too."

No one says anything for several moments. Everything seems so quiet it's almost eerie.

After a minute, I realize that I'm getting chilly—my erect nipples butting up against my legs tell me so. I stand with my hands covering my chest and look out the door. At last, whoever the person was has left. "Thank God," I say. "I think we're safe. I don't think he saw anything."

I gesture for everyone to follow me. We scurry back to the pool and get dressed. "I need to go dry my hair so nobody knows what we were up to," I say.

"Me too," Jenna says.

"Let's go back to Carmen's mother's bathroom. She'll have a hairdryer."

The four of us go back upstairs to her bathroom and dry our hair. My hair doesn't look nearly as cute as it did when we first arrived, but that's what I get for going on an illicit nude swim.

We go back outside to the wedding and learn that Carmen and Anthony have already left to go to a hotel in Madison before they leave for three weeks for their honeymoon in Fiji.

"Oh, we missed them cutting the cake," I say. "The cake is the very best part of the wedding."

"There are still some pieces left. I'll get us some," John says.

"I'll come with you. You'll need help carrying the plates," I say. We walk up to the table, which is covered in crumbs and small plates with slices of cake on them.

"There's chocolate and vanilla. Which do you want?"

I give him a look. "John. I'm a woman. What do you think?"

"Chocolate?"

"Excellent guess. Hey, it looks like some people have taken some of the little dollhouse furniture as a keepsake."

There are still a few pieces lined up behind the slices of cake.

"Do you want one?" he asks.

"Yeah. Do you?"

"What am I going to do with doll furniture?"

"It'll help you remember tonight."

"I don't need a piece of furniture to remember tonight."

I look into his eyes and smile, but it's a sad smile. I think life throws you nights like this to remind you why it's worth getting through hard times—because every now and then there are evenings spent beneath the stars dancing with a handsome man.

"You should take one. Which piece do you want?"

"The bed, of course." He raises his eyebrows up and down. "How about you?"

"I don't know. The rocking chair is pretty cute. But so is the pool table. And the couch is fun too."

"I wonder if this could be a personality test."

"What do you mean?"

"Have you ever played that game where you try to figure out what animal you are most like? Like if you're a free spirit, you're most like a horse. If you're lazy you're like a bear, and so on."

"Maybe. What does my choice say about me? That I have a hard time making decisions?"

"That you are well rounded. You like a nice quiet night at home, you also like to have fun, and you like a place where you can just kick back and relax."

I smile. "I guess. So which should I pick?"

"Take all three."

I look around. It seems like everyone has already had their cake. The party is winding down. If I don't take the furniture, it might just go to waste so I take all three. John has to carry all the plates by himself after all.

We join Jenna and David at the table.

"So David," John asks, "what do you do for a living?"

"I'm a music reviewer for the *Chicago Reader*."

"I love that paper," John says. "Are you the one who did the review of Spiral?"

David nods.

"I love that band."

"I love that band too," I say. "I didn't realize they tour in California. I didn't realize they'd gotten that big." I take a bite of the cake. The sugary white frosting melts on my tongue.

"California? I don't know if they tour in California," John says. "I see them at Harry's on Wabash."

"Harry's on Wabash? In Chicago? Do you visit Chicago on business?"

"I live there."

"You live in Chicago?"

A flash of confusion crosses his face. "Yes." He says it like we've already talked about this. Believe me, I would have remembered this particular detail.

"I thought you lived in California."

"I grew up there, but I moved to Chicago four years ago when I took the job that I have now. I thought we talked about this."

"We talked a little about your job, but not about the fact that it's located in Chicago or that you've lived there for the last four years."

"I was talking to somebody tonight about the best Italian restaurant in Chicago. That wasn't you?"

"That wasn't me," I say, reeling from this information grenade.

"Oh. Well, would you like to come out for Italian with me next weekend? You and I can decide together what the best Italian restaurant in town is."

He lives in Chicago. He's single. And most important of all, he's seen me naked, yet he wants to see me again anyway. "Yes, I'd like that a lot."

This is too good to be true. There has to be something wrong with him. I just haven't found it yet. Probably he's going to fail on my last criteria, but it's an important, nonnegotiable point. I betcha he's an absolutely terrible kisser. He might be like the first guy I ever French-kissed, who made his tongue as hard as a concrete tube and he darted it in and out of my mouth like a boa constrictor. Or he might be your run-of-the-mill saliva-fest kisser, the kind of guy who makes it feel like he's hocked a loogie into your mouth every time you smooch. Or maybe his kissing style is simply unimaginative and dull. It's not the kind of awful that turns you off first thing, but over time you get bored. That's perhaps the trickiest sort of bad kissing of all.

"We'll have to be very scientific about how we decide. We might have to go to a lot of restaurants and eat a whole lot of pasta," he says.

"And a lot of garlic bread."

"That's mandatory."

"The garlic bread is really my favorite part. I don't need that silly dinner stuff. Just give me bread dripping in butter and garlic and marinara sauce."

"I feel the same way."

"Then it's a deal."

We finish our cake. My heart and my limbs are trembling slightly. I feel nervous and thrilled at once. "Well, I guess we should get going."

"I'll walk you to your car if you promise to give me your phone number," John says.

"I'm looking forward to it."

We go to the arched driveway and wait for the valet to bring around our cars. Jenna and David exchange phone numbers and John and I do the same.

"Where in Chicago do you live?" John asks.

I tell him the major cross streets close to my condo.

"That's only about ten minutes away from me."

Ten minutes away! He lives ten minutes away!

The valet brings my car around.

"I guess this is it," I say.

He smiles. "I had a wonderful time tonight."

"I did too."

He looks into my eyes, a hint of a smile on his lips. His gaze is so intense it makes my heart flutter as fast as a humming-bird's wings. I try to warn myself that it will be a terrible kiss, but I can't help but feel optimistic. When he leans in to kiss me, I inhale sharply. His lips touch mine softly. His tongue slides into my mouth, gently meeting mine as if he were licking a drop of melting ice cream from the side of a sugar cone.

I cannot believe my luck. He is a bona fide good kisser.

I realize that just because he seems like my perfect guy in every way, that is no guarantee things will work out between us. Relationships are hard, I know that. But what I feel right now in the warm night air, with the taste of John's mouth on my lips, is hope.

Before tonight I would have never believed I could fall for somebody so hard in just a few hours.

And the thing is, I never even saw it coming.

CLEO BARNES: WORST BLIND DATE EVER

Holly Chamberlin

As always, for Stephen
And this time, also for Rusty

Acknowledgements

I would like to honor Lilly Gordon Einstein. After raising three boys until they were old enough to attend school, she returned to her dream and became a dedicated writer whose stories touched a generation of women; whose generous spirit inspired many hopeful young writers; and whose sparkling wit, genuine warmth, and creative gifts live on in those who knew and loved her.

I would also like to thank John Scognamiglio for his ceaseless support.

Chapter 1

If you lose your temper and throw a dish at him,
remember girls: he absolutely deserves it.
—You're Perfect; He's Not

We were walking through the lobby of the Porter Building when The Predator I'd been watching for months came strutting through the large glass doors.

I grabbed my friend Jane's arm. "Look at that guy," I hissed. "He has macho idiot written all over him."

Jane extricated her arm and looked at me quizzically. "That guy?" she asked, nodding toward The Predator, who now stood in three-quarter profile by the middle elevator. "The one in the beautiful suit? The one with the dark, wavy hair?"

"That's the one," I said.

Jane considered The Predator with almost clinical interest. Finally, she said, "He looks perfectly harmless. Gorgeous, in a sexy, young Al Pacino sort of way, but perfectly harmless."

"Are you kidding?" I hissed. The Predator lifted his hand to his mouth and cleared his throat. "Did you see that fake cough? He's a total poser."

Jane sighed. "Cleo, you're insane," she said. "You're biased, prejudiced, whatever. What's the reverse of a misogynist? You hate men."

"I do not hate men." The Predator stepped onto the elevator; I watched, narrow-eyed, as the doors closed on his suspiciously broad shoulders. "Besides," I added, turning back to Jane, "don't I have a reason to?"

Jane put her hands on her ample hips, which were accentuated by ultra-low-rise jeans. Jane is my fashionable friend. Me? I have no sense of style whatsoever.

"Let me get this straight," she said. "Because Justin is a jerk all guys are jerks?"

"No, of course not. It's just that—"

"Look." Jane took my arm and pulled me along toward the lobby doors. "You know nothing about that guy with the great suit. For all you know he could be a total sweetheart. Come on, Cleo, how would you like it if he decided you were mentally unbalanced based on the color of your sweater? Which, by the way, does nothing for you. That wouldn't be very fair, now would it?"

"No," I admitted, "but I wouldn't care. Why would I want to be involved with a guy like him anyway? He's obviously a cheater and a liar."

We emerged into the cool evening air of a Boston spring. Jane shivered and buttoned her blush-colored ultrasuede jacket. "You're impossible. You'll never get another date for the rest of your life if you believe everyone with a penis is a jerk."

"Who said I want another date? I just might be through with men. Finished, over."

"Do you think Marty's a jerk?" Jane challenged.

I thought of Jane's mild-mannered, amusing, successful corporate boyfriend and about all the nice times we'd had together and about how he'd told Jane, who'd told me, that he'd never trusted Justin, and I felt a teeny stab of guilt. "Marty's an exception," I said.

"Uh-huh. Look, Cleo, you can't let your slimy ex-boyfriend destroy the rest of your life. Justin is history. Besides, he's just one guy."

True, I thought, Justin was history—at least, I wasn't dating him anymore—and he was just one guy—just one popular, handsome guy—but why then did he exert such influence on my life almost a year after I'd kicked him out?

Fool me once, shame on you; fool me twice . . . Well, you know the saying.

Suddenly, I was eager to drop the subject of men—current or expired—entirely. "I'm in the mood for a burger," I said brightly.

"Nice change of subject," Jane said. "Fine. Let's go."

Chapter 2

Every single member of the male sex—without exception!—is morally decrepit.

—Men Suck, Get Used to It

"What's a cute kid like you doing in a dump like this?" That's the first thing Justin said to me, the night we met at a bar called Soiree, which was, in fact, not a dump. No one had ever called me cute before; I'm tall and I wear a size 10 shoe, not really cute material, and in my late twenties, not really a kid. But Justin smiled down into my eyes and oh, did I suddenly feel cute. Cute and young and desired.

Bluff, buff, and blond, Justin was a former college football player and Big Man on Campus. At twenty-eight he was still immensely popular; every time we were out together at a bar or a club he ran into someone he knew. Sure, once or twice—maybe three or four times—the person Justin accosted heartily didn't seem to remember him but, you know, that sort of thing happens in a big city. You meet so many people you just can't keep track of them all and if Justin remembered every person he'd ever met, it simply attested to his superior social skills.

That or his overinflated ego.

Justin was successful too. Sure, maybe he hadn't gone to

law school or gotten an MBA, and he wasn't a doctor or a computer whiz, but he was a rising star at the manufacturer of home appliances where he worked as a manager in the personnel department.

All the time we were dating I never knew Justin's official title; it was only months after the bitter end that I ran into a guy who worked with Justin and learned that the man I'd thought a powerful player at StayHome Tech was in fact lower midlevel management and not likely to rise much further.

Until the disastrous end of our relationship I believed everything Justin told me, including all the clichéd compliments I'm sure he picked up from some cheesy daytime soap opera. (Justin called in sick to work at least twice a month, usually because of a hangover.)

"Cleo, you're a special girl."

"Cleo, I've never met anyone like you."

"Cleo, you're a really sweet kid."

A really sweet kid who was rendered totally brain-dead by a guy so full of himself he barely noticed that I existed— except when he wanted sex or his laundry done.

Why would a young woman most people considered intelligent and levelheaded fall so hard for such a worthless guy? The answer is embarrassingly simple: because he looked at me. For the first time in my life a big, popular guy looked at me. And Justin Barrow, being big and popular, knew a good deal when it fell into his arms.

In the almost two years we were together I never had the slightest suspicion that Justin was cheating on me. It was Jane who had the guts to confront me with the sorry truth about my big, popular boyfriend. She dropped by my apartment one evening last July. After ascertaining that Justin wasn't lurking in the background, she got right to the point. "Marty and I saw Justin at Venue last night."

"So?" I opened the fridge and said: "Do you want a soda?"

"No thanks. Did you know where he was?" she asked.

I didn't know where Justin had been the previous night. All

I knew was that he'd come to bed around four A.M. I remember because I hadn't been able to get back to sleep; Justin had a bad snoring habit.

"I don't own him," I protested lightly. "He told me he was out with some buddies."

Jane gave a bitter little laugh. "Yeah, well, this buddy was female and she was all over Justin and he didn't seem to mind one little bit."

"What are you saying?" I felt my cheeks redden. I put down the can of soda I'd popped opened.

"I'm saying that what I saw, and you can ask Marty too, was not appropriate behavior for a guy who's in a committed relationship."

I reacted as any loyal girlfriend blinded by misplaced adoration would have reacted. "You're lying," I said to Jane.

"No," she replied, "I'm not."

"I'm sure there's a perfectly legitimate explanation." I thought for a moment but no perfectly legitimate explanation came to me. Finally, stupidly, I said: "Maybe the girl is his cousin."

"Then there's a whole new meaning to kissing cousins, trust me."

"It's not a joke. You just accused my boyfriend of cheating on me."

Jane had the good grace to look greatly sympathetic. "I'm sorry, Cleo," she said. "This wasn't easy to tell you. But Marty and I agreed it would be wrong not to let you know what we saw."

"Marty's never liked Justin," I snapped.

"That's true. But like you said, this is not a joke and neither of us would lie about something so serious."

I turned away from Jane; I couldn't bear for her to see the growing humiliation on my face.

After a moment Jane said, "Are you going to confront him?"

"I don't know," I said. "I have to think about it."

For a while after Jane left I stomped around the apartment, feeling very angry with my best friend. Jane, I decided, was the problem, not Justin. Who did she think she was? Everything was 'Marty and I' and 'me and Marty.' I'm sick of those two, I decided. They're so smug. They think they're the perfect couple. They think every other couple should be just like them, all loyal and loving and, and—perfect!

I didn't stay angry for long. I'm not entirely stupid. I knew there was a chance that Jane was right and that Justin had cheated on me. It was in the realm of possibility. It was conceivable.

But: what then? What, I wondered, should I do? Should I confront him? Or should I just try to forget about Justin's . . . indiscretion. After all, we'd been together for close to two years. Men got bored; they were genetically wired to stray. It didn't necessarily mean our relationship was over. Besides, could I really function without him? I began to feel panicked; I wished I'd accepted those antianxiety pills my friend Sam had offered me when I'd had to give a big presentation the month before.

When drugs aren't available, cats will do nicely. Around ten o'clock I settled in bed with Gargoyle and Goblin, five-year-old littermates, one gray with white, the other white with gray. To my left was a stack of mindless magazines; by my right hand the TV remote. And I waited.

Around midnight, I fell asleep. Justin didn't come home until almost three. Gargoyle and Goblin were snoozing on my feet but when Justin crawled into bed, they leapt onto the floor and stalked off. I was too groggy to focus on anything other than the fact that Justin was home, in my bed, with me, where he belonged.

"Hey," he said. I smelled beer on his breath but that was nothing unusual. "Sorry I woke you."

" 'Sokay," I mumbled, touched by his concern. And then he kissed my forehead, a sort of sloppy kiss, but it was such a nice, comforting gesture that I fell back to sleep absolutely sure that Jane and Marty had been mistaken.

Still, in the bright light of morning I felt less certain about Justin's innocence. Maybe, I thought queasily, listening to Justin rumbling around the bathroom as he showered and shaved, maybe Jane was right and Justin had been out with another girl. But did I really want to confirm that unhappy suspicion?

Justin swore. He must have dropped his toothbrush again, I thought. He was rather clumsy in the morning. It was an endearing trait actually. I would miss Justin's morning bumbling. I would miss Justin.

And at that moment I decided to let the whole cheating thing drop.

Justin left the apartment already a half hour late for work. Once he was gone I hurried through my own morning routine, which included picking up after my sloppy boyfriend. Balled-up socks, dirty underwear, a used tissue . . .

"What is it, Goblin?" I bent down to take whatever it was from the cat's jaws and stopped cold. Goblin was gnawing on the expensive silk tie I'd bought for Justin just weeks before, for no other reason than I'd wanted to give him a present.

And here it was, stained, crumpled, tossed under the bed to be retrieved by a curious cat.

Did Justin expect me to pay for the dry cleaning? Probably. He never seemed to have any money for the essentials.

Plenty for playing, though. I wondered how many drinks Justin had bought that girl at Venue. I remembered that he had failed to pay his portion of the rent for the past three months. I thought about that mysterious charge on my credit card, the one from a store called PartyHoppers.

Goblin, bored with munching on Justin's tie, stood, stretched, and stalked from the bedroom. I finished getting ready for work. But once at my desk I could focus only on Jane's damning accusation. Why, I wondered, would my friend lie to me? Why would she want to hurt me? Finally, I emailed Jane on her home account.

"Are you really, one hundred percent, totally sure?" I

asked. When I got home from work at six thirty that evening, Jane's answer was waiting.

"Yes."

I poured myself a glass of wine. I put on a favorite jazz CD. I threw away the remains of Justin's tie.

"Well, boys," I said to my ever-faithful kitties, "wish Mommy luck. Things are about to get ugly."

Justin got home around seven thirty that evening, unusually early, as he made it a habit to stop at a bar after work with a few of his colleagues.

"You're home early," I said.

"Yeah," Justin replied.

"Any particular reason?"

Justin yanked open the refrigerator. "There's nothing in here," he said disgustedly.

"I didn't get to shop."

Justin looked around the apartment as if seeing it for the first time and finding it sorely lacking. "I think I'll call Bob," he said. "Maybe we'll go get a pizza."

And then I said, as casual as you please, "You know what Jane told me? She told me that she and Marty saw you at Venue making out with some other girl. Can you believe it? I don't know why she would lie to me like that."

There was dead, heavy silence. Justin stood like a hulking bear; his eyes were focused on the fridge. When he finally looked at me, what I saw on his face confirmed that Jane had, indeed, been telling the truth.

I laughed. I couldn't believe I was laughing but I was. "You cheated on me," I said.

Justin sighed the sigh of a long-suffering man. "Look," he said, "it was no big deal, okay? It was just like, I was there alone cause Tony hadn't shown up and I met this girl and we got to like, talking, and then, you know, maybe I had one too many beers, and we hooked up a bit. That's all."

Justin took a step toward me and I backed a step away.

Who was this person in my home? "Hooked up a bit? What does 'a bit' mean?" I demanded.

"Look," he said, "we never left the booth. I swear. I didn't go home with her or anything."

The absurd laughter had passed; now I was inarticulate with grief. Like someone in physical pain, I eased onto the couch and stared down at my folded hands. Why, I wondered, were they folded? I didn't remember folding them. Maybe, unconsciously, I was afraid I'd hit my boyfriend.

Justin mumbled something. I'm sure it wasn't "I'm sorry." I looked back up at him and said, "You need to leave. Now."

"Whoa, Cleo," he said, "don't overplay this!" I watched, fascinated, disgusted, as he lazily scratched his stomach through his shirt. "I told you it meant nothing."

"And that's supposed to make me feel better?" I demanded. "Just go."

I watched Justin take in the stunning fact that meek, mousy Cleo had just ordered him out of her apartment, and her life.

"But it's like, night," he said. "Where the hell am I supposed to go now?"

"Call one of your buddies," I snapped. "I'm sure one of them will let you sleep in his bathtub."

Fact: Justin's friends' apartments were grim. Nobody had taught those boys anything about housekeeping, not even the basics. No wonder Justin had given up his lease only a month after we'd started to date. With me he got sex and a spotless home.

Justin looked at me with his wide blue eyes and for a moment I almost relented entirely. "That's harsh," he said, and his voice was low. "Look, just let me stay on the couch tonight. It's the least you can do for me."

I didn't have the energy to argue Justin's dubious logic. I let him sleep on the couch that night but the moment he opened his eyes the next morning I handed him his clothes and his walking papers.

Justin Barrow was history.

Chapter 3

Don't be shy about asking to see his financials. Love is a lot easier when you're not on a tight budget.
—Love and Marriage in the Twenty-First Century

I'd like to say that the relationship ended once and for all that morning but the truth is that I missed Justin almost immediately.

Being with him had made me feel special. All my life I'd pretty much assumed that an average, unexciting girl like me should expect to date only average, unexciting boys, boys like Billy Newman of the Junior Rotary Club or Cliff Pitt, who worked in produce at the local grocery store. Nice enough boys but nobody you'd actually admit to dating, as my sister, Ashley, pointed out when I made the mistake of bringing them home to meet my family.

My sister, Ashley Barnes: beautiful, brainy, and compelling. For twenty-six years I'd lived in her shadow, and then Justin had come along—big, blond, bluff Justin—and he'd chosen me, Cleo Barnes, Girl Ordinaire.

And now he was gone.

At first I wondered if Justin had cheated on me because I wasn't thin enough. It was possible; Justin was always ogling other girls when we were out together. Then I was convinced he'd cheated on me because I was too straight-laced. How many times had Justin begged me to go to an after-hours club on a weeknight and how many times had I refused because I had to be up early for work? Justin mocked my job as an editor of technical manuals; he couldn't understand how I could waste my time on such "boring crap."

The bottom line, I decided, was that a guy like Justin needed a skinny girl who liked to have fun, not a fat stick-in-the-mud like me. A guy like Justin needed a girl like Ashley.

Less than two weeks after I'd thrown Justin out, I called him. He was cold at first but after I begged and pleaded he finally agreed to meet me for a drink at a popular, expensive steak house. Drinks turned into dinner, which I paid for. And the sad story is that I took him back. I don't know why he came back; maybe he was tired of crashing in dirty bathtubs and eating spray cheese straight from the can.

Sam Nashe, my good friend from college who is now the senior vice president of corporate security at a financial services firm downtown, was barely able to hide his disgust with me.

"I was so proud of you when you kicked him out," Sam said. "What happened? Did you have a ministroke or something?"

"Of course not," I said. "I just think he deserves a second chance. Doesn't everybody deserve a second chance?"

"No," Sam said emphatically. "Absolutely not."

Jane wasn't much more supportive. "I think," she said, "that you're making a big mistake."

"I'm sorry you feel that way," I replied loftily.

Marty's opinion was stamped clearly on his face. Justin was a bum and I was an idiot for trusting him.

Marty, it turns out, was right. It took less than a month for Justin to cheat on me again. At least, it took less than a month for me to find him on my couch with our acquaintance Melissa, half-dressed, limbs entwined, empty beer bottles littering the coffee table. Maybe worst of all, Justin had locked Gargoyle and Goblin in the bedroom where they were howling furiously.

In retrospect the scene was kind of funny, Justin hobbling to the door, pants around his ankles, two angry cats swiping at his legs—I'd released them, of course—Melissa mumbling, "Oh my God, oh my God, oh my God," as she gathered her things and fled alone into the night.

"I don't ever want to see you again!" I shouted when my errant ex-boyfriend finally managed to pull his pants up around his waist. (Had Justin gained weight? For the first time I noticed an unsightly bulge around his middle.)

"Don't worry," he muttered, as he hightailed it down the hall. "This is so not worth it."

What Justin really meant by that parting comment was that I was not worth loving.

And that's why, nine months after I threw Justin out of my apartment for the final time, I was a full-blown, totally committed, she-devil man-hater.

Chapter 4

Never, ever apologize, even if he's twisted the facts to make it appear that you are guilty because you are not guilty. Ever.

—It's All His Fault!

"Guys like him make me so sick. I swear if I look at him for one more second I'm going to projectile vomit all the way to the vending machines."

Roughly, Sam turned me away from the creep lounging across the theater lobby. "I thought," he said with a significant look, "that we came to the movies to have a good time."

I looked over my shoulder. The creep had been joined by a woman. She looked nice and clean and smart.

"Just look at that guy!" I hissed into Sam's face. "Ugh, my flesh is creeping. How can that woman stand to be within five feet of him?"

With a long-suffering sigh Sam peered back at the creep in question.

"What, exactly, are you objecting to?" he asked. "And don't say his hair because it's fabulous."

Fabulous hair. Jane had said the same thing about The Predator, who did, as a matter of plain fact, have fabulous, dark, shiny hair, which he surely used to seduce hordes of weak-willed women.

"I'm objecting," I informed Sam haughtily, "to everything!"

The theater lobby attendant removed the velvet rope before us, and the crowd of people waiting to see the latest Wes Anderson film surged forward. Sam and I made our way to the snack counter. "Okay," he said, "I'm an empathetic kind of guy, I can see why you're angry, but I do think you're taking it too far. And by the way, why don't you hate all women too? Didn't Justin cheat on you with someone who was supposed to be your friend?"

"Melissa wasn't a close friend," I pointed out. "Besides, Justin probably lied and told her we'd broken up."

"Then why did he take her to your apartment?"

I had wondered about that. Didn't Melissa, who knew my apartment because she had been at a party there, wonder what Justin was still doing with a key?

"I don't know, exactly," I said archly. "But I'm sure he was totally to blame. He's such an asshole."

Sam frowned. "You've developed quite the potty mouth, Ms. Barnes. I must say it's not a very attractive quality."

"All right then," I said, slightly embarrassed, "what would you prefer I call Justin and all slimeballs like him?"

"Libertine, rake, rogue, lecher, satyr, lothario. Would you like to me to go on?"

"Just because you're smarter than me—" I began.

"Smarter than I am. And I'm not smarter, I just have a larger vocabulary."

I looked up at my friend. Sam wasn't particularly handsome; his nose was a bit too large and his hair was thinning at an alarming rate. I'd known him for ten years and not once in all that time had he had his heart broken. Was it only because he was lucky, or was it also because he chose the right sort of man, the kind who would end a relationship, if need be, in an honest, careful way?

"You are smarter," I said. "You don't date ass—I mean, libertines."

"I have a good sense of self-esteem. I'm not full of myself but I don't allow idiots to waste my precious time."

Clutching a tub of popcorn and two sodas, Sam and I settled in seats in the exact middle of the theater. The lights dimmed and movie music surged.

"How," I whispered, "do you achieve that balance of, I don't know, humility and self-respect?"

I asked Sam this question as if my life depended on it. In a way, I suppose, it did.

Sam turned to me; I could hardly see his face in the dark. "It's a gift," he whispered back. "Now be quiet. The previews are about to start."

Chapter 5

Any woman who expects to get a straight answer from a man in response to a straight question—e.g., Q: Do you want to eat out tonight? A: I dunno.—is a hopeless idiot.

—Excuses, Lies, and Prevarications:
Learning the Male Language

"Oh great! What rotten luck!"

I didn't actually say these words aloud but I thought them all right. Because just as the elevator doors were starting to close, the dark-haired guy Jane thought was so cute slipped in next to me. It was just we two.

I took a giant step to the left to put some distance between The Predator and me. I kept my eyes on the floor. It was going to be a long ride. I'd already established he worked at Luna Design, on the tenth floor, two floors below Arbiter Publishing, where I work. I had no idea what exactly he did at Luna Design but what did it matter? The last thing I wanted was to get into a conversation with The Predator.

We must have been nearing the fourth floor, my eyes still trained on the ground, when suddenly I noticed The Predator was wearing a pair of very nice shoes. They were black and contemporary; they looked like something I'd seen in one of Jane's fashion magazines.

And in the next second, absolutely unbidden, I found myself wondering about The Predator's toes. What, I thought, were his toes like? Were they plump or scrawny, knobbed or straight? Whatever they were like—and I felt suddenly sure they were attractive—they were right there, in his very nice shoes, covered by his socks, very close, in fact, to my own toes in their size ten pumps.

By the sixth floor I felt ready to die of embarrassment. Feet are so terribly intimate. Why was I daydreaming about such an intimate, vulnerable, altogether humble part of The Predator's body? A witness to my thoughts would assume I liked him or something.

The elevator came to a smooth halt. The doors slid open and the dark-haired, lovely-toed Predator stepped out. I didn't raise my eyes until I'd reached my desk.

"Let's move down a few seats," I hissed.

"Why?" Jane asked. "What's wrong with these seats?"

Jane and I were at the art deco-style bar at Communique after work one evening. And we were not alone. I nodded and gave Jane what I hoped was a significant look.

"What's wrong with you?" she demanded. "Are you having a fit?"

I gathered my bag and jacket, hopped off the stool, and strode to the far end of the bar. Jane had no choice but to follow.

"That guy to your left," I explained when we were settled in our new seats. "I caught him looking at you."

For a moment Jane stared at me with a completely blank expression. What didn't she understand? Finally, she shook her head.

"You made us change seats because a guy looked at me? So what? He's allowed to look. There's no ring on my finger. He doesn't know I'm involved."

It was true that all sorts of guys routinely looked at Jane. She is eye-catching. Her hair is thick and brown with artful blond highlights. Her figure is camera-ready. Her clothes are all bought at discount from the hip clothing store she manages.

Before the Justin debacle it never bothered me that guys gave her the eye. Now, what had been a harmless, possibly flattering gesture seemed an act of supreme violation and arrogance.

"Cleo," Jane said now, with an air of someone who'd studied at the feet of the Dali Lama, "did you ever think that maybe you're angry at yourself and not at Justin?"

Where, I wondered, do people come up with these theories?

"Absolutely not! What did I do wrong? Nothing. I'm the injured party."

"Well," she persisted, "if you are angry at yourself for believing Justin's lies—"

"But I'm not."

"Of course not. But if by any chance you were, I'd like to point out that you're wasting a lot of time being angry at the wrong person."

The bartender brought our drinks then, which allowed me to take a deep breath before having to answer.

"I am not," I repeated, "angry at the wrong person. I'm angry at Justin."

"And at every other person with testicles."

The conversation pretty much fell apart after that. Jane declined a second glass of wine.

"I've got to go," she said, slipping off the stool and shouldering her bag. "Marty and I are having dinner with one of his colleagues from the Seattle office. Are you going to be okay?"

"Of course I'm going to be okay," I said. "Why wouldn't I be?"

Jane shrugged and was gone. There was no way I was going to sit alone at the bar with that guy just waiting to pounce on me. Sure, he'd been looking at Jane, but guys will try to bag any girl just so they have something to tell their buddies.

On the way out I gave the guy a dirty look. I'm not sure he actually saw it because he was busy fooling around with his Blackberry. Still . . .

As I was rummaging in my closet that evening, hoping to find something decent to wear to a big meeting the following day, I came across an envelope stuffed with photos of my sister. For the past ten years Ashley had made it a point to have her portrait taken. With the arrival of each new 8 x 10, the previous year's portrait went into this envelope and the new one took its place in a cut-glass frame.

I sat on the bed with the envelope of Ashley through the ages. Fifteen-year-old Ashley in a white cashmere sweater she'd bought with money borrowed from me. (Money never paid back, but I really didn't mind. Ashley looked wonderful in white.) Twenty-one-year-old Ashley in a mink stole that had belonged to her husband's mother. (I wonder what happened to that stole after the divorce.) Twenty-four-year-old Ashley in a genuine Dolce & Gabbana suit she'd gotten as a gift from an admirer.

I slid the photos back into the envelope and sighed. Ashley got couture and I got dumped. And suddenly, just like that, I realized that Jane was right. I *was* angry with myself, I was furious with myself for being so stupid and trusting. Yes, I hated Justin, but I also hated myself. I'd allowed my heart to be broken.

I pulled last year's portrait of Ashley from the envelope again and looked hard at it. Ashley had never had her heart broken; even her short-lived marriage had hardly caused a ripple in her emotional state. Maybe it really was because she was so beautiful; maybe her beauty gave her strength. Maybe it was also because she didn't date losers. Even the husband hadn't been so bad. Just old and rich.

I went to bed then and burrowed far under the covers. Gargoyle and Goblin settled on my legs and chest, effectively pinning me in safely. I lay there in the dark and wondered: how do you forgive yourself for having a big heart?

Chapter 6

An iguana makes a fine animal companion for the woman allergic to pet dander.

—Men: Who Needs 'Em?

"I think," I said, "that I'm going to be sick."

"You're not going to be sick." Jane yanked me further into the shadows of Club Milano to a place from where we could see and not be seen, because the last thing I wanted was for Justin to see me standing there in my chinos and demure cotton sweater.

Justin, in all his bluff blond glory, his tongue halfway down the throat of some Britney Spears-looking specimen wearing a skirt that barely covered her admirable butt and a top that barely covered her considerable breasts.

Compared to her I was a dried-up old crone. Worse, I was dateless on a Saturday night.

"You can do so much better than Justin," Jane said firmly.

"Forget him," Marty urged. "Forget you ever wasted—I mean, just forget him."

"It's okay," I said grimly. "I know I wasted two years of my life with him. I'm aware of my own stupidity."

Marty turned forty shades of red. "I didn't mean—" he began, but Jane put a hand on his arm and he shut up.

Soon after, I claimed a headache—not entirely untrue—and took a cab home, leaving Jane and Marty to enjoy the rest of the night without my depressing company.

Later that night, in bed with Gargoyle and Goblin squatting like sentinels watching for bluff blond invaders, I thought about why it mattered to me that Justin was out with another woman. It wasn't like I was still in love with him. In fact, the sight of him had brought on that headache.

The local news. A rerun of *Dharma & Greg.* Why, I wondered, did I even bother with TV? I stopped for a moment on a new reality show, something called *Pathetic Losers,* in which a group of so–called friends sent the most innocent, trusting person they knew on a date with the most unbelievably wretched specimen of the opposite sex.

Huh, I thought. I could be that Pathetic Loser. And then it came to me. It mattered that Justin was out with another woman because that meant he had won. He'd broken my heart and found another girl—just one?—long before my heart had mended and long before I was ready to find another guy. Me and my innocent, trusting heart.

The Pathetic Loser on-screen was meeting his blind date. I squinted hard at the screen. The date looked remarkably like my sister. And that's when I decided, just like that, that I was going to steal Justin's victory away from him. I was going to show him—show the world!—that Cleo Barnes was alive and well and dateable.

I was going to get myself a new boyfriend whether I liked it or not.

Chapter 7

Believe it: every man wants a wife not quite as smart as he thinks he is. Act slightly ditzy on the very first date and chances are good you'll be sporting a two-carat diamond within the year.

—The MRS. Files

"It doesn't seem," Jane said carefully, "that you're in the right frame of mind for dating."

It was a rainy Saturday afternoon and Jane and I were killing time at the Barnes & Noble in the Prudential Mall. Jane hefted the most recent copy of British *Vogue* from the wall-to-wall magazine rack. I was just about to protest that I was indeed in the right frame of mind for dating when something absolutely sickening caught my eye.

"Look at that couple," I hissed, "over there, by the discount table. I swear I'm going to vomit. I hate, hate, hate when guys do that!"

"Do what?" Jane asked, shifting only her eyes.

"Put their arm around a girl's waist, like they own her. Like she's some sort of possession. Ugh."

Jane shrugged. "I think it's kind of sexy. I don't know, Cleo. Your attitude is so nasty and suspicious. What guy is going to want to go out with a nasty, suspicious girl?"

"I am not nasty and suspicious!"

"Okay," she said, flipping open the massive glossy magazine, "I'll pretend I believe that. But why do you want to go on a blind date? What's the rush? Why not just wait until you meet someone you like?"

"I'm never going to like a guy ever again." The words were out of my mouth before I could stop them.

"Oh yeah," Jane drawled, "this is going to go well."

"So," I said, undeterred, "can you fix me up? Marty must know someone."

Jane closed the copy of British *Vogue* I wasn't letting her enjoy. "Cleo," she said, "you're my best friend, but honestly? I'm not sure I want to set up some nice, unsuspecting guy with the man-hater you've become."

I was hurt by Jane's words but not so self-delusional that I couldn't see a wee bit of truth in them.

"Fine, then don't," I said. "And don't ask Marty either. But maybe you can ask someone you sort of know if she sort of knows someone so that if the date doesn't work out you won't be embarrassed because nobody really knows the guy so nobody will have to feel responsible."

"That's really ridiculous, Cleo."

"Please?"

Jane eyed me critically for what seemed like forever. "All right," she said finally, "I'll ask around at work. Maybe one of the girls knows a guy desperate enough to go out with you."

"Well," I said, "I'll never get a date if you tell everyone I'm horrible! Anyway, I'm not horrible, I'm just cautious. I'm smarter than I used to be. I'm a strong woman who's not going to allow a man to take advantage of her ever again."

"Cleo," Jane said, in that "I know best because I have a wonderful relationship with a perfect boyfriend" way I'd come to despise, "relationships are built on trust."

"Not the ones I've been in," I retorted. "And if you say

'Just look at Marty and me' I'm going to start screaming and have a very hard time stopping."

Jane bought the British *Vogue*. We spent the rest of the afternoon wandering the mall. And not once did she mention her wonderful relationship with her perfect boyfriend.

Chapter 8

Never underestimate the power of cleavage. If you don't own a push-up bra, buy one. Now.
—Guys & How to Bag Them

His name was Ben. A girl who worked for Jane, Alison Somebody-or-Other, set us up. Ben was about thirty-five and, Alison informed me, back in graduate school part time preparing for a career change.

Ben sounded nice on the phone. We talked for all of two minutes, long enough to agree to meet at six o'clock in Porter Square in Cambridge. I was nervous but excited to finally start Life After Justin.

I arrived five minutes early; Ben showed up exactly at six. He was a nice-looking guy in that small-town news-anchorman sort of way, the kind with a very precise haircut and a sincere expression he probably acquired in Cub Scouts. I found him bland but not in the least repulsive. Things boded well.

And then . . . it happened. I don't know how to describe it other than to say I was possessed, literally taken over by another being, someone not at all like the me I knew. I'll call this other being The Hag.

"So," Ben said, when we were seated at a small rectangular

table at Full-A-Falafel. There was a dinner special for $5.99. It came with a can of Coke. "I guess Alison told you I'm changing careers."

"From what to what?" I asked challengingly.

"Right now I'm a computer systems analyst," he said, "but I'm training to become a special education teacher. It will be a big cut in salary but it's a sacrifice I'm willing to make."

Cleo might have been impressed by this statement of selfless social responsibility. The Hag was not. I looked down at the largely gray-and-taupe dinner special, and then back up to Ben's innocent, unsuspecting face.

"So," I said, "what you're saying is that you can't make up your mind about what you want to be when you grow up."

Ben seemed confused; he dropped his plastic fork to the floor. "Uh, no," he said, "that's not it at all. It's just that—"

"Now you're going to tell me that all your money goes toward school and you have no money to spend on dates so that's why you took me to this lousy place and if I want to see you again I have to understand that I'll be paying for everything?"

Poor Ben. For almost two full minutes he struggled mightily to say something, anything. I'm sure the sneer on my face wasn't helpful.

"I like hummus." The words finally came bursting from Ben's mouth. "I know lots of people who like hummus. I just thought—"

"You might," I interrupted, "have had the courtesy to ask me where I would like to eat. You might have had the intelligence to pick a sort of neutral place, you know, maybe even one with a wine list and without ripped plastic seats. I've cut my thigh, you know."

I hadn't really cut my thigh—I was wearing heavy twill pants—but The Hag, it seems, was not above lying for effect.

Ben looked ashen. "You've cut yourself?"

"I'll be fine," I replied coolly.

And then came another two minutes of awful silence. Ben labored. I waited.

"So . . ." he said finally.

I looked at him nonencouragingly. How slow-witted was this guy? Ben began to fidget. I'd never actually seen a guy nervously twist a napkin.

"So, what you're saying is . . . what you're saying is you're not interested in seeing me again?"

"Frankly, Ben," I said, "I'm not interested in seeing you right now." With great dignity I stood and with one finger pushed the brown plastic tray with my untouched dinner across the table. "Enjoy."

There was a metallic crash from behind the food counter but I heard Ben's words loud and clear. This is what he said: "And to think I passed up poker night for this."

Chapter 9

Be sure to keep the GIA certification in a safe place for every diamond you receive, and to have the stones reappraised at least once every two or three years. Know what you're worth!
—To Hell With Love, Jewelry Lasts Longer

"I'm out." Jane's voice over the phone sounded oddly foreign. "I give up. From now on you're on your own with this blind-date thing. Alison said Ben was really broken up. He called her as soon as he got home. She said he was crying. He's a very sensitive guy."

I winced. Ben had cried? Justin had never cried in the two years we were together. Not even when his older brother had been diagnosed with cancer.

"Then why doesn't Alison go out with him?" I said flippantly.

"Alison, as you know, is gay."

"Oh. Right." I felt chastened. "Really, Jane, I don't know what came over me. My intentions were good. I wanted to be nice. Maybe I was just really nervous. Nothing like that has ever happened to me before. I'm sorry."

"You should be," Jane replied smartly. "My authority with

Alison has been undermined. I mean, it's salvageable, but I've taken a hit. A manager needs to have the respect of her staff. If I—"

"Okay, okay," I said, "I get it."

Truth is, I really didn't get it. What had happened to me on that date with Ben? One minute I'd been nice, normal Cleo and the next I was a complete harridan. By the time I got home that night I was sick with regret. Okay, I'd felt no attraction toward Ben but that was no reason for my abominable behavior. Most weird had been my objection to the Middle Eastern cuisine. I'd eaten at Full-A-Falafel lots of times. The $5.99 dinner special was a fantastic deal.

I could only hope my appalling behavior was attributable to blind-date jitters and not to some nascent multiple personality disorder. Who else besides The Hag was inside me? The Butcher? The Pathological Liar?

"I'm sure I'll be okay on the next blind date," I told Jane with false certainty.

Jane didn't immediately reply.

"Hello?" I said. "Are you still there?"

"I'm here. I'm just trying to process your last statement. The next blind date?"

"Sure. Why not? I mean, if someone will set me up."

"That," Jane replied, "is the big question."

At three o'clock I took the elevator down to the lobby for a pack of sugarless gum. I don't chew gum. But I'd already gone down to the lobby twice that day and both times I'd bought a candy bar. There are an awful lot of calories in the average candy bar.

I narrowed my eyes in anticipation of sighting The Predator. It had been a week, five working days, since I'd seen him. Where, I wondered, was he hiding?

I lingered by the magazine stand for a while, pretending to be interested in the latest news about Julia Roberts's twins. I checked my watch. Five minutes. No sighting.

I strolled over to the circular rack of pantyhose, pulled a packet from its slot, and pretended to read the label.

Maybe, I thought, he's on vacation. Maybe he lured some poor, unsuspecting girl to Jamaica where he's forcing her to smoke dope and be his bleary-eyed sex slave.

I returned the packet to the rack and watched an elevator spit its contents into the lobby. Still no Predator.

The proprietor of the lobby concession gave me a strange sort of look. Hurriedly, I bought a bottle of water and a pack of gum—this seemed to mollify him—and stationed myself against a wall, out of his line of vision.

Ten minutes and counting. Maybe, I thought, The Predator is sick. Maybe he got a really bad cold from staying out too late and partying too hard. Maybe—and even at the time I knew this thought was really unworthy of me—maybe he caught some icky STD and can't even wear underwear because of the severe itching and burning. That would serve him right, I thought, his being a bum and all.

Nonchalantly I checked my watch. Thirteen minutes since I'd left my office. And for what?

It wasn't that I missed The Predator in any personal way. How could I? I'd never spoken a word to him. It was that I'd come to regard him as a sort of lab rat, a specimen of disgusting male attitude and behavior. I was the social scientist and The Predator was my subject.

I finished the bottle of water and stuck the pack of gum in my pocket. The Predator wasn't coming. And if I didn't get back to the office, I'd be fired. Then I'd have no legitimate reason to linger in the lobby of the Porter Building and continue my study.

Chapter 10

A course of tetanus shots will counteract the bite of a rabid dog. But no amount of medicine will guarantee a quick or complete cure after a man has broken your heart.

—Men: The Disease That Kills Slowly

"Thanks for doing this, really."

"He's a bit older than you," Patti told me, as we stood in the ladies' room checking our teeth after lunch. Patti, who works in the production department, set up the next blind date. Jim was a longtime friend of her husband and a respected road engineer with a respected engineering firm.

"That's okay," I'd told her, "I'm fine with older guys."

"He's been married."

I shrugged. "Whatever."

"And," Patti went on, "he has a ten-year-old daughter. He's a very good father. Just so you know."

"Sounds good," I said. I wasn't opposed to the notion of children in general or the reality of someone's in particular. I was an intelligent, levelheaded woman.

I smiled at Patti in the mirror; she smiled back.

"Have a great time," she said.

"I will," I told her. Silently I vowed to be as relaxed, fun, and bright with Jim as I'd been tense, angry, and humorless with poor Ben.

Jim chose Attache, a long-established steak house, for our blind date. It was, I thought, a good choice. The crowd was generally over thirty and the mashed potatoes were to die for. My hopes for a nice evening were high.

But the second I saw Jim's handsome, slightly craggy features and his piercing green eyes and his wavy, lightly salted hair, it happened. The Hag took possession and no amount of struggle could make her go away. Jim, The Hag decided, was a horrible person. He was the guilty party in his divorce, and, in spite of what Patti had told me, a neglectful, possibly even abusive father.

"I assume Patti told you I'm divorced," Jim said once we were seated at the bar.

"She told me you were married before," I replied enigmatically.

Jim traced the edges of the napkin set under his drink. "Yes. It didn't work out. It was nobody's fault, it just wasn't meant to be."

"Ah," I said, "I see."

Jim smiled awkwardly. "Excuse me?"

"I see," I said, speaking slowly, enunciating carefully, "that you're just one of those typical midlife-crisis men. I bet you drive an outrageously expensive convertible. I bet that so-called hair on your head is a weave. And I'd lay money that you trade in your current wife for a younger model every other year. How clichéd. Don't you bore yourself?"

Jim gaped like the proverbial fish flopping on the deck of a boat, gasping for air.

"Who," I went on, perfectly calm, "do you think you are, Michael Douglas? At least Catherine Zeta-Jones gets a famous association out of the deal. What does a girl get with you? Free tape measures and highway plans?"

Jim closed his mouth. He cocked his head and opened his mouth again. But nothing came out.

"And while we're on the topic of age," I said, "why in the world did you suggest this place? It's full of old fogies who should be home in their rocking chairs nice and close to their defibrillators. You might be over the hill, Mr. Hill, but I'm not."

It was that last comment that sent Jim running. Well, not exactly running but it made him hop off the bar stool as if it were on fire. His formerly wide eyes were now narrowed dangerously. Through the layers of The Hag's insanity Cleo felt a flicker of trepidation.

"I gave up Red Sox tickets for this?" Jim hissed. "I don't need this kind of abuse. From now on I'm sticking to speed dating."

Jim grabbed his trench coat and stormed off. His departure was the signal for The Hag to disappear and for my stunned and deeply remorseful self to return. I slapped my hands over my eyes and moaned.

"Your table is ready."

Slowly, reluctantly, I lowered my hands. The tall, red-haired hostess, who was no more than twenty-five, stood smirking before me. I was sure she'd heard at least part of my mortifying performance.

"Oh," I said, "my date didn't feel well. We won't be needing the table after all."

The hostess sneered. With bowed head I slunk out of the restaurant and made my way home.

Chapter 11

Face it, ladies: expecting a man to remain faithful is like expecting a cat not to have a hairball once every few days, the pope not to be Catholic, the Earth not to turn on its axis.

—'Til the Affair Do You Part

"So," I said bravely, "I suppose you heard from your friend."

Patti had been giving me the cold shoulder all that Monday morning, which took some skill and effort considering I had to address her directly in the weekly production meeting. Finally I came upon her in the tiny kitchen. After our elbows bumped while reaching for the coffee and creamer, I broke the awful silence.

Patti looked at me with wide eyes, as if she had just noticed me. "Oh, yes, indeed. We had quite an interesting conversation."

I imagined Jim's reconstruction of our very brief encounter. I felt queasy.

"It just didn't work out, is all," I said with a practiced shrug of indifference. In truth, I still felt sick about my behavior toward Patti's friend. "He shouldn't worry about it."

Patti's smile was bright and brittle. "Oh, he's not worried," she said. "There are plenty of women out there who would be thrilled to date Jim Hill. Did I mention he's got a house on the Vineyard? Well, not that it matters since you won't ever be invited."

Patti left the kitchen, head high, and I slunk back to my office.

What luck! It was four o'clock and there I was, about to leave the lobby of the Porter Building on my way to a dentist appointment, when who should come through the big glass doors but The Predator. I dashed back inside for a closer look.

Honestly, there was no denying The Predator was extremely good-looking. Sure, not every woman likes the heavy-lidded, liquid brown eyes, dark brown hair, Mediterranean thing. In fact, until I saw The Predator for the first time I didn't even know I liked the Mediterranean thing.

While I lurked just out of The Predator's line of sight a vibrant, powerful image flashed across my mind. A gorgeous white sand beach. Calm, sparkling blue water. A fresh calamari salad and a bottle of good local wine. The Predator pulling me toward his tanned naked chest, his lips coming down to meet mine . . .

I stumbled and put my hand against the cool marble wall. And the ridiculous, purely chemical reaction to The Predator's dark good looks was immediately transformed to annoyance as he flashed a brilliant smile at a woman who'd joined him at the elevator. She began to talk and The Predator nodded as if he were truly interested in what she had to say, which, of course, he couldn't be, not someone with that incredibly sexy smile. Grimly, I wondered how many women he'd seduced with his teeth alone.

I leaned fully against the wall. Was I to be plagued for the rest of my life—at least for the rest of the time we worked in the same building—by this lady-killer, this scoundrel?

The Predator got on the elevator with the poor, unsuspecting woman and I wondered: did women really need men? Not for money. Sex? Huh. Lots of women could take it or leave it; besides, any woman could buy a pretty good replica of a penis online. Romance? Only a means to an end. Once a man married, his interest in romance virtually disappeared.

The fact is, I thought, as I stalked from the lobby, that before long women might not even need men for reproductive purposes, and wouldn't that be a huge blow for them and a fantastic victory for us!

By the time I got home that afternoon my head was pounding horribly and it had nothing to do with my new filling. I took three aspirin and collapsed on my bed. Gargoyle obligingly sat on my head and his weight helped ease the pain so that eventually I fell asleep.

I dreamed of white sand beaches, brilliant blue water—and him.

Chapter 12

Trust in another human being's virtuous nature is, in this writer's opinion, just plain stupid.
—Better Safe Than Sorry: The Virtues of a
Prenuptial Agreement

"Please just ask Marty to consider setting me up. I promise I'll be good."

There was silence on the line for a long moment. "What about what happened with Ben?" Jane asked finally. "And with Jim? What if you erupt into The Hag again?"

"I won't," I swore. "I've got everything under control, really. I'm sure it won't happen again."

"Just try to be normal. You do remember how normal people behave, don't you?"

"Absolutely," I lied heartily. "I'll be totally normal."

Two days later Jane called to tell me about my date. David DeCraene was an up-and-coming chef on the local restaurant scene. At twenty-nine he was ambitious, independent, and, of course, creative. Already he'd garnered good reviews from notoriously critical food critics and had a bit of a celebrity following.

"Marty eats at Boffo at least twice a week," Jane told me.

"He's gotten to know David pretty well. He thinks you'll like him. So remember—"

"Be normal," I said. "I will."

At David's suggestion we met for coffee one Friday morning at eight o'clock. He apologized for the odd hour; his work schedule was crazier than usual as he was filling in for a sous chef on vacation. I assured him it was fine.

I arrived at the café five minutes early, as usual. David was already seated at a table and had ordered a selection of pastries for us to share.

"So," I said, once our coffee had arrived, "you work in a restaurant."

So far, so good, I thought. The Hag hadn't shown any sign of popping in to unfairly destroy another man's fragile ego.

David had a quick smile. It suited his almost boyish looks. Someday Chef David might be battling a weight problem, but at twenty-nine the heft was working for him, the heft and his amazingly blue eyes.

"Yes," he said. "Actually, I'm a chef. I got my degree from CIA. That's the Culinary Institute of America."

"Yes," I said, "it's highly respected."

"Anyway," David went on, "ever since I was a kid, like six or something, I've loved to cook. Sometimes I can hardly believe I'm actually living my dream."

And then, it happened. One minute I was enjoying the pleasant company of an attractive, talented man and the next minute all I wanted to do was poke him in the eye with my fork.

What had Marty been thinking? This guy worked in a kitchen. Like he'd ever be home at night? Like he wouldn't be cheating on me with every hot young thing who cat-walked into the place?

"So, what?" I said. "You have delusions of grandeur? You think you're suddenly going to become the next celebrity chef, the next Emeril Lagasse, the next Mario Batali, the next Bobby Flay?"

Chef David, it turned out, wasn't going down without a fight. Ah, I thought, barely able to control a smirk, the portly passionate chef.

"Look," he said, leaning in toward me as if to emphasize his words, "my career is a career of sweat and blood, it's a labor of love, and let me tell you, nothing comes easily, especially not fame. I'll be happy if someday I can own my own restaurant, to hell with a TV show."

I dismissed David's noble protestations with a snort. "Oh please. Of course you want your own TV show. And a line of cookware in Williams-Sonoma and cookbooks on the Barnes & Noble bestseller list and a cheesy restaurant in one of the big Vegas casino hotels. And don't give me this 'poor hardworking me' thing either. Do you think I care that you work hard? Who doesn't work hard?"

Chef David, a vein in his forehead now throbbing dangerously, rose to his unimpressive height and threw his napkin on the table.

"Marty told me you were feisty," he said, "but he didn't tell me you were a bitch."

I was stunned. No one had ever called me a bitch to my face. I wanted to burst out crying. It didn't help matters that there was some truth to David's insult. Maybe a lot of truth.

Before David stalked off he looked down at me with an expression of supreme disgust. I wanted to look away but I couldn't seem to. "I can't believe I gave up my one free morning for this," he said. "From now on I'm only dating models."

Chapter 13

*Love is a social construct that has outlived its useful-
ness. Deal with it.*
    —Men, Women, and Romance: The Myth Exploded

"**D**o you know how awkward you made things for
Marty?" Jane demanded. "Every time he has to take a
client to Boffo he's going to be worried about laxatives in his
soup!"

Jane and I met for a quick lunch only hours after the Chef
David debacle. I felt I needed to offer an abject apology in person.

"I'm sorry," I said, "really! Don't hate me. I tried to be
nice."

"All I asked was that you try to be normal."

"I did try to be normal, I swear, but . . . but . . . Oh, look,
Jane, I'm really sorry. How can I make it up to Marty?"

Jane frowned. "You could apologize to him, though it
won't change what you've done."

"I'll call him this afternoon," I promised.

Jane and I parted. She headed toward the Back Bay and her
store; I dragged myself back to my office.

It was official: Cleo Barnes was The Blind Date From Hell.

The Worst Blind Date Ever. The Black Widow of Boston Proper. I felt terribly low, very close to crying. I was only a block away from the Porter Building, where I could hide in a stall in the ladies' room for a while, when I saw her. My back-stabbing former acquaintance, Melissa. There she was, tall, trim, and tan (Melissa's parents had a time share in Anguilla) and walking right toward me, a look of determination on her perfectly pretty face.

"Cleo, hi. I—"

"I have to run," I said, hoping she didn't hear the catch in my voice.

Melissa reached out as if to touch my arm but thought better of it. Something about the way she hesitated made me stay put.

"Please," she said, "just let me apologize. I should never have gone with Justin that night knowing you guys were still a couple."

I suppose on some level I'd always known the truth: that two people had knowingly, consciously betrayed me that night. Still, hearing it then from Melissa was a blow. Just to be crystal clear I said, "So, Justin didn't lie to you about us?"

Melissa frowned. "No. I'm sorry. I know it was wrong, I don't know what I was thinking. I didn't want to hurt you but you know how Justin can be, so persuasive, so . . . I guess I just didn't care that he was still seeing you."

"Still living with me," I corrected coldly. "In my apartment, where I pay the rent."

A trace of annoyance flickered in Melissa's eyes. "Look, I said I'm sorry, okay?"

"And that's supposed to make it all better?" I snapped.

Melissa made a face. "Whatever. I shouldn't have bothered to apologize."

"No," I said, "you should have. You owed me an apology. But it's a funny thing about apologies. Sometimes they're not sincere and even when they are, they don't have to be accepted. And if you're the one apologizing and your apology isn't accepted, you have no right to get all pissed about it because you're the one who screwed up in the first place."

I'm not sure how much of my speech Melissa heard; she started to walk away long before the end. I stood there on the sidewalk and watched until she was lost to the crowds around Filene's.

Chapter 14

*Men can smell desperation a mile off—as clearly as
they can smell nachos baking in the oven.*
                    —Accountability and the Single Gal:
                              Are You Driving Men Away?

"Gay men," I said, "are the only men worth knowing."
Sam rolled his eyes at me. "Earth to Planet Cleo: Gay
men are men. Men are people. All people are scum at some
time in their lives. Besides, you can't sleep with gay men."

I was at Sam's apartment for a night of cocktails and the
first season of *Seinfeld* on DVD. We both knew the episodes
by heart but that was part of the fun.

"No," I agreed, idly running my finger along the edge of a
sleek end table, "but I could marry one. Cole Porter had a
wife. That woman on *Sex and the City* married the Nathan
Lane character and he was gay. They even had a baby."

Sam handed me the pretty pink cocktail he'd whipped up in
his retro blender. "Listen, Cleo, don't seek out heartache, okay?
Don't make life more difficult than it has to be."

I took a sip of the concoction Sam called a Rosy Dawn. It
was beyond yummy. "How do you know I would be miserable
married to a gay man?" I asked defiantly.

"I don't," Sam admitted. "But I'm pretty sure he would be miserable married to you. All due respect, honey, but nothing makes up for a lack of the right equipment."

Maybe Sam was right. Maybe it would be weird having your husband go out on dates every Saturday night. Maybe, I thought, I should just stick to cats. Every woman knows there are a million reasons why cats are better than men.

"You were never this bitter," Sam said, suddenly. "You used to be so much fun. It's like there was the pre-Justin Cleo and now the post-Justin Cleo and they're not at all compatible."

"What was I like when I was with Justin?" I wondered aloud.

"Justin's hand puppet, but we're not talking about her."

"Ouch," I said. Had I really been such a thing?

Sam patted my knee. "Sorry. Sometimes the truth hurts. That's why it's not all that popular."

The truth. The truth about Justin had hurt all right. But would I really have been better off not knowing it?

"Maybe," Sam said then, "you should just try to forgive Justin. I mean, really forgive him, just let it all go."

"I don't know if I have it in me to forgive," I admitted.

Sam persisted. "Have you really tried?"

Had I? I wasn't sure how to answer so I said, "I know I'll never forget what he did to me."

"Of course you'll never forget," Sam said, and his tone suggested he thought me stupid for making the point. "The memories will grow dim but they'll probably always be there. So what? They're just memories."

I wondered: if they were just memories, why did they hurt so much?

"Can I have another one of these?" I asked, lifting my empty, pink-frosted glass.

"*May* I have another, not *can* I. Of course you *can*. The question is will I give you another?"

I smiled. "Just make the stupid drink."

Chapter 15

*Remember the old adage: all is fair in love and war.
This is especially true for women over the age of thirty-
five who haven't yet achieved social victory in marriage.
Ladies, it's time to abandon your scruples.*
—Take No Prisoners: How to Win the Dating Wars

"Cleo? You're attacking the wool. What did it ever do to you?"

I looked up at the fifty-something, caftan-wearing instructor. "Nothing," I admitted.

Knitting, it is said, can help relieve stress. So far, all it had done for me was raise my blood pressure and increase my sense of personal failure.

The instructor gently but firmly took hold of my hands and tried to guide me through a few stitches but it was hopeless. My hands just wouldn't do what they were supposed to do.

"Sorry," I said finally.

"Why don't you give it a try yourself," she said with a sigh of resignation. "Just be careful with those needles, okay?"

For a moment after the instructor dashed away to compliment some burgeoning knitting genius, I sat forlorn, staring at the mess of wool in my lap.

"Do you want me to show you that stitch again?"

I looked up at the woman sitting next to me. She had the lush beauty of an Italian cinema star of the 1950s.

"Thanks," I said, "but I'm afraid I'm hopeless."

"No you're not. You're just inexperienced. We all are."

They were simple words, simply delivered, but suddenly I felt all teary.

"Thanks again," I said when I'd recovered my composure. "I'm Cleo, by the way."

The woman introduced herself as Liz. She was a patient teacher. Under her tutelage I actually completed three rows of stitches without disaster.

"See?" she said. "You did it!"

"I did. And I'm sorry but I just can't help but notice that you're engaged."

Liz looked down at the ring on her left hand and blushed. "It's kind of big, isn't it?"

"It's huge," I agreed. Clearly her fiancé was one of those bums who tried to buy a woman's affection.

Liz smiled sheepishly. "Sometimes I just can't stop looking at it. I mean, it really is beautiful. Sometimes I can't believe that it's mine."

So, his ploy had worked! Liz was besotted by the bling and oblivious to the fact that the man she was going to spend the rest of her life with was a bounder, a lothario, a libertine.

"Did he pick it out?" I asked, smugly assured I knew the answer.

"Oh no," Liz said. "It's been in my fiancé's family for generations. It meant so much for Brad to give this to me."

I felt a teeny bit disappointed to learn that Brad was a good egg. Not that I wanted Liz, who seemed like a very good egg, to be engaged to a bum. It was just that . . . Well, misery loves company, doesn't it?

"I don't mean to pry," she said then, "but are you seeing anyone?"

"No." I tried to laugh but it came out more like an aborted screech.

"Well," said Liz, undeterred, "if you're interested, my brother Max is single and I know he wants to meet someone. He's really great. Of course I'm prejudiced but trust me, I'd never set up another woman with a jerk."

I believed that Liz wouldn't consciously set up a woman with a jerk; but aren't jerks skilled at deception?

"If he's so great," I challenged, "why does he need his sister to fix him up?"

"Why does anyone need to be fixed up?" she replied. "Life is hard. Dating is hard. Why not help people when you can?"

I thought about Liz's offer. I was on a spectacular losing streak. Why continue the agony? Why not just give up? And then the image of Justin with that blonde booby bimbo flashed across my mind and the next thing I knew I was saying, "Okay, sure. I'll go out with your brother."

"Great!" Liz flashed a brilliant smile. Something about it looked familiar but before I could make a connection the smile was gone. "Uh, Cleo? You've stuck the needle into your thigh. Don't you feel it?"

I looked down at the pink metal needle sticking into the worn blue of my jeans. "No," I admitted, "I've developed a thick skin."

Chapter 16

Sex without negative consequence, lying without guilt, more money just for showing up with a penis. What's not to envy?

—Strap On a Pair: How to Beat Men at Their Own Game

"Sam? Do you have a minute?"

I was spending the morning at my desk fiddling with paper clips, calling friends, and obsessing over my love life instead of working on the latest deadline project.

"A minute," he said. I heard his keyboard clacking madly.

I told Sam about meeting Liz at knitting class and agreeing to go out with her brother.

"Sounds good," Sam replied.

I harrumphed.

Sam sighed. The keyboard fell silent. "Is there a problem I'm not seeing?"

"It's just that every woman with an engagement ring wants to play matchmaker." I heard the petulance in my voice. "Why is that? It's very annoying."

Sam's fingers were flying across his keyboard again. "Maybe they just want other women to be as happy as they are."

"Yeah, right."

For a moment Sam didn't answer. The clacking of his keyboard was thunderous. And then he said, "If the whole thing pisses you off so much, just don't go out with this guy. Look, Cleo, I've got to go. I've got a meeting."

"Oh," I said, stunned by Sam's annoyance, "sorry. 'Bye." I hung up and sat there fighting back tears and an onslaught of self-pity.

Everybody was getting tired of me. I was getting tired of me.

When, I wondered, would this craziness just go away?

There was a message from Max Cooper on my answering machine when I got home that evening. He had a good voice, low and rich. It was, I thought, a sexy voice.

I felt very afraid and therefore very brave dialing his number. When an answering machine picked up I felt very relieved.

"Hi," I said. "It's Cleo Barnes. Liz's, um, friend. I got your message. Thanks. I'll see you at Marlowe's at eight o'clock."

Short and sweet.

It seemed I was going through with the blind date after all. But only for Liz's sake. And it would be my last blind date ever.

Chapter 17

Go on the date for the good restaurant, the stimulating conversation, the fabulous sex. But leave your expectations of true love behind.
        —Why Bother? He's Only Going to Screw You

The Predator stood. He smiled the devastating smile. "Cleo?" he said.

"Max," I replied.

The buzzing in my head threatened to knock me to the floor. No wonder something about Liz's smile had seemed familiar. I stuck a fingernail in my palm and felt the pain. No, this wasn't a bad dream.

The Predator was indeed my blind date.

He pulled a chair from the café table. "Please," he said, "have a seat."

I sat. I crossed my legs. I uncrossed them. I didn't know what the hell to do with my hands.

The Predator sat as well. He wore a white linen long-sleeved shirt open at the neck. His left hand on the table, I noticed, was beautifully formed. I had an insane desire to slip my hand under it.

"This," The Predator said, "is amazing. I know you. I mean, I don't know you but I've seen you."

"Oh?" I remarked in an extraordinarily high voice. "You don't look at all familiar."

The Predator sat back just a wee bit. "We work in the same building," he said. "I've seen you in the lobby and a few times on the elevator. You get your breakfast from the coffee place next door."

Ah, I thought, the makings of a stalker! Never mind that I'd been stalking him. The Predator didn't need to know that.

"I'm sorry," I said in a more ordinary pitch, "I've never seen you before in my life."

The Predator seemed to deflate somehow, as if he'd really been bothered by my coldness. Oh, he was good. "I guess," he said, "there's no reason you'd have noticed me."

The Predator's reply made my flesh creep. False modesty is so unattractive in a man.

"Why does someone like you bother with this sort of thing?" I asked suddenly, angrily. "What's in this blind-date setup for you?"

"I'm sorry," The Predator said, "I don't understand."

"Please," I spat. "I know what this sweet, 'oh, I'm nothing special' act is all about and it's just not going to work with me. Look, I lied, okay? I do know you. I've seen you chatting it up with women in the building. I know what you're up to. You're the classic love 'em-and-leave 'em type. Believe me, I've seen it before."

The look on The Predator's face was priceless. It was a combination of disbelief, anguish, and a tiny bit of anger. Maybe he'd actually taken acting lessons. "Cleo," he protested in an appropriately pained voice, "I don't know where you got that idea. I—"

I shoved my chair back, stood, and tossed a twenty-dollar bill on the table. "Keep the change," I said over my shoulder. It seemed an appropriately dramatic way to leave such an obvious phony.

Two blocks from the restaurant I ducked into a dark and dirty alley. My heart was pounding madly; I had trouble breathing; I wondered if I was having a heart attack. Suddenly, my stomach heaved but all that came up was bile.

Chapter 18

Ask yourself: am I sabotaging every chance at a healthy relationship? Am I really working for happiness?
—Why Are You Still Alone? Tough Questions for the Single Woman

"I went out with your brother."

I didn't exactly look Liz in the eye when I said these words. I was staring somewhere in the region of her left shoulder. I held the knitting needles so tightly my fingers began to cramp. I could barely believe I had the nerve to show up for class.

"I know," she said. "He told me."

"It didn't work out."

"Yes," Liz said, "he told me that too."

Neither of us said anything for a moment. I continued to stare at Liz's shoulder.

"I thought you'd hit it off," Liz said finally. Her voice was tight. "I thought you might enjoy each other's company."

"Yeah, well," I said, and my voice was as shaky as hers was controlled, "not everyone is who you think they are."

"Obviously."

Liz got up and took a seat on the far side of the room. I frowned down at the knotted lump that was my knitting project and wondered who I could ask to help me untangle the mess.

Chapter 19

Substitute mother figures can be found in a variety of places. If your birth mother strictly controlled your diet when you were a budding young woman, look for a full-figured-and-proud-of-it older friend at work, church, or the local bakery and latch on to her like a barnacle on a boat.

—No Man Will Ever Love Me:
Surviving a Negligent Mother

"Am I bothering you?" I asked Jane.

It was five thirty. I'd snuck out of the Porter Building an hour earlier and had been walking aimlessly since.

"I am working," Jane pointed out. "But if you keep out of the way you can stay. You know, it would be nice if you bought something every once in a while."

I pulled a hot-pink satin bustier off the rack to my left, and frowned. "I'm not really comfortable in this sort of thing."

"At least buy a T-shirt, Cleo. Ten dollars. Everyone wears T-shirts."

"Next time I'll buy a T-shirt. A white one."

"Your sartorial risk-taking takes my breath away."

"Ha. Look, I didn't come here to talk about clothes. I came

here to talk about the guy from my building, the creep by the elevator, remember?"

Jane frowned. "Vaguely. What about him?"

"Well, you are not going to believe this. You know that woman I met at my knitting class, the one who set me up with her brother?"

"Yeah."

"Well, are you ready? Her brother is the creep from my building! And I went on a date with him! Well, it wasn't really a date since I left after about ten minutes. Of course."

"Of course," Jane murmured. "Boy, that is a coincidence. He has great hair. I remember that."

"Hair!" I cried, recalling vividly not only his hair but his smile and his eyes and his perfectly shaped hands. "Who cares about hair? You would just not believe this guy. He's obviously one thing, which is a Casanova, and yet he pretends to be something totally opposite: a nice, respectful guy interested in a long-term relationship."

Jane, I saw, was keeping an eye on a repulsively overtanned woman who was yanking pants off hangers like a bulimic yanking bags of potato chips off a grocery store shelf. "What are you saying?" she asked finally. "That he's a Gemini or something?"

"Maybe. I wouldn't put it past him. He's definitely two-faced. One of his faces is false, it has to be."

Jane sighed. "Maybe," she said, "neither of his faces is false. People are complex, Cleo. People are multifaceted."

"Huh!" I said. The repulsively overtanned woman headed for the changing rooms, arms loaded. Jane nodded to an assistant; the assistant made her way straight to the woman's side.

"Are you sure," Jane said, "that The Hag didn't take over again?"

"No," I said, perhaps too forcefully. "This guy is not like the others. He's really and truly awful. I'm sure of it."

Jane motioned for me to follow her to the checkout counter, where she began to sort a pile of hangers.

"So?" I said.

Jane sighed again. "I'm sorry, Cleo. I don't know what to say. I just don't understand what repulses you about this guy. Frankly, it sounds to me like it's all in your head."

I felt as if she'd slapped me, hard. "I'm sorry I bothered you," I replied haughtily.

"Don't be sorry," Jane said with a shrug. "I wish I could be of some help, I do, but I really don't know what you want from me."

I looked my friend right in the eye. "Neither," I said, in a voice barely above a whisper, "do I."

Chapter 20

So he chews with his mouth open! So he defaulted on his car payments! So he's been divorced three times! Are you so perfect?
  —Your Standards Are Too High: How to Reassess
  Your Checklist and Find Satisfaction
  (If Not Real Happiness)

"Hey."
"Hey."

It was a Thursday evening and about thirty people were milling about the hall outside two locked classrooms. The Basic Cooking instructor and my knitting instructor were both running late.

"You're in the knitting class?" the guy asked. He was tall and lanky, not terribly good-looking but not ugly. He wore a long-sleeved T-shirt and chinos, standard-issue casual clothes for someone who looked to be in his early thirties.

"Yeah," I said. "You're in the cooking class?"

The guy nodded. "Yeah."

For about a minute we had nothing more to say. The guy whistled a few bars of some tune. I sighed and checked my watch.

"I'm Mark, by the way."

"Cleo."

Mark nodded. And then his mouth turned up in a grin. "Do you think they're making out in the janitor's closet?"

"Who?" I asked, a bit taken aback.

"Our instructors."

I smiled. "Could be. Do people over fifty do that sort of thing?"

Mark shrugged. "All I know is that Mr. DuBois better show up. I paid a lot of money for this class."

"Why do you want to learn how to cook?" I asked, for lack of anything better to say.

"Girls like a guy who cooks. Right?" Mark grinned again.

"All I know," I said, "is that Ms. Brown better show up. Guys like a girl who knits, right?"

"Are you good at it?" Mark said. "You know, at knitting."

"No," I said, "not at knitting. Are you good at it? You know, at cooking?"

"No, I'm really bad in the kitchen."

Can this be happening? I wondered. *Am I actually flirting with a guy I just met? Maybe I'd turned over a new leaf without even knowing it! The Hag had been replaced by The Flirt. Cleo Barnes was back and better than ever!*

"How bad?" I asked coyly.

Mark leaned down closer to my face. "Okay," he said, "this is embarrassing. One time I actually tried to toast an egg."

"What?" I laughed. "In a toaster? How—"

"Believe me," Mark said, "you don't want to know the details."

"You'd better pay serious attention tonight. What's the lesson?"

"How not to slice off a finger."

"Ah. It's good to learn the basics."

Just then Ms. Brown loomed into view. "Here's my instructor," I said.

Mark laughed. "Ho, ho! And she's with my instructor! What did I say about the janitor's closet?"

I laughed too. Mark was a pretty funny guy. "So," said the better-than-ever Cleo, "do you want to maybe have a drink sometime?"

Mark beamed. "That would be awesome. Like, this weekend?"

I was caught off guard. Was asking a guy out always this easy? "Sure," I said and I scribbled my phone number and address on the cover of his notebook. "We can meet at my place and then go to this fun café just down the block."

Mark followed the crowd into the practice kitchen. Just before disappearing he winked. I winked back.

When I turned into the classroom I caught the look on Liz's face. It was subtle but it was a look of disappointment, I was sure.

Chapter 21

Only a few years ago the average couple was uncom-
fortable around the perpetually single woman. Now, no
dinner party is complete without an unmarried or other-
wise unattached female!
    —The Twenty-First Century Spinster and
     How She's Challenging Society's Rules

"So I told him, look, I just can't make the deadline, what
are you going to do about it?"

"Rats!"

"What?" Barbara said. I'd bumped into the newest addition to the editorial staff a block away. She'd been complain-
ing about our boss and her workload all the way to the lobby
of the Porter Building.

"I just remembered I forgot to stop at the drugstore," I lied,
keenly aware that The Predator was only yards away at the elevator bank. "I'll see you upstairs."

Leaving Barbara frowning after me, I scurried from the
lobby. But once on the sidewalk I hesitated and turned back.
From a certain angle I could see The Predator's face without, I
hoped, his seeing mine. Did he look . . . sad? Just a wee bit
forlorn?

I harrumphed; Emily from accounting gave me an odd look as she passed through the doors of the Porter Building. I ignored her and watched as the elevator doors slid open and The Predator stepped on, followed closely by Barbara, and then by Emily. Suddenly, I was facing all three and they were facing me.

The Predator lowered his eyes. My colleagues smirked.

Chapter 22

Positive Single Fact #15: The toilet seat is always in the closed position, preventing your cats from drinking unclean water.

—Single and Surviving: How to Tolerate,
If Not Love, Your Lonely Life

"Hey."
"Hey."

Cooking-Class Mark stood at the door to my apartment. He looked okay, not as goofily charming as he'd looked when I'd last seen him disappearing into the classroom next to mine. But maybe, I thought, I was just nervous. Here I was, the new-and-improved Cleo, going out on her very first date with a guy she'd picked out all on her own!

I grabbed my jacket from the coat stand, opened my mouth to say, "I'm ready"—and was barreled onto the couch by a tall, lanky guy who suddenly seemed terribly, terribly strong.

"What the hell are you doing!" I cried.

Mark laughed. "Tease!"

I pushed with all my might against his shoulders but it didn't result in much. His right knee dug into my thigh. My heart began to pound. "I mean it, Mark, what the hell is going on?"

Mark laughed again. "We're going to have sex, right?"

"What! Get off me, now! Get off!"

Mark tried to slobber on my cheek. I cringed.

"Well," he said, a bit petulantly, "you did ask me out."

"So?" I demanded.

"So that means you want to hook up. You know, you want to do it."

I did? Mark lunged again; I turned my head sharply to the right to avoid his lips on mine.

"Stop it!" I shouted. "I mean it, Mark, if you don't get off me this second I'm going to sic the cats on you!"

As cats will, Goblin and Gargoyle responded to the sound of my distress by leaping onto the couch and hissing madly.

"Cat scars never heal," I added ominously. "They continue to fester for years." That final remark seemed to do the trick and Mark, obviously protective of his minimal good looks, backed off me and stumbled to his feet.

"All right, all right. Jeez, what a waste."

"Just get out," I said. "Now."

At the door Mark turned back to me. "You're a freak, you know that?"

I didn't have the energy to respond. Mark slammed his way out and I locked and bolted the door after him.

Chapter 23

*Love your skin tags, embrace your sagging chin, and
welcome the occasional liver spot! These are all perfectly
normal marks of the aging beauty!*
—It's Never Too Late for Love:
Dating Past Your Prime

"**I**n conclusion," I said, with what I thought was a saucy
smile, "he was more interested in boning me than in de-
boning a chicken."

Jane frowned. "That's not very funny."

"Sorry. I'm trying to be all witty and adult about this."

Jane and I met for a good, old-fashioned greasy breakfast
the morning after the wrestling match with Cooking-Class
Mark. Marty was supposed to have joined us but had come
down with a rare case of "wine flu" and was sleeping in. I was
glad in a way that he wasn't there. It would have been beyond
embarrassing to talk about what had happened with Mark in
front of another guy.

"Are you a masochist?" Jane demanded suddenly.

"What?"

"Why are you doing this to yourself? Cleo, your judgment
is totally impaired."

"No, it's not," I protested.

"Please. You throw away a guy whose only visible flaw is that he's over forty; you toss aside a guy whose only visible flaw is that he wants to better himself; you reject a guy who's on his way to fame and fortune; you reject another one who comes with a sterling recommendation from his own sister; and you ask out a guy who tries to rape you. Why did you invite a stranger to your apartment anyway?"

"He didn't try to rape me," I said lamely.

Jane looked disgusted. "You said no and he kept pawing. That's attempted rape. Look, Cleo, why don't you just give up on dating? Take some more time to get over—"

"I am over Justin." I spoke too loudly; the couple at the next table gave us a dirty look.

Jane leaned closer. "I was going to say to get over hating yourself for believing he loved you. It's not your fault you got hurt. You're blaming the victim."

I poured more cream in my coffee. I stirred it. I rearranged the untouched eggs on my plate. I took a bite of cold toast.

"Have you considered seeing a therapist?"

Clearly, ignoring Jane wasn't going to make her go away. "I can't afford a therapist."

"Do you really know that?" Jane demanded. "What about your health insurance? Doesn't it cover even a few visits?"

"Okay, okay," I said. "Maybe I can afford a therapist, I don't know, but I just don't think it's necessary."

Jane took a final sip of her coffee and tucked her napkin under her plate.

"Fine," she said. "It's your call. But I have to be honest with you, Cleo. This is getting a little boring. I told you in the store the other day, I just don't know how to help you anymore."

I called for the check. Like Sam said, the truth is not popular for a reason.

Chapter 24

If, on occasion, your heart leaps at the sight of a man, don't panic. It's just habit. Immediately reach for a book by Virginia Woolf or pop in a tape of The L Word *and relax.*

—Switching Teams at Halftime: The Unexpected
Satisfactions of Becoming a Lesbian

"You know what's going to happen?"

"What?" I asked. Why had I called Sam anyway? What could he do to help me out of the mess I'd made of my romantic life?

"You're going to change teams. You're going to try to become a lesbian."

"I am not!" I cried, startling Goblin off the couch. "That's ridiculous."

Sam clucked like an old mother hen. "I've seen it before. You got burned by Justin and you can't forgive him and you won't forgive yourself for being fooled so you're going to give up and pretend to be gay because you think women are kinder and more honest than men. But it will all be a big mistake because one, you're not gay and two, women aren't necessarily kinder or more honest than men."

"I am not going to change teams," I insisted.

"Want to put money on it?"

"I don't gamble."

"Aha! You know I'm right!"

"No," I said with emphasis, "that's not it at all. I am not going to change teams for a lot of reasons but the main reason is that I'm hopeless when it comes to romance. I'd ruin every relationship with a woman just like I've ruined every relationship with a man, sometimes even before it gets to be a relationship."

Sam sighed. "You're not hopeless, Cleo. You're just going through a bad time. Remember, this too shall pass. Everything does."

"Including," I said, "this phone call. Look, Sam, I should go. It's time for the kitties' dinner. You know how they get when they're hungry."

"I do. I have the nightmares to prove it."

Once Gargoyle and Goblin had eaten and were busy with their postprandial ablutions, I flopped on the couch. An Anita Shreve novel sat on the coffee table but I had no interest in reading. HBO On Demand was probably playing a decent movie but I didn't have the energy pick up the remote control. Instead I stared across the room at the front door and indulged in a bout of self-pity.

The answer to the question of my romantic woes was obvious. I would stay single until the day I died, rather than risk choosing another loser or throwing away a perfectly fine guy for no good reason. Yes, I decided, staying single forever sounded great, absolutely fantastic.

As long as I could find a way to block thoughts of Max Cooper from haunting me. I sighed so dramatically Goblin jumped straight up into the air. I'd made a horrible mistake when I stalked out of the restaurant that night. If my instincts about men really were off—and how could I argue that they weren't?—I'd probably misjudged Max right from the start. It might just be that The Predator wasn't a predator at all.

But now I'd never know for sure.

Yes, I thought, reaching for the remote, staying single forever would be absolutely fantastic.

Chapter 25

A simple gold band worn on the ring finger will be perceived as a wedding band. Subsequently, you will be asked to dance by those married men present who are eager for a little action on the side from a woman who's ultimately unavailable.

—The Singles' Table: How to Negotiate
Social Events Without a Date

"The usual?" the counter server barked.

I nodded and stepped aside to wait for my breakfast order: a coffee with cream and a corn muffin. The diner was crowded with nine-to-fivers. I glanced around, killing time by noting who was eating what, and then I saw him.

Max Cooper.

Of all the rotten luck! For weeks I'd successfully avoided him, sneaking into work early and leaving at erratic times, getting my morning coffee and lunchtime sandwiches at a diner blocks away from the Porter Building.

And now . . .

I turned away and took a shaky breath. I didn't have the nerve to say hello to the man I had treated so unmercifully. And there was no way he'd want to say hello to me. No. Way.

"Cleo?"

Slowly, I turned to face him. He smiled a brief, social smile. It gave me some nerve, not a lot. "Hi," I said, eyes lowered.

"Hello."

"How are you?"

"Okay," he said, in that lovely low voice. "You know. And you?"

"Okay. You know." My head shot up; I looked beseechingly into his wonderful dark eyes. "Oh, I'm so sorry! I didn't mean to repeat what you just said! Really, I'm sorry. I'll just be going . . ."

Max nodded toward the counter. "What about your breakfast?"

I waved my hand in lieu of a spoken answer. I thought that maybe I'd cry.

"Stay," he said.

"Why?" I blurted. "Why would you possibly want to be nice to me?"

For a moment Max just looked at me. And I just looked at him. And in that moment something very big happened.

"Would you like to go out sometime?" he asked suddenly.

"After how I behaved on our blind date?"

"You think I'm nuts."

"No," I said quickly, "I didn't mean it that way. Yes, yes I'd like to go out with you."

Max smiled that unbelievably brilliant, gorgeous smile. "Okay, then. Great."

I reached for my bag. "Do you want my number? I think I have a pen in here . . ."

"That's okay," he said, "I still have it."

"Oh."

"Is that strange?"

"No," I said sincerely. "It's nice. It's very, very nice."

Chapter 26

It's true: love is on its own schedule. You never know when and where it will appear—the canned goods aisle at the grocery store, coffee hour after Sunday services, even in line at the Department of Motor Vehicles. Keep your eyes open, ladies!

—When You Least Expect It: Letting Love Happen

"I wanted to ask you out a long time ago," Max told me, "when I first saw you in the lobby."

I don't think I'd ever been more nervous getting ready for a date. I wasn't able to eat breakfast or lunch. My hands shook ridiculously as I tried to blow-dry my hair. I dropped a bottle of liquid makeup on the tiled bathroom floor. Glass and tan goo were everywhere.

But so far, so good. The Hag wasn't at all in evidence and I'd actually relaxed enough to take a sip or two of wine.

"Oh," I said, "why didn't you?"

Max smiled. "It's one thing when you've gotten to know someone a bit. But approaching a total stranger is not easy, trust me."

"Well," I told him, "I probably wasn't available anyway. I was with someone for two years. Until about a year ago."

"Oh."

"You want to know what happened, don't you?"

"Yes."

"But you're too polite to ask."

"Yes again."

Why not? I thought. Why not just admit to the shame? "He cheated on me," I told Max. "Twice. Maybe more but I only know definitely of two times."

"Two times is two times too many," Max said shortly.

"You're telling me."

And then the strangest thing happened. I laughed. I actually laughed. I thought of Justin, of lazy, sloppy Justin and I laughed.

"Are you okay?" Max leaned closer and put his hand on mine for just a moment. His touch was exhilarating.

"Yes," I said, suddenly sober. "I'm fine. Wow, I can't believe I just laughed about my ex-boyfriend. I think that's a good sign."

Max agreed. "You know, a long-term girlfriend cheated on me," he said. "But it was two years ago. I'm long past the pain and the laughter. Time really does heal all wounds. Most of them anyway."

"I'd like," I said, "to think we have more in common than betrayal. Tell me about yourself."

That night I learned some basic information about the real Max Cooper. Things like the fact that he and Liz and Chuck have always been close; that Chuck, the oldest, lives in Seattle and plays sax in a jazz band; that Liz, the youngest, is a third grade teacher; and that Max—my Max—loves blues and Greek food and the *Thin Man* movies. I found out too that Max is the senior designer at his firm, that their specialty is office design, and that after hours Max is an avid amateur photographer, who's still shooting film and uses his linen closet for a dark room.

Max, for his part, discovered that I take lousy pictures when I take them at all, that I am a fan of Agatha Christie novels, that I too like blues, and that I have two giant cats and two best friends.

"What about your family?" Max asked finally.

Was it odd that I hadn't mentioned my family once in telling Max about myself? "I have parents, of course," I said.

Max raised his eyebrows. "I was pretty sure you didn't sprout from a fungus."

"Ha ha. And I have one sister. Ashley's wonderful. Actually, I haven't heard from her in a while. She's really busy and she lives in the suburbs so . . ."

"Have you ever been to a tractor pull?"

Max's bizarre and unexpected question made me laugh. "No! Don't tell me you have!"

"I was in college. It seemed like a fun thing to do."

"Was it?"

"No, but I did get to try a corn dog. I was a real wild man in those days."

I looked across the table at Max's sleepy brown eyes and hoped fervently that he still was.

Chapter 27

Stop ignoring the oil deliveryman! What about the postal worker? Your son's bachelor science teacher? The busboy at the local Italian restaurant? Men are all around you—and some might even be eligible!
—Wake Up! Finding the Love Right
Under Your Nose

"This guy just might be different," I said. "Pass the syrup?"

Jane, Marty, and I met for brunch one Sunday morning shortly after Max and I started to date. I hadn't felt so energized in years. I could hardly keep from bouncing in the seat.

"The question is," Jane said promptly, handing me the sticky bottle, "are *you* different? I mean, have you gotten past all that anger and mistrust? Because even if Max is the catch of the century it's not going to work out if you can't bring yourself to trust him, even a little."

"Thanks," I said, with blatantly false cheer, "you've completely harshed my buzz."

"Sorry, but I just—"

"Jane." Marty's tone was firm. "Cleo gets your point."

"Oh."

"Tell us about him, Cleo," Marty said.

I told them every little thing I knew about Max. "I can't believe I was so wrong about him," I admitted. "Just because he looks good doesn't mean he acts bad. What was I thinking?"

"You weren't yourself," Marty said soothingly.

I saw the look on Jane's face. "What?" I challenged.

"Nothing. I just really think that before you get further involved with this guy you should determine if you've completely worked through your issues with abandonment and self-esteem."

Abandonment and self-esteem. "All I wanted," I said, "was to eat some pancakes."

Marty sighed. "Jane, can't you let Cleo live her own life for once?"

"I just want her to be cautious."

"I'm not saying she should marry the guy tomorrow. Of course she should be cautious, especially after, you know, what she's been going through."

I tapped my fork against the water glass. "Uh, guys? I'm right here. Could you stop talking about me as if I'm not?"

Jane and Marty both looked back to me.

"Oh," she said, "sorry.

"Yeah," he said, "sorry."

"It's just that—"

I cut Jane off. "I'll be fine," I said. "I promise. I can handle this relationship."

Jane shrugged; Marty nodded.

And suddenly I wondered: could I really?

Chapter 28

Grooming tools are only as effective as the user. Become acquainted early on with the workings of an electric shaver.
—Disgusting Habits, Horrid Odors, and Unsightly Body Hair: Living with a Member of the Male Tribe

"So," I asked, "is Max short for Maxwell?"

Max and I were taking an after-dinner stroll through the Boston Gardens. It was a warm evening in early May, the tulips were in bloom, and all was feeling very right with my world.

Max laughed. "The question. I knew it would happen sometime. Ready? My real name is Maximus."

"Oh no!"

"Oh yes."

"It's . . . interesting," I said, trying very hard not to laugh.

"That's one word for it."

"Why Maximus?"

"Supposedly," Max explained, "my mother wanted to name me Michael, after her brother, but my father had these grandiose notions about his sons. Oddly, he never gave my brother or me much support or encouragement. I think we were supposed to be spectacular all on our own, right from the start. Needless to say, in our father's eyes neither of us did achieve spectacularness."

I smiled. "I don't think that's a word."

"See? Even my vocabulary is defective."

"You can make up a word if you want. I think it shows creativity."

"Thanks," Max said. "Actually, I think so too."

"Wait a minute. Your brother's name is Chuck, right? Chuck isn't a grandiose name."

Max agreed. "Chuck's real name is—ready?"

"Maybe."

"Caesar. As in—"

"The salad," I said. "Or as in Julius Caesar, ruler of the Roman Empire. Well, Caesar isn't as bad as Maximus. I'm sorry. I didn't mean that as an insult."

"I didn't take it as one."

Max and I continued to stroll, arms linked, out of the Common and then up Charles Street.

"I love Beacon Hill," I told him.

"I live here," he told me.

And before long we were at the door of his charming old apartment in a charming old red brick building.

"I have to warn you," Max said as we stepped inside, "it's pretty small. Space isn't something you get a lot of in this neighborhood."

But I found Max's home wonderful. Not surprisingly, it was neat and more, it was clean. Max opened the two small windows in the living area. "Do you mind?" he asked. "It's such great weather."

I told him I didn't. Max got us each a glass of wine, put on a Madeleine Peyroux CD, and there we were, standing hand in hand by the open windows.

"I don't know what your sister was thinking when she set us up," I admitted. "I wasn't exactly exuding sweetness and light. Are you sure Liz really likes you?"

Max laughed. "I'm sure. I guess she saw in you something of what I see in you."

"Oh yeah?" I asked, my heart suddenly thumping. "What's that?"

Max put down his glass of wine; then he took mine and set it next to his on the windowsill. He drew me to him. "A person," he said, "worth knowing."

Well, you can imagine what happened next. It was our first real kiss and it was intensely passionate and when it was over I wasn't sure of my own name.

Max ran his hands to my waist and I leaned against his chest.

"I'm scared," I whispered.

Max put his lips to my ear. "Can we be scared together?"

And then we kissed again and I don't have words to describe how perfectly his mouth fit with mine.

"By the way," Max said, finally, "what are we afraid of?"

"I can't remember," I replied. And for a while, I really couldn't.

Chapter 29

Maybe he really was thinking of you when he was having sex with your sister. Stop whining and lose those five pounds already!
                    —It's All My Fault: Learning How to Take
                        Responsibility for Your Happiness

"His name," I told Sam, "if you can believe this, is Maximus."

We were walking across the Arthur Fiedler Footbridge, on our way to the Charles River Esplanade. It was a lovely Saturday morning, made even more radiant by the fact that I saw everything through a lens of sparkling emotion.

"Well," Sam replied, "I hope it refers to his endowment."

Playfully, I smacked his arm. "I wouldn't know. I've only been out with him a few times."

"And? Oh I see. You're taking things slowly."

"Can you blame me? I slept with Justin almost immediately. And look what happened there."

"Cleo, honey, even if you'd held out until the tenth date the relationship still wouldn't have worked. Justin is a jackass."

"Ooh, foul language!"

"Jackass is not a foul word. It means a male donkey or a stupid person."

"I know," I said. "I'm just teasing."

For a while we strolled amicably without talking. That's one of the best things about a good friendship, the ability to be quiet together. When we reached the bank of the river, crowded with joggers, cyclists, dog walkers, and even a few sunbathers, Sam broke the silence.

"You seem okay," he said. "Certainly happier than you've been since Justin."

I smiled over at him. "I think I am happy. At least, I'm on my way to being happy."

A sailboat-class race slipped by and I imagined Max and me on the deck of a boat, soaking up the sun. The summer, I thought, will be so much fun.

"How does it feel?" Sam asked. "To be happy again?"

"I don't know," I admitted. "Scary, but also nice."

"You deserve a big lot of happy, Cleo."

"I don't know if I deserve it."

Sam turned to me. "Yes," he said, "you do. You deserve to be happy in yourself and to be made happy by a wonderful man."

I opened my mouth to protest again but Sam quite effectively shut me up.

"If," he said, "you demure, I will be forced to toss you right in the path of those sailboats."

Chapter 30

Why are you necessarily any better than the guy on death row? Maybe he was framed. Maybe his mother didn't love him. Send a letter. Take the first step!
—Letting Go of Your Pride and
Taking a Chance on Love

"Er, how much does Goblin weigh?" Max sat stiffly, which was a good idea, given the clawed beast on his head.

"Oh," I said, struggling not to laugh, "about fourteen pounds. Don't you like cats?"

"I've never really known a cat," he admitted. "I'm kind of freaked out right now."

Gargoyle chose that moment to poke at Max's leg with his massive clawed paw.

"They know. They're kind of enjoying it."

Max gave me a funny look. "They enjoy people's discomfort?"

"Cats are in charge," I explained. "Some people don't understand that so cats have to demonstrate their supremacy."

"I see," Max said carefully. "So, you don't own a cat, you serve one?"

"Exactly. You're a fast learner, Mr. Cooper!"

"Next time I'll bring them a treat. Do they like catnip?"

Goblin chose that moment to leap off Max's head and onto Gargoyle's back. With a massive thud they rolled off the couch and onto the floor where they engaged in a spectacular wrestling match.

"Don't worry," I told Max, who was eyeing the tumbling beasts warily. "They do this once or twice a day. And yes, they love catnip."

While I made two cups of tea Max poked around the living room.

"Who's this?" he asked after a moment. Max stood by the tall bookshelves, looking at the most recent 8 x 10 framed photograph of Ashley.

"Oh," I said, "that's my sister." I joined Max and handed him his tea. "We don't look much alike."

Max looked more closely at the portrait. "You think so? I see a strong resemblance. Your facial structure is almost identical."

"Oh no," I declared, "Ashley is perfect."

"I've never," Max said, turning back to me, "met a perfect person. I'm not sure I'd want to. I think they'd be intimidating."

"Oh, Ashley's not intimidating," I assured him. "Everybody loves Ashley."

Max raised his eyebrows. "Oh? Tell me about her."

Where, I thought, should I begin? I'd never been reluctant to sing my sister's praises, only occasionally overwhelmed by their abundance. But if Max was going to know me he would need to know Ashley too.

"Well," I said, "for one thing, she could have been a model if she didn't spend so much time winning academic awards and perfecting her tennis game."

Max glanced back at the portrait. "She's still in school? You look about the same age."

"Oh we are," I told him. "Ashley's two years younger than

me, twenty-six. She's getting her second master's degree. Or maybe it's her third, I've lost count."

"I see." Max settled next to me on the couch, his mug of tea on his thigh. "So, what does she do, besides go to school? Does she work?"

"She doesn't really have time to work," I explained. "What with attending lectures and writing papers and all."

Max nodded thoughtfully. "So," he asked, "where does Ashley live?"

"With our parents," I said. "They have a really big house. Ashley's got her own suite, really. Except that she doesn't like to cook so my mom makes dinner for the three of them every night. That is, when Ashley's not out with a friend or on a date. She's very popular."

For a moment we sipped our tea in silence. I thought about Ashley's charmed life. I guess Max did too, because then he said, "So, I guess Ashley prefers not to get her own place?"

"Well, rent is pretty high these days."

"I know. I pay rent. So do you."

Sure, I thought. But what does my paying rent have to do with Ashley? "She did live with her husband for a year," I said.

Max took a large gulp of tea. "Just a year?" he said when he'd swallowed.

"The marriage didn't work out," I explained. "He was a lot older. He accused her of being spoiled and he told the court that she'd almost bankrupted him in less than six months. It was a mess."

"I'll bet."

"I mean, the guy did lose pretty much everything, his business and houses and all, but I'm sure the bankruptcy had nothing to do with Ashley. The last I heard he'd had a stroke and was living in a nursing home."

Max winced. "I'm sorry. I mean, for him."

I was kind of sorry for Mr. Tuttle too. I'd met him only once, at the wedding, but I'd thought he seemed pretty nice. He was definitely madly in love with my sister.

"Anyway," I said to Max, "she's out of that ugly situation."

"Yes," Max agreed, "an ugly situation."

"Actually, she was engaged once after that."

"She was?"

"Yes, but the guy broke it off. I'm not sure why. That was just around the time Ashley's driver's license was taken away on some technicality. Something silly. Come to think of it, that was also about the time she signed up for another two years of school."

"Uh-huh." Max drained his tea.

"Would you like another cup?" I asked.

Max shook his head. "No thanks. What's this about Ashley and tennis?"

I was glad Max was a good listener. Justin always blanked out when I talked about anything personal.

"Oh, Ashley is a really good player," I told him. "She could easily have gone pro but she just didn't think it was worth all the practice."

"Yes," Max said, "to be a professional tennis player you certainly have to practice a lot."

"I remember when Ashley was about twelve," I said. "This coach came to see my parents. He was all upset about Ashley being lazy and uncommitted. He said that she was throwing away a great talent. Anyway, my father kicked him out. Literally, he kicked the coach right out the front door. After that, Ashley had a few other coaches but nobody ever stuck with her."

"Oh."

"I guess nobody ever really appreciated her," I said. "Nobody ever really inspired her."

"Sure, I bet that's it. Look, Cleo." Max took my hands in his. "Don't take this the wrong way but I've heard enough about Ashley. You're the Barnes sister I want to spend time with."

Max and I said very little else that night.

Chapter 31

Remember: it just doesn't matter that you're not the most beautiful woman at the party. If you're the one who listens to him with sympathy (real or not), you're the one he's going to marry in the end.
— Slow and Steady: How to Get Your
Man the Old-Fashioned Way

"**I** got the feeling," I said to Sam the following evening, when we'd met for a drink at Spy, "that Max wasn't all that impressed by Ashley's accomplishments."

"That," Sam replied, "is because there's not a lot to be impressed about."

I looked at my friend in outrage. "What a horrible thing to say!"

The bartender brought us our drinks and Sam took a sip of his Manhattan before answering. "Look, Cleo, I met Ashley, remember? At our college graduation? She was bored to tears, literally."

"I remember," I said. "She was crying only because she had to miss a party to be at my graduation. Can you blame her?"

Sam rolled his eyes at me. "Do you remember the scene she made at the parents' reception that Friday night? When nobody was focusing on Little Miss Perfect because they were focusing on you, the magna cum laude graduate?"

I did remember. Suddenly, the whole embarrassing scene came roaring back.

"Let me tell you," Sam went on, "you're just as beautiful as La Ashley. In fact, you're even more beautiful because you don't come with her insufferable attitude. Cleo, that girl is ugly when she wants to be."

I stared blindly at the Cosmo in front of me. I'd never heard anyone talk about my sister that way—so brutally, so critically. The disturbing thing was Sam was usually right about people, about everything, really.

I wondered: could it be that Ashley wasn't all I'd made her out to be? Could it actually be that I was the more impressive sister?

"Do you want to get something to eat?" Sam asked.

"Sure," I said absentmindedly, "whatever."

By the time I got home that evening I'd rejected the idea of my superiority as not only absurd but also deeply disloyal. For whatever reason, I'd decided, Sam just wasn't equipped to appreciate Ashley's special qualities.

After feeding Gargoyle and Goblin, I picked up the phone and dialed Ashley's private line. I hadn't talked to her in over a month.

"What?" my sister said.

"Ashley? It's me."

"Who?"

"Cleo. Your sister."

"Oh. What do you want?"

"Nothing. I just called to say hi. How—"

"Hi. Look, Cleo, I can't talk right now. I'm running a bath and if I don't soak soon my nerves are just not going to recover."

Before I could reply Ashley was gone. I heard another familiar voice in the background, and then my mother was on the line.

"Were you nice to your sister?" she said by way of a greeting.

"Hello, Mom," I said. "Of course I was nice."

"You should call her more often," my mother went on. "She's under a lot of stress. That awful friend of hers, that Elaine character, I think she's going insane or something. She actually showed up at the door the other night at midnight—midnight!—ranting and raving about I don't know what. Anyway, I called the police immediately. Your poor sister needs her sleep you know. She—"

"Mom," I said loudly, "speaking of sleep, I've got to go. I've got a big day at work tomorrow. Good—"

"But Ashley needs—"

"Night."

Chapter 32

Reason #657: My girlfriend is a suspicious old nag.
   —Why Men Cheat: A History of
   Infidelity in the Western World

"Guess what's playing at that tiny revival house out in Somerville?" Max said one night on the phone, not long after the aborted conversation with my sister and mother.

"I'm very bad at guessing," I admitted.

"How about I give you a clue? It's based on a book by one of your favorite authors—"

"Murder on the Orient Express!" I cried.

"Do you want to go tomorrow? There's a show at seven."

We made plans to meet and I went to bed that night savoring the fact that my new boyfriend was kind and attentive and that thus far, I hadn't destroyed our blossoming relationship by any ugly fits of unwarranted suspicion.

The next evening after work I took the Red Line to Davis Square. The air was a little damp and chilly. I walked quickly, shoulders slightly hunched. About a block away from the theatre I looked up and stopped short.

There was Max standing outside the movie theatre talking animatedly with a petite, blonde woman wearing an ultrafeminine, flounced, sleeveless dress. Clearly, she didn't feel the damp and chill. I watched as Max laughed and the woman put her hand briefly on his arm. Then, with a perky little wave the woman walked off. I continued toward my boyfriend.

"Cleo, hi!" Max leaned down and kissed my cheek. "You just missed my old friend Susie. We worked together about five years ago."

I tried to smile brightly. "We should go in," I said. "The movie starts in ten minutes."

"We have some time," Max said. "I already bought our tickets."

"I'm cold."

"Of course." Max tried to take my hand but I slipped ahead of him. I felt slightly sick, like how you feel when you've been on a bus for too long.

"How about sharing some popcorn?" Max asked when we were in the lobby.

"No thanks," I said. "I'm not hungry."

Max looked at me with concern. "Cleo," he said, "are you feeling okay?"

I saw not a trace of duplicity in Max's lovely brown eyes. In my heart I knew the woman he'd been chatting with outside the theatre really was just an old friend from the office. In my heart I knew that Max was a good man.

But something bad had lodged in my brain.

"I'm fine," I lied. "Let's just take our seats."

Chapter 33

Chances are you were passed over for a promotion because your male boss is a pig. Consider shortening your skirt.

—Today's Working Bachelorette and
What She's Doing Wrong

"Okay people, listen up. The last bit of business for today's meeting is the TechKnowledgy project."

I nodded at Simon, my boss. I tried to appear calm and professional but under the table my fingers were crossed. I was so hoping to work on the TechKnowledgy project. Arbiter Publishing had worked long and hard to get this new contract and we stood to make a lot of money over the next few years.

Simon glanced at each of us before going on.

"I'm giving the project to Barbara," he announced. "Rob? You're off your usual assignments for the duration. You're going to work closely with Barbara. This project is far too important to blow."

Barbara beamed. I sat with my hands still in my lap, fingers uncrossed, shocked. All Barbara did was complain about her workload. I had seniority, more talent, and more patience than my colleague. Why had Simon chosen her over me?

Maybe, I thought, because for months I'd spent too much time lingering in the lobby hoping for a glimpse of The Predator. Maybe because since that stupid little blonde outside the movie theatre I'd been spending too much time sitting at my desk worrying about my relationship with Max instead of working.

Barbara continued to beam. "Anybody have anything to add?" Simon asked. "Fine. Meeting over. Everybody back to work!"

Chapter 34

You've moved across the country, changed your name, and assumed a false identity. But he still tracks you down. What to do? Hire a personal bodyguard. See the Appendix for suggestions.
— When Ex-Boyfriends Rear Their Ugly Heads:
How to Handle the Situation Without
Going to Prison for Manslaughter

There was one message on the answering machine when I got home that night. I played it through twice.

"Cleo, hi, it's Max. I'm really sorry, I hate to do this, but I have to cancel our date tonight. One of our most important clients changed their mind about a design we submitted, and now I've got to rework the whole scheme and get it into Fed Ex before the last pickup at ten. Clients. Can't live with them . . . Anyway, I'll call you later when I get home. Again, I'm really sorry. 'Bye."

I sat heavily on the couch. Gargoyle and Goblin, at the other end, looked up from their prebedtime nap with annoyance in their bright green eyes.

"Sorry," I said automatically.

I took a deep breath. I wondered if I could believe Max.

He'd never betrayed the slightest bit of insincerity. Or had he? Maybe, like with Justin, I'd just been too blind to see the signs. Wasn't "working late" the classic excuse men gave their wives and girlfriends when they were having an affair?

I rubbed my forehead with the tips of my fingers. It didn't ease the dull ache that was forming. Too many things on my mind. Sam's honest assessment of Ashley was troubling. He'd shaken loose a whole slew of assumptions I'd held for most of my life. I no longer knew what to think about my sister or about me. Especially since losing the project to my new colleague. That had been a blow to my professional self-esteem. Now I started to wonder if somehow I'd lost the editorial talents I'd worked so hard to acquire in the seven years I'd been at Arbiter.

Now I started to wonder about a lot of things.

A memory of the petite blonde outside the movie theatre flashed to mind, followed by a memory of Max's lips on my cheek. I went into the bathroom and took two aspirin. Then I returned to the couch and waited.

The phone rang around nine. I knew it was Max. He'd finished work early. I so wanted to hear his low, soothing, sexy voice and feel reassured that he was mine. I grabbed the receiver.

"Hello," I said eagerly.

"It's Justin."

I swear I had to think for a moment before placing him. Yes. Justin.

"What do you want?"

Justin laughed. "Whoa, what's with the attitude?"

"What is it, Justin?"

"I think I left my Metallica CD at your place."

Now it was time for me to laugh. "Ten months ago? No, Justin, there's nothing here, trust me."

Justin snorted. "I'm telling you it's missing and I know I left it there. And now I want it."

"And I'm telling you it's not here!" The sound of my voice,

loud and angry, caused Gargoyle and Goblin to leap to the floor. "Believe me I went through this place after I kicked you out and got rid of every last trace of you."

I heard the sound of slurping. Big surprise. Justin was drinking a can of beer. And then he burped loudly, right into the phone.

"Look," he said, "I swear I'll smash down your door and find the CD myself!"

My whole body began to tremble; my cheeks felt all prickly. "You come anywhere near me or my home," I spat, "and I swear I'll call the police. I'll get a restraining order against you. I mean it, Justin. Don't push me."

Without waiting for his rude reply, I hung up. When Max did call at ten thirty, I let the answering machine take his message.

Chapter 35

If you're very lucky, your medication will so dull your sensibilities that you won't even know you're disappointed with your boor of a date.
—When All Seems Lost: Antidepressants and Dating

"Too bad about your not getting the TechKnowledgy project."

Patti cornered me in the kitchen the next morning. Her smile seemed unusually bright.

I shrugged and reached for a tea bag. "Oh," I said, "it's okay."

"Everyone," Patti went on, pinning me with her eyes, "thought Simon would give the project to you. Well, some of us did."

"Well," I said, "he didn't give it to me."

Patti sighed. "No. I guess Simon knows best. Oh, and did I tell you?"

What else, I wondered, could this woman do to me? Hadn't she punished me enough? Could I accidentally on purpose spill boiling water on her? I said and did nothing.

"Jim Hill, you remember him? The guy I set you up with? Well, he got engaged! He met this fabulous woman, as smart and successful as she is gorgeous, and they just clicked right off the bat. They're getting married this summer."

Patti's smile grew even brighter as she waited for my reaction. What did she want to see? Tears and histrionics, a woman in the midst of a total breakdown?

"That's just great, Patti," I said evenly. "It's all just great."

Somehow I made it back to my office where I broke Simon's rule against closed doors. I tried to concentrate on work, I really did, but for almost two hours my mind was a whirl of fractured thoughts about the mess that seemed to be my life. Justin's abusive behavior. My sister's self-centeredness. My mother's indifference. My boss's lack of faith in me. Ben, Jim, David, Mark.

Max. Oh, what was I going to do to Max?

At about eleven thirty the receptionist, a young man named Jeff, buzzed me.

"There's a Max Cooper on the line for you."

"Send it to voice mail," I said without hesitation.

I sat staring at the phone for what seemed a long time. And then I got up, gathered my bag and jacket, told Jeff to let everyone know that I'd gone home sick, and headed for the elevator. I held my breath as we approached the tenth floor. The elevator didn't stop. At the lobby I stepped off—and there was Max, my Max, holding the door open for a very stylish young woman, ushering her out before him. Together they turned right on the sidewalk. For a split second I thought of following them.

I didn't return my boyfriend's calls. I considered spying on him. What kind of person was I?

Someone not at all ready for a real relationship. I watched Max and the stylish woman disappear, and then I too left the Porter Building.

I got home around one o'clock. I locked the door behind me and pulled down the shades. Goblin and Gargoyle were happy to see me. At least, I thought, I know what I'm doing with four-legged males.

Chapter 36

Just because you're single doesn't mean you have to live like a slob. Forget about peanut butter on pretzels for dinner. No more barbeque sauce on undercooked pasta. It's time the single gal learned some basic kitchen skills.
—Meals for One: Treating Yourself Like You Matter

"I'm glad you asked me to come over this afternoon," Max said. "When I didn't hear from you all day yesterday I got a little worried." Max stood on one side of the kitchen counter. He wore black jeans and a white shirt, the cuffs rolled back. I stood on the other side of the counter, out of reach.

"Oh?" I said. "Why?"

"Well, I began to think you were avoiding me. Please tell me you're not angry with me for canceling our date the other night."

"No," I said, "of course not. These things happen."

"Good. I hate to let work interfere with my personal life. But sometimes it's unavoidable."

"Of course," I said. "I totally understand."

Max came around the counter. I took a step back. If I touched him, if he touched me, I could never go through with it.

"You know," he said, "if you felt sick at the office you could have called me to take you home."

"I'm sure you had other things to do." I opened the fridge and took out a bottle of orange juice. It kept my hands busy.

"Of course, but not more important things. Just a very trying business lunch with our tragically hip new client."

I opened a cabinet and reached for a glass. I felt Max very close.

"Come here," he said. "I have something for you."

Slowly, reluctantly, I turned and followed him into the living room. He took a small square box from his jacket pocket.

"I know," he said, "we haven't been seeing each other for long, but I saw this the other day and I had to get it for you. Cleo?" Max stepped closer; he took my hand, kissed it, and gave me the box. "I'm falling in love with you."

It was the worst thing he could have done, the worst thing he could have said. As if in a trance, against my will, I opened the box. Inside was a lovely silver bangle, etched with the image of a leafy vine. Tears filled my eyes.

"Do you like it?" Max asked softly. "I thought it was more you than tickets to a tractor pull."

I didn't laugh. I couldn't.

Max touched my hair. "Sorry. I thought it was kind of funny. Remember, I told you I'd been to a tractor pull in college?"

I nodded. The bracelet was so beautiful. Max was so beautiful. But I—

"I can't," I cried. "I can't do this anymore. I'm sorry, Max. I'm so sorry."

The look on Max's face broke what was left of my heart. "What do you mean 'can't do this'? Can't do what?"

"You know what I mean. I can't see you anymore."

"Why not?" he demanded.

"I can't—" I turned away from him, unable to stand the sight of him so hurt.

"Stop saying you can't." Max grabbed my shoulders and pulled me around to him. "Look at me, Cleo. Look at me."

There was so much in his beautiful dark eyes. I thought about never touching him again and the thought almost killed me right there and then. How would I survive without him?

How would I survive with him?

"I can't explain why," I whispered. "It's just that everything is all messed up inside me."

"No it's not," he whispered hoarsely.

"You don't know me!"

"You won't let me know you!"

I broke away and held the box out for him to take. My hand was trembling.

"Please," I said. "I'm just going to mess it all up. I can't—"

Max laughed bitterly. "There's that word again."

I put the box on the coffee table. "It's better this way," I said. "Believe me."

Max stood very still. Suddenly, the skin around his eyes looked bruised, as if he'd been hit. I guess he had.

"Better," he said, "for who?"

Chapter 37

Think twice before you dump your current less-than-spectacular man for the guy down the hall. Chances are good you'll just be trading one set of problems for another. Better the hell you know than the hell you don't.
                                     —The Grass is Always Greener:
                                     Living With the Man You Have

"I'm thinking of sending a note of apology to those three guys I went out with. The blind dates."

Sam, Jane, and Marty exchanged looks of alarm. We were finishing brunch one Saturday morning about two weeks after I'd broken it off with Max. It was the first time I'd been out of the apartment other than to sneak to and from work.

Jane put her coffee cup down with emphasis. "I say leave well enough alone. What makes you think they'll even open the envelope? Once they see your name they'll probably tear it to shreds. Or burn it."

Marty cringed but didn't protest Jane's opinion.

"I'm with Jane," Sam said. "Leave those guys alone. Haven't they suffered enough? Anyway, maybe they've recovered from you by now."

I doubted it. "Well," I said, "maybe you're right."

The waitress brought our checks. Marty tried to pay for me but I wouldn't let him.

"Are you sure you don't want to come to the movies with us?" Jane asked, as she checked her lipstick in her compact.

"I'm sure," I told her. "Thanks anyway, I've got a bunch of things to do at home."

Sam took my hand and squeezed. "As long as you're not going home to mope. Will you promise me you're not going home to mope?"

I squeezed Sam's hand in return. "I can't," I said, "promise anything."

The doorbell rang at about five that afternoon. It was my sister, Ashley. I wondered how she'd gotten my address. It wasn't like she was in the habit of visiting or sending birthday cards.

"Ashley," I said, "hi."

Ashley barreled past me, loaded down with Louis Vuitton luggage. "I need to stay here for a while," she announced, dumping the designer bags on the floor. Gargoyle jumped at the unexpected noise. Goblin shot under the coffee table.

"Oh," I replied. I noted that my sister's hair was unusually unkempt. And that it was badly in need of a color touch-up. "How long is a while?"

Ashley rolled her eyes. "Does it matter? I don't know, a month, maybe two months."

"Why?"

"Oh my God, Cleo, what's with the third degree?" Ashley looked around the room and frowned. "I just need to stay here. I'll take the bedroom and you can sleep on the couch."

Gargoyle chose that moment to chase an imaginary mouse into the bathroom. Goblin shot out from under the coffee table and followed.

"And keep those animals away from me," Ashley cried. "I don't know how you can stand all that fur flying around."

Ashley stepped into the kitchen. I watched as she yanked

open the refrigerator door. "There's nothing in here!" she whined.

Suddenly, I remembered Justin standing at the same fridge, uttering the same complaint just before admitting he'd cheated on me. I squinted at my sister. Like my former boyfriend, had she, too, gained weight?

"Do Mom and Dad know you're here?" I asked.

"I don't know. Where are your take-out menus?"

I pointed to a basket on the counter. Ashley grabbed a handful of menus; several fluttered to the floor. "Look," she said, "I'm a bit low on cash so you'll have to pay the delivery guy. I think I'll have the beef chow mein."

I picked up the fallen menus. "Why are you here, Ashley?" I repeated. "Is something wrong at home? Are you in trouble?"

Ashley moaned like she was being tortured and threw herself onto the couch.

"God, you're a pain, Cleo!" She rested her head on the back of the couch and looked up at the ceiling. "Okay, if you must know, I had sex with Elaine's fiancé—"

"Elaine?" I repeated. "Your best friend?"

Ashley grunted. "Whatever. She's always been pretty useless."

I thought of Elaine. Even-tempered, endlessly patient, loyal to Ashley since grammar school. How could Ashley have betrayed her?

"So, she found out?" I said.

"Yeah, her dorky fiancé confessed, can you believe it? What a loser! He wasn't even worth it, frankly."

"So," I said, "you're hiding from Elaine because she's mad at you? I know Elaine, Ashley. She's not a vindictive person."

"There's more to it, okay?"

My stomach clenched. For the first time in my life I battled a surge of pure anger toward my beloved sister.

"Tell me," I demanded.

Ashley looked at her hands, not at me when she spoke. "I

borrowed some money from her about six months ago and I just haven't been able to pay it back. God, I mean, she's got a job, she can afford it."

"How much money?"

Ashley shrugged. "I don't know."

"You don't know how much money you borrowed from your best friend?"

"Look, it was a lot, okay?"

"How much, Ashley?" I demanded.

"Twenty thousand!" Ashley jumped up from the couch, eyes blazing. "Jesus, get off my back!"

"It was Elaine's wedding fund, wasn't it?"

Ashley laughed a little. Was she the tiniest bit embarrassed? "Yeah. But if she was going to be such a pain about it she shouldn't have given me the money in the first place, right?"

For a moment I wondered if I was imagining this whole scenario. Was I really related to someone so entirely without a conscience? "So," I said after a long moment, "you're here because . . ."

"Because Elaine's got some collection agency or something after me."

"A collection agency? Or a hit man?"

Ashley rolled her eyes at me.

"What did you need the money for?" I asked. Though at this point, did it really matter?

"Stuff," she said. "Look, I'm really tired. I think I'll take a nap while you call for the Chinese food, okay?"

And then I opened my mouth to say, as I had all my adult life, "Well, I'll put fresh sheets on the bed for you," but something else entirely came out.

"No," I said emphatically. "You cannot stay here. In fact, I want you out of here now. This minute. It's time you started cleaning up your own messes, Ashley." And then I picked up her Louis Vuitton overnight bag and matching suitcase and hauled them unceremoniously into the hallway.

"Good-bye, Ashley."

My sister finally found her voice. "You," she spat, "are so going to regret this."

A big laugh burst from me. "What are you doing to do?" I asked. "Borrow my allowance and never pay it back? Steal my boyfriend when I'm sick in bed with the flu? Tell Dad I was the one who stole that lipstick from the drugstore?"

Ashley stumbled into the hallway. And just like that I shut the door on my sister and on a whole lot of wasted time.

Chapter 38

Consider embracing a life of eccentricity, as eccentric behavior is both entertaining to friends and a successful cover for your debilitating grief.
—Picking Up the Pieces: Life After You've Destroyed the Best Relationship You're Ever Going to Have

"What?" I asked.

They stood at the door to my apartment like white-coated medics ready to haul a crazy person off to a mental institution. At least, that's what they looked like to me.

"Hello to you too," Jane replied. "We're here to convince you to come out with us tonight."

"And we're not taking no for an answer." Sam stepped forward so that I had no choice but to back into the apartment and let them all in.

"I have nothing to wear," I said.

"I'll pull something together for you." Jane strode into my bedroom.

"I have to go to a cash machine."

"I've got plenty of cash," Marty said. "You can pay me back some other time."

I looked at Sam.

"You know you can't win," he said. "I can always out-argue you."

I sighed. Really, what was the point in spending another night alone and miserable, bemoaning my idiocy? It was almost three weeks since I'd destroyed my last chance at true happiness. But I was still alive. Miserable, but alive.

"Okay," I said. "I'll come along, but on one condition. We can't go anywhere Max might be."

"How can we guarantee that?" Sam demanded.

"Wait," Marty said. "I have an idea. There's this new place called Monsta. A guy in my office told me about it. It's huge, it's on three floors, with pool tables and pinball machines and a band. The point is it's big. I'm sure there's plenty of room for two people who aren't talking to each other."

Sam and Marty looked at me expectantly. Jane reappeared holding up a pair of jeans and a sparkly lilac-colored top I had absolutely no recollection of ever having owned.

"This will do," she said. "You can throw my scarf around your neck. You'll be very LA."

I looked at Goblin and Gargoyle; they were asleep in one giant mound on the couch. I couldn't use them as an excuse for staying home; cats don't need any help with sleep.

"Give me five minutes," I said.

Jane looked at my hair and frowned. "Better make it ten."

Chapter 39

Take a deep breath, count to ten, and then open your eyes. You just might be surprised at what you see.
—Deep Breathing and You: Relaxation Techniques
Are Cheaper Than Drugs

"Oh, crap, oh crap, oh crap."

No sooner had the four of us settled at a circular booth on the second floor of Monsta than I'd spotted Max Cooper walking determinedly toward the bar.

"Where are you going?" Jane hissed.

From the floor under the table I replied, "The floor under the table."

"Careful of my shoes," Sam warned. "They're new and they cost a fortune."

"I thought," I said, "that this place was big enough for two people trying to avoid each other!"

"We shouldn't have backed ourselves into a corner," Marty protested.

"I like sitting in a corner booth!" Jane said.

"Well," I told Jane's sandal-shod feet, "you should have thought ahead. You should have planned a quick and easy getaway. You should—"

Jane's frowning face suddenly appeared very close to mine. "I should," she said, "have let you stay home to rot."

"Sorry." It really wasn't anyone's fault, other than perhaps my own, that I found myself on the floor under a table on a Saturday night. "What's Max doing?" I asked. "No, don't tell me. Just hand me my drink. Are you sure he didn't see me?"

"I'm pretty sure," Jane said. "He hasn't looked this way once. In fact, he looks like he'd rather be anywhere but here."

"Max and I don't really like clubs," I explained, suddenly tortured by a memory of the two of us holed up in my apartment, drinking tea, listening to music, laughing, kissing . . .

"You dumped that guy?" Sam demanded, peeking under the cloth. "Are you insane? He's gorgeous."

Sam disappeared.

"Yes, I dumped him. And yes, I'm insane."

"Does he have a brother?"

"Yes, but I don't think he's gay."

"Let me worry about that," Sam said. "Here's how it's going to go down. You're going to get back together with Max and get me an introduction to the brother."

"I can assure you," I replied, "the last thing Max wants is to get back together with me. Look, as soon as he leaves, we're out of here."

But things were about to get much worse before they had the chance to get better. I heard a dull roar, the coarse laughter of drunken guys, the shrill laughter of girls desperate enough to want them.

"What's going on?" I asked. "What's all that noise?"

None of my friends replied.

"Hello! Is anyone up there?"

Jane's face appeared again. "Um, Cleo? We might be here for a while. Justin just showed up. And he's standing right next to Max."

"What!" I cried.

"They never met each other, right?"

I sighed. "Right. The last thing I need is to witness my two ex-boyfriends engaged in a Cleo-bashing session. Get back up there and see what's going on!"

There was another roar of laughter, this time without the addition of female voices.

"A few members of Justin's posse are drifting off," Sam informed me. "See? Everyone finds his supposed charm short-lived."

"To hell with Justin," I replied. "What's Max doing?" No one answered. I poked Jane's ankle. "Hello?"

"You really want to know?" she asked.

"Yes." Did I?

"Justin just turned to face Max. I think, yeah, Max is saying something to him. He looks . . . angry or something."

"Something bad is going to happen," Marty said then, and his voice sounded odd, slightly strangled. "I've seen that look before."

"What's going to happen?" I demanded. But before Marty could reply I peered above the rim of the table—just in time to see Max deliver a solid right hook to Justin's chin!

"Holy shit!" Sam cried.

Jane screamed.

"I knew it," Marty mumbled.

I climbed to my feet and with my friends rushed to join the crowd around Justin's prone body. A man had just been knocked out cold but no one seemed very concerned.

A guy about twice Justin's girth shook his head. "Barrow's had it coming for a long time."

"Maybe now," said a girl with the attenuated look of a professional dieter, "he'll think twice before trash-talking his ex-girlfriend in public."

A guy, wearing a Red Sox hat backwards, laughed. "Not likely. One right hook doesn't change anything for idiots like Justin."

Jane shot me a significant look. She'd heard it too. And it was clear to both of us what had happened. Justin had been trashing his ex named Cleo. Max had heard enough to recognize Justin's Cleo as his former Cleo. Max had asked Justin, nicely, to shut up. Justin had said, "Make me" or some such stupid thing. So Max had.

I looked past the gloating crowd around Justin and caught Max's eye. He looked sort of stunned. A guy strode up to him and slapped him on the shoulder. "Dude," he said, "that was amazing!"

I looked back to the prone figure of my ex-boyfriend.

"Is he unconscious?" Jane asked indifferently.

Sam poked Justin with the toe of his new shoe. "He's coming around. I've seen worse."

"There are fistfights in gay bars?" I asked inanely.

Sam rolled his eyes at me.

"He's going to have a killer headache," Marty said.

Good, I thought. And then Jane gave me a shove and I was stumbling over to Max, who had moved farther away from the scene of the crime.

I don't think he'd ever looked more attractive to me than he did at that moment.

"Did you see that?" he asked me.

"Yes."

"Where were you?"

"Under the table in the corner."

A hint of a smile appeared on Max's beautiful face. Suddenly, his eyes didn't look so bruised. "What were you doing under the table?"

"Hiding from you."

"Ah. I thought you hated going to clubs."

"I do. My friends dragged me here. They felt sorry for me sitting home alone."

Max nodded. "It's good to have friends."

"What about you?" I said. "I thought you hated clubs too."

"My sister and her fiancé nagged me to meet them here."

"Are we that pitiful?"

"We seem to be." Max grimaced and looked at his right hand. "I think I sprained it."

I took a step closer to Max. He didn't seem to mind. "I don't like violence."

"Neither do I."

"But it was a pretty amazing punch." I tried but I couldn't hide a grin.

Max grinned back. "So, you like me now because I decked your old boyfriend?"

"Well, not exactly. I mean, yes, I like you, I've always liked you but . . . Max, I'm an idiot."

"No you're not," Max said in that low, sexy voice. "You're adorable."

"And you're sophisticated, and yet not above delivering a solid right hook. I like that in a man."

"Did I mention I'm a Gemini?"

"I knew it!"

There was a groan from the vicinity of the group behind us. Justin, it seems, was coming back to consciousness. Max looked hard at me. "I can't," he said, "believe you went out with that specimen."

"Neither can I," I admitted. "But that was the old Cleo. The new Cleo has higher standards. I made some bad mistakes in the past."

"Are there any good mistakes?"

"Some are worse than others. Leaving you was one of the very bad ones."

Max took my hand. I held his gently. "Thinking you couldn't make things work between us was worse," he said. "You underestimated yourself, Cleo."

My hero. "Boyfriendius Maximus."

Max grinned. "You mean it?"

"If it's okay with you."

"It's wonderful with me. I promise no more bar fights."

"Good. And I promise to remember you're Max and not some standard-issue idiot."

And then we kissed and though I'd never been much for public displays of affection, at that moment I just let myself love him. Interesting noises from Justin's crew finally distracted us from each other. We looked in time to see Justin slumping out of the room, his arms flung around the shoulders of two loyal buddies.

I turned back to Max. "I'm going to knit you a scarf for Christmas."

"Cleo, Christmas is months away."

"I know. It will take me that long. I'm really bad."

"I'll love it anyway," he promised.

"I believe you," I told him. And I did.

"Max!"

It was Liz, coming toward us with a look of surprise and yes, a bit of wariness on her pretty face. With her was a big, jolly-looking guy I assumed was Brad, her fiancé.

"Your brother," I said by way of greeting, "is giving me another chance." Max put his arm around my waist. I smiled up at him. "And this time I won't let him down."

LOVE IS LIKE A BOX OF CHOCOLATES

Marcia Evanick

Chapter 1

Sometimes you feel like a nut.

The worst job in any hospital had to be housekeeping. Okay, maybe the second worst job. Working in the deep, dark bowels of the hospital's basement and through creaky metal doors marked 'Morgue' had to be the bottom rung of the medical ladder. Dead bodies scare the hell out of me, and I'm an RN. That's me, Judith Elizabeth Howland, RN. Those initials sound impressive, until you meet my two brothers, both with a lovely MD after their names. Both are brilliant, handsome, and total idiots.

Those two very expensive initials give our parents major bragging rights in their circle of friends. Of course my parents still have that second mortgage on their home, years of loans still to be paid back, and my father just figured out he can finally retire at eighty-three, providing he lives that long. The amazing part is, both of my parents seem to think this financial hardship is a way of life, some sick, sadistic badge of honor to prove what wonderful, self-sacrificing parents they are. My mother would rather eat bugs than to ask her "Doctor" sons for a penny to lighten the load. My father, for the sake of peace and harmony in their marriage, agrees with whatever my mother says. Besides, he isn't stupid, he likes living.

Neither of my parents understood why I never had the burning desire to become a doctor. It's simple, really, I care about people and have no desire, burning or otherwise, to play God by making life-and-death decisions on a daily basis. Hell, half the time I roll out of bed and can't decide what outfit to wear. I prefer to give it my all to make patients' lives, usually in a tough situation, more comfortable. If I wanted to slice and dice, I'd buy a Cuisinart.

John, my older brother by four years, is a plastic surgeon for the rich and vain. Granted, he isn't making life-and-death decisions, but he is playing at being God in a different way. John even married the poster child of his profession. Vanessa schedules surgery on her body like most people schedule an oil change for their car. For Christmas last year, John bought Vanessa cheek implants. What a guy. Now there's a present I would love to find under my own Christmas tree. Not!

How in the hell you wrap cheek implants is still a mystery to me. Maybe John stuck a fancy gold bow on them and dropped them into her stocking hanging on the mantel Christmas Eve, along with the sugar plums and a 10 percent discount coupon for her next liposuction session.

Dr. Frankenstein was using Franklin University Hospital's operating room to create his own monster. John still hasn't forgiven me for my comment during Christmas dinner about someone implanting Abby Normal's brain in Vanessa's plastic body. Hell, Vanessa's face, boobs, and ass are so taut, that Barbie has more jiggle in her stride. Vanessa's skin is stretched so tight that when she sneezes her asshole slams shut and she can't poop for a week.

Paul, my other older brother, by two years, is an extremely gifted cardiologist. If you think living with a plastic surgeon in the family is tough, try having a cardiologist for a brother. Unless I find a cure for cancer, initiate world peace, or finally give my mother that grandchild she has been begging for, my name will never come first when my mother brags to all her friends and fellow members of the Red Hat Society about her children. I accepted that fact a long time ago, and try not to let it bother me too much.

It gives me great comfort to point out, during family get-togethers, that since John and Vanessa got married first, Vanessa should have the honor of carrying that first grandchild. I usually try to snap Vanessa's picture right at that exact moment . . . you know, capture that look of pure horror on her face. Of course, that's the photo I always put in my photo album. Once I even snapped a picture of her with a mouth full of wine. I had just suggested she should do her wifely duty and carry on the family name and that ten-pound babies ran in the family. The wine had been red, and her cashmere sweater had been a brilliant, expensive white. I had that photo blown up to a lovely 8 x 10, and gave it its own page.

As you might have guessed, Vanessa and her size two jeans and I don't get along.

Before you get the wrong idea and think I'm a total bitch, I want to tell you that I honestly like my other brother's wife, Matilda. Paul married Matty, a dear, sweet woman whose heart is in the right place, but a bowl of Fruit Loops has more intelligence. Matty is determined to save every animal in the world, whether they want to be saved or not. Their home is filled with four dogs, six cats, cages of reptiles and birds, a ferret, and the last time I visited them, a Shetland pony, which had been living in their garage. Paul hadn't even noticed the pony until I pointed it out, and then his only response was a small grunt about the smell before burying his nose back into some medical journal.

Matty could have Big Foot staying in the guest bedroom and Paul would never notice . . . unless Big Foot wolfed down a bowl of fettuccine, causing his arteries to slam close, and suffered a heart attack in the upstairs hallway. Paul would undoubtedly be glad to perform a triple bypass on the missing link for the challenge and a big splashy article in one of his beloved medical journals.

Paul is an ass sometimes for the way he ignores Matty. He never notices what goes on around him and prefers to be elbow-deep into someone's chest cavity, while John sculptures his own trophy wife.

John and Vanessa have matching red BMWs bought with profits from bigger boobs for the Hooters waitresses and smaller noses for those private-school kiddies. God forbid should the little Tiffanys and Stephanies of the world not be invited to the next Country Club Junior Mixer because their honker isn't perfectly formed.

And my parents wonder why I never felt the need to join the ranks.

I prefer to keep what little empathy, humanity, and sympathy I have for the human race intact. Besides, I want a life outside the hallowed walls of Franklin University Hospital. Not that I have one—a life, I mean. But I'm an optimist. I'm not looking for Prince Charming, just a good, decent man. One that I could train without too much of a hassle.

The career part of my life had me standing outside of Cubicle Number 2 in the emergency room at midnight on a beautiful spring night. I was thinking about the daffodils that were finally in bloom and with a sense of dread I realized bikini season wasn't far behind. I would rather get every one of my eyelashes plucked out by chickens than try on swimsuits. If I thought last year's humiliating shopping spree was bad, I couldn't imagine what this year's was going to be like. I was eight pounds heavier, and I didn't need a full-length mirror to tell me where those pounds had adhered to: my ass.

Visions of a hippo in a yellow string bikini were filling my mind when the patient behind the curtain christened the floor again. I cringed at the sound, knowing my friend and fellow RN, Claudia, was in with the patient. I wasn't tempted or fool enough to go offer assistance. Claudia was more than capable of handling the situation. Besides, Claudia, the rat, had hid last night while I got stuck handling a screamer for nearly an hour.

Screamers were the worst.

Little kids screaming because they are hurt and scared

break my heart. Thirty-year-old yuppies screaming because of a few stitches and needles usually make me want to break a bedpan over their fat heads. A full bedpan. Men usually make the worst patients.

I walked over to the counter, picked up the phone, and dialed the intercom. When it clicked on, I said, "Housekeeping to the ER. Housekeeping to the ER." and quickly hung up. I hate hearing my own voice. To my inner ear, my voice sounds classically normal, with a hint of seductive huskiness. Think Meg Ryan with a touch of Katharine Hepburn thrown in to drive the men wild. What I just heard come over the loudspeakers sounded like Minnie Mouse huffing on some helium balloons.

Claudia, looking green around the edges and disgusted, emerged from behind Curtain Number 2. The slight splattering on Claudia's pants told the story. "Still haven't learned to move fast enough, huh?" Claudia always had been slow off the mark, while I could break the land-speed record at the first sound of a gag.

"Stuff it, Howland." Claudia wasn't having a good night.

Claudia hadn't had a good night since Christmas, when she had worked herself up into believing her live-in boyfriend, Chris, was going to pop the question, complete with a big ass diamond ring and bended knee. When she had gotten off work Christmas morning and rushed home, she discovered a 57" big-screen television sitting in their living room, complete with a big-ass red bow.

Things between Claudia and Chris haven't been the same since.

Claudia marched over to the industrial mop and bucket and started to wheel it toward Curtain Number 2. Don't let the fancy RN behind our names fool you. We do a lot of cleaning up, especially when it consists of bodily fluids. The housekeeping department has been known to take a week to respond to a page.

"I already paged Housekeeping for you."

"I heard, thanks." Claudia held onto the mop handle as if it was supporting her weight. She looked exhausted, and since it was only an hour into our shift, I couldn't imagine what she was going to look like around four in the morning. Working the night shift wasn't for the vain. No matter how nice and well-rested you are at the beginning of your shift, by seven in the morning you look like an extra on *The Night of the Living Dead* movie set.

"Rough night?"

"Rough day." Claudia swished the mop around in the sudsy water, releasing the stench of bleach, disinfectant, and Lord knows what else the hospital uses to kill every known germ in the universe. "My mom's 'Let's meet for breakfast' turned into an all-day affair with lunch, shopping, and a lecture on living in sin with Chris."

"I thought she'd be used to that by now." Claudia and Chris had been cohabitating for three years.

"She's still of the opinion that Chris isn't going to buy the cow if I keep giving away the milk for free." Claudia rolled her eyes. "I don't know what's worse, my mother referring to me as a cow, or referring to sex as 'milking' someone."

I tried not to laugh. My own mother wouldn't mention the word sex in mixed company. Heck, I never heard her mention it in private either. "Sex and milking have a lot in common, Claud. There's tits and getting those juices flowing, things like that."

"It's teats."

"What's teats?"

"Cows don't have tits, they have teats." Claudia shook her head at my barnyard ignorance.

"Oh, someone's *Green Acres* roots are showing." Claudia had been born and raised about thirty miles outside of Franklin's city limits. Where the women made biscuits from scratch and the men rode around on John Deere tractors all day.

"Sorry, but after spending the entire day walking the mall and listening to my mother tell me how to live my life, I came home only to discover Chris had invited half the town over to watch the Pay Per View boxing match on *my* television. They all showed up three hours before the fight bearing foot-long subs, bags of chips, and cases of beer. I managed to catch about an hour's worth of sleep, tops."

It was painful, but I held my tongue. Most of the time Chris is an inconsiderate a-hole and I have no idea what Claudia sees in him. Okay, he has a nice bod, but broad shoulders and a tight ass don't make up for taking Claudia's milk for free. "So how's your mom?"

"Worried about Hugh." Claudia took the change of subject with grace.

"What's wrong with him?" Hugh is Claudia's older brother, who has just moved back into the area. For the past six years he had been living out in LA. I've never met Hugh, but if Claudia had her way we would be married by now with a house filled with little Hughies. Hugh's been back on the East coast for about two months.

"Nothing's wrong with him." Claudia frowned at Theodore, the night shift lab tech, as he slipped silently behind Curtain Number 1. The striped curtain barely fluttered in his wake.

Theo, whose job consists of drawing blood from patients, and then running the numbers, gives me the willies. He didn't earn the nickname Drac, short for Dracula, for drawing blood all night. He looks the part. Even his complexion is paler than his white lab coat. Once, I swear, I looked into the metal paper towel dispenser while he was in the room, and he didn't have a reflection.

"So why is your mom worried?" I could hear my patient talking to Theo, but I couldn't hear Theo's response. Theo is the quietest human I ever ran across. The man doesn't make a sound when he walks. Hell, half the time I don't think he *is* human.

"She thinks he's lonely." Claudia seemed to appraise my mood. "I think she's right."

I knew what was coming. I had known it since Hugh's name

was mentioned. "I'm not going to go out with your brother, Claud. We went over this before. I don't do blind dates anymore. You know that."

I'm the queen of disastrous blind dates. I've been on one calamitous blind date after another. I've been left holding the check, escorted out of some of the nicest restaurants in town, groped, and proposed to. Sometimes all in the same evening. Five weeks ago, I declared an end to all well-meaning matchmaking by friends and family.

I shouted that declaration while nearly pulling out my back putting my second cousin's third wife's nephew onto his couch. We met downtown one afternoon at a local bar-slash-restaurant. I wanted to order lunch, he wanted to drink it. By three o'clock he was so smashed, I had to drive him back to his apartment and pour him onto the couch. The second time his fingers squeezed my ass, I hauled off and elbowed him in the stomach. He was moaning something about needing a bucket when I slammed his apartment door behind me.

The dozen red roses I received the next day didn't even put me in a forgiving mood. Nor did it make me change my mind about swearing off all blind dates.

"Come on, Judith, your first marriage proposal came on a blind date." The corner of Claudia's mouth twitched.

"That should tell you something." It told me something too. I had actually hesitated before politely, but firmly, turning down Herman Tremount. Something about his mother having plenty of room at her house for me had soured the deal. I was desperate, not pathetic. "Look, Claud, I like you. Heck, I consider you one of my best friends. No man, brother or not, is worth ruining that friendship over."

One of Claudia's brows kicked up. "Not even if you would be perfect for each other?"

"Last time someone said someone was perfect for me, I ended up being subpoenaed to appear in court to testify against him."

"Chad only got a fine and six months' probation." Claudia

giggled and lowered her voice. "Besides, he was cute and you did make page seven of the local paper."

"Being called 'an unidentified woman' isn't how I want to make the papers. Besides, the nice officer gave me his coat so I could hide under it when the news van showed up. The pushy photographer only got a picture of me from the chest down."

"Yeah, but your T-shirt was soaking wet and clinging to you like Saran Wrap."

"I had a bra on." The humiliation of that night was burned into my memory forever. To top it off, it had been freezing out, and all a person had to do was look at my wet T-shirt to get that weather report.

The date with Chad had started off okay with a nice dinner and normal conversation, so I agreed to go to Paddy's Place with him. Paddy's is an Irish pub that specializes in darts and Irish music. Sounded perfect to me, because I was stupid enough not to have known that Sunday nights at Paddy's is Wet T-shirt night. When all the gents in the pub that night started to shout, "The good Lord be praised," I knew something wasn't right and no way was it a spontaneous Bible Study class breaking out. When it dawned on me what was happening, I stood up and wanted to leave immediately. Chad, being either stupid or drunk, decided his date, that being me, should win the contest, and proceeded to dump an entire pitcher of ice water down the front of my shirt.

That's when the fight broke out. And to my dying shame, I'm afraid I was the one to throw the first punch. The patrons of the pub, not wanting to be left out of a good fight, quickly joined in and a brawl ensued. Bar stools went flying, glass broke, and someone ended up with a dart in his thigh. Through it all, the bartender merrily squirted down any women within his range. The cops, who responded to the scene, questioned every woman in the place for hours while the men resumed their dart game and drinking.

And people wonder why I won't go out on blind dates any longer.

"Hugh doesn't drink, Judith. I already told you, he has an occasional beer once in a while."

"One beer was all it took for Brad to start singing about whiskers on kittens and his favorite things during a black-tie affair honoring the mayor." Brad Commums, a local news reporter my sister-in-law Matty had fixed me up with, hadn't been *humming* the song either. Brad had stood on a chair and started to belt it out like he was in the cast of *Cats* and there were critics in the banquet hall.

"Brad was on medication that reacted with the beer, Judith. You can't count that. You're a nurse, you should have sympathy for the ill."

"Not when I spent three hundred and fifty bucks on a red-sequined evening gown, only to have my date get physically ill on me while riding in the back of an ambulance."

"He offered to have it cleaned." Claudia failed to keep the laughter out of her voice. "I must say you do live an interesting dating life. On second thought, Hugh might be too tame for you."

Oh I could see what she was trying to do. Tell me I wasn't right for her precious brother, and I would be jumping at the chance to go out with him. I wasn't stupid. I took Psychology 101 and quite a few other psych courses. "Don't you have a patient to clean up after?" That would wipe the smirk off her face.

"Don't you have one too?" Claudia glanced at Curtain Number 1.

"Drac's in there siphoning blood." Edna Klein was resting comfortably, with her son sitting next to her bed. Edna showed up about five times a year, claiming to be weak and dizzy, and not able to catch her breath. Physically, seventy-four-year-old Edna was fine. Mentally, she just craved some attention from her kids once in a while.

"Drac left about three minutes ago." Claudia smirked, and headed for Curtain Number 2 and a mess I was grateful it wasn't mine to clean up.

Hugh James sounded a little too perfect to be true. He had a college education, was single with not even a divorce or kids to weigh him down, and had just started his own business in town. I've never dated an architect before, and I really shouldn't be thinking about it now. I work with Claudia five nights a week and there is no way I'm going to put her brother between us. Life experience has taught me there has to be something seriously wrong with Hugh if he is still single at thirty-three.

Then again, maybe not. I'm single and thirty-two and the only thing wrong with me is my stunning ability to date nothing but losers. And the fact that I wasted five years of my life on Todd Bently, Dr. Todd Bently. My mother almost forgave me for living in sin with Todd because he had that all-important MD after his name. If I won't become a doctor, marrying one is a well-respected second place in her opinion.

Problem was, there was a reason Todd chose to specialize in gynecology. After looking at the female body all day long, he went chasing it all night long. The real problems started when I wasn't the one he was chasing.

Thankfully, right after our breakup two years ago, Todd took a position down in Atlanta, so I didn't have to worry about running into him in the hospital parking lot. And I do mean literally running into his cheating ass if he had ever gotten stupid enough to walk in front of my car. I pay insurance premiums for a reason and I have five hundred in the bank to cover the deductible. Of course he didn't take the new job because of me, or out of any sense of guilt. Todd Bently, MD had been caught in bed with the wife of the dean of Franklin University and had left town in a hurry, without said wife.

Franklin University Hospital, affectionately referred to as F.U. Hospital, is a teaching hospital, and has a close tie to Franklin University right next door. Over time I have found the old saying "those who can't, teach" proved remarkably true. In one of the amazing, horrifying twists of fate, it is those teachers training the crop of new doctors who would be called upon to save your ass.

Now you understand why everyone calls it F.U. Hospital. The billing department still uses their fingers to count, the bedpans are cold, and the doctors are horny. At least the nurses are nice. Okay, I'll qualify that: some of the nurses are nice. F.U. Hospial employs a couple of nurses that scare the crap out of me. I can't imagine what they do to poor bedridden patients.

I was heading back toward Edna when the phone on the counter rang. Dr. Garmond, who was probably down in the X ray department flirting with whoever was working the night shift, would never lower himself to answer a phone. He also isn't very particular as to whom he flirts with: old, young, barely breathing—it doesn't make a difference to him. The coordinator who was supposed to be manning the phones disappeared into the bathroom about ten minutes ago, and the rest of the staff were making themselves scarce. Not that I blamed them. It was a quiet night, so far.

I answered the phone, "ER, Howland speaking."

"I've got a patient for you whenever you're ready, Judith. He's a real clown." I could hear the laughter in Millie's voice.

"Great, that ought to brighten my night. I'll be right there." Whenever a patient comes to the ER there is paperwork to do, insurance cards to copy, and wristbands to attach before you even get to see a doctor. Millie is our night admission gal, and she has a wicked sense of humor. The clown out in the waiting room must really be a joker and a half. The way my luck runs, it was probably some teenage boy who thought it would be hysterical if he shoved a goldfish up his nose.

I stopped in and checked on my patient. "How are you doing here, Edna?" There was color back in her cheeks and her breathing seemed to be easier.

"Better, Judith." Edna was holding her son's hand. "You always take such nice care of me."

I tucked another blanket over her legs and glanced at the bandage Drac had put over the injection site. "A nurse from the X-ray department will be up in a minute or two to take you back for a chest X-ray. Once we get that back, and some numbers from the lab, the doctor will be in to see you."

"Thank you, Judith. I think I'll rest till then." Edna gave me a small smile. In about a week's time, Edna will have one of her children deliver a plateful of chocolate chip cookies to the ER.

"I'll be back in a couple of minutes." I looked at her son. "Give a holler if you need anything."

"Will do."

I pulled the curtain closed behind me for Edna's privacy and headed for the joker in the waiting room. This ought to be good. Millie usually didn't make personal comments over the phone. I pushed open the swinging doors, took one step, and froze.

There was a real live clown sitting in a wheelchair. One of his feet was up and a woman—wearing a low-necked and high-cut sequined pink bodysuit, pink fishnet stockings, and a silver tiara with a huge pink feather in it—was holding a bag of ice on his foot. Two interns were standing in the hall with their mouths hanging open staring at the woman's ass, which was halfway out of the body suit.

Great, no one told me the circus had come to town.

Millie handed me the chart and I glanced at the name. "Emmett Lockwood?"

The clown raised his head and stared at me. Beneath the red fright wig and white greasepaint, I could tell the guy was in pain, but a real smile broke out beneath the gigantic red painted-on one. "Just what the doctor ordered, a beautiful nurse."

Okay, so it was a stupid line, but it made me smile. I looked at his bare toes peeking out from beneath the ice bag. They were pink from the cold. He had a white sock on the other foot and I had to wonder where his clown shoes were. He looked ridiculous sitting in the wheelchair dressed in baggy purple-and-yellow plaid pants, a lime green shirt, and red suspenders. A pink polkadotted tie set the outfit off swimmingly.

"What happened? The dancing bear step on your foot?"

"No, one of my horses did." The woman turned and smiled at me. "I'm Kelly, and I'm afraid Ginger stepped on his foot."

I pushed the wheelchair through the doors and headed for Curtain Number 3. "I take it Ginger's the horse?"

"Bingo," said Emmett.

I locked the brakes on the chair and handed Kelly, whose top half was now falling out of the sparkling body suit, the ice pack. Emmett's foot was swollen and appeared to be frozen. "Your wife's horse doesn't like you?"

"I'm not his wife, I'm his sister."

"You know, Emmett and Kelly? Emmett Kelly?" He looked at me as if I should see a connection.

I drew a blank. "Who's Emmett Kelly?" The only part on his face that wasn't covered in heavy makeup was the tip of his nose. He must have taken off the fake one on the way to the hospital. His eyes were a crystal blue, and it wasn't pain I was seeing in them now. It was interest. Interest in me. My, how fast one's life could turn around. The night was definitely looking up. First, I wasn't the one to get the hurler, now I got Bozo. A single Bozo.

Hey, I'm thirty-two and single. At that age you start looking beneath the fright wigs and makeup.

"Emmett Kelly was the world's most famous clown." Kelly looked aghast at my ignorance.

The Emmett before me looked amused, and still interested. "He played Weary Willie."

I shook my head. The only clowns I knew were Bozo and Ronald McDonald. "Your mother named you both after a clown?" Maybe their mother was psychic and knew her son was destined to run away and join the circus.

"Our family comes from a long line of clowns." Emmett winked.

I grinned back. "Then you should be darn glad they didn't name you Bozo." I studied his foot. Most of the damage seemed to be in the toes. "You are going to need an X-ray."

"Will you hold my hand?" Emmett's gaze was locked on my ring finger, my unadorned ring finger.

"No, but if you are a good boy for the technician I'll give you a lollipop."

"Grape?"

"I'll see what I can do."

I left the exam room and nearly ran into Claudia as she wheeled the mop and bucket back to the corner. Hopefully Housekeeping would replace the water within the next hour. "I've got a real clown in Number 3." It was against the rules to fraternize with the patients. But bringing a clown a sucker couldn't be labeled as fraternizing.

"What did he do, grab your ass?" Claudia and I both have been grabbed before. Usually by drunks and doctors.

"No, I mean he's a real clown. Rollins Circus must have put up their tents on the outskirts of town."

"What's his problem? Bowling pin land on his head? Fell off the tightrope and his parasol got jammed in a very sensitive area?" Claudia chuckled.

"No, his sister's horse stepped on his toes."

"Which ones?"

"This little piggy had roast beef, this little piggy had none, and this little piggy went wee wee wee all the way home." It was common knowledge that I could never remember all the fancy names for the bones in the fingers and toes. Fingers are easy, you have the pointer, the pinky, and the index finger. You even have "The Finger." You have a big toe and the rest are just toes. I've found over the years that the little-piggy analogy works just fine.

"Sounds painful."

"I think he's cute, and he's interested."

Claudia blinked. "What do you mean, 'think he's cute'? He's either cute, or he's not."

"It's kind of hard to tell with all the greasepaint on his face. The tip of his nose is cute, good bone structure, and he has the most devastating blue eyes."

"You mean he came to the hospital in his clown outfit?" Claudia lowered her voice and stared at the curtain to the Exam Room Number 3.

"They're his work clothes." I've attended patients who wore everything and anything. From pajamas to bathing suits to firefighting gear. Granted, Emmett was my first clown, but hell, if a clown isn't a good guy, who is? I read somewhere once in *Cosmo* that most women think a man's sense of humor is more important than his looks. You couldn't get funnier than a clown.

"I think I'm going to ask him out. You know, show him the town while he's here."

Claudia's eyes widened so far I was afraid her eyeballs were going to fall out. "You'd go out with a clown," she sputtered, "but not my brother."

"If I ask him out, or better yet, if I can get him to ask me out, it's not a blind date. I would know exactly who I'm going out with." Made perfect sense to me. "How much trouble could I get into in broad daylight with a clown?"

Chapter 2

Sometimes you don't.

I was never going to live this one down. Emmett Lockwood was certifiable, and not in a good way.

I really didn't mind having to drive on our date. Emmett's transportation was also his home. It would be a little hard parking a 24'-long recreational vehicle in the Wok and Roll restaurant's parking lot. I love Chinese, and Emmett said he'd eat anywhere that didn't have corn dogs and cotton candy on the menu. Lunch had been semienjoyable.

I amused Emmett with some hysterical emergency room stories. No one believes what some people do to themselves, usually when they are drunk, or in the name of love and a good time. Emmett had reciprocated with some circus stories of his own. If his stories bordered more on the *questionable* side of decent, I wrote it off as a male trait. We were both adults, and I did appreciate a good raunchy joke on occasion.

I just felt a little funny about Emmett using our first date as that occasion. Other than that, he was the perfect gentleman, and even picked up the entire check.

After leaving the restaurant, I was at odds about a suggestion as to where we should go. With three broken toes, Emmett wasn't up for walking around the park. It was bad enough he had to perform that night under the big top. With a couple hours to kill, Emmett offered to show me around the circus, and a personal introduction to Roberta the Wonder Elephant.

How could I have refused such a tempting offer? Besides, I was curious to see how circus entertainers lived. Who didn't think about the glamorous life of a trapeze artist, or the illusionist who could saw a woman in half? I admit it, I'm a sucker for a sad-faced clown and a bagful of roasted peanuts.

My glorious illusions were shattered within the first twenty minutes of the tour. Within the next twenty minutes I wanted to call Health and Human Services and have the Rollins Traveling Circus shut down. No one had cleaned up after Roberta the Wonder Elephant, who pooped the size of a Volkswagen. Georgio, the ringmaster, was drunk and holding a game of craps next to the popcorn stand with a bunch of questionable-looking men. Poodles wearing tutus were running everywhere and marking their territory.

The one redeeming good spot so far was the fact I hadn't ruined my shoes yet by stepping in crap.

"Come on, Judith, guess." Emmett, who was leaning against his postage-stamp-sized kitchen sink, had just finished blowing up a pinkish-colored balloon animal and he wanted me to guess what it was. Either he was the worse balloon animal maker in the world, or he had just blown up an eighteen-inch penis. A circumcised eighteen-inch penis.

"I really should be going, Emmett." I stood up and tried not to touch anything in his RV. As my mother would have gladly pointed out, I didn't know where it had been. "It has been fun." Oh well, I just spent my Friday afternoon with a clown who made pornographic balloon animals to entertain his dates. Emmett Kelly, the once world-famous clown, had to be rolling over in his grave.

I'd officially sunk to the bottom of the dating pool, and there wasn't a lifeguard in sight.

"You don't have to leave yet, Judith. I don't have to go on for another two hours." Emmett slowly started to release the air from the balloon. When it was halfway deflated, he grinned. "Now it's Weary Willie."

I blinked. My God, I was right. It *had* been a penis instead of some deformed caterpillar with no legs. *I'm out of here.*

Emmett pulled two beers out of his ancient refrigerator, on which someone had graciously painted a half-naked brunette. The woman was holding a whip in one hand and a tiger was curled around her feet. Charming. Emmett opened both bottles and tilted one toward the sadistic-looking woman. "That's Clarissa, my first wife."

"She was a tiger tamer?" What I really should have been asking was how many wives did he have, but the tiger threw me off stride.

"Tigers, lions, and leopards." Emmett tried to hand me a beer, and when I refused to take it he placed it on the counter with a shrug. "She even had a pet jaguar named Crissy." He took a big pull on his beer. "Crissy scratched the hell out of my ass one night." Emmett wiggled his brows. "Want to see my scars?"

"No thank you." Okay that settles it. I will never date another circus performer if I get out of this in one piece, and without the cops being involved. "I really have to head on back now, Emmett. It's been interesting." I took a step toward the door. I was ten miles from my apartment and somehow I didn't think Roberta the Wonder Elephant would come to my rescue if I started screaming. I've learned a little self-defense, but more importantly, I know the male anatomy. I knew exactly where to kick if Bozo got frisky.

"Come on, Judith, relax."

"No can do." I kept a smile on my face as I took another step to the door.

The door opening behind me caused me to jump and spin around. The woman barging into the trailer had me backing up into the padded bench I had just been sitting on. The woman wore a see-through robe and a microscopic red outfit that consisted mostly of fringe. Fringe barely covered her breasts and ass. Bleached blond hair was piled high on her head, and she reeked of perfume and scotch as she teetered on red high heels.

"Emmett, darling, I need your help." The woman pressed her massive breasts against Emmett's chest and pouted up at him. I could have sat a glass on her deep-red pouting lower lip.

"Judith, this is Phoebe, the prettier half of our trapeze team." Emmett eyes were on Phoebe's chest.

Phoebe turned to me and glared. "I'm also Emmett's wife." The seductive pout turned into a snarl.

My first thought was if Phoebe went flying through the air with the greatest of ease, she better be working with a net. Gravity would definitely play a part in that act. Those breasts weren't meant for flying, unless she just pumped them up with helium. My second thought was this date was turning into another episode of the *Jerry Springer Show*. I could picture the headlines now: "Local RN and Aerial Artist Get Into Fight Over Some Clown."

"She's my ex-wife. My third ex-wife." Emmett didn't seem to be in a hurry to push Wife Number 3 away.

"Nice to met you, Phoebe. I was just leaving." I hurried to the door and was down the one step before Emmett could utter a protest. " 'Bye!" I cheerfully waved and hurried in the direction where I'd parked my car.

If my luck held, I just might make it there without getting my shoes fertilized.

Claudia was never going to believe this one. Then again I might not tell her. She was still ticked at me for accepting Emmett's invitation for lunch, while I wouldn't even consider meeting her brother. I carefully made my way between two other parked recreational vehicles, which had also seen better days. Both had their windows open. In one it was quiet, while the other had the unmistakable sound of two people in the throws of ecstasy.

And the afternoon just kept getting better. What was with these people?

I tried to quietly hurry past, but I nearly stumbled when I heard the sound of a duck coming from the same trailer. My eyes crossed as the distinct honk filled the air again, followed by a woman's giggle. No way did I want to know what in the world was going on behind those rusting aluminum walls. Two poodles dressed in blue tutus ran by, chasing a poor, scared bunny. I sympathized with the rabbit.

Maybe I should call Animal Abuse Services—but tell them what, I have no idea. I would come off sounding like a nut if I told them that the elephant's poop was huge and ducks honked while watching, or God forbid participating in, sex. In the distance someone was checking out the loud-speakers under the big red-and-white-striped tent and circus music filled the air. Roberta let out a loud cry, either because the organ music startled her, or she was trying to sing along.

My fingers fumbled for my keys, and I didn't stop looking over my shoulder until I was pulling out onto the road. Two miles away from the circus grounds I pulled over to the side of the road and began to laugh. I laughed until I had tears rolling down my cheeks.

My track record was still standing. I dated nothing but losers, whiners, mama's boys, cheaters, drunks—and now I could add a perverted clown to the list. Somehow the tears didn't seem to be coming from laughter anymore.

Eight thirty that night I was pulled from my sleep—and a troubling dream about being on a trapeze with Emmett, dressed as a clown ready to catch me—by a pounding on my front door. It was dark outside, and I had only been asleep for about an hour.

I was hoping like hell that the dream hadn't meant anything. Visions of me flying through the air with only Emmett to catch me was disheartening.

I tried to remember if there had been a safety net in my dream as I stumbled to the door and peeked out the peephole. If I spotted a red rubber nose or a balloon penis, I was calling the cops. My brother Paul stood on the other side of the door. He looked lost, confused, and troubled. I quickly opened the door. I could count on one hand the number of times Paul had come to my apartment in the two years that I have lived here. My heart started to pound as I fumbled with the chain and opened the door. "Paul, what's wrong?"

Paul stepped into my apartment. "I, uh . . ."

"Is it Mom? Dad?" By my brother's paleness I was prepared for the worst.

"No, they're fine, Judith. I didn't mean to upset you." Paul just stood there, looking lost.

"Matty? What's wrong with Matty?" I could feel my heart lurch in my chest. I like Matty when she isn't trying to get me to take in a stray dog or cat. Thankfully, it's in my lease that pets aren't allowed or I would be knee-deep in kitty litter by now.

"Nothing's wrong with Matty." Paul blinked. "At least I don't think so." He blinked again. "She threw me out, Judith. Matty threw me out." Paul's voice broke on the last word.

I gently took his arm and walked him over to the sofa. "Sit down and tell me everything." There was no way Matty threw Paul out of their home and her life. Matty loved Paul. Any fool could see that.

Paul lowered himself to the couch, bent forward, and put his face into his hands; his gifted hands that saved people every day. Hands that now trembled. I had never seen my brother's hands tremble before and it scared me. Okay, maybe it was bad and Paul hadn't misheard Matty. "Take a couple of deep breaths and relax. I'll go make us some tea."

I put the kettle on to boil, and made a quick dash into my bedroom to change. Paul is my brother, and I love him dearly, but there was no way I was going back out into the living room to discuss his troubled marriage wearing an old Pittsburgh Steelers' T-shirt and a pair of black lace panties. The water had just started to boil when I reentered the kitchen. Two minutes later I rejoined Paul. He hadn't moved an inch.

"Paul, you still take tea with honey?" I hadn't seen either of my brothers drink tea in about fifteen years. Tea laced with honey was my mother's specialty. She had given it to us kids that way to cure anything from a sore throat to a stubbed toe. It usually worked.

"Honey's fine." Paul leaned back into the couch. "I'm sorry I woke you up."

"No problem." It was the weekend, and I didn't have to be at work by eleven, but I still try to stick to my normal schedule as much as possible. It isn't like I actually have a life outside of my job to interfere with my sleeping schedule.

In a way I was honored that Paul had sought me out with his problems. Both of my brothers seem to live charmed lives. Both had found women who love them, careers that are rewarding, and financial success. It was nice to know that even the great mighty MD's could screw up once in a while.

But somehow I still can't picture either of my brothers dating a clown.

I cradled my cup of tea in my hands and concentrated on my brother and his problems. "Want to talk about it?" Short of Paul committing adultery, I couldn't imagine one reason why Matty would have thrown him out. If my brother was stupid enough to cheat on his wife, I was throwing him over the railing of my balcony. I was only on the second floor. The fall might not kill him, but it would get my feelings across pretty nicely.

"I said I was sorry, and that I didn't mean for her to take it that way." Paul looked at his cup as if he had never seen a cup of tea before. The strongest thing in the apartment that I had to drink was white wine, flavored with strawberries. Somehow I didn't think it fit the occasion. Tea would have to do.

"What were you sorry for?"

"Matty's been trying to get pregnant for about three years now."

I grinned, but it really didn't surprise me. I could see Matty as a mother. "Really?"

"It wasn't working. I was tested, so I'm not the problem." Paul ran his hand through his hair. "Matty just couldn't conceive."

"You didn't blame her, did you?" Oh my God, no wonder Matty tossed him out of the house. Paul should be thankful to have been able to walk away. I would have sliced off a very important piece of his anatomy before I threw his sorry ass out onto the street.

"Of course not! What kind of husband do you take me for?"

"Honestly?"

"Yeah, honestly."

Since he asked, I gave him the unvarnished truth. "Inconsiderate, absentminded, rude, arrogant. I think you are a great doctor, Paul, but a lousy husband to Matty."

Paul's face crumbled further. "Really? I'm that bad?"

Damn, I felt like I'd just kicked a puppy. "Some of the time, Paul. I don't live with you, and I really don't see you all that much, but I do feel as if you ignore Matty. Your job is more important. Your medical journals are more important. The hospital is more important. Matty, your home, your marriage come in a distant last to all of that. I honestly don't know how she has put up with you this long."

"I love her."

"I know, but saying you love her and showing that you love her are two different things." Poor Matty. All that maternal instinct going to stray animals, instead of her own baby. "She needs your understanding, Paul. Being infertile, to a woman who wants a child, is devastating."

"You didn't let me finish." The corner of Paul's mouth kicked up. "She's pregnant. I'm going to be a daddy."

"I'm going to be an aunt?" The cup of hot tea nearly slipped out of my hand. I quickly put it back on the coffee table and hugged my brother. I was going to be an aunt, but more importantly, my mother would get off my back about giving her a grandchild. "When?"

"I'm not sure." Paul hugged me back.

I leaned back, smacked him in the chest, and glared. "What do you mean, you're not sure?"

"I just found out tonight."

"Matty told you she was pregnant, and *then* threw you out of the house? What did you do? What did you say?"

"Why does it have to be my fault?"

"You're the one sitting on my couch, aren't you?"

Paul was quiet for a moment. "I was supposed to be home from work at six. Matty called the office, said she had something important to tell me. I told her I'd be there at six."

"What time did you show up?"

"Seven thirty. Matty had dinner ready. The meatloaf looked burnt, if that was her attempt at meatloaf. There was a bottle of something on ice, the fancy china was out, and there were about a dozen balloons throughout the kitchen and dining room. Pink and blue balloons."

"Sounds like a lot of planning on Matty's part. You should have been home on time." Okay, I can see where Matty might be upset, but still, Paul's wife knew long before their marriage about his crazy hours.

"She wasn't upset about me being late. She knows my schedule is totally unpredictable." Paul glanced away. "Do you know what she said the moment I walked into the room?"

"No, what?"

"We're pregnant!"

I hid my smile. "What did you say to that announcement?"

"I believe my exact words were, "How did that happen?""

"You didn't?" I stared at Paul as if he was nuts.

"I was in shock, Judith. Matty hadn't even hinted that she was late or that there was a chance."

"Don't you know how it happened?" I teased.

"Of course I do. I said I was sorry, but she was crying. Then she threw the meatloaf at me, and started screaming for me to get out. The dogs were attacking the meatloaf, one of the cats popped a balloon, which startled the parrot, which started to scream obscenities that his last owner had taught him. Matty was getting hysterical. She was crying and throwing corn at the parrot to shut him up, and still screaming at me to get out. I didn't know what else to do. I was afraid she was going to hurt herself or the baby, so I asked her if I left would she calm down, she said yes, so I left."

"You left her like that?" Men weren't idiots, they were frickin' morons.

"What was I supposed to do?" Paul stood up and started to pace the room. "What should I do?"

"Go home and keep apologizing until she accepts it. Matty loves you for some reason I have yet to figure out." I glanced at the clock. It was five minutes til nine. "If you're smart, stop at the mall on the way home. They're open til ten on Fridays. Be romantic for once. Buy her flowers, diamonds, and an abandoned pet."

Paul headed for the door. "Judith?" He stopped with his hand on the knob. "I'm going to be the best dad."

I smiled. Maybe this little episode had been a wake-up call for Paul. "Be the best husband first, the dad part will fall into place." Wouldn't it be nice if all of life's problems were settled so easily?

Paul hurried out the door and I headed back for bed with a silly grin on my face. Aunt Judith. It had a nice ring to it.

Two o'clock Monday morning, and the emergency room was hopping. All seven exam rooms were full, and one Immediate Care unit was occupied. An ambulance was on its way in with an injured firefighter. I barely got to say hello to Claudia, never mind about reliving my date with Bozo and having her tell me "I told you so."

The good news was, Saturday morning a bouquet of flowers arrived at my door from my brother Paul. Matty and he had made up and were celebrating impending parenthood and planning a second honeymoon before my niece or nephew's arrival.

My mother had gone to Babies-R-Us and bought out half the store.

I read the chart for the obnoxious, foul-mouthed teenager in Bed Number 4. The boy's mother was doting on him as if he was the next in line for the crown. Stupid woman. Stupider kid. Justin wasn't sick, as the mother had claimed. Justin was a smart-ass who knew how to work his mother. He also was high as a kite. I was leaving it to Dr. Garmond to tell the modern-day June Cleaver her little boy had popped one too many pills. "The doctor will be in shortly to see you, Justin."

"What's taking him so long?" The mother fussed with the blanket. Justin kicked the blanket away and uttered something I was tempted to wash his mouth out for saying.

I always like how people just automatically assume that the doctor is a he instead of a she. "He's with another patient right now." It galled me that in this case she was right.

"We've been here for over an hour." Justin's mom was getting a little testy. I didn't blame her. If Justin was my son, I'd be testy too.

Maybe she should try getting a little testy with her *son*. Smacking him alongside the head a couple times a day might knock some sense into him. Then again, maybe it wouldn't. "The doctor has just stabilized a patient who suffered a heart attack. Once that patient has been moved upstairs, he'll be free to check on Justin."

I left Justin to his mother, and went to prepare our last remaining room for the incoming firefighter. Of course since I prioritize the order in which my patients are seen, I decided to make sure Dr. Garmond would first see the four-month-old in Exam Room Number 2, who is running a high fever. Then there was the sprained ankle in Number 3. And who could forget the incoming firefighter. Dr. Garmond would be one busy doc, and who knew what Claudia and the other nurses had lined up for him.

Claudia hurried past me muttering something about the full moon and crazies. I had to agree. It was definitely a full-moon night in the ER. I know a lot of people say there isn't a connection between the moon's cycle and human behavior. I'm just not one of them. Ask any medical, fire, or police personnel, and I bet you at least 90 percent tell you that there is a noticeable difference in accidents, injuries, and plain-old craziness when the moon is full.

Two years ago, during a full moon, the cops brought in a guy who thought he was a werewolf. He was about twenty-six, long hair, hadn't shaved in a while, and drooled when he growled and snarled. The cops picked him up running around Farley's Woods totally naked, rolling around on the ground and howling at the moon. Most of the nurses had been scared to death of him. Not me. I figured that with a haircut, shave, and some decent clothes he'd clean up pretty good in a rustic, outdoorsy kind of way. Besides, he was hung.

What can I say, I'm pathetic.

The double doors pushed open and two paramedics wheeled the gurney carrying the firefighter into the ER. The firefighter was in the upright position, and in the process of taking off the oxygen mask. "I told you I don't need to see a doctor." He coughed again, in a way that had me relaxing. The firefighter was probably right.

"You heard your captain. Better safe than sorry." Ed, a paramedic I've known for years, grinned at me. "Hey Judith, which room you want our hero in?"

"Trauma 2, Ed." I smiled at the soot-covered fireman. He was young and probably good looking underneath all the black carbon. Thick brown hair, dark eyes, and brilliant white teeth. "Your captain is right, you know." Cops and firefighters always got special treatment. Them and kids.

The fireman grinned. "You'll be my nurse?"

"Sure will." I followed them into the room. "For the whole

twenty minutes you'll be here." Dr. Garmond would be releasing the local hero faster than it was going to take to write up the chart.

"I don't know about that. All of a sudden I don't feel so good."

I stopped what I was doing and studied his face. His deep brown eyes were smiling at me and I relaxed. Romeo was flirting.

"The Italian Stallion strikes again." Ed shook his head as he and his partner maneuvered the firefighter off the gurney and onto the hospital bed. "Easy, Tony. Give Judith a moment to fill out your chart and listen to your heart go pitter-patter before asking her out."

I wasn't positive, but Tony the Italian Stallion might have blushed. Interesting and cute. Two of my favorite qualities in a guy. That and the fact he seemed perfectly sane. He was even a hero. Sometimes the full moon can be a wonderful thing.

Before I could take Tony's blood pressure an administration-worker clone was next to his bed getting all his vitals. Insurance carrier, marital status, and next of kin. When the single, twenty nine-year-old Anthony Mincarelli said his mother was his next of kin, he looked at me and said, "Don't you dare call her and tell her I'm here."

"Why? Don't you think she'll care?" I wrapped the blood-pressure cuff around his bicep. Now that Tony had stripped down to a T-shirt and pants, my appreciation for the male anatomy grew. Tony definitely worked out and my knees grew weak.

"She'll work herself up into a panic, and then call every relative, friend, and neighbor I have ever known. They will all rush down here, thinking I'm at death's door, even though I'm sure you will tell her I'm fine. My mother won't believe you. Nothing against you personally, she wouldn't believe our priest if he was on the phone either."

"She worries about you?" Okay, having a fireman for a son could be a bit nerve-racking.

Tony snorted. "Is the Pope Catholic?"

"Last I heard he was."

"You're not Catholic?" Tony clutched his chest and frowned.

"Methodist. Why?" The administration gal looked bent out of shape because Tony had stopped answering her million and one questions and she hadn't even gotten to the Workmen's Comp forms.

"You'll need to convert."

"I will?" I pressed the stethoscope to his chest. "Take a deep breath."

Tony took a deep breath, and then said, "Grandmom Sophia won't come to the wedding if it's not in the Catholic church. She's very religious that way."

I glanced up and saw the laughter in his eyes. He was teasing me. Either because he liked me, or he wanted to piss off Ophelia Snodgrass, the sixty-year-old paper pusher who was now tapping her pen against her clipboard and sighing loudly. I moved the stethoscope to his back. "Take another deep breath." Tony's lungs sounded clear to me. "Are you asking me to marry you?"

Ophelia choked.

"Not yet." Tony turned his head so Ophelia couldn't see him wink at me. "I'll do that over dinner Saturday night."

"And if I say no?" I tried not to grin. He was cute and mischievous. He was also three years younger than me, and probably didn't know the first thing about balloon animals.

When I was eight, against my wishes, I was forced to spend a week at horseback-riding camp. The first day there, I fell off the horse. Thankfully I didn't break anything, but I did learn a very important lesson that summer: if you fall off a horse, the best thing to do is to get right back up on it. By the end of the week I not only knew how to ride, but to trot too. I came home thinking I was Dale Evans and I bugged my parents at least a hundred times a day for the rest of the summer for a horse of my own.

My mother, sensing the error of her ways, never sent me to horseback-riding camp again.

Tony's smile brightened his soot-covered face. "I'll ask you again Sunday morning," his voice dropped seductively. "Over breakfast."

Chapter 3

Hungry . . . why wait?

I opened my locker and reached for my purse and jacket. I was beat, wiped out, and ready to crash. All I wanted was a hot shower and cool sheets. The shift had been one nonstop emergency after another, and I'd never been so relieved to see seven o'clock—and the arrival of the day-shift nurses and doctors—roll around.

Drac had prowled the Emergency Room all night, drawing blood and staring at me every chance he got. He hadn't been staring at my boobs either—his intense, weird gaze had been zeroed in on my neck. Tonight when I show up for work I will be wearing a turtleneck and a necklace made of garlic cloves under my uniform. I didn't care how bad I stank, Drac was starting to freak me out.

My inner bitch had made an appearance. She handled two passes—one from a visiting doctor and one from an intern. The doctor from Boston had seemed to like the bitch, while the intern had blushed at my amazing ability to string curses together so creatively.

To top matters off, Tony, the cute firefighter, hadn't asked me out. He teased and flirted with me the entire time he had been here, but when one of the guys from his station came to pick him up, he left. No passing of phone numbers, no date set, not even a teasing mention of what I might like for Sunday's breakfast.

No wonder my inner bitch nearly took the intern's head off.

"You never got to tell me how your date with the clown went." Claudia opened her locker and stretched the kinks out of her back. "I looked in the papers, but didn't see any news of you being hauled away in handcuffs."

"Smart-ass." I debated telling her the truth, but decided she couldn't handle it. Claudia would either die laughing when I told her about the balloon penis, or pee herself. Both would be humiliating to her, so I was going to be generous and spare her feelings. "Let's just say me and Bozo didn't hit it off, and leave it at that."

I knew it had been the wrong thing to say when Claudia grinned. "Oh, this I got to hear."

"There's nothing to hear. We had a nice lunch, then he gave me the nickel tour of the circus grounds. I got to meet Roberta the Wonder Elephant, and a couple other performers. Then I left." If I kept it short and sweet, she might drop the subject.

"What are you leaving out?" Claudia slipped on her jacket and reached for her purse. "You dated a professional clown, something funny had to have happened."

I zipped my jacket and dug my car keys out from the bottom of my pocketbook. "He made me a balloon animal." I was proud of myself for saying that with a straight face. We left the locker room and headed for the parking lot.

"It must have been bad."

"What must have been bad?" There was no way she could have guessed.

"Whatever happened." Claudia grinned. "You usually tell me every hysterical detail that happens on your blind dates."

"That wasn't a blind date." Even I couldn't get around that

one. I had no one to blame my latest dating disaster on but myself. Now *there* was a depressing thought.

"So a real date, with a guy you picked and met beforehand, didn't turn out so well after all."

"Listen Claudia, I'm not going out with your brother." I knew exactly where she was heading with this conversation. After my date with Bozo and his pornographic balloon animals, I didn't even want to think what an architect could do with Legos. We walked outside and crossed the pavement. "I handled the date just fine. I didn't end up with my picture in the paper, I didn't get hurled on, and I didn't get stuck with the lunch check." Beneath all the frustration of the past two years, one thing galled me the most and I practically screamed it at Claudia, with her perfect-for-me brother, Hugh. "And I most certainly didn't end up with third prize again in a Wet T-shirt contest."

"I would have to say either a bunch of blind men judged that contest, or the judges were paid off." Tony Mincarelli had walked up behind us in time to hear my last comment.

I felt the blush sweeping up my face while Claudia laughed. "She only got third place because she had a bra on under the T-shirt." Claudia, being a good friend, felt she had to defend my dismal placing.

Tony tried to hide a grin, but failed. "Never entered one before?"

"I didn't enter that one. Someone dumped water on me." There was no way I was telling Claudia or Tony that I kept the yellow ribbon the bartender had handed me on the way out. I figure it will make a very interesting memento for my grandchildren to find when I'm about ninety and gumming my oatmeal in some nursing home.

"She's modest," explained Claudia with a smirk.

"She's cute," Tony said.

Claudia stared at Tony for a moment before recognition set in. "You're the firefighter who decided to take up smoking all at once."

"Guilty."

Lord, he did clean up nicely, but I would have recognized him anywhere. It was the voice. Tony's voice was deep and he had just a touch of an Italian accent. Ten to one he probably could speak or at least curse fluently in Italian. There was only one reason I could think of as to why Tony was waiting for me in the employees' parking lot. I could feel myself getting right back up on that dating horse again.

"I have to run, Judith. See you tonight." Claudia gave Tony a smile. "Nice meeting you."

"You too." Tony stood there as Claudia walked away, and then softly said, "I'm not stalking you, just in case you're worried about that. I looked you up in the phone book, and unless you're Joseph or Jerry Howland, you're not listed."

"I'm unlisted." I found my love life ran a lot smoother if guys couldn't reach me after the first disastrous date. If I give a guy my phone number, I really want him to call. "Are you feeling okay?" He looked good enough to snuggle up against, while I looked like something Drac wouldn't even drag into the crypt.

"I'm fine." Tony jammed his hands into the pockets of his jeans and gave me a crooked smile. "I was wondering if you would like to go out Saturday night?"

There wasn't a woman alive who could refuse that smile. "I would love to." I was sitting on that horse, straight and proud. I was about to ride the Italian Stallion. "Sunday's breakfast isn't included, right?" It would be better if I found out now how crazy Tony was, before I invested an entire night on him.

"I only said that to tick off Hatchet Face. She didn't have a sense of humor, and besides, I was in need of emergency treatment and some TLC. I wasn't in the mood to spout off my Social Security Number and date of birth while hacking up a lung."

"What were you in the mood for?"

"Impressing a beautiful nurse."

Damn, he said the sweetest things. "I'm not supposed to fraternize with patients."

"I know. That's why I'm here now. I'm no longer a patient and you're no longer on duty. We can do what we want."

"What time Saturday night?" I reached into my purse and quickly wrote down my address.

"Five, and dress casually." He took the piece of paper, glanced at the address, and slipped it into his pocket.

"Want directions to my place?"

"I'm a firefighter. If I can't find an address, someone is going to need a whole bunch of marshmallows." Tony grinned and started to walk away. "See you Saturday."

I watched him walk around the side of the hospital to where visitors park their cars. Tony looked as good going as he did coming. Saturday night couldn't come fast enough.

I stood in front of the full-length mirror on the back of my bedroom door and frowned. What in the hell did men mean by casual? Was it little-black-dress casual, or "Do you want fries with that?" casual? Tony was due any minute and so far I had tried on three outfits, and wasn't happy with any of them. Jeans were too casual, and besides, they make my ass look fat. The flowered dress that I had worn to church Easter morning was too frilly and girly.

That left me with my in between outfit: a khaki skirt that ended a couple of inches above my knees, a solid green blouse, and a plaid green blazer. I suffered the indignity of pantyhose because it was too early in the season to lie out by the pool, and I hated tanning salons.

I studied my reflection in the mirror. At work I usually pulled my hair back and up off my neck. I decided to go all out and give my long brown hair, with its pale golden highlights that Mother Nature had overlooked, a few twirls with the curling iron. My makeup was minimal, so were jewelry and perfume. I frowned at my reflection.

I looked like a freakin' schoolteacher.

The doorbell rang before I could strip off the outfit. I was out of time. Prim-and-proper schoolmarm it was going to be. I walked out of the bedroom and wondered what kind of lesson I was going to learn and did I have enough credit left on my Visa to make bail.

Half an hour later I found myself sitting where Tony claimed the best Italian food in all of Franklin was served: his mother's kitchen. Not the best beginning to a date, but amazingly enough, I'd had worse.

"Here, Judith, I want you to try this." Rosina Mincarelli, Tony's mother, placed a plate in front of me with a lone meatball on it. It was covered in sauce and smelled delicious. "Tell me if it tastes okay to you."

"Mom, you're going to ruin Judith's appetite before dinner." Tony leaned over my shoulder, sliced the meatball in half, and swiped the bigger piece. "Besides, you know your meatballs are perfect."

Rosina playfully whacked his hand with a wooden spoon while I quickly forked the remaining portion of the meatball into my mouth. Who could refuse the perfect meatball? Especially since I'd slept through lunch, and breakfast had consisted of a cup of strawberry yogurt. Those extra eight pounds on my ass needed to come off before a bikini bottom went on.

Lying on the beach, soaking up the rays, and minding my own business was my idea of the second closest thing to heaven. Being naked in bed with Brad Pitt would have to rank number 1 on my list. If some bleeding-heart animal lover rolled me back into the ocean, screaming about beached whales, I would be spending the rest of my summer vacation wearing a bright-orange prison jumpsuit.

Rosina beamed at me, making me wonder how often little Anthony brought home his dates. Did that make Tony desperate, a mama's boy, or cheap?

"So? So?"

My taste buds were throwing a party in my mouth. Since I couldn't marry Momma Rosina I was wondering if she would adopt me. I swallowed. "Delicious."

"Delicious?" Rosina seemed disappointed in my compliment.

Before she uninvited me to dinner, I quickly added, "Deliciously perfect." Rosina started to smile again. "I really think that has to be the best meatball I have ever eaten." I wasn't lying. Rosina should open her own restaurant and make a million bucks. There are a lot of hungry people out there who would pay top dollar for something that good.

Rosina swept up my empty plate and piled on two more meatballs. "You think?" She plunked the plate back down in front of me. "Try again." Rosina waved her spoon at her son. "You no touch Judith's meatballs. She's too skinny."

My heart went pitter-patter and I fell in love with sixty-year-old Rosina. Her hair was more gray than brown, she was a good seventy pounds overweight, and without an official blood test, I would guess her cholesterol was in the 300 range. To me, she was perfect.

"Mom, the meatballs taste the same as they always do." Tony chuckled as he poured us both a glass of wine. "Is that lasagna I smell?"

"Stay away from the oven." Rosina maneuvered around the kitchen with a fluid grace that only years of cooking had perfected. I dug into the meatballs while watching the culinary ballet. Rosina handed Tony a cucumber and a knife. "Peel and cut for the salad."

Tony took the vegetable and started peeling. I was impressed. Neither of my brothers know which end of the peeler to use. Paul could perform a heart transplant, but give him a box of Quaker Instant Oatmeal and he'll starve to death.

"Your Grandmother Sophia told Maria and Teresa after mass on Sunday," Rosina quickly crossed herself, "that her meatballs were better than mine." Rosina grunted and muttered something in Italian while stirring a huge pot of bubbling sauce. Every surface in the kitchen was covered with food, dishes, or pots and pans. Rosina was cooking enough to feed a small third-world country.

"Last time Grandmother Sophia made meatballs she forgot to add the oregano. She's eighty-seven and forgets where she lives half the time. I don't think you have to worry about her outdoing you in the kitchen, Mom." Tony kissed his mother's cheek. "You're still the best cook I know."

Rosina beamed. "See, Judith, he's such a good boy." She wiped her hands on her flowered apron. "Just feed him lots of pasta and he's happy."

Pasta I could do. It's all those other ingredients that you have to add to the noodles that throws me. I'm selfish enough to want my dates to take me out for dinner, instead of me cooking for them. I am a firm believer in not scaring off eligible men with my ability to cause instant heartburn with the simplest of meals. Dessert at my table has a name: Tums.

Cooking isn't one of my strong points and I fully believe tomato sauce comes from a jar and that microwaves were discovered for a reason. Strike three in the Date With Tony game. First strike, I'm not Catholic. Second swing and a miss was the fact he had taken me to his mother's on our first date. The third swing I missed the ball by a mile: I don't like to spend hours upon hours in the kitchen.

I pictured a fancy box of chocolates, just like the kind Forrest Gump had had in the film. Instead of "Life is like a box of chocolates," I substituted the word love. Love is like a box of chocolates and I usually manage to choose the piece crammed-packed with nuts. This particular piece of chocolate was sweet, but not very satisfying. I hated nuts.

"Is everyone coming for dinner?" Tony reached around his mother and popped a cherry tomato into his mouth.

"Yes. Your uncles Sal and Giuseppe are already here and in the back room talking on the phones again. Always the phones."

Rosina took out a pot, roughly the same size as a fifty-five gallon drum and started to fill it with water. "I ask you," Rosina shouted above the sound of running water, "what could be so important that they haven't come out to meet your date?"

"They are probably taking odds on Anna Santangelo's wedding."

Rosina sniffed. "Ha. My money's on the groom wising up and not showing up at all. The marriage will never work. Even in the old country, the families hated each other's guts."

I felt sorry for that couple, having odds placed on their wedding even taking place. Didn't bode well for them celebrating that silver anniversary. Then again, it was a guaranteed interesting reception.

"Oh, both Anna and Joe are stubborn and in love," Tony said. "The wedding will go on, it's the reception that has Uncle Sal and Uncle Giuseppe working the phones and raising those odds. Seems Anna is three months pregnant and her father wants to kill Joe." Tony grinned at his mother's shocked expression.

"How do you know this?"

"I work with Anna's second cousin, twice removed. Or it her third cousin, once removed? Either way, someone is going to end up with an assault-and-battery charge against them, and Joseph's mom hired the Bruno Brothers to protect him during the ceremony."

Rosina crossed herself while muttering a prayer in Italian to the ceiling. "The wedding must go on, there is a baby's future at stake." Rosina allowed Tony to carry the big pot of water over to the stove and set it on the back burner. She twisted the knob to high. "Besides, I already bought a new dress for the occasion."

I tried not to choke as the last bite of the meatball went down my throat. I didn't know what tickled me the most: two uncles in the back room running a bookmaking operation, hiring bodyguards for the wedding, or Rosina thinking a new dress was reason enough for the wedding to go on.

All this drama was going on around me, and for once I wasn't smack dab in the middle of it. I quietly sat at the small breakfast table enjoying the show and Rosina's meatballs.

"Rosina, after further tasting"—I used the paper napkin with little hearts and flowers printed on it to wipe my lips—"I came to the conclusion your meatballs are the best I have ever tasted." I just might make it to dinner now without embarrassing myself by either having my stomach growl or drooling over the plate stacked with handmade ravioli. I didn't even want to think about the smell of lasagna bubbling away in the oven.

There were definitely good sides to dating Tony: he was cute, three years younger than me, and his mother could cook. Maybe I was being too hasty in closing that particular box of chocolates.

"Sorry, Judith, but do you mind if I borrow Tony for a few minutes?" Vince Mincarelli entered the kitchen looking a little frazzled.

"Not at all." Heck, I was having more fun with Rosina than my date.

"What's up, Dad?"

"What's wrong?" Rosina crossed herself.

"One of the Carvelli boys just called. Mom just showed up at their house, claiming they invited her for dinner."

"What do you need me for?" Tony continued slicing the cucumber.

Vince smiled. "Seems the Carvelli boys' parents are out of town and they were throwing a private party with a bunch of girls. My mother is down there praying for their sins." Vince looked at me and shrugged. "The Carvelli boys have this thing against nice girls. They like them wild. So we can only imagine what my mother walked in on."

I tried not to laugh. It was so nice just to sit on the sidelines and watch someone else's drama for a change. "How old are the Carvelli boys? Twenty? Twenty-one?" At that age there was no telling what Grandmom Sophia interrupted.

"One's eighteen, the other three are younger." Vince looked at his son. "Let's go. I'll handle your grandmother, you handle the Carvelli boys. Matt didn't sound too happy on the phone."

Tony looked at me, and I laughed. "Go, I'm fine. I'll help your mother with the salad."

Vince and Tony left the kitchen and Rosina piled four ravioli on a plate, dumped a generous amount of sauce over them, and sat it before me. "You are a guest in my house. You will sit there and tell me if they need more salt. Sophia is always telling me they need more salt. That woman is never happy with what I cook. Forty years of marriage to her precious son and I still can't boil water to suit her."

I really didn't want to get into the middle of a family dispute, so I dug into the cheese ravioli.

The sound of a slamming screen door and yelling kids destroyed the peace. Rosina cocked her head, listened to the shouts, and smiled. "That's my eldest son, Francis, his wife, Rosemarie, and their kids. Rosemarie, the poor girl, can't cook to save her soul, but she gives me beautiful grandbabies."

A tide of kids swept into the kitchen and immediately surrounded a laughing Rosina. Between hugs, kisses, and shouting, Rosina introduced the kids to me, but most of the names I couldn't hear. There were seven kids, and the oldest looked to be around ten. Rosina gave each of the kids a cookie and shooed them out back.

The amount of food Rosina was cooking was now explained, but I was still stunned. I picked up my wine glass and drained it. I nearly choked on the last mouthful when a woman walked into the kitchen. She had a baby boy riding on her hip and she looked ready to go into labor at any moment. Nine kids! What, was she out of her mind?

"Hi, Mom." Rosemarie lowered the little boy to his feet, and then slowly stood back up.

"Rosemarie, this is Judith, Tony's date."

"Hi, Judith. You're a very brave woman coming here for the weekly family dinner."

A man, who looked like an older version of Tony, came up behind her and wrapped his arms around her huge stomach. "Hi, I'm Frank, Tony's brother."

It didn't seem appropriate to tell them I had had no idea I was coming to family night at the Mincarellis when Tony had asked me to dinner. I had been picturing something a little more intimate. "Hi, Rosemarie, Frank. Were all those kids yours?" Maybe there were four more pairs of parents in the living room. No one had nine children in this day and age. Think of the college cost.

"Yep, we haven't been able to buy a school bus yet, so we travel in two separate minivans." Rosemarie gave a serene smile and patted her belly as the little boy toddled over to his grandmother, who swept him up into her arms. "This makes nine and ten."

"Twins?" I tried to control it, but I knew there was pure horror in my voice by the way Rosemarie's smile faded. "I mean, are you sure?"

"We have pictures to prove it." Frank seemed quite pleased by this accomplishment.

Of course they had pictures. Ultrasound is now done on a routine basis, and doctors aren't fooled by twins any longer. I stood up and offered my seat to her. "When are you due?" I knew most expectant mothers loved to talk about the pending arrival.

"Not for another three months." Rosemarie shook her head at the chair. "Thanks, but I should help Rosina with dinner. When I sit down, I tend not to get back up."

"Hey, Mom," asked Frank, "where were Dad and Tony heading off to? I saw them walking down the street when we pulled up."

"To get your grandmother. She wandered into the wrong house again." Rosina handed Frank his son, who was now clutching a cookie. "Go get out the other tables."

"Boy, the kids' table is going to be crowded." I teased Rosemarie, hoping to make up for my earlier reaction. My parents, on the rare family occasion, never had enough people over for dinner to warrant a kids' table.

Rosemarie laughed and started peeling another cucumber. "Oh just wait. Eugene and David aren't here yet with their families. I just hope you're not claustrophobic."

Rosina dumped a couple boxes of noodles into the boiling water. "Judith, will you go to the back of the house and tell Sal and Giuseppe dinner is almost ready?"

"Sure." Even though I hadn't met the uncles yet, I figured it was an easy task. I wished Tony hadn't left me alone with his family, but it wasn't his fault his grandmother wandered into people's homes demanding dinner. Then again, maybe it was. Someone really should do something about Sophia, before she got hurt or lost.

I headed toward the back of the house. I could hear the kids playing out back. A partially closed door was at the end of the hall. I hesitated and listened.

"Fifty on Twinkle Toes in the third?" asked a male voice.

"You're already into us for a one spot, why should we extend your credit?" A deeper male voice spoke from the opposite side of the room.

A cell phone started to play the "Star Spangled Banner."

Another cell phone played the theme from *Star Wars.*

"Yeah?" the first male voice answered the Star Wars phone. "Okay, twenty on Snoopy in the second." There was a pause. "Are you sure you want to do that, Nate? Snoopy hasn't won a race in two years." Another pause. "It's your money to piss away."

The uncles weren't betting on some wedding. They were bookies taking bets on the ponies. Rosina and Vince had an illegal gaming operation going on in their back room. I was torn between laughter and running. Laughter won. I'd never met an actual bookie before. That night was my lucky night. I was about to meet two.

I raised my hand and knocked loudly. "Sal? Giuseppe?" I pushed open the door and smiled at the two gentlemen on either side of the room. Both sat before tables lined with yellow notepads and cell phones. "Hi, I'm Judith Howland, Tony's date." Three of the phones were ringing, but neither gentleman was answering them. I figured it was best if I ignored the phones too. "Rosina sent me back here to tell you both that dinner's almost ready."

One of them looked at the clock and said, "Three minutes til seven, Rosina's right on time."

Somewhere toward the front of the house there was another commotion. It sounded like an entire preschool was racing into the house. Babies were crying, feet were running, someone was yelling something about slowing down and walking in the house.

"Good. David's here. He'll help us get the rest before the windows close." One of the uncles looked at me and said, "Could you please go tell David we need him for a minute or two?"

"Sure." I walked out of the room and wondered if I could be arrested for aiding a bookie operation. Wouldn't that look swell on my resume?

I spotted a man in the living room in the process of taking a screaming infant out of a car seat. "David?"

"Nope, I'm Gene." The baby's cries drowned out every thought in my brain.

"I'm David." A tall, slender man, with a two-year-old perched on his shoulders stepped into the room.

"Hi, I'm Judith. Your uncles need your help in the back room for a couple of minutes." There. I passed on the message.

David handed the two-year-old to Gene, who in turn handed me the crying baby. I instinctively cradled the baby and started to bounce. Six months working in the maternity ward had taught me how to handle a baby. The baby quieted down.

Gene smiled. "Amazing. Sophia loves to hear herself scream."

"She didn't like the seat. She likes to be held." I lightly bounced the little girl, who let out a loud burp, and then proceeded to lose about three ounces of formula onto my shoulder. Green silk and formula didn't mix very well.

"Oops," said Gene as he lowered the boy to the floor, reached into a diaper bag, and handed me a burp cloth. "I forgot to mention, Sophia's formula isn't agreeing with her lately."

I wiped Sophia's mouth and handed her back to her father. "No problem." I wiped as much of the formula off my blouse as possible. "Have you called the pediatrician yet?"

"Yes. If Sophia isn't keeping it down by morning, she has to go on the soy kind." Gene looked at my blouse and cringed. "I'm taking it that you're Tony's date."

"That's me."

"Where's Tony?"

"Helping your father to either rescue your Grandmother Sophia from the Carvelli boys or the Carvelli boys from your grandmother."

Gene laughed. "My money's on the latter."

Placing bets seemed to run in the family. "Could you point me in the direction of a powder room?" I wanted to at least try to wash most of the formula off of my shoulder before it smelled too badly. Now this was more like my usual dates.

"Down the hall, first door on your right."

"Thanks." I headed for the hall and waited my turn. Frank was in the bathroom, and he wasn't using the facilities. He was talking on his cell phone, loud enough for me to hear just about every word.

"I don't care how you do it, I want him gone. Out of the picture." A moment later he added, "Yeah, like he had never been there in the first place." Another pause. "Money's no object, you know I'm good for it."

I blinked at the closed door. At first I thought Frank might be either taking or placing a bet. What I was hearing now wasn't about Twinkle Toes in the third. It sounded like Frank wanted someone gone. Taken out of the picture.

Tony's brother was arranging a hit!

I accepted a date with a cute fireman, and ended up in a bad remake of the *Godfather*.

Chapter 4

Give me a break.

"So you're not going out with Tony again?" Millie took another spoonful of her yogurt.

"Afraid not." We were in the lounge area eating lunch. At three in the morning I was eating a salad with low-fat blue-cheese dressing and a bottle of water. Dinner at the Mincarellis Saturday night had caused my jeans to shrink half a size. Millie, as always, ate her usual container of yogurt, a Diet Coke, and three candy bars.

"You could always convert to being a Catholic." Claudia smirked as she unwrapped an Italian sub she had picked up on her way into work. "And no one said you have to have ten kids. I'm sure his mother would be happy with another six or seven grandbabies to spoil."

Some nights Claudia really got on my nerves. This was one such night. She sat there with that silly-looking smirk on her face as I recounted my Saturday-night date with Tony. Of course I didn't mention the illegal numbers operation going on in the back room, or Frank possibly ordering a hit while sitting on the can. If some guy named Gino turned up floating in the river, I was moving and changing my name. I wasn't stupid. I've seen a couple episodes of *The Sopranos*.

Millie had thoroughly enjoyed my recounting of the date, and I use that term loosely. I've always figured a date requires some time together and conversation. A time to get to know one another, see if you had anything in common. Saturday night there had been conversation, nonstop conversation. I talked with Rosina, Rosemarie, David, Vince, and everyone else there. The kids' tables had overflowed out of the dining room and into the kitchen and living room.

Once Uncle Sal and Uncle Giuseppe realized I was a nurse, they bombarded me with health questions, looking for free medical advice. At the dinner table Sal had even gone so far as to take off his shoe and show me the bunion on his toe. I changed diapers, bandaged a scraped knee, and looked at a strange rash on one of Gene's kids. Or at least I think it was Gene's kid. There were so many there it was hard to keep them straight. Rosina had that "I want another grandbaby" gleam in her eye every time she smiled at me.

I had not walked away from Tony at the end of our first date. I had run as fast as my size sevens would carry me.

"I don't know, Judith." Millie scraped the bottom of her plastic container, getting every last drop. "Being part of a big family like that could have its advantages."

"Name one." Unless I wanted to contract out a hit or place fifty bucks on Mr. Ed in the fourth to show, I couldn't think of one.

"Think of all the babysitters you would have." Millie tossed the empty cup across the room and made a perfect basket. "Think of all Rosina's cooking you will be missing." She crumpled up her napkin and shot it. It bounced off the rim and into the trash can. "I could think of worse things than going to confession, having beautiful babies with a man who is actually younger than you, and eating pasta for the rest of my life."

Millie was in her early forties and a widow for the last ten years. I knew Millie could think of worse things... working full time because you won't be able to afford two fifty? Six

"Think of the stretch marks, the night feeds on a fireman's salary, and topping the scales at wh

gnancies and a steady diet of pasta will do that to you."
audia's smirk turned gleeful as she bit into her hoagie.

The smell of the Italian sub was causing my mouth to water. Who wanted to munch on rabbit food when there was salami and provolone cheese three feet away?

"I don't remember ever saying I want one baby, let alone six of them."

Claudia was in a rotten mood, again, or maybe it was still. Claudia and Chris must be fighting again. Ever since I started to refuse to go out with her brother, Claudia hadn't talked to me much about what was going on in her life. Here I was trying to save our friendship, and she was the one clamming up.

"You don't want kids, Judith?" Millie frowned as she unwrapped the Hershey's bar with almonds.

"Maybe." I thought about it for a second. "Probably. I'm only thirty-two. Sure I've got a biological clock ticking, but it sure as hell isn't ringing. There's plenty of time left for starting a family." Out of the top ten important things in life that I wanted, a baby ranked about a six. Maybe a five.

Claudia studied her hoagie with sad eyes. "What if you got pregnant?"

I snorted. "Well then I'd be joining the Catholic church because it will be by immaculate conception. Last I heard you actually have to have sex to conceive." I tried to think of the last time I had had sex. I drew a blank. Now *there* was a depressing thought.

"Not in today's society." Millie polished off her first candy bar, and started in on number two: Reese's Peanut Butter Cups. "My neighbor, who's a lawyer and single, went to a sperm bank nd picked out the father of her baby by glancing through some b k."

ou mean they had pictures of the donors?" I could picture ne Brad Pitt lookalike spending a lot of time in the collectio om to meet the demand, with a jar and a *Playboy* magazi

"No, had completed questionnaires that the donors

filled out. You know: height, hair color, ethnic backgrou_ education, and medical history. Cost her a nice penny, but took the first time. She's about seven months along and is talk ing about hiring a professional decorator to do the nursery."

"Who did your neighbor pick?" I couldn't imagine picking the father of your child out of some loose-leaf notebook. Kind of takes all the fun out of it, if you ask me. Go down to any local bar on a Friday night, and for the price of two beers you could probably get your pick of men and at least a night to re-member that hopefully will put a smile on your face come morning.

"She told me she chose a six-foot Scotsman, who loves po-etry, fishing, and hiking."

I blinked. "You're kidding. I want him." Maybe I was doing this find-your-mate thing all wrong.

Claudia rolled her eyes. "What's wrong with a perfectly good man of English descent who loves fishing, hiking, and crime novels?"

"I didn't say there was anything wrong with your brother, Claudia. He sounds perfect. Too perfect."

"Hugh has flaws. Lots of them."

"Name one."

"He reads the newspaper from beginning to end. He doesn't skip around or read the sports section first."

"That isn't a flaw. It means he's logical and systematic."

Millie joined the conversation about Hugh. I knew from experience that Millie was on Claudia's side of the argument. "It means while the sports section will give him pleasure, he forgoes it until after he has finished reading the important stuff, which might affect his life and livelihood, first."

"Meaning, he'll pay the mortgage before going out and buying a 57" television so he can watch ESPN ten hours a day." Claudia bit into her sub with a resounding snapping of teeth.

I looked over at Millie and whispered, "Someone's got un-resolved issues."

"What?" Claudia narrowed her eyes and glared at me.

"I said, "What other flaws does Hugh have?""

"He's a horrible driver."

"How many accidents has he been in?" If he is that bad of a driver it would be the perfect excuse not to risk life and limb by going out with him.

"None." Claudia lowered her sub. "He drives too slow. It drives me nuts."

"See, I told you he's too perfect." I was grasping at straws. "He's thirty-three years old and has never been married. That should tell you something. There is a rule to this kind of thing, Claudia, and you know it as well as I do." I rolled my eyes and recited it: "All good men are either gay or already married."

"Hugh's not gay." Claudia looked mad. "If you must know he lived with his girlfriend for six years in LA. He was the one pushing for a commitment and possibly starting a family. Tiffany, the bitch, moved out of their apartment while he was away on business." Claudia lowered her hoagie back to the paper it had been wrapped in. "The bitch broke my brother's heart."

Damn. I didn't want to know that. Hugh and I had something in common after all. "How long ago was that?"

"A year before he left LA." Claudia's smile was small and hopeful. "He's not on the rebound, Judith. I wouldn't do that to you. Dinner, maybe a movie, that's all. If nothing clicks, fine. It's one date." Claudia's smile grew, along with her laughter. "Hell, you are the Queen of Blind Dates."

"That's not what I want chiseled on my tombstone." I glanced at the clock. My lunch break was over. "How about if I think about it? I'm not promising anything."

"But you will think about it?" Claudia looked suspicious.

"Promise. I'll let you know by Thursday." Hopefully by then I would meet Prince Charming, who would sweep me off my feet and make all my fantasies come true. I snorted as I left the lounge area. I'd have better odds at being the only one to hit the Power Ball lotto Saturday night.

* * *

I lugged my third, and final suitcase into my brother Paul's house. How I got talked into animal sitting was beyond me. I didn't particularly have anything against animals, I just didn't have anything for them. Paul and Matty were going away for a long weekend, and they were putting me in charge of the ark.

Paul hurried down the steps and took the suitcase from me. "Here, give me that."

I tried to catch my breath without panting. "Why? I already lugged two of them up to the guestroom."

Paul started to carry the suitcase up the flight of stairs. I smiled when he started puffing by the fourth step. "I would have taken it up for you. For a cardiologist you're in horrible shape."

"I am not."

I could tell he was holding his breath so he wouldn't pant. He also had sucked in his stomach. Men, they were all the same.

"Who's going to do your first bypass: Karmen or Goldstein?" Call me petty, but I loved pressing my brothers' hot buttons. "You really should get out and exercise more." With my brother John, I tease about a second chin, and then innocently claim it must have been a shadow. After that comment I have caught John staring into mirrors from every possible angle.

"Like I have the time." Paul nearly dropped the suitcase on the last step.

"You better make the time or you'll never see your baby's college graduation, let alone any medical degrees she might go for."

Matty stepped out of the master bedroom looking radiant and ready to go. Her navy blue slacks were covered in cat hair, and four dogs followed her out of the room. Matty placed her hand on her flat stomach. "Judith, do you really think it's a girl?"

For Matty's sake I hope the baby isn't allergic to animals. "I guess I have a 50–50 chance, so my vote will be for a girl."

"Paul wants a boy." Matty stood on her toes and kissed my brother's cheek.

"Whatever it turns out to be, he decided." I think it's totally unfair that the male determines the sex of the baby, while the poor female has to carry and deliver it. Talk about an unbalanced division of labor. "What are you hoping for, Matty?"

"It doesn't matter to me, as long as he or she is healthy. That's the main thing." Matty pushed Sarge, a blind-in-one-eye German Shepherd, down when he tried to jump up on her. "Down."

Sarge immediately sat.

"Good boy." Matty rubbed the top of his head. "Are you ready for your instructions, Judith?" She hurried down the stairs while Paul put my suitcase in with my other ones in the guestroom.

"Sure." I followed her. How hard could taking care of a few animals be? Open up a couple of cans, and voilà, dinner. Thankfully Matty had found a nice farm for the Shetland pony the other week. I wouldn't have to use the snow shovel as a pooper-scooper.

Matty stopped at the kitchen counter, picked up a stack of papers that looked about fifty pages high, and handed it to me. "I wrote it all down for you."

The pages were typed and single-spaced. I tried not to groan. "You're kidding, right?" I glanced through the top couple of pages. Matty hadn't been kidding. Each animal had over a page of personal instructions. Since Matty had over a dozen animals, it made for an entire book on What's What in Animal Care.

"We do have one problem." Matty led the gang of canines over to the patio door, and then shooed them out back.

"What's that?" I could think of over a dozen problems. Each of them had four legs, expected to be fed, and pooped everywhere. Not a one of them knew how to use the john. The other two problems had feathers and liked to nip at fingers. The two parakeets were yellow and green and named Sunny and The Hulk. It didn't take a genius to figure out which was which.

"Vicky's pregnant." Matty looked worried.

"Who's Vicky?" Matty had a sister, but her name was Amanda.

"Victoria."

"Victoria who?" But more importantly, why should this be a problem for me?

Matty rolled her eyes. "Victoria's a cat."

I glanced around the room. I saw a long, skinny black cat draped over the back of the sofa. A white cat with a black-and-brown face was curled up in a recliner. Neither looked pregnant to me, but I knew Matty had at least half a dozen cats living in the house. "Which one is she?"

"Vicky's the orange tabby and she's carrying a full litter." Matty walked over to the laundry room and glanced inside. "She's sleeping right now."

I peeked into the room and saw a fat orange cat sleeping on an old blanket. Vicky didn't look pregnant. She looked like she'd swallowed a watermelon. "When is she due?"

"Any day now. I would like to stay here with her, but this is the only time Paul can get a few days away." Matty knelt next to the cat and gently scratched the top of her head. "How are you doing, Mommy?"

Vicky purred.

"Don't you worry, sweetie, Auntie Judith's a nurse. She'll know what to do if you run into any problems."

I cringed. I might have agreed to handle the ark so Matty and my brother can go play smoochy-smoochy on some sandy beach before Matty starts to show. But I didn't agree to play nursemaid to a basketful of kittens. "Matty, maybe you can drop Vicky off at the vet's on your way to the airport. I don't want to be responsible, in case something goes wrong." I've seen dozens of babies enter the world, but never a kitten. There was a reason I wasn't assigned to the maternity ward. I didn't want to be.

Paul came into the kitchen carrying their luggage. "We don't have time to stop at the vet's, Judith. Besides, it's a cat. It comes naturally to them. Vicky will know what to do when the time comes."

Matty gave Vicky another good scratch before standing back up. "Don't worry, Judith. She'll do all the work and you won't even have to boil water."

"I am not worrying about boiling water." What I was worrying about was something happening to the kittens or to Vicky herself. Matty would never forgive me.

"There are some clean towels and old blankets in case she needs them." Matty pointed to a stack of folded towels and blankets sitting on top of the dryer.

"Come on, hon, we don't want to miss the plane." Paul kissed my cheek as he passed me. "Thanks, Judith. If you need us I have my cell phone on, and the name and number of the hotel is on the refrigerator."

Matty quickly followed Paul. "Call us if Vicky delivers. Any time, day or night."

Paul winked. "Make it day, sis." He hustled his wife out the door. "See you Monday night."

I stood there and listened to their car drive away. I was trapped in a *Doctor Doolittle* nightmare. Four dogs, ranging in size from Sarge, the largest, to Pedro the tiny Chihuahua, sat on the other side of the patio doors staring in at me. Goldie, a mix of Golden Retriever and possibly a collie, and Wilbur, the ugly smashed-face Pug with a terminal sinus condition, completed the sad-looking group.

I glanced in at Vicky. "You, cross your legs until they get back Monday night." Vicky gave a jaw-popping yawn and settled back down on the blanket. There was no way she was waiting until Monday night. My luck wasn't that good.

I looked at the dogs and shook my head. Sarge had a drool-coated tennis ball in his mouth. Pedro was trying to drag a Frisbee, but he kept tripping over it. Goldie, the dink, was licking the glass door, and Wilbur had his smashed face pressed against it and seemed to be smearing snot all over the glass. I was not cleaning the door, but I would go out back and toss a few balls.

I wasn't totally inhuman. It just felt that way some days.

It was Thursday night and my time was up. Claudia wanted to know if I would go out with Hugh or not. By one o'clock Friday morning I still hadn't made up my mind. It was a damned if I do and damned if I don't situation. If the date turned out like one of my usual blind dates, I'd probably end up in jail or strangling Claudia. If it turned out Hugh was as great as Claudia was building him up to be, and something did click between us, who was I going to talk all the good stuff over with? No way could I talk about Hugh and sex with his sister.

I mean, what if things got interesting and I find out he likes to wear girl's panties to bed or something equally embarrassing? Who was I supposed to share that little bit of knowledge with? There was no way I could do that to Claudia, she would need therapy for the rest of her life. I couldn't see me sitting down with my mother and sharing that little tidbit of information over a cup of tea and warm chocolate chip cookies. I just wasn't that close to either of my sisters-in-law. Grandmom Howland would probably get a good chuckle out of it. We seemed to be the only two in the entire family with a sense of humor. She didn't like Vanessa, the plastic-boob bimbo, either.

Claudia had been giving me the look since our shift started at eleven. She wanted an answer, and she wasn't going to wait all night. I still wasn't sure what the answer was going to be. No sexy knight in shining armor had ridden into the hospital's ER to sweep me off my feet. The closest thing I had had to a conversation with a man was this afternoon, when Matty and Paul's sixty-year-old neighbor started yelling at me because Sarge had escaped the backyard and had taken a dump in his precious petunias.

To shut the neighbor up, I had to pick up the horse-sized turd out of his award-winning flowerbed. To get back at my brother for volunteering me for kennel duty, I used his fancy spatula that had been hanging from his gas grill on the back patio. The expression on the neighbor's face, as I made my way gingerly back to the trash can while holding out the offending spatula and its fragrant load, had been worth the hassle as I dumped not only the turd, but the spatula into the can and slammed on the lid.

I had severely reprimanded Sarge, who then looked at me, with his one good eye, as if I was torturing him. My heart caved. I ended up giving him two large Milk Bones and a doggie treat.

So far the score was: Animals 16, Me 0. Even Conan, the bearded-dragon lizard, had a certain charm about him as he munched on the lettuce I put in his cage.

"Hey Judith, we got a hot one coming in." Megan, one of the nurses I worked with regularly, grinned at me and winked.

By the smile I knew it wasn't a life-or-death situation. "Hot ones" could mean anything from a ten-car pileup with multiple injuries to a Chippendale dancer pulling out his back while performing for the ladies down at the Prancing Stallion nightclub. It could also mean a patient who had done something hysterical and injured themselves. Those were the hard patients to handle. Laughter had no place in the ER, but sometimes it couldn't be helped. People did the stupidest things.

"How hot?" If it was of the dancers, I wanted to go put on some lipstick and fix my hair. Knights in shining armor could be hot.

"Does the saying 'Like a rock' mean anything to you?" Megan was smirking.

"Chevy trucks."

Megan rolled her eyes. "How about, 'We bring good things to life'?"

"GE." I didn't get Megan most of the time. At twenty-four she seemed to be listening to a different drummer out there. "We got an ad executive?"

"How about this one, 'This is your penis. This is your penis on drugs.' "

"Viagra." I finally figured out Megan's twisted thinking. We had a patient who took the wonder drug and was suffering the consequences. As the ads on television say: if erections last for more than four hours, seek immediate medical attention. Someone wanted to be a big bad boy, but then he couldn't get any relief. "Tell me he has no idea about how that particular side effect is handled."

"Not yet he doesn't." Megan's smile was pure evil. "He's still out there with Millie, filling out the paperwork and looking red in the face."

"I'm amazed he has that much blood flow left." Oh God, sometimes life hands you a plum instead of a lemon. This was a definite plum. "Dr. Garmond is going to love this one." Not! Dr. Garmond was homophobic and now he had to get up-close and personal with his worse fear.

"Maybe he'll have Drac do it."

"Could be. No one can take blood better than Drac." I'll give him that much credit. It's eerie how Drac can hit the vein the first time, every time.

"I'm going to bring him back and put him in Number 3." Megan actually had a skip in her step as she headed for the waiting room.

A moment later I was pretending to read a chart as Megan escorted the embarrassed-looking male patient into Exam Room Number 3. The patient was holding a jacket in both hands, conveniently placed in front of his pants. I recognized him and nearly choked on the wad of Juicy Fruit I was chewing.

Megan closed the curtains to give the patient some privacy, and then came over to me. Her grin wasn't just evil, it was pure wickedness.

I leaned in close and whispered, "Professor Witman?"

"Oh yeah." Megan slapped a hand across her mouth to prevent a giggle from escaping. "Five years ago the man accused me of being a Neanderthal for not understanding Shakespeare, and now he pops a double dose of Viagra to please his honey."

"I didn't see his honey." Most patients have their loved one or guardian come back into the ER with them. The professor from the English Lit department at Franklin University had come alone.

"I'm sure she was too embarrassed to drive him here." Megan grinned and waved the professor's chart. "Now for the highlight of my night: I get to drag Garmond away from the new X-ray tech he's been trying to hit on, and tell him he's got a patient waiting for him."

I stood by the counter in the center of the ER and waved Claudia over. No way was I missing this. I didn't want to see the procedure. I just wanted to hear the professor's reaction when Dr. Garmond told him what had to be done. Maybe the ads on television should explain what happens when you pop a pill and your woody lasts more than four hours. I bet men would think twice, if not three times, before swallowing that little blue pill.

"What's up?" Claudia leaned against the counter. She looked exhausted. There were actual shadows under her eyes.

I laughed at her unintentional pun. "Professor Witman, English Lit."

"Huh?"

"He's what's up."

Claudia made a face. "He gave me my only C. How could I forget him?"

I nodded toward Curtain Number 3. "Guess who took a double dose of Viagra, the current drug of choice, and four hours later his pants still don't fit."

Claudia bit her lower lip and her eyes filled with laughter. "Does he know yet?"

"Megan just went to get Garmond. She's going to let him tell him."

"We get to hear his reaction." Claudia rubbed her hands together and grinned.

"Unless you want to go in and assist. I think I can talk Megan into letting you take her place."

"Not in a million years." Claudia picked up a folder and pretended to be busy with me. A moment later Megan and a put-out Dr. Garmond came down the hall and entered Number 3.

There was a murmur of voices. I could pick out Dr. Garmond's soothing tone. The next minute we could hear Witman shouting, and he sounded like a little girl, and not the boring, and oh-so-proper English professor.

Claudia nudged me. I nudged her back as the professor's voice rose in disbelief. Men were such sissies about certain things. Megan slid out from behind the curtain—I'm sure to give the men privacy—while they discussed the procedure. Megan took one look at Claudia and me and went running for the nurses' lounge with her hand over her mouth. She wasn't going to be sick, she was trying to hold back the laughter.

"Should we go after her?" Claudia asked.

"Nah, let her enjoy the moment. He called her a Neanderthal." Laughter was such a precious thing in our line of work, we preferred not to waste it.

I went to the supply cabinet and started putting together the tray Dr. Garmond would need. By the time I had it ready, Megan had composed herself. "Thanks, Judith."

"My pleasure." I placed the tray on the cart and allowed her to wheel it to Room Number 3.

The patient in Room 1 was sleeping, waiting for some lab results. The patient in Room 2, my patient, was down in X-ray getting some lovely shots of his wrist. It was a slow night so far.

Millie poked her head through the door just as the professor was voicing his objections. What men fail to realize is that all the blood that pools in the penis, which makes it hard, has to be relieved. There is only one way to do it: use a needle to siphon out the excess blood.

It's a good thing females give birth. Given all the noise and shrieks the coming from the professor, he would never be able to survive childbirth. And this was only a little needle.

I was just finishing my peanut butter-and-jelly sandwich when Claudia entered the lounge and pulled her bag out of the old refrigerator. "So, Judith, what's your answer? Technically it's Friday now, not Thursday."

She sat down in front of me and pulled a hoagie out of the bag. What was with Claudia and the hoagies lately?

"I'll do it on one condition." I held up my hand when Claudia opened her mouth. "It has to be a double date, with you and Chris."

My requirement had a twofold advantage: One, if the date went horribly wrong, Claudia would be there to witness the disaster, so there couldn't be any finger pointing later on. Two, I wanted to see what was up with Claudia and Chris. I was beginning to worry about them—things clearly weren't rosy on the home front.

"Deal." Claudia smiled. "You'll see. Hugh is a sweetie and I think he'll be perfect for you."

"Don't start planning a bridal shower, Claudia. I agreed to one date, and one date only. A double date at that. Technically it isn't even a blind date." If I looked at it as a double date instead of a blind date, I just might be able to make it through the night.

"We can pick you up at your place." I could see Claudia's mind spinning.

"I'm not at the apartment." I opened the small bag of chips I had gotten from the vending machine out in the waiting room. "I'm staying at my brother Paul's house. I'm animal sitting while he and Matty get some sun and quality time together."

"I bet they're thrilled about the baby."

"Matty's on cloud nine. She's already decided the nursery will be done in a Noah's Ark theme. She likes animals. All kinds of animals." I chuckled. "Paul wanted space ships, but he was vetoed because they won't know if it's a girl or a boy until the birth. Neither want to know beforehand. Matty gave him the honor of being the one to pick out the theme to the baby's room once he or she outgrows the nursery."

"Matty's the one with all those cats and kittens you keep trying to foist off on me, right?" asked Millie, who had just entered the room.

"She only has six cats right now, and a litter of kittens due at any moment." I tried not to think about poor Vicky at the house. She was getting bigger by the hour. I wasn't sure if I would prefer her delivering while I was at work, or if I wanted to be there in case she needed some help. "She also has four dogs, two parakeets, a parrot, three lizards, and a ferret named Roscoe." I wanted to add "and a partridge in a pear tree," but I refrained.

"Holy cow," Millie whistled.

"No cows, Millie." I took a sip of my Diet Coke. "But there had been a Shetland pony living in their garage for about two weeks until Matty found a great home for him."

Claudia laughed. "Give me Paul's address and we'll pick you up there. Unless you just want Hugh to pick you up, and Chris and I will meet you at the restaurant?"

"Definitely not. You all be together when you pick me up and let's make it casual. I didn't pack anything fancy and I don't want to have to run over to the apartment. The feeding and watering of the herd is taking all my free time." Casual dinner I could do. I could even manage to be polite to Claudia's brother for one night. Who knew, I might even enjoy myself.

Chapter 5

Get the sensation.

"Claudia, you can't do this to me," I shouted into the phone at six o'clock Saturday night. They were supposed to be by any minute to pick me up, and Claudia and Chris were backing out of their end of the bargain.

"It's not my fault Chris got sick." Claudia didn't sound sorry at all. In fact there was definitely a smile in her voice. "Hugh should be there any minute."

The ring of the doorbell caused all four dogs to bark and run around like idiots. Claudia had very short minutes. "I'm going to hurt you, Claud."

Claudia chuckled on the other end of the phone. "Be nice to him, Judith. He is my only brother."

I hung up, with Claudia's laughter ringing in my ear and a headache forming behind my right eye. I had prepared myself for a double date. Now I was stuck holding the bag all on my own. For two cents I'd let the dogs greet him. No one could be as perfect as Claudia built Hugh up to be. He probably hated animals, talked with a lisp, and smelled like week-old shrimp left out in the sun.

I opened the patio door and shooed the canines out back while mulling over Claudia's description of her brother: 6'1" tall, same dark brown hair and eyes as Claudia, broad shoulders, and a killer body. I snorted in disbelief. Still, there was no sense scaring Hugh off within the first two minutes with the canine greeting committee. He was single and available, even if he didn't match his sister's description.

I'm not stupid. Stranger things than someone exaggerating a potential blind date or family relative had been known to happen. I was once again about to blindly select a piece of chocolate from the dating box and I was praying this one didn't contain any nuts or other unexpected surprises. All I wanted was a nicely sweet and smooth buttercream.

I reached for the doorknob and opened it to Claudia's brother. My stomach dropped and my spirits soared. Hugh James wasn't an ordinary piece of chocolate. He was Godiva, and wrapped in gold foil with a pretty bow on top. "Hugh?" No way was my luck this good. The gorgeous hunk standing on my doorstep had to be at the wrong house.

"Judith?" Hugh's smile was just a bit crooked.

"Hi, come on in." I opened the door wider and kept an eye out for escaping felines. Albert, a part-Persian-and-Lord-knew-what-else cat, had a bad habit of slipping outside as soon as someone opened a door. I was going to kill Claudia the next time I saw her. Why didn't she show me a picture of her brother? I would have dated him on his looks alone.

Hugh stepped into the house and looked around curiously. I didn't blame him. It was like living in a pet shop. Matty really had to do something with some of the animals before the little one arrived. There wasn't any room left for the normal baby clutter I've seen in some people's homes.

Matty and Paul had cats everywhere, the parakeet cage was in the eating area of the kitchen, and three separate reptile cages were in the formal living room. The ferret's pen was in the family room. There was nothing formal about Matty or her decorating tastes. Every room had the same theme: Noah's Ark á la pet shoppe. Every electrical outlet had an air freshener plugged into it.

All four dogs were staring in through the patio doors.

Pedro, the Chihuahua, was barking its fool head off. Sarge looked ready to attack if I gave the order. Goldie was chewing on a 3'-long branch covered in oak leaves, which I had no idea where she got, since Paul's enclosed backyard didn't have an oak tree. Wilbur, as usual, was smearing more snot on the glass door.

If first impressions meant anything, Hugh was probably thinking he just bit into a pecan cluster.

"None of them are mine," I was compelled to explain. "I'm animal sitting for my brother and his wife."

"I know, Claudia explained."

"Did she also explain how Chris is supposed to be sick and couldn't make it tonight?"

Huge's mouth curved into that crooked smile again. "I didn't believe a word of it." He didn't appear to be too upset with his sister.

"I think we have been had."

"Only think?" he asked. The crooked smile grew.

"Okay, know. I *know* we have been had." And I didn't care one bit. From Hugh's reaction, neither did he. "I have the world's worst record when it comes to blind dates," I confessed. Maybe if I gave him some type of warning he wouldn't go running and screaming into the night at the first sign of trouble.

"Ever have a first date do a reenactment of the famous restaurant scene from *When Harry Met Sally?*"

I tried not to sputter. "Ummmm . . . no." Okay, maybe there were some seriously disturbed females out there. Maybe we should fix up orgasmic Sally with Bozo and his perverted balloons. I didn't want to imagine the fun those two could have together. Some things in life were better left unimagined.

"I can promise that if I get an urge to um . . . show you my acting ability in the restaurant I'll pick a scene from *Hamlet* or *Dirty Harry*."

"You know *Hamlet*?" Hugh seemed impressed.

I really hated to bust his bubble. "About three lines from *Hamlet* and a couple more from *Romeo and Juliet*."

"Just don't do the dying scene." He flashed me that killer smile and my toes melted. "I really don't want to end our date with me being dragged out of the restaurant in handcuffs for poisoning you."

"Now that sounds like my usual first, and last, dates." His smile was going to get me into serious trouble. I could feel it.

"Do you like country music?" Hugh walked over to the couch and started to scratch one of the cats behind its ears. I think it was Mary, or it could have been Richard. Both Mary and Richard looked identical, which wasn't surprising since they were from the same litter.

"As long as you don't expect me to square dance." Country music wasn't bad, but I deplored the heavy metal crap people were trying to pass off as music.

"My sister told me casual, so I didn't make reservations." He gave the cat a tickle under the chin, and the gray tabby seemed to melt beneath his touch. It had to be Mary, the little hussy.

I glanced down at my outfit. Khaki slacks and a silky pink shirt. You couldn't get any more casual than that. Okay, jeans, but as I told you before, jeans make my ass look big. "I'm the one who said casual. I didn't feel like running across town to my apartment for dress clothes." Hugh was dressed in dark gray Dockers, and a yellow-and-gray plaid button-down shirt. He looked comfortable, and yummy.

"How do you feel about going to the concert in Franklin Park?"

Anyone who lived within a hundred miles of Franklin knew about their Saturday-night concerts in the park. "Cheeseburgers on toast!" I closed my eyes in ecstasy. I hadn't been to one of the concerts in years, but I could still remember the taste of the local Lions Club specialty. Instead of the traditional hamburger bun, the Lions used two slices of toast and a square hamburger patty.

Franklin Park is the place to be on a Saturday night. Local organizations sell refreshments, bands perform on the stage, and couples snuggle on blankets under the trees and the stars while young children run wild or feed the growing duck population at the pond. I hoped like hell that Hugh had packed a blanket. A very small blanket.

"It's been years since I thought about those cheeseburgers." Hugh grinned. "You game for listening to songs about broken hearts, bar fights, prison, and dogs?"

"Sure am." The planets had to be aligned. There was no other explanation for such a promising start of the evening. Claudia had been right. Hugh was perfect. "Let me get a jacket and check on Vicky one last time." The last time I peeked in on her she was sleeping.

"Who's Vicky?"

"Victoria, a very pregnant cat. My sister-in-law Matty named all the cats after queens and kings." I headed for the laundry room where Vicky's bed was all ready for her and the new arrivals. Of course Vicky preferred to sleep on some threadbare blanket than in the cute wicker basket Matty had bought for the special occasion.

Hugh followed and peered over my shoulder as I carefully pushed the door open and groaned. Vicky was in the process of delivering the first kitten. "Tell me she's not doing what I think she's doing."

"What do you think she's doing?" There was laughter in Hugh's voice.

"Tap dancing," I whispered hopefully. I looked at Vicky again, just to make sure I wasn't hallucinating. Nope, that little wet blob was a kitten. I turned and faced Hugh. Lord, he was handsome. It was going to break my heart to cancel our date, but there was no way I could leave the house now.

"She's not doing what you think she's doing." Hugh gave another peek. "I do believe she just became a mother." Hugh's soft smile was genuine as he took in the sight of Vicky cleaning her firstborn.

My heart gave a funny little lurch. Hugh was not only handsome, he was nice. I glanced back into the laundry room. The situation hadn't miraculously changed. Now this was more like my luck. A twenty-pound fur ball was ruining my date. "I can't leave her alone, Hugh. Matty would never forgive me." Heck, I wouldn't be able to forgive myself.

"I wouldn't expect you to." Hugh shook his head in wonder as the little wet blob wiggled. "By the size of Vicky, I've got a feeling it's going to be a long night."

By the size of Vicky, I thought she would be delivering lion cubs instead of egg-sized kittens. I had a sinking feeling there were a lot more where that one just came from. "Do you have any idea how many kittens a cat usually has?" Was it two, three, twelve?

"None whatsoever." Hugh chuckled. "How about if we order in? I'm sure we can get pizza or Chinese."

I tried to ignore the rapid pounding of my heart. He wasn't going to desert me. "You won't mind?"

"As long as you don't order anchovies or pineapple on the pizza." His smile was teasing.

"What's your opinion of hot wings?" I wouldn't eat an anchovy if someone paid me, and I had a rule about pineapples. They belonged on a ham, or speared onto a long stick stuck into my drink as I lounged beside a pool.

"The hotter the better." Hugh raised a dark brow and waited for my reaction.

"Good Lord, a man after my own heart." I fanned myself and hopefully sounded like I was teasing him. I wasn't too sure if I was or not.

Hugh chuckled. "Point me in the direction of the phone book and I'll see what I can do about rounding us up some dinner."

"Sweet talker." I pulled open a kitchen drawer and handed him the phone book.

"I'll handle this, you go help Vicky."

"Why me?" I didn't want to play nursemaid to a bunch of

kittens and Vicky. I wanted to go snuggle with Hugh on a blanket, eat cheeseburgers on toast, and listen to songs about pickup trucks, horses, and cowboys.

"You're the nurse."

"I've never delivered a kitten before."

"Don't look at me. I've never owned a cat." Hugh started to flip through the yellow pages. "Any preferences?"

"Nah, I'm not a picky eater." I headed for the laundry room and prayed that Vicky knew what she was doing.

Four minutes later Hugh joined me in the small room. "It will be half an hour." He frowned at Vicky and the dark-colored kitten. "Got a towel?"

"Yes, why?" I was standing back, allowing the new momma to do her thing. I reached for the towel on top of the pile Matty had left.

"I think number two is about to make an appearance." He took the pink towel I was holding out. "We can finish drying number one for her while she's busy delivering number two."

"Are you sure you aren't a vet?"

"No, but as the commercial says, I spent the night in a Holiday Inn Express." Hugh chuckled along with me, and then handed me back the towel. "Since Vicky knows you, and I'm a complete stranger to her, why don't you pick up number one?"

"That sounds so impersonal." I knelt down and tenderly picked up the kitten with the towel. Vicky didn't bother sparing me a glance. She was busy with number two. "We'll call this one Baby, and Number two, Kitty."

"What about three and four?"

"We'll worry about that as they come." I stood back up and gently rubbed the miniature fur ball. Hugh stood close to me and watched the little fellow. Or maybe it was a she, but I wasn't looking. I had no idea if you could tell the sex by looking, even when kittens were only five minutes old; but I wasn't taking the chance. What kind of RN would I be if I couldn't tell the difference?

"This one has dark hair," Hugh said. "I wonder who the father is?"

"Probably one of Matty's other cats. There are three girls and three boys."

"Any of them have dark hair?"

I tenderly rubbed the dark hair dry. "Richard is gray striped, Albert's a Persian mix, and Henry the Sixth is light colored with brown spots."

"You weren't kidding when you said they are named after kings."

"The girls are all named after queens. There's Victoria here; Mary, who I think you were scratching earlier; and Elizabeth, she's solid black and tends to be quite snooty."

Number two, or Kitty, made his or her appearance. It was hard to tell, but Kitty might be orange like mom.

"Why Henry the Sixth? I thought Henry the Eighth would have been more familiar." Hugh carefully took Baby from me as I knelt down to make sure Kitty was breathing. The little bundle wasn't moving.

Mom did her job and Kitty started to move. "I think Matty had five other cats named Henry before this one."

"She goes through a lot of cats?"

"No, she tries to find good homes for them." I smiled as Kitty wiggled some more. "Matty brings home strays like J.Lo brings home husbands."

Hugh knelt next to me and gently placed Baby near Vicky's belly. He slowly picked up Kitty. "How about I finish this one for you, Momma? By the size of your belly, I've got a feeling there's more to come. Get some rest."

It was ridiculous, I know, but watching Hugh with Vicky made me glad we didn't go down to Franklin Park. I would have missed seeing this side of him.

Thirty minutes and two more kittens later, the food arrived. Vicky's stomach was smaller, but nowhere near its normal size. Which didn't mean a thing. I've seen women deliver eight-pound babies, and their stomach never went flat in the delivery room.

All four kittens were dry and figuring out on their own how to feed. Vicky lay there exhausted.

"How about we leave them alone and eat while the wings are still hot?" Hugh ushered me from the room and partly closed the door.

By midnight Vicky was the proud mother of five kittens, three light in color, two dark. All of them appeared healthy and Vicky hadn't protested when we moved them to the cute wicker basket and cleaned up the room. The wings and salad Hugh had ordered were long gone and we had raided my brother's pantry for a snack. A ten minute phone call to Matty and Paul had covered all the bases. Matty wanted to ask a hundred more questions. Paul wanted to get back to whatever they had been doing before they had been rudely interrupted. I cut the call short.

It had been the most enjoyable evening of my life. Hugh had found an old Mel Brooks movie on television and we spent two hours trying to outdo one another on who knew most of the lines by heart. I think we were tied when the credits started to appear at the end of the movie. I hated to see the evening end.

"I should be going." Hugh stood up and stretched.

"Thanks for all your help with Vicky and for being such a good guy when your plans for the evening were changed." I was trying to figure out how to ask him out without sounding too desperate.

"I didn't do anything. Vicky did all the work." Hugh walked over to the front door. "Besides, I love *Blazing Saddles.*"

"Really? I didn't notice," I teased as I followed him. Goldie and Pedro came along. Sarge was snoring by the unlit fireplace and Wilbur was in the kitchen munching on some doggy food. Not only did Hugh like cats, he loved dogs. Goldie was in love with him and hadn't left his side since we let them all in earlier. "I had a great time tonight."

Hugh smiled but didn't open the door. "So did I." He

leaned against the door. "Now that Vicky and her little ones are all settled, any chance you might be interested in going out to dinner tomorrow night?"

I glanced at the clock on the living room mantel. It was past midnight. "Tonight you mean?" I was trying for a nonchalant look, but I was failing miserably. "I would love to."

"Great, I'll pick you up at six." Hugh stepped away from the door. "What about Franklin Park next Saturday night? I think it's Blue Grass night."

The butterflies in my stomach were put to rest. Not only was Hugh asking me out, but he was asking for two dates. Now there was a man who knew what he was feeling and acted on it. "I love blue grass music." I would have said yes to heavy metal or even disco music.

Hugh's fingers lightly cupped my chin. His thumb tenderly rubbed my lower lip.

I forgot how to breathe.

"Now that I walked you to your front door, can I kiss you good night?" he softly whispered.

"I'd be very disappointed if you didn't." There was something incredibly sexy about a man who asks to kiss you good night. Most of my dates just assume they have the right to stick their tongue down your throat and their hand up your blouse just because they pay for dinner.

Hugh's mouth was gentle and warm as he lightly kissed me. I sank into the sensation, wrapped my arms around his neck, and deepened the kiss.

One of us groaned as Hugh pulled me tight against his chest and what had started out as a gentle kiss went into melt-down. I had no idea where the kiss would have led, because Goldie, either thinking it was a game or was jealous, jumped up on us.

I stumbled backward, but Hugh's hands steadied me as he gently scolded Goldie.

Hugh appeared to be having as much trouble catching his breath as I was. "I guess I better get going."

"Good night, Hugh."

He gave me a quick, gentle kiss that held a lot of promise of things to come. "Good night, Judith."

I stood in the doorway and watched as he got into his car and drove away.

My fellow nurses at F.U. were wrong. Not all the good men were taken. You just have to search through life's box of chocolates, until you find one that's just right.

I closed and locked the door, and turned off the outside porch light. I licked my lower lip and could still taste Hugh. He tasted like a sweet buttercream.

JUST
JENNIFER

Lisa Plumley

Chapter 1

Everyone wants to skip the preliminaries, but with a few simple precautions, you can avoid redness, frustration, and unsightly bumps in the future. Be smart! Before getting started, take a nice, long bubble bath, exfoliate thoroughly, and plan your approach.
    —Tips courtesy of "The Girls' Guide to Getting Smooth" (Goddess Razors, Inc.)

66 "I still don't see what you're getting so worked up about." Not answering, Jennifer Merryn wiggled impatiently at the downtown San Diego street corner, waiting for the light to turn. She loved Stephanie, her favorite stylist from the salon where they both worked—and the originator of the question she was determinedly avoiding—but now was *not* the time for Stephanie's trademark sunny-side-up routine.

"Seriously." In the neon-spangled light from a nearby thrift-store window, Stephanie gestured at the thing that had started this whole mess: a rolled-up magazine shoved beneath Jennifer's elbow. "Lighten up. It's only an ad."

Only an ad. Ha. She wished.

Too impatient to wait any longer, Jennifer made her move. She didn't like waiting for anything—including clueless tourists in Hertzes looking for the Gaslamp Quarter. Dodging a yellow Sunshine Pool Cleaning truck before it squashed her, she made it to the other side with Stephanie still on her trail.

They hurried along the sidewalk, heels clicking and hand-bags swinging, their requisite stylists' black-on-black ensembles melting into the twilight. Springtime humidity filled the air, making Jennifer's clothes stick to her. Worse, making her hair frizz. If she didn't find their destination soon, she'd have a full-on California-girl 'fro on her hands.

"It's 'only an ad' that calls my whole *life* into question," Jennifer pointed out as she squinted up the street, searching for the supposedly obvious purple door—sans signage—that would identify their target. "I *can't* lighten up."

"Chill. You're taking this way too seriously."

"No, I'm taking Nyla's directions too seriously. She *did* say two blocks from Fourth, right? A purple door?"

Stephanie shrugged. Jennifer stopped, temporarily defeated by the Nancy Drew routine they always had to go through to meet up with their friend these days. Foot traffic surged around them, composed of office workers and tourists and residents of the area's funky, semigentrified neighborhood.

No sign of a purple door.

Or, for that matter, of a much-needed, fortifying cocktail.

Arrgh. The perfume-strip inserts in the January issue of *Cosmopolitan*—which really was, as Stephanie had indicated, responsible for this entire imbroglio—were making Jennifer giddy. Also, she hadn't eaten anything since before lunchtime, not counting the Fritos she'd snagged between clients. It was a stylist's routine, but skipping meals always made her woozy.

As if she didn't have enough to cope with. Why did Nyla's new "finds" always have to be so damned cryptic? It was like cracking the freaking Da Vinci Code just to locate the latest restaurant, club, or hangout her best friend had trend-spotted.

"Let's try that way." Jennifer pointed.

They set off again. The magazine flapped beneath her arm, reminding her with every step of the problem at hand. Jennifer was three steps away from a stopgap Rubio's fish taco and a heart-to-heart with Stephanie—just to revive her flagging blood sugar—when she spotted the purple door.

Nirvana! Jennifer yanked it open. She and Stephanie sailed inside, stumbling in the unexpected gloom. The place was noisy, crowded, and apparently very popular . . . at least with those in the know. Amid the music, past the jostling heads and shoulders of the nine-to-fivers, Jennifer caught sight of an industrial-looking steel bar, a swooping modern-art installation, jammed tables, and Nyla.

Her friend—and roommate—waved them over. They slid in her choice corner booth, taking their positions—by long habit—with Jennifer in the middle. Amazed, she looked around.

"I don't know how you do it. This place is incredible." According to Nyla, it had only been open a week or so. "It's like going from black and white to Technicolor."

"Just a modest neighborhood watering hole." Grinning, Nyla gestured for cocktails. "All you need is an ear to the ground. The bartender is a *genius*. He used to work at the Valencia in La Jolla before he got stolen away. And the food is decent too."

"Good, I'm starving." Stephanie grabbed a menu. "Four donuts and a lukewarm coffee *don't* last all day. Especially when you've got Freaky McFreakerson, over here, to deal with."

She jabbed her chin meaningfully toward Jennifer.

"Hey!" Jennifer protested. "I have *reason* to freak out. This is serious." To prove it, she slapped her magazine on the table and jabbed her finger at the dreaded ad. "Look!"

Nyla did. She wrinkled her nose. "A stick-figure teenager with ten pounds of makeup pretending to worry about wrinkle cream? So what? That's just business as usual."

"Not that. The other page. The *other* ad."

Just glancing at it, Jennifer felt a renewed pang of unease. She'd never been prone to ruminating or deliberating or even questioning herself. She'd spent most of her life flitting blithely from thing to thing, never worrying about goals or problems or the future. But this time . . .

"Who do you want to be today?" Nyla read. She glanced up from the caption, her face a study in confusion. "Well, judging by this model's picture and the hideous lipstick she's wearing, I'd say she wants to be Queen of the Fugly."

Nyla did have a way of cutting straight to the point.

"No, you don't get it." Urgently, Jennifer poked the ad. "*Who do you want to be today?*" she repeated. "Who? Who! And the minute I looked at it, I realized the truth."

Miserably, she paused. Her friends stared at her, clearly missing the significance of the revelation she'd experienced.

"I . . . don't . . . know," Jennifer said. "I don't know! I'm a twenty-eight-year-old woman. I have a cosmetology license, a job, and half a rent payment every month. I have a twelve-point plan for picking the perfect pair of butt-flattering jeans! But I still don't know *who I want to be today*."

"Ahhh." Nyla exchanged a knowing glance with Stephanie. "I should have ordered before you got here. Clearly, Miss Cosmo Girl needs a blood sugar boost. Don't touch that—"

It was too late. Jennifer downed her cocktail with a clatter, smacking her lips. Yes. She needed that. "Mmmm . . . tasty. Let's get more."

"Oh God. We can't let her drink on an empty stomach."

Stephanie slid the empty glass to the table's edge. Her tactical maneuver didn't bother Jennifer a bit. She felt better already.

"Wow, you guys are miracle workers. I mean it." She beamed at her friends, her two favorite people in the whole world. "I must have really needed to get that whole 'Who do you want to be today?' thing off my chest."

"Off your chest?" Stephanie gawked. "You were blabbering about it, nonstop, all the way here from PB." PB—Pacific Beach to out-of-towners—was where their salon was located. "I thought we were going to cause a ten-car pileup on I-5, the way you were waving your arms around like that."

"Please. I was having an existential crisis."

Nyla nodded. "That explains the gibbering text message you sent me. I wondered what 'Who M I?' meant."

Optimistically, Jennifer surveyed her empty glass. Now that her problem was in the wild, she knew she could solve it. She just needed a little reinforcement first.

"What was that anyway? A margarita?" She signaled for more. Stress made her thirsty. "It was delicious."

"It was a kiwi daiquiri." Nyla sounded resigned, which was easier to face than sunny-side-up any day. "The bartender's originally from Melbourne."

"An Aussie *and* a genius. Let's get more."

"Fine by me." Stephanie was a notoriously moment-to-moment person. She forgot her clients' hair-color processing times, her locker combination at work, her own allergy to shell-fish. "Mmmm, coconut prawns! Let's get some of those too."

"You two need keepers," Nyla groused.

Ten minutes later, they had a second round, two shared plates of food, and enough energy to consider a plan of action.

"Earth to Jenn." Stephanie snapped her fingers.

Nyla waved a French fry. "Focus, girl."

Jennifer wavered. The hottie at the end of the bar was look-ing her way, and he was just her type. Blond hair, killer bod, easy smile. A surfer, if she didn't miss her bet. The kind of guy who took things easy, kept in shape, and had plenty of time for nookie—unless the waves were good.

A fry bounced off her nose. Nyla guffawed. Despite the rari-fied, technochic atmosphere, the food here was "ironically" old school: buffalo burgers, barbecue ribs, and jalapeno-dusted French fries. It had suited Jennifer perfectly. At least until she'd noticed *him*. Maybe all she needed was distraction.

Seductively, she tossed her hair.

Its kinky length fluffed out from her head.

The surf god blanched.

Too late, Jennifer remembered the humidity. For a naturally curly-haired person like her, San Diego was the worst.

"Hello?" Nyla prodded. "What about your identity crisis?"

Oh. That. Unhappily, Jennifer swiveled to face her.

"I'm serious. It might seem like I'm overreacting, but that ad really bugged me." Fortified by her happy-hour munchies, she dredged up the courage to study the lipstick ad more closely. "I know it looks just like any other stupid ad, but that caption is . . . chilling."

"I think it's supposed to be fantasy-provoking." Stephanie craned her neck as she munched a barbecue rib. "You know: Who do you want to be today? Va-va-voom red, innocent pink, etc."

"Yeah. It's like the slogan says"—Nyla fanned her hands as though holding a banner—"Easy. Breezy. Psycho Girl."

"Har, har." Jennifer dragged the magazine closer. As her gaze fell on that innocent-seeming question, she shivered. *Who do you want to be today?* "Shouldn't I *know* who I want to be by now? I mean, I've had twenty-eight years to figure it out."

"You're probably having a delayed quarter-life crisis." Nyla scammed a fry, looking unconcerned. "I read about it at the spa. A sense of purposelessness, confusion about life goals, the feeling that everybody else has things figured out already. Don't worry. You'll snap out of it."

"Yeah." Stephanie leaned forward, an earnest expression on her face. "Just give it some time. And another kiwi daiquiri."

But somehow, Jennifer felt as though she *couldn't* just "give it time." That ad was a call to action. A challenge.

A dare.

And she'd never been one to refuse a dare.

"No. I need to define myself," she insisted. "Figure out who I really am. The question is . . . how?"

They pondered it for a minute.

"I've got it!" Excitedly, Stephanie sat straighter.

Her chest bobbled with the movement, catching the eye of every man in the place. At times, Jennifer really envied her pal's gutsy twenty-first birthday gift to herself: a visit to the renowned "Doctor Ta-Ta." Her upgrade from a 34B to an overflowing C had really boosted her confidence. And her tips.

"That new stylist does hair analysis. We can yank out a few strands and see what *she* has to say about who you are!"

"Yeah," Nyla deadpanned. "Either that, or we can consult Madame Fortune Cookie, psychic connection."

"Come on, hair analysis is a science!"

"Sorry, but my personality is *not* a split end."

Undeterred, Stephanie brainstormed. "Or . . . what about a makeover? A total makeover!" Eagerly, she shifted in the booth. "On those TV shows, they always say they finally feel like *themselves* afterward. For the first time ever."

Visions of before and after wafted through Jennifer's head. She felt more terrified than ever.

"No way. I'm not letting a stranger get their hands on my head." She put her palms protectively over her curls, cursing her lack of Frizz-Ease. "I'll look like a giant Brillo pad."

Her hair was very delicate. Its trials and tribulations had been instrumental in leading her to cosmetology school.

"Look. Just because we're women doesn't mean we have to approach this from the outside in." Nyla signaled for more daiquiris. "Let's be analytical. Is your job bugging you?"

"No. I love being a hairstylist." That was partly what made this so frustrating. Jennifer didn't feel unhappy per se. Just undefined. As though her whole life had happened by accident. "Things are really picking up at tease lately too."

Her friends nodded. Stephanie worked there, of course, and Nyla was in the beauty industry, if somewhat tangentially— but everyone in town knew that *tease* didn't need a capital T to be recognized. Or a more obvious beauty salon name. Especially not with San Diego's elite, its news anchors, and its most stylish citizens all jockeying for chair space.

Some of them even at Jennifer's station.

"Okay, then. What about your hobbies? Your interests?"

At Nyla's prompting, they ran through them all, searching for an answer. Overall, Jennifer felt satisfied with her life. She had a good job, wonderful friends, and an awesome beach-front apartment she shared with Nyla. But despite all that, she couldn't help wondering if it meant anything.

"I never really *chose* any of that stuff, though. I just kind of went along for the ride. Who's to say any of it reflects the real me? The authentic me?" Shoving aside her remaining fries, Jennifer regarded her friends with honest curiosity. "I mean, maybe I should have been a librarian. Or a gymnast. Or a high-powered executive."

"No good. You can't talk quietly *or* spell." Nyla grinned. "You almost dislocated your kneecap the one time you invaded my yoga class. And high-powered executiveness requires a variety of bloodthirsty ambition you just don't have."

"How do you know? Maybe I'm secretly vicious."

Her friends scoffed.

"Yeah, and I'm Einstein's sister," Stephanie said.

Tactfully, Nyla sipped her drink.

"Still," Jennifer persisted, feeling determined. No measly lipstick ad was going to ignite a quarter-life crisis, screw with her self-image, and get away with it. "There's got to be a way to find out *who I want to be today*."

"Just put on some lipstick," Nyla advised, tapping the ad like a true child of advertising. "Resistance is futile."

Stephanie shook her head. "Lip gloss is the only way to go. It's more moisturizing."

They stared at her.

"Are you sure Doctor Ta-Ta didn't operate farther north?" Nyla squeezed Stephanie's hand sympathetically. "Like, on your head? Because ever since you got those things—"

"Har, har." Not bothered by Nyla's ever-cynical outlook, Stephanie rolled her eyes. "I suggest a shopping trip," she told Jennifer. "New shoes *always* perk me up."

"Try on men's clothes. Maybe you're a dude in disguise."

"Very funny, Nyla." Stephanie shook her head, then wrapped her arm around Jennifer's shoulders. "This is a crisis! Cross-dressing? Seriously? Do you want to make her more confused?"

"It was a *joke*, brainiac."

"I'm pretty sure Jennifer isn't a man."

"Maybe not, but it looks as if she's hooked herself one."

Guiltily, Jennifer dragged her gaze from the cute surfer at the bar. Something about him, combined with Stephanie and Nyla's conversation, tickled her brain. Like a word stuck on the tip of her tongue, it teased her with possibilities.

"Don't bother," Nyla advised, nodding toward him. "You know how it'll end already. Everything will be great until the surf comes up. Then he'll head out for the waves and you'll be kicking yourself for succumbing to that surfer-boy charm."

"Again," Stephanie added, stirring her daiquiri.

Neither of them met her eyes. That was when it hit her.

Men. Men were the key to finding out who she really was.

It was brilliant! After all, dating comprised the biggest rut Jennifer had ever been in. Time after time, she stuck with happy-go-lucky surfer types, falling for their irresistible blend of laughter, sinewy muscles, and ocean-blue eyes.

No wonder she didn't know who she really was. She'd been limiting herself without realizing it!

Men were the perfect try-on vehicle, Jennifer realized in a burst of revelation. They were the ultimate accessory.

With the right men for inspiration, she could test-drive new parts of her identity and find out which ones felt most authentic. By the end of her experiment, she was bound to gain new insight into herself . . . and whip her quarter-life crisis into submission at the same time. It was pure genius.

"I'm going on a voyage of self-discovery," Jennifer announced. Her gaze dropped to the drippy Heinz ketchup bottle on the table. Unexpectedly, it offered up further inspiration. "Fifty-seven men in fifty-seven days."

Nyla choked. "*What?*"

Stephanie crinkled her brows. "Why fifty-seven?"

Jennifer shrugged. "Why not?"

A broad smile spread over her face. Yes, this could work.

"Oh wow," Nyla said. "You're going to need a *lot* of condoms. I suggest buying online. Unless you want to give the Ralph's checkout guy an embolism."

"I'm not going to *sleep* with fifty-seven men! I'm just going to date them. Sheesh." Jennifer downed the rest of her kiwi daiquiri, feeling thrilled with herself. Now that she was on the path to subduing her identity crisis, she felt a million times better. "For once in my life, I'm going to be proactive in my choices."

"In your *dating* choices."

"Right. But it's perfect. Don't you see?" Jennifer spread her hands, trying to explain. "Dating is the ultimate microcosm of life. Especially *my* life. I wait around for a guy to ask me out, then I wait around for him to kiss me. Then I wait around for him to call. I leave all the decisions in somebody else's hands!"

"I recommend a push-up bra," Stephanie advised inexplicably.

Undaunted, Jennifer forged on. "This is a new millennium. Yet I'm *still* waiting around for men to make all my relationship decisions—especially when it comes to getting the ball rolling. But not anymore. For the next two months, I'm becoming the player instead of the played." Gaining enthusiasm, she shouted out her big finale. "I'm *seizing control* of my destiny!"

Jennifer sat back, waiting for the applause to start.

And waiting. And waiting . . .

"Ummm, I hate to be a buzzkill." Nyla *loved* to be a buzzkill. She was paid to do it professionally as an undercover salon "secret shopper" for an industry magazine. "But if it's really your destiny, seizing control of it is pointless."

"Yeah," Stephanie put in. "Hello? It's your *destiny*."

Pedantic did *not* mesh with cocktails. Or inspiration.

"You both need more vision," Jennifer argued. "Come on, just picture it! I could be Goth girl. Granola girl. Uptown girl." The possibilities were limitless. Exciting. And best of all, potentially self-revelatory. "All I need are the right accoutrements."

"Or the right *man*-cessories."

"Exactly!"

"Let me get this straight," Nyla persisted. "You're going to *date* as a path to self-enlightenment?"

"Yes!"

She waited. Still no applause, damn it.

"I don't know," Stephanie said doubtfully. "Fifty-seven men in fifty-seven days is a lot." She stretched, making her belly-baring top ride up—and unknowingly causing a near riot at the table of businessmen next door. "You might want to pace yourself. What if you have a bad hair day?"

"We're stylists. We don't *have* bad hair days."

Nyla's gaze skittered upward. "Tell that to those faux Rasta dreadlocks you're sporting, Vidal Sassoon."

"Hey, don't malign my professional expertise. I don't tell you what goes into a proper bikini wax, do I?"

"Sorry."

They lapsed into thoughtful silence. Jennifer scoped out her project's unwitting first target, still in place at the end of the bar. She took in his easygoing stance, his telltale sun-bleached hair, his entourage of buddies. They hefted Coronas and hooted with laughter.

Despite their obvious good cheer, Jennifer held back. He was just her type, but his retinue of wingmen was pretty intimidating. Even to a woman as determined—and as liquored up on kiwi daiquiris—as she was.

None of the *wingmen* had frizzy, naturally curly hair.

"Ohmigod." Stephanie widened her eyes, realizing where Jennifer's attention was focused. "You're serious. You're really going to do this, aren't you?"

No time like the present. New me? Here I come.

Jennifer grinned. "Just watch me."

Chapter 2

You might be eager to get started, but take time to explore your options! Pivoting heads, spring-mounted models, and state-of-the-art micropulse technology—combined with sensible lathering up beforehand—ensure a far more enjoyable experience.

—Tips courtesy of "The Girls' Guide to Getting Smooth" (Goddess Razors, Inc.)

The only thing Gavin Collaro didn't understand about women was why they always made everything so dramatic. Broken fingernail? Disaster. Uncoordinated clothes? Trauma. Relationship "issues"? Catastrophe.

He just didn't get it. Really, all anyone needed were a sharp pair of nail clippers, a convenient dose of situation-activated color blindness, and a few laughs with a nice girl once in a while. Whenever the waves weren't good.

But noooo. That was too simple for most women.

Take his sister, Nyla, for instance. She took *everything* seriously, including the beach sand Gavin had accidentally tracked in on his flip-flops while visiting her today, the deadline on her salon-spy column (reportedly overdue), and the ups and downs of her friends' dating lives.

Okay, he also didn't understand why women wanted him to divulge his innermost thoughts, which were ordinarily pretty mundane. But that was it. Seriously. He thought.

"So *then* she said, 'But he was a professional *wakeboarder*, not a surfer!' " Nyla gestured wildly from her chair. On the desk in front of her, her laptop showed the ghostly imprint of her unfinished column. "As if *that* makes any difference at all. I swear, she's completely delusional."

Nyla stared up at him in a huff. Sensing he was supposed to be indignant too, Gavin frowned. "You're kidding me."

"I know. One down, and already she's blowing it."

"Totally. *Totally* blowing it. As if."

"I mean, I understand the impulse. Everybody feels as if their life is happening in spite of them, sometimes, but—" His sister broke off, her eyes narrowing. " 'As if'? What's that supposed to mean?"

Damned if he knew. He'd just been trying to play along. Life was too short for all this drama.

Caught, Gavin thrust out the item he'd brought. "Thanks for the use of your toaster. I cleaned out the crumb tray and serviced the dials. I'll let you get back to your column."

When Nyla didn't take the toaster, he knew he was screwed. She was in a talkative mood, filled with concern for her mysterious wakeboarder-dating friend.

Nobody stopped his sister when she was on a roll. However, Gavin was an optimistic guy. So he shoved the toaster on the peninsula between the kitchen and living room, then backed away anyway. Real slow.

Outside, just visible through the open patio door and way down the crowded beach past the bustling boardwalk, he caught a glimpse of the Pacific. At the sight, his whole body relaxed. The sparkling waves beckoned, tangy with saltwater. Gavin figured he still had time to catch a few swells.

"*Wait a minute,*" Nyla said.

Hell. He recognized that *gotcha* tone. She was going to ask him about Carmen, the woman he'd borrowed the toaster for.

Gavin didn't want to discuss the sappy romantic breakfast in bed he'd planned . . . for a woman who, as usual, *hadn't* been interested in bagels and coffee. Or anything else from him besides sex.

Not that he had anything against sex. Hell, no. He'd enjoyed Carmen's enthusiastic version of "making the bed" as much as the next guy would have. Possibly more. It was just that lately . . . Gavin didn't know . . . he wanted something else.

He couldn't say what, not being prone to drama himself.

But he knew he wanted . . . *more.*

His sister, older by two years, eyeballed him with her arms crossed. A disturbingly thoughtful gleam came into her eyes.

"Hey. *You're* a guy," she accused. "Sort of."

"Sort of?"

Nyla waved off his protest. "So you tell me: what would *you* say if a woman told you she'd decided to date thirty guys in thirty days?"

"I'd say sign me up."

"Be serious," Nyla pleaded. "I am."

Awww, hell. Mingled with his relief that he *wasn't* about to be interrogated about Carmen came a brotherly sense of concern for his sister. It sounded as if she *meant* this thirty guys in thirty days stuff. Not even Nyla—with her nagging and her stubbornness and her refusal to let him dominate in Ping-Pong when they were kids—was immune to being hurt by a wacky scheme like that.

Not that Gavin wanted to get all mushy about it.

"Okay." He drew in a breath, frowning. "I think it's a little ambitious, but hey . . . you always were an overachiever. Let me know if any of your twenty-four-hour boyfriends gets out of line. I'll beat the crap out of him for you."

"Sweet, musclehead."

"No prob."

"But I'm not talking about me. I'm talking about—"

"But that thirty guys in thirty days thing is way too much," he interrupted, thinking about it some more. "You'll cramp up. Get dehydrated. Lose perspective. You should scale back a little."

Nyla walloped him with a back issue of the glossy magazine she wrote for. "I said, it's not me! Besides, thirty guys in thirty days is a *big* back off on the original plan. Originally, it was supposed to be fifty-seven."

"Guys? Or days?"

"Both."

"Whew." He couldn't help but grin. "There's not enough Gatorade in the world to fuel up for a sexapaloosa like that."

"It's not about sex," Nyla said. "It's about . . . finding yourself. I *told* Jennifer it was a crazy plan, but would she listen? Noooo. Not until Stephanie and I both—"

Gavin's focus sharpened. "Jennifer?"

She was going to date thirty guys in thirty days?

His sister nodded, looking bewildered. His belly lurched. His stupid heart pounded faster too. Gavin didn't want to give himself away, but . . . damn. *Jennifer.*

He'd been crushing on her since high school.

But she'd never looked twice at him.

"Yes, Jennifer." Nyla sounded exasperated. "Who did you think I was talking ab—"

"Yeah. I'm going to need to move in here with you," Gavin announced. He straightened his spine, then gave the apartment a manly once-over. "Keep an eye on things."

Nyla gazed at him as if he'd just declared his intention to join the ballet team. Club. Huddle. Whatever.

"For safety," he added, lowering his voice.

He scratched his beard stubble for good measure too. It was damned hard to look tough to a person who'd once held him down and clobbered him with his He-Man action figure, just for calling her new Pretty Pony "lame," but he did his best.

"What?" His sister shook her head. She still wore the ballet-team look. "That's crazy. You can't move in here."

He had to. He absolutely had to. He'd never been more

sure of anything, aside from his need to tackle that sweet fifty-footer at Maverick's last spring.

But Nyla wasn't buying it.

And Gavin was about to miss his likeliest chance to get closer to Jennifer. While she was feeling experimental.

After all, *he* could fit in with twenty-nine other guys.

He'd blow them all out of the running. No problem.

And he'd finally get his Jennifer jones out of his system.

Thinking on his feet, Gavin tried to look forlorn. It felt completely unnatural, but it seemed to be working. His sister squinted at him thoughtfully, and her sigh suggested she was weakening. He went on staring outside, macho-style.

Be the strong, silent type, he ordered himself.

Damn, those waves looked good.

"I didn't want to tell you this." Amping up the stakes, he tightened his shoulders and looked away. "But I'm . . . having a hard time right now. My company's having some issues. I could really use a place to crash."

So I can get close to Jennifer.

"Oh Gav." Nyla's voice softened. She levered from her chair to put her arms around him in a big-sisterly hug. "What happened? Did you lose your—"

"I can't talk about it," he choked out.

Jesus, he was a horse's ass to do this to his sister. But if he was going to get into Jennifer's datathon lineup, he needed to act fast. Like now. If he wanted to make any headway with Jennifer, being nearby—even underfoot—was crucial.

Otherwise, she might overlook him again.

"Jeez, Gav. Why didn't you say something before? I thought you were just returning the toaster." She squeezed him tighter, with the same exuberance and caring his whole family sported—when they weren't giving each other a hard time. "Of *course* you can stay here. As long as you need to."

"Thanks. I, uh, don't think it'll take long." Gavin patted Nyla's hair, catapulted back to their days of swimming lessons and Kool-Aid and Pac-Man. He set her at arm's length and mustered a stoic smile. "Do you think Jennifer will mind?"

"Jen? Nah."

"I don't want to interfere with her dating . . . thing. You know: the thirty guys in thirty days, finding-herself routine."

"You won't." His sister waved her hand. "A charging horde of shoe salesmen couldn't put her off track now. Once Jennifer's mind is made up about something, it's made up. Although now that you mention it, it's funny . . ."

Nyla scrutinized him. Gavin had the weird sensation she was measuring him. Evaluating him. Being *surprised* by him.

"What's funny?"

She shook her head. "Nothing . . . it's just that . . . I never realized it before, but you're exactly Jennifer's type."

His heart kicked into high gear again, and the sun-bleached hair on his arms stood on end. "I am?"

Why the hell had no one mentioned this before?

To, oh, he didn't know . . . *Jennifer*, maybe?

"Yeah." Nyla nodded. "We had to debrief Jennifer on all her preferences as part of the wakeboarder-versus-surfer debate last night, and it turns out she definitely has a type."

"A type like me."

"Weirdly enough, yeah. *Exactly* like you. But don't worry. You're safe to carry on your usual life of debauchery and board waxing." His sister breezed to her desk, typed something as though inspired for her article, then grinned at him. "Jennifer's sworn off happy-go-lucky, adorably rumpled surfer types till after her 'experiment' is finished. So, no worries!"

"Awesome." Painfully, Gavin mustered a smile.

"Hey . . ." Nyla glanced to the toaster, then to him. "Whatever happened between you and Carmen? Did she like your surprise?"

He shrugged, feeling less bummed about things than he had when he'd arrived. "It turns out mutual toasting was more of a commitment than Carmen was ready for."

"Awww, Gav." His sister scrunched her nose. "Sorry. Hey,

do you want some distraction?" Nyla's gaze lit on her froufrou cache of spa product samples. With enthusiasm, she snatched one from the array on her desk. "You can help me test out this new take-home exfoliating system with squash-blossom extract and real butter. It's guaranteed to tone, tighten, and refresh—"

He held up both hands to ward her off. "I'll stick with soap and water, thanks."

"Come on. Live a little. Call it the price of admission. You *are* going to be staying here a while, you know. You might as well indulge me in some trials. I need a male subject."

Catching her meaning, Gavin examined the fancy bottles, squat jars, and aqua-colored tubes that comprised Nyla's "homework." She had more *stuff*—girly stuff—than anyone he knew. And she was dedicated to evaluating all of it in painstaking detail. How had he forgotten that about her?

At his hesitation, her eyes lit up. Apparently, Nyla viewed his decision not to bolt immediately as acquiescence. She grabbed another tub of something pink and came toward him.

"You're going to love this line," she enthused. "This prickly pear-and-sagebrush shaving cream is totally—"

"Wait." He stopped her in midadvance. "Just hang on."

She frowned.

"I need to think."

She rolled her eyes.

There were obvious drawbacks to this get-close-to-Jennifer plan, Gavin realized belatedly. Drawbacks that smelled weird, looked even weirder, and would do God only knew what to his skin—not to mention his sense of machismo. Seriously. Prickly pear-and-sagebrush shaving cream? If he wanted to smell like the desert, he'd go roll around in El Cajon. If any of his buds caught him with pink fizzy crap on his face, he'd get a worse hazing than he'd ever had as a grommet.

Then Gavin thought of Jennifer, and it all seemed worth it.

If he could only get her to look twice at him . . .

"Tell you what," Gavin said decisively. "When I get back with my stuff, you can test out whatever you want on me."

To his horror, Nyla almost hopped up and down with glee. Damn, but he hoped the sacrifice would be worth it.

Jennifer. With a little luck, she *liked* pink.

"Right now," he added, "I've got packing to do."

Gavin opened the door, gave the nearby waves a longing look, then went to get the things he needed for an impromptu crash with his sister and his crush.

Ready or not, he was on his way.

"Dakota is right." Jennifer's fourth client of the day, Vanessa, peeked up from beneath her highlighting foils. Her exquisitely groomed brows furrowed in thought as she pondered the blow-by-blow account Jennifer had just given of her night out with Nyla and Stephanie. "You can't be trusted to choose your own thirty men in thirty days. I know you. You'll fall back into your rut for sure."

Unfortunately, that was exactly the conclusion Stephanie and Nyla had come to last night . . . after Jennifer had returned with the surfer stud's—no, the *wakeboarder* stud's— phone number and plans to meet him for smoothies in PB. But come on. Jennifer *had* been feeling the effects of all those kiwi daiquiris. Her lapse of judgment wasn't entirely her fault.

Besides, a wakeboarder was *completely* different from a surfer. Everybody knew that. She was breaking out already.

"That's what I'm *saying*!" Dakota, the salon manager and head stylist, put her hand on her hip. From her station came the smells of hot irons and styling cream. "If you really want to get anything out of this experiment, Jennifer, you'll have to let other people pick your rut-busting dates for you."

"That's brilliant!" Across the salon, Stephanie nodded. "They'll be like blind dates. Only with more variety."

"Ohhh! *I've* got one for you," Vanessa volunteered.

"Me too!" Dakota's client added. "The guy in my—"

"Blind dates? Uh-uh." Jennifer shook her head, needing to put a stop to this idea before it gained momentum. She raised her comb to continue sectioning Vanessa's hair, then grabbed a foil in her most professional manner. "I'm going on a voyage of self-discovery, not humiliation. The last thing I need is—"

"Is *you* choosing your own dates," Dakota said. The client in her chair made a knowing face, adding insult to injury. "You'll only pick the same old, same old, and you know it. If you want to get anything out of this plan of yours, you need to broaden your horizons, for sure."

"Uh-huh," Stephanie and Vanessa chimed in, "that's right."

Jennifer gaped at them. It was bad enough that everyone thought she was incapable of choosing good test-run men. Apparently, they also thought she had infallible loser radar too.

"I *intend* to broaden my horizons!" Jennifer informed the salon at large. Raising her chin, she brushed on some bleach, then folded the foil. "That's the whole point. To broaden my horizons, discover parts of me I've overlooked, and find myself." *And quit freaking out about that lipstick ad.*

"Right. Like you did last night?" Stephanie rolled her eyes. "Those might be your intentions, but trust me. You'll revert to your usual type by day two—"

"And torpedo your whole project," Dakota put in.

"I will not!" Jennifer protested.

Vanessa met her gaze in the mirror. She shook her head. *Poor, delusional loser bait,* her expression said.

"You sound like me before my nose job," she said sorrowfully. "Always rationalizing away the truth."

"I'm *good* at choosing men," Jennifer insisted. "I am."

Her voice carried across the salon, overriding the techno music playing over the state-of-the-art sound system. Tease wasn't terribly busy this early on a weekday, but her announcement was greeted with several chortles anyway.

"Good at choosing men? Hello?" Stephanie wielded her shears with precision as she focused on her client's shoulder-length cut. "Surfer number 227, anyone? You might as well install one of those deli-counter number machines down at Mission Beach, then stand next to it."

Now *that* was just insulting.

"I don't go through men that quickly."

"But you loooove those surfer types," Dakota confirmed.

"I swore off them last night, okay? I did."

Stephanie and Nyla had made her do it. But Jennifer was glad she had. With her usual dating type clouding her vision, she'd never show that stupid lipstick ad—and her resulting quarter-life crisis—who was boss. She'd never find herself.

"There *would* be potential benefits to doing the blind-dating thing, you know," Vanessa cajoled, her head half-covered in foils as she twisted to rejoin the conversation. "Between the five of us, we could offer you a much wider dating pool."

"Of a much greater variety of men," Dakota's client added.

Behind her chair, Jennifer sagged, hands full of foils and brush. From her rolling supply cart, the tang of bleach stung her nose . . . or maybe that was just the truth, finally sinking in.

Was everybody right? Did she need help?

Around her, the salon hummed with activity, stylish with its midcentury modern furnishings and designer lighting scheme. The mirrors reflected the clear San Diego skies and the busy PB street. She'd spent the past six years here, and her coworkers and clients knew her pretty well.

But did they know her well enough to choose her dates?

"If you're reluctant," Dakota prodded, never willing to leave anything well enough alone, "you can always screen your potential blind dates with a haircut. Once they're in that chair, they don't have *any* secrets, and we all know it."

"Comb-overs, weirdos, chronically pomade-addicted poseurs," Stephanie ticked off on her fingers. "None of them get away with it for long, once you slap them in a haircutting cape and start snipping."

Jennifer bit her lip, thinking about it.

"Do it," Dakota urged. "Why not? If nothing else, it'll bring in new business. We can always use clients."

"And gossip fodder." Stephanie grinned. Her gaze shot to

the salon's front windows, caught by a movement there. Her eyes widened. "Hunk alert. Ten o'clock."

Every head swiveled to the front door. It opened to admit a man in beat-up jeans, a black T-shirt, and a tool belt. He paused by the receptionist's station, chatting with Amber, his smile wide and his demeanor casual.

Jennifer watched him too. She couldn't help it.

In offices, women looked forward to the arrival of the UPS man or the FedEx guy. At tease, the stylists eagerly awaited the arrival of their own personal fantasy man: the hunky plumber. Good with his hands, gainfully employed, handy with moving parts . . . Hank the plumber was a necessary part of every week.

At something Amber said, Hank glanced toward the stylists' stations. One thick, dark brow rose in question.

They all froze. There was something about being pinned by that curious, good-with-his-hands gaze that just stopped a woman in her tracks.

Dakota snapped out of it first. She tittered, then waved her comb toward a nearby shampoo bowl, the first in their gleaming black array. "It's that one. A huge clog."

With an agreeable nod, Hank strode across the polished floor. He looked twice as burly up close . . . and a gazillion times more rough-and-tumble when contrasted against the salon's sleek furnishings. He didn't fit in, but he was all the more delicious because of it.

His steady booted footfalls made his low-slung tool belt jangle with a seductive rhythm. They all followed its arresting movements, then, when he turned to examine the problem, focused on its natural follow-up: Hank butt. One hundred percent Grade A fantastic.

"Mmmm, mighty fine," Stephanie murmured.

"Worth every minute of stuffing hair down the drain," Dakota agreed, ogling along with her client. "Every week."

They kept their voices low, hidden beneath the clang of Hank's tools as he grabbed something metallic, industrial, and efficient looking, then went to work beneath the shampoo bowl. None of them would admit to occasionally meandering over to that sink and cramming a handful of clippings down the hatch. Not while they could share the group illusion that Hank's visits were a natural outgrowth of the salon's work-days.

"I don't know why this one's such a troublemaker." Hank swiped his hand over his forehead, giving them all a devilish grin. The tool in his hand looked intimidating and earthy. His taut biceps merely looked incredible. "I swear I unclogged this same S-trap last week."

"Maybe we just enjoy seeing you, Hank," Jennifer mused.

Dakota kicked her. Then, apparently called from her Zen-like contemplation of Hank's backside, she glanced from Jennifer to the plumber and back again. Her expression turned devious.

Uh-oh. *That* couldn't bode well.

"Or maybe that sink just gets a lot of use," Stephanie said. Then *she* too, gave Hank a measured look and glanced at Jennifer. A smile quirked the corners of her mouth.

Double uh-oh. If Stephanie and Dakota were teaming up . . .

The clients in their chairs exchanged conspiratorial glances. Vanessa even grinned unabashedly, Botox be damned.

"Say, Hank . . ." Dakota tossed her hair, then focused on the plumber's impressive shoulders as he went on working. "Are you seeing anyone special right now?"

"Dakota!" Jennifer whispered. "You're married!"

"But *you're* not." Eyes sparkling, her boss awaited an an-swer. "And he's perfect for your plan. If *I* can't have him, somebody else might as well."

Hank dragged over a bucket, glanced up at them, then wrenched one of the pipes beneath the sink. Beneath his T-shirt, his back muscles rippled with the movement.

"Nope. Not seeing anybody," he said.

Even his voice was sexy. Deep and sure. Jennifer felt a little tingle of anticipation. She'd never dated anybody so blue col-lar before. Hank's hands were clean, but his jeans were smudged with dark swipes, suggesting a healthy appreciation of hard work. She liked a man who wasn't afraid of getting dirty.

"Wow." Stephanie ladled on her best wide-eyed-blonde impression. "Neither is Jennifer. What a coincidence!"

Hank looked directly at her. His eyes were nice too.

Jennifer resisted the urge to blurt a denial. She didn't like being trapped this way—but if a girl was going to get bamboozled into blind dating her boss's secret plumber fantasy man, the only thing to do, she guessed, was roll with it.

"You two would make a lovely couple," Vanessa said.

The whole salon seemed to beam at them. Hank rose, wiping his hands on the seat of his jeans. Those were pretty nice hands. Capable looking. Jennifer figured she could do worse for her second finding-herself date. But first . . .

"Do you surf?" she blurted.

Hank looked surprised. "Surf? Hell, no. The only thing I want between me and the water is a fishing rod. Or maybe a boat." He sauntered nearer, his gaze dipping over her in an unmistakably macho once-over. "You like boats?"

Jennifer pictured herself on whatever boat Hank had in mind—probably a fast-flying speedboat—and envisioned a whole new persona to try on. Pigtails, bubblegum, cut-off denim shorts, and a halter top. Maybe even a bandanna in her hair, for that casual, blue-collar-dating vibe. Yeah. She could do this.

"I love boats," she said, unable to hold back a smile.

They made a date for the following morning.

She'd have sworn the whole salon cheered her on.

"Okay." Watching Hank leave, Jennifer shrugged. She turned to her coworkers and clients. "Let's do this. I've got twenty-eight more men to get through, so . . . bring on the blind dates!"

Chapter 3

Choose accessories wisely. Yes, you should pamper yourself—but remember, unexpected irritants lurk every-where . . . even in the most appealing packages! Before being seduced by promises of a smooth glide and effort-less finish, check for undesirable elements such as men-thol, peppermint, and excessive alcohol content before applying to your skin.
> —Tips courtesy of "The Girls' Guide to Getting Smooth" (Goddess Razors, Inc.)

"Hey, Nyla!" Jennifer surged into her apartment, glad to be home at last, bearing her handbag, a new cell phone, and a red bandana cadged from the boardwalk seller down the block. She wanted to be prepared for tomorrow's stint as Blue Collar Jennifer. "You'll never guess what I—"

She stopped, staring in puzzlement at the two surfboards propped in their tiny foyer. Beach sand puddled at the short-boards' bottom edges, crusty against the tiled floor. They smelled of saltwater and surfwax, rousing a million memories of boys Jennifer had chased, dated, and been dumped by.

Good thing she'd sworn off surfers.

"I've got it all planned out," she went on, looking for her

roommate as she slung her handbag from her shoulder. More than likely, there was a good explanation for those boards. In the meantime, she wanted to share her news. "The wake-boarder was a bust—he's headed to Waikiki for a competition next week—but everybody at the salon came up with an idea for me. Nyla?"

She dropped her handbag on the sofa and almost smashed the acoustic guitar already occupying the cushy space. Befuddled, Jennifer blinked. Nyla didn't play the guitar, and neither did Jennifer. Although she had dated a coffeehouse musician once.

Too jumped-up on the events of the day to consider it for long, Jennifer headed to the kitchen. She was starving. One smoothie, even with wheatgrass, didn't exactly constitute dinner.

"So I'm going to have all these blind dates," she called toward the bathroom. Jeez, it was unsatisfying to share her news like this. Probably Nyla was busy applying a beauty-treatment mask made up of coffee grounds, cinnamon, and milkfat. For the past few years, her spa products had trended toward the edible. "I got a new cell phone with unlimited text-messaging minutes, just for my blind-date project, then stopped at Sephora for some lip gloss—"

There was a man in her kitchen.

Or, more accurately, there was a man rummaging through her fridge in her kitchen. All she could see of him were board shorts, the back of a T-shirt, bare legs, and one long, sinewy arm as he peered into the depths of their Frigidaire, but he was unmistakably male. That arm told a story all its own.

"What flavor?" he asked, his voice muffled.

"Huh?"

"What flavor lip gloss?"

He straightened, glancing over his shoulder at her. His hair looked sun-streaked and tousled, his features blunt and affable and familiar. Something amber-colored, long-necked, and smooth gleamed in his hand. He offered it to her.

A beer. Automatically, Jennifer accepted it.

"I was just stocking up." He angled one shoulder toward the refrigerator, then snagged another beer for himself. The fridge closed with a nudge. "You girls don't have anything but salad dressing and Diet Coke in there."

"We eat out a lot."

He nodded. "Awesome."

That was when it hit her. *Gavin.* This was Nyla's little brother, Gavin. She hadn't seen him for a while—for some reason he'd quit visiting shortly after she and Nyla had gotten this place together—but the family resemblance was unmistakable. So was the easygoing smile on his face.

It all made sense. The surfboards. The guitar.

The six-foot-whatever of sun-burnished man looking at her right now. He seemed perfectly happy to let her realize what was going on at her own pace. But then Gavin had always been that way. Happy. Easy. Perfect.

Perfect enough to incite a *major* crush on him.

Jennifer had kept *hers* going for years now. Too bad Gavin had never noticed it . . . or her. He'd never looked twice at her, much to her undying mortification.

"So." He reached for her beer, chivalrously opened it with an efficient twist of his wiry forearm, then handed it back. Apparently he'd grown up and turned gallant. "What flavor?"

She tasted. "Ummm, it's . . . beer . . . flavor?"

His smile, wide and sunny, made her heart stutter. Stupid, *stupid* crush. She ought to be past this stuff by now.

"Of lip gloss," he explained, leaning companionably against the counter. "I like cherry. Do they still make that kind?"

Frankly, it was hard to remember with him looking at her that way. All friendliness and intensity and interest. Gavin's knack for conversation—for *connecting*—was a major component of her interest in him, Jennifer realized. Most men couldn't be bothered to look higher than her collarbones.

While Gavin . . . couldn't be bothered to look lower.

Damn it.

"I don't think it's flavored. It's berry-colored, though, so maybe it's got a flavor. I don't know." Wow, she was some kind of articulate tonight. Even worse, Jennifer couldn't seem to quit staring into Gavin's eyes. They were blue, with funny speckles of gold. Like sunset on the ocean. "Where's, uh . . ." She forgot her question. "Where's Nyla?"

"Crashed. She was out late shopping for a bikini."

Ahhh. "New assignment?"

He nodded. "Some resort opening in Monterey. She thinks twelve inches of different-colored spandex will put her under-cover. I didn't want to disillusion her."

He winked. More beer. Jennifer watched his tanned throat flex as he swallowed, feeling stupidly transfixed. His fingers on the bottle were mesmerizing. Long . . . nicely shaped . . . strong.

"Don't you like yours?" Gavin nodded at her bottle.

Jennifer snapped out of it. What was the matter with her? Gavin was her roommate's baby brother. Her *best friend's* baby brother. What was she, some kind of perv?

Except . . . Wow. He'd done a lot of growing up lately.

And he was exactly her type. *Exactly.*

Had been, in fact, for years and years and . . .

"It's great. Fine. I'm just"—she gestured toward the other half of the two-bedroom apartment—"really tired. Long day. I should be getting to bed pretty soon."

Except she didn't move. *Get out of here!* her brain com-manded, but her body wanted to linger and apparently it was calling the shots. Jennifer leaned her hip against the counter.

She'd almost have sworn Gavin looked there. At her hip.

Then he lowered his gaze to her legs, bared in the swishy black skirt she'd worn to work today so she wouldn't have to change for her smoothie date with Mr. Wakeboarder.

If Gavin thought it was weird that she'd announced her in-tentions of sleeping—only to stay planted in place—he didn't let on. If anything, he seemed to understand. To want to hang out with her too. Which didn't make sense at all.

"Yeah, I'm like that too—insomnia." His tone was husky

and confiding. Intimate. Especially in the darkened kitchen. "Some nights, I feel as if I'm the only person in the whole universe, you know?"

Jennifer stared. "Me too."

Something passed between them then, some kind of connection or understanding or . . . yearning. It felt positively seductive. This was what she got, Jennifer guessed, for swilling beer after a busy day of rut-busting, lipstick-ad-defying date planning.

Still it felt nice. Really nice.

"That's when I grab my board and head out." Gavin nodded toward the foyer. "Night surfing is unreal. So peaceful."

Oh yeah. He was a surfer.

Strictly off-limits, if her plan was going to go forward.

And Jennifer *really* wanted it to go forward. Her whole sense of self-identity hinged on it. Disappointment surged.

Inanely, she nodded. "So . . . yeah. Good seeing you again, Gavin." Another nod. "I'll see you around, okay? Okay."

Without waiting for his reply, she set down her beer, then headed for her room. Intent on . . . escape, really.

"Hey, good night, then," Gavin called after her, blissfully unaware of her need to get away. "Thanks for the company."

Without thinking, Jennifer paused. She glanced over her shoulder, drawn to do so by . . . curiosity. Sure, that was it. Curiosity. It wasn't that she wanted another look at Gavin, something to remember him by in case he made himself scarce—again—for another few years.

He lifted his beer in a salute.

She caught herself smiling. That *thing* zinged between them again, heady and thrilling and almost irresistible.

When had Gavin grown into such a hottie?

Why had she promised not to date any more surfers?

Either way, it was too late to stop now. She told him good night, knowing he could let himself out, and trailed away. Her dorky parting wave probably explained a lot, in retrospect, about why Gavin had ignored her—and her crush—all these years.

Men like him could pick and choose from *non*geeks.

Jennifer's only saving grace, she decided as she closed her bedroom door and sank against it in relief, was that Gavin didn't know she wanted him. Nyla didn't know Jennifer wanted him. Everybody was oblivious to her feelings for him.

With a little luck, Jennifer could keep it that way.

At least until her dating experiment was done.

Gavin awakened with a sense of urgency. Also with a feeling that he'd slept on something hard, pointy, and—surprisingly, given the autoaroused state of his body south of the beltline—*not* capable of making the earth move.

For him or anybody else.

Ignoring his usual morning hard-on, he rolled sideways to investigate. Half the covers slid with him. Everything Nyla had provided him with for sleeping on her sofa was flowery, lacy, and freakishly slippery—as though it was made of lingerie material. While Gavin was as much of a lingerie fan as the next red-blooded Victoria's Secret catalog connoisseur, he sure as hell didn't want to sleep beneath a gigantic teddy.

That stuff was made for looking at, after all.

Then for taking off. Sloooowly.

After some squinty-eyed groping beneath the sofa cushions, he came up with the pointy, hard-edged culprit—a snack-sized box of Chips Ahoy! that had been wedged in place—just as Jennifer strolled into the room. In the sunlight, she looked fresh and tawny-haired and delectable. Also, surprised as hell to find him there.

" 'Morning." The word emerged as a croak. His insomnia rap hadn't been a joke last night. Gavin was as big a night owl as they came, whether he wanted to be or not. "How's it hanging?"

His efforts to be more sociable earned him a look.

One of *those* looks. Women specialized in them.

This one said, ". . . the hell? Get off my sofa."

Then Jennifer spotted the cookies in his hand. Her cheeks flushed guiltily, turning almost as red as the bandana in her hair. Interesting. She had a sweet tooth.

Plus, apparently, a downright puritanical resistance to indulging it. That was surprising.

Gavin offered the Chips Ahoy! anyway. "Cookie?"

He added his best, most awake grin, hoping to sweeten the deal. It probably looked pretty lopsided and ridiculous this early in the AM, but he had an opening and he was seizing it.

"No, thanks. That's not a very nutritious breakfast." Jennifer paused, actually managing to seem as though she *hadn't* noshed cookies in secret, probably while couch-potatoing to *The O.C.* She was quite a woman. "But enjoy. I'm late for a boating date."

A date? Already? Jesus, it couldn't be much past seven o'clock. Even the seagulls were napping. Probably.

Gavin didn't want to let her get away. He searched for a likely topic of conversation—not easy while Jennifer stood there absently adjusting her halter top—and came up with . . .

"Uh, isn't it kind of early for a date?"

"No." She popped her gum. "Not if you're seeing a very studly, very eligible plumber who has his own speedboat."

Damn it. "Seriously?"

She nodded, looking like a sexed-up version of the girl next door. Especially her hair, with its twin pigtails.

He liked it. Liked *her*. All of her.

And he would have liked her to stay a while—at least until he was coherent enough to muster a more tempting incentive than chocolate chip cookies. He knew he had it in him.

Unfortunately, it wasn't awake yet. Gavin frowned. "I've got to tell you, I'm not sure you're the plumber-dating type."

It was exactly the wrong thing to say.

"Well, I'm about to find that out, aren't I?"

Jerking her chin high, Jennifer sailed into the kitchen with her denim cut-offs swinging, probably following the aromatic trail of life-giving coffee Gavin suddenly detected. But before she did, before she left, Jennifer did something else. Something that gave him hope.

She ogled his bare chest, revealed by his droopy covers.

Then she ogled his naked legs, hanging over the stumpy sofa. Then she ogled his bed-headed hair, his face, and his mouth. *His mouth!* With—he felt compelled to point out to himself with a sense of jubilation—clear and evident interest.

So long as she did that, Gavin knew he had a chance. Never mind Jennifer's disappearing act last night. Never mind her nose-in-the-air routine today. That was all in the past, and Gavin was not a man who got overly hung up on the past. He believed in the here and now. In the *right* here and *right* now.

Jennifer was interested in him, he realized.

Or at least a part of her was. That was all that really mattered. From this moment forward, it was up to Gavin to ensure that the rest of her got in on the action too.

He couldn't wait to get started.

"I hope you don't mind about Gavin." Nyla propped her foot on the closed toilet lid, applying salt-and-Tabasco anti-cellulite body scrub to her thigh. "He's going through some issues with work and needed a place to crash for a while."

"No problem." Jennifer reached for her smoky-gray eyeliner. *Unless one of you discovers my crush on him.*

Which would completely wreck her self-discovery plan.

"Good. I told him you'd be cool with it."

"I am. Totally." *Unless I can't quit staring at him.*

Which was definitely not helping her self-discovery plan.

Like this morning. The last thing Jennifer had expected to find on their sofa had been a crashed-out Gavin, all casual nakedness and miles of muscles. The long, lean kind of muscles that surfers had, fit for paddling out against the waves.

She'd barely been able to drag her gaze away. The covers had slid, the sunlight had shifted . . . The view had been spectacular. And Gavin's grin! Apparently, he woke up as cheerful and uninhibited as he always was.

Trying not to think about it, Jennifer edged closer to the vanity mirror. She squinted, smudging the line she'd drawn. Tonight's blind date was with an ad exec who worked downtown, so she was going for a sultry, sophisticated look.

It was tricky to pull off after a full day's work at tease. She'd have to start scheduling these things for lunchtimes.

"I'm just a big softie at heart," Nyla said, wiping her hands clean. "When Gavin gave me that fake macho routine of his, I couldn't say no. I could tell he needed me."

Jennifer fought, and lost, an urge to find out more.

"Did he tell you what happened? With his job?"

Nyla shook her head. "He was too upset to talk about it. But I know he's been doing this pool-cleaning gig for a while now, so most likely it has something to do with that."

"Pool cleaning? I thought he went pro years ago, and that was why he wasn't around much." Jennifer kept her voice low, so Gavin wouldn't overhear. Although with his guitar strumming in the next room, that seemed unlikely. "But it's probably pretty tough to make it on the pro circuit, I guess."

"Pro? Surfing?" Nyla arched her brows. "Gavin's not a pro—strictly amateur. He only goes out for fun. I mean, don't get me wrong. He's good enough to turn pro for sure, but . . ."

She shrugged, giving a "What can you do?" look.

"But . . . what?" Jennifer prodded.

"But he's always had other interests. Gavin's never been big on playing by the rules."

For an instant, Jennifer felt a heart stopping yen to follow his lead. To go her own way and damn the consequences.

How did Gavin do it?

"So." Nyla elbowed her, grinning. "How'd it go this morning? With Hank the hunky plumber?"

"Mmmm, not that great."

"Why not? What happened?"

"Turns out I'm prone to seasickness. Especially in a small

boat on the open water." Jennifer made a face, then reached for her lip gloss. Two men down . . . twenty-eight to go. "Blue Collar Jennifer is strictly a landlubber."

"But what about Hank? Are you going to see him again?"

For a moment, Jennifer thought she heard Gavin's guitar music stop. But the chords picked up again right away.

She shrugged. "After my experiment? Maybe."

But the truth was, once she'd found Gavin on their sofa, once she'd experienced his husky good morning and his teasing invitation to cookie-noshing, she'd had trouble thinking about anything else. Including Hank's renowned mechanical abilities.

"You should," Nyla urged. "Stephanie told me he's totally gorgeous. And sweet too. He sounds amazing."

"Yeah. I guess so." But he was no Gavin.

Oh hell. Deliberately, Jennifer plastered on a smile. "In the meantime, blind date number 3. Don't wait up!"

Not meeting Nyla's bound-to-be-knowing gaze in the mirror, Jennifer checked her hair—now ironed straight—and closed her handbag. She popped an Altoid from the economy-sized, blind-date-designated tin she'd bought, then headed into the living room to grab her new cell phone from its place beside the answering machine. One short search for her keys, then . . .

"I'm off." She paused, waiting . . . For Gavin to notice her cocktail dress and slammin' heels? If that was her motivation, she was sorely disappointed. "See you later."

Gavin glanced up, still strumming. He looked as puzzled by her farewell as she felt giving it. Jennifer stood there awkwardly for a second, then deliberately checked her cell.

The guitar music stuttered. She glanced up again.

"Wow, you look incredible. Is all that for the plumber?"

He gestured at her dress and shoes—or maybe, Jennifer thought crazily, at her hips and legs, liking what he saw.

Either way, the appreciation in Gavin's gaze made her feel all glowy. Whether he was enjoying *her* or her fashion sense didn't quite matter. He'd noticed her! She suddenly felt like doing a pirouette, or maybe just Vogueing.

God, she really *was* a geek around him.

"Nope, it's for Andy, an advertising exec I met."

Gavin gave a noncommittal sound. "Don't trust a guy who lies for a living." Then he went back to playing.

Jennifer gaped at his bent head, with its tousled hair and intent posture. Where did he get off giving her advice? It wasn't as if he was offering *himself* as a substitute date.

Whoa. Spooked by the very notion, she jangled her keys and headed out the door. Her old surfer dating rut was obviously calling her name, and Jennifer felt determined not to answer. Whatever else happened, that lipstick ad was *not* going to win.

Ordinarily, Jennifer liked sushi. Maguro, Susuki, even Unagi . . . they were all delicious. Give her a tasty plate and a glass of Hakutsuru draft, and she was good to go. San Diego had no shortage of fine dining options, but the dodgy coastal sushi bar Andy the Advertiser agreed to meet her at had a decidedly slimy atmosphere. So, unfortunately, did Andy.

Jennifer didn't get it. He hadn't seemed all that bad while he'd been in her chair at tease. Then, he'd mostly e-mailed nonstop on his Blackberry, too in demand to take time out for a mere trim. Occasionally, he'd glanced up, examined his reflection in the mirror, and flashed her a smile.

He'd also left a big tip. Generally speaking, generous tipping boded well for a person's inner self, so she'd let herself be swayed when Andy had asked her to dinner.

"Do you have a big deal going on? A new ad campaign?" she asked, eyeing his hands-free headset. It dented his perfectly styled hair, but Jennifer tried to overlook that. "We could do this another time, if that would work better for—"

"Are you kidding me? And let you miss out on the complete Andy Experience? We're seeing this through, baby."

Oookay. Maybe he was a *Swingers*-style indie movie fan.

Hence the "baby." Maybe sounding like a cheesy Sinatra imitator was the Next Big Thing. She didn't know. But Andy *did* look the part of a successful downtown executive, and Jennifer wanted to give him a fair shot. He was probably just nervous.

Across the table, Andy grabbed her hand. "Romantic, right? We've practically got the whole place to ourselves."

"Thanks to that pesky C- health-code grade in the window." She mustered a smile. "Yay, bureaucracy."

"People are like sheep." Andy waved dismissively, giving her a toothy grin. "They follow the pack. But not me."

Jennifer felt pretty sure sheep traveled in herds, not packs. But this was supposed to be fun, so she let it slide.

Andy's phone pealed. "Gotta get this, baby." He snapped his fingers to summon the waiter. "Yo, order me a platter of something pricey, okay? I'm expensing this."

She stared. He was expensing their date?

Soon enough, Jennifer found out why. When Andy wasn't on his cell phone "networking," he spent the whole time—between ravenous bites of food—selling her.

On himself. On his work credentials, his career trajectory, his penchant for traveling to exotic locales. Expensed, of course. He just didn't shut up.

When he paused for breath, she leaped into the fray.

"You *do* realize this"—she gestured between them—"is a date, right? I thought we were supposed to be—"

His bark of laughter cut her off. "You've gotta get the appetizer before you sample the goods! Right, baby?" Andy's "seductive" look made her cringe. "I haven't even started on the personal details. Feelin' hungry yet?"

Ugh. How had she gotten into this?

Andy pointed at her untouched food. "Because if you're not going to eat that—"

She regarded her C- plate with dismay.

"We could skip all this chitchat." He guffawed. "You look pretty sexy tonight actually. Even better than I'd hoped from my little, uh, preview this afternoon."

He leered openly at her breasts. Too late, Jennifer remembered that he'd done the same thing while she'd trimmed his hair. True, they were right there, unavoidably in the way while she worked. But most decent men tried to be respectful.

"Besides," Andy continued loudly, "the way I see it, somebody like you probably isn't all that interested in conversation anyway. Am I right?"

She could *not* have heard him correctly.

"Somebody like me?"

"You know," He chuckled. "A beautician. Cute but dumb, no big goals except to finish beauty school and make big tips." A smarmy smirk. "I've got a really, really big *tip* for you."

Ohmigod. She *did* have loser radar.

She'd chosen this guy herself, on impulse, and look where it had gotten her. Botulism on a plate with Mr. Me-Me-Me.

From here on out, she would definitely let other people—any people!—choose her dates. But for now . . .

"Tell me, Andy." Jennifer leaned back and steepled her fingers, completely fed up. Not in the literal sense, unfortunately for her growling stomach. "You're a smart guy. How much do *you* know about the technical and engineering aspects of performing spherical geometry on an imperfect sphere?"

He stopped in midbite. "Huh?"

"Because that's what I specialize in," Jennifer informed him sweetly. "Artistic and creative spherical geometry."

"You wha . . . ?"

"As a hairstylist, I spend all day cutting three-dimensional shapes on three-dimensional heads. To be specific, thanks to thousands of hours of training and experience, I have the expertise to create two-dimensional cuts that collapse into another shape and still make people look fabulous. Do you really think *you* have the brains to do that?"

He gawked at her, openmouthed.

"No? I didn't *think* so."

The only thing more satisfying than tossing down some cash for her share of the dinner bill and heading outside for some fresh air, Jennifer discovered next, was spotting a familiar fast-food sign three blocks away.

Dodging between two parked Sunshine Pool Cleaning trucks, she headed in that direction. Right now, a Whopper with cheese sounded just about perfect. So did anything except a blowhard ad exec and his "sophisticated" seafood.

Three down . . . and just about a million to go.

When she told him the whole story, Gavin laughed out loud.

"Spherical *what*? Holy Brainiac, Batman. You'd better slow down before my head explodes." His admiring gaze focused on her face, then meandered to her lap . . . where the rest of her drippy Whopper lay nestled on its crumpled wrapper. "I always knew you were smart. That guy deserved a comedown."

He snagged a French fry, companionably munching it in his place beside her on the chipped concrete seawall. Jennifer didn't know why it seemed so natural to talk to him. She only knew that when she'd trouped up the boardwalk on her way home—Burger King bag in hand and disappointment in her heart—spying Gavin coming out of the surf had been like seeing an old friend.

He'd had his shortboard under his arm, carrying it by the rail with the leash flopping behind. Watching him walk toward her in the sunset, all easy athleticism and wetsuited joviality, had loosened something inside her that Jennifer hadn't been aware of holding tight.

Of course, watching him change out of his wetsuit, all gleaming skin and flexing muscles, had tightened another part of her altogether. Despite Gavin's gallant care not to flash her, Jennifer had *accidentally* gotten an eyeful anyway. But she wasn't going to think about that now.

Feeling better in spite of her newly activated unrequited crush—not to mention the naked-Gavin flashbacks whooshing through her brain—she took another bite of her Whopper. She kicked off her sandals and let her feet dangle from the seawall, watching the city lights twinkle along the coast. The warm off-shore wind ruffled her hair, hauling the disappointments of the day out to sea.

Ahhh . . . Life was better out here. Maybe that was why she liked hanging out with surfers.

"Either way, it looks as if Sophisticated Jennifer is a bust." She swabbed up some ketchup and sucked it from her finger, unconcerned with looking sultry for Gavin's sake. She already knew he wasn't interested in her. "Maybe I'll have better luck with Sea World Jenny tomorrow. My next date is with an aquatic trainer who works at the park."

"Hmmm, you're diverse, I'll give you that."

"What I am is desperate." Jennifer gave him an honest look. "If I don't make some kind of sense of my life . . ."

Gavin watched her. "If you don't . . . then what?"

She hadn't thought of it that way. "I'm not sure."

"I mean, what's the rush?" His gaze was kind, his eyes dark in the twilight. "You've got a lot going for you already."

She smiled at him. "Nyla's been tutoring you."

At that, Gavin looked aghast. Murmuring a denial, he reached for the Baja-style pullover he'd left on the seawall after changing out of his wetsuit. He dragged its colorful wool over his head, letting the hood flop down his back.

"Pretty much, I do what I want," Gavin said. "No matter what Nyla, or anybody else, says. It's not easy, but it's worth it in the end. Worth it to look at myself straight-on every day without regrets."

She regarded him curiously. "For a guy who's having career issues, you seem pretty upbeat."

Gavin's smile flashed. "Actually, things are looking up."

"How can you say that? You're sleeping on your sister's sofa, you've got work problems, the French fries are gone . . ."

He seemed momentarily discomfited by the fry shortage, but it didn't last. Gavin shrugged, then wadded up her empty wrapper. He pitched it into the nearest shore-side trash can.

"I've also got plenty of time to surf. To play guitar." He

nudged her with his shoulder, bringing unexpected heat to her chilly arm. "To hang out with you. What's not to like?"

"Oh, I don't know, unemployment, homelessness—"

"You don't get it, do you?" His interested gaze whisked over her, calm and carefree. "Life is like surfing. You've just got to let it flow. If you try to control it, it'll fall apart on you every time."

Jennifer shook her head. "'Letting it flow' only leaves you washed out—at a time when everybody else has already hit solid ground."

"Nah." His voice was easy, sure. "It only looks that way from the outside. Trust me."

Exasperated, she stared at him. This *feeling* of hers, of having her whole life happen by accident, was hardly as Zen as Gavin's philosophy made it out to be. She didn't like it.

"Well, I guess I've had enough of getting tossed around in the soup." The surfer expression—referring to mushy white-water—seemed to make sense to him in a way her other explanations hadn't. "I'm sick of getting sidelined, of waiting for the next thing to carry me along. From here on out, I'm taking charge."

"Okay, sure." Gavin's thoughtful look roamed over her face, giving her a crazy, fluttery thrill. He touched her hand, their palms flattened together against the cold concrete seawall. "I get it. Can I just recommend one thing first?"

Jennifer nodded. *Here it comes. Some sort of Buddhist-mentality, surfer-sage, New Age mantra about getting "loose."*

"While you're doing all that," Gavin said, "keep this in mind too."

He slid his hand over her cheek, his fingers warm and deft in her hair. Then he leaned nearer and kissed her.

The first touch of his mouth felt electric; the second, seductive. By the time he pulled away, looking at her through dark and somehow needful eyes, Jennifer felt limp.

And taut. And elated, all at the same time.

Wow. What the . . . ?

"If you forget that," he said, his voice as rumbling and familiar and appealing as ever, "I can arrange a repeat."

"Uhhh . . . I, uhhh . . ."

Gavin's smile flashed again, making her wonder if he'd meant that remarkable kiss at all. But before Jennifer could ask, he slid from the seawall, picked up his board and wetsuit, and strode away toward home.

Chapter 4

Once you've assembled everything, proceed slowly. Modern technology makes it easy to get very close, very quickly, but remember to use careful strokes! For best results, be sure to apply even pressure. And no matter how tempted you may be to rush, take your time. You'll be oh so glad you did.
                    —Tips courtesy of "The Girls' Guide to Getting
                                    Smooth" (Goddess Razors, Inc.)

From there on, Jennifer's days took on a distinct—if bizarre— rhythm. Every day she worked her shift at tease, as usual, and she went out with Stephanie and Nyla whenever she could, keeping them updated on her project. But at least once a day she fielded a potential blind-date candidate too.

Their exchange typically went something like this: A man would wander into the salon, sometimes stiffly, sometimes defensively, sometimes filled with cocksure certainty, and other times twittering with nervousness. He would peek furtively past the furnishings to the bustling salon floor—scoping out a preview—then ask for Jennifer. (A few scaredy cat souls bailed out at this point—much to Amber's chagrin.) Then, after a short wait, he would find himself in Jennifer's chair, draped and shampooed and defenseless.

Just to level the playing field, her gambit was always the same: a friendly smile, coupled with, "How would you like your hair cut today?"

The various answers were telling.

"Counterclockwise," said the rock-climbing doctor suggested by her elderly neighbor. His precision—and appealing sense of manual dexterity—earned him a "Why not?" first date.

"Stop when you get to my ears," said the sculptor, recommended by her dentist, with an exhibit at Balboa Park. His sense of humor—coupled with his avant-garde joie de vivre and his trendy-nerd eyeglasses—merited a first date too.

"So people won't recognize me," said the cable guy suggested by her friendly local bartender. After a few more minutes, he confided that he'd been abducted by aliens and wanted to throw them off the track "for next time." While his story made for good laughs over mojitos that night, Jennifer thought it would be better *not* to volunteer a follow-up date.

"I thought this was the self-service chair," said the affable coffeehouse barista recommended by Stephanie—his eyes wide and trusting. Jennifer fixed him up with Stephanie—his obvious soul mate—instead and moved on to the next contender.

All in all, the predate (discounted) haircut turned out to be an excellent maneuver in her search for (nonsurfer) blind-date material. But it was only one item in her arsenal. After the haircut came the next crucial consideration in Jennifer's evaluation: tips.

It started out innocently enough. After the sushi fiasco with Mr. Big Tipper turned Mr. No Way, Jennifer began refusing cash tips from her fix-ups. She didn't want to be swayed by a candidate's perceived largesse, or lack of it.

But her potential blind dates were craftier than that, and they refused to be dissuaded. Over the next couple of weeks, Jennifer discovered "tips" of all kinds left at her station. Business cards, matchbooks with phone numbers scrawled inside them. Toupee tape mementoes. Even, unforgettably, a strip of foil-wrapped Trojan Magnums . . . size XL.

"*Call him,*" Dakota urged unabashedly.

"At least he practices safe sex," Stephanie prodded.

But Jennifer only dropped all her "keepsakes" into a designated tip jar and went on to the next blind date. She didn't have time to ruminate over the potentialities of her whacked-out tips. Because everybody and their mother knew *somebody* Jennifer ought to add to her blind-dating roster.

Her cell phone beeped with calls and text messages. At home, her answering machine overflowed with suggestions and "finds" and follow-up calls. It seemed that plenty of people wanted to vicariously blind date through Jennifer.

Once she fully caved in to getting fixed up, she had no trouble lining up a date per day. And although none of her chosen man-cessories turned out to be the key to unlocking her authentic identity, at least not so far, there was a lot of satisfaction in taking control of her quarter-life crisis at last. *Take that, lipstick ad!*

As a bonus, several of her dates did unwittingly help her to weed out the absolutely, no-freaking-way options too.

For instance, she learned that she wasn't Sea World Jenny, happy feeder of fish to the park's dolphins—much to the disappointment of Dolph (no pun intended), the aquatic trainer. She wasn't librarian-chic Jennifer, much to the Dewey-decimal dismay of Jeremy, the bookworm bookstore employee. And she definitely wasn't Jen², the hyperfashionista perfect match for "M" ("Just like P.Diddy," he'd told her, "only without the Diddy."), the budding fashion designer from LA.

After two-and-a-half heady weeks, though, Jennifer found her enthusiasm waning for her finding-herself dating project. She still went on dates, but she enjoyed her hilarious postdate recap sessions with Gavin even more. She still decked herself out in test-mode outfits, trying to discover which date-inspired personas suited her best, but she savored Gavin's appreciative and funny reactions to her getups even more.

She still kissed several of her dates good night, but she reminisced about Gavin's surprising surf-side kiss even more . . . and yearned for a repeat too.

Despite their growing closeness, though, despite their flirtatious talks and shared-apartment intimacy and casual get-togethers, Gavin didn't make another move. Not overtly, at least. Jennifer was stuck in limbo between wanting him, resisting him, and sticking to her plan. It drove her crazy.

What he did with the better part of his days, she wasn't sure. But when she prepped for a date, Gavin was there, playing his guitar and making her pirouette for a final inspection before leaving. When she came home afterward, Gavin was there, relaxed from surfing and smelling of the sea, with beers in hand for each of them. And when she woke in the morning, he was there, drowsy and naked and ridiculously tempting.

Didn't he know what the sight of fantastic abs like his could *do* to a girl? Didn't he realize what kinds of fantasies his smiles and touches and heated looks caused?

If Jennifer hadn't known better, she'd have sworn Gavin was trying to seduce her . . . with humor and understanding and a smokin' hot bod. But that was silly. Or maybe it was just wishful thinking. Because Nyla had told her brother about Jennifer's vow to swear off surfers, and she knew he respected her wishes. If anything was going to happen between them, Jennifer knew, it would have to start with her.

The question was: did she dare risk her whole sense of self-awareness, just for another taste of Gavin? Did she dare blow off her plan, just to indulge her longtime crush?

Did she dare not to?

Gavin sprawled on the sofa, immobilized by Nyla's latest spa-treatment test, his cell phone to his ear. Staying at his sister's apartment was seriously starting to complicate his life, in more ways than one.

"Just handle it the best you can, brah," he said in a low tone—the closest he came to furtive. "I'll try to tackle a few of the regular clients myself, just to pick up the slack. In the meantime . . . I'm still kind of tied up here."

He listened as Bobby, one of the most hardworking people

he knew, kicked off a monologue about the latest in pool service. Before long, Gavin was knee-deep in a discussion about pH tests, in-line chlorinators, and the complications of expensive underwater fiber-optic lighting. He couldn't be caught talking like this, but Bobby was a good guy. Gavin didn't want to leave him hanging any more than he already had.

Jennifer sailed past, fortunately not looking at him, then stepped out the creaky front door. Moments later she returned, carrying a copy of the *Union-Tribune* under her arm, giving Gavin just enough time to end his phone call without making her suspicious.

Wearing track pants and a tank top—an ensemble closest to the real her, he'd learned—Jennifer flopped down on a chair. She flipped over the newspaper, quickly becoming absorbed by something on the back page.

Gavin grinned. He didn't know anybody who read that way—back to front. But Jennifer always did. It was uniquely her.

He watched her, idiotically entranced by the way her mouth puckered as she browsed the local news. By the way her lithe, curvy body curled up in the chair, emanating sensuality and comfort in equal measure. By the way she kept on showing up here, every morning, for their now-routine "Get Gavin a job" comb-through of the daily want ads.

Her concern touched him. It affected him in ways he hadn't anticipated when he'd started this thing and made him want to tell Jennifer the truth—the whole truth. But if he did, he couldn't be near her anymore. So Gavin only soaked in another few minutes of her company, then spoke up.

"What's up with that?" he asked, pointing. "The back-to-front reading. Are you just impatient, or what?"

"What, this?" She shook the newspaper, then glanced to him for confirmation.

Her lips curved in a smile as she noticed—for the first time—the coffee-and-cocoa masque his sister had made him slather on his face and chest. He'd swear it was giving him a caffeine buzz. Not to mention a craving for a Hershey's bar.

"I was just reading, waiting for you to either harden in place or sign up for full-time spa membership," she said breezily. "You can probably get a discount through Nyla."

"Very funny."

"Come on. I think it's sweet—you helping her test-drive new products for men." She sniffed. "That one smells good. How long are you supposed to stay there like that anyway?"

"I'm not supposed to move for at least thirty minutes. Nyla made that explicitly clear—something about antioxidants—before she handed me the tub of goo and bailed out of here."

"How long ago was that?"

Gavin peered at the clock. "Ten minutes? Give or take."

"Aha. You're my prisoner then." A teasing pause. "If I wanted, I could have my way with you."

Grinning, Jennifer perused him as though considering it. She started at his toes, swept up past his boardshorts, then ended on his torso, which, as it happened, was nude except for a thick coating of granular, muddy masque.

Her playful, suggestive look was killing him.

Biting back a groan, Gavin struggled to keep his tone light. "You're doing it again, you know . . . just like with reading. Starting bottom to top, back to front."

"I always do that." She didn't look away. If anything, Jennifer's gaze turned even more deliberate. Even more daring, as though she'd come to a decision of some kind. "I read the endings of paperbacks before starting with page one. I buy knickknacks to decorate rooms I don't even have yet. I get shoes and earrings first, then drive myself wild looking for an outfit to match my accessories afterward."

Her gaze moved to his biceps, then swerved to his mouth. Jennifer licked her lips. Speaking of driving someone wild . . .

"I think it's a haircutting thing," she explained, warming to her subject—and warming him too. "Every new design starts with the ends, you know. With a level perimeter and a plan."

That sounded reasonable. Except right now, Gavin felt anything but *level*. And his *plan* was quickly careening out of control too. He hadn't meant to do anything but quell his crush on Jennifer. So why did he feel willing, even eager, to do something as simple as keep listening to her talk?

Just as he realized it, Jennifer lapsed into unexpected silence, still looking at him. Her gaze softened, making her eyes look dark and affecting and sensual. Trapped motionless, Gavin fought an urge to squirm. Or to invite her over to the sofa for an up-close sampling of antioxidants.

Speaking of *hardening in place* . . .

"So you're definitely stuck there, huh?" she asked.

"Yeah. But if you want to kill time before we get started with the want ads, this stuff is edible," he supplied helpfully.

Whoops. His voice sounded hoarse as hell. Thick with yearning. *Not* the carefree tone he'd been going for. But as long as he'd started this . . .

"You could lick off every inch of it, if you wanted. It's supposed to taste exactly like chocolate-mocha frosting."

She actually seemed to consider the idea. Gavin couldn't help but join her. Vividly, he pictured Jennifer straddling him, licking his chest while she moaned in enjoyment—of the chocolate or him, he didn't care.

He imagined the two of them smudging caffeinated body masque all over as they kissed and rolled and came together. Somehow, Jennifer's tank top disappeared beneath his grasp, baring her completely to him, and she was beautiful. Gavin knew he had to touch her with his bare hands. His bare, cocoa-smudged, aching—

"Yeah, we should probably look at the want ads," she said.

His reverie melted like so much cocoa butter.

But when Gavin met her gaze, he saw that she hadn't even opened the paper, still slack in her grasp. His hopes soared.

"Or try to find a music gig." He nodded to his guitar.

"Right." Jennifer's voice sounded husky. Dreamy. She cleared her throat. "We've also got your résumé to work on."

She'd been helping him with it all week, beefing up the descriptions of his credentials and fine-tuning the page layout. Gavin had to hand it to her. Jennifer was really smart, incredibly generous, and funny as hell. There was no one else in the world he'd have openly accepted pity-help from.

Even if it *was* a little misguided.

But right now, the last thing he wanted to do was read the fine print on classified job ads or stamp résumé envelopes. He wanted to finish what he'd started on the seawall. And more. Gavin dug his elbows in the cushion, pushed upward, and—

"Hey, stop it. You're not following orders."

Suddenly beside him, Jennifer shoved him back down. She braced both hands on the arm of the sofa beneath Gavin's head, then, to his gawking delight, lowered herself over him.

"You're my prisoner, remember?"

Her thighs squeezed his boardshorts. Her pelvis grazed his. Her upper body descended, beginning with a shining trail of curls that headed lower and lower, all the way toward—

"Careful. Your hair." He caught a soft hank in his hand, moments before it dragged through the caffé mocha sludge of his semihardened chest masque. "You don't want to mess up—"

"Right." Jennifer hesitated. She glanced down at their position, taking in their nearness as though gauging its likely consequences. "I don't want to mess up . . . anything."

The questions in her eyes told him more than her words did. She wanted to know if he wanted this too. If what was about to happen between them would ruin their friendship . . . or affect her dating plans somehow.

Gavin didn't know. It wasn't like him to be introspective. But all the same, as he gazed back at her, a fierce sense of protectiveness welled within him. He didn't want to hurt Jennifer. Yet resisting her now felt about as impossible as goofyfooting a frontside wave.

"If we're careful," he urged, "I think we can—"

He never finished. Jennifer's mouth came down on his, and

the next thing he knew, he was holding fistfuls of her wild curly hair instead of a single wayward tangle. Gavin buried his hands in her hair, pulling her to him, kissing her back with all the need and honesty and desire he'd hidden for so long now.

As though sensing all of it, Jennifer moaned and swirled her tongue around his mouth. Her enthusiasm felt as sexy as he'd ever dreamed it might . . . and somehow twice as intoxicating.

Drunk with it, drunk with *her*, Gavin let his hands roam lower. He swept his palms across her back and downward, dying to arch higher, to drag her nearer . . . to feel all of her pressed taut against him, skin on skin. No longer able to resist, he groaned and levered his knee gently upward. Jennifer gasped with the heat that rose between them.

"Careful," she murmured. "Careful, careful . . . "

But the words rapidly lost meaning. Jennifer was kissing him, Jennifer *wanted* him, and Gavin knew he was supposed to be taking this slowly, but he simply couldn't remember why. All he understood was the warm, sleek feel of her beneath his hands, the urgent press of their bodies coming together, the necessity of getting closer, closer, *closer.*

Cocoa and coffee grounds smushed between them, sending their heady scents into the air. Gavin inhaled and felt himself growing even giddier. This wasn't like him. This was just a kiss, just a friendly coming together, just a sexy, slippery, mind-blowing . . . where was he? Yeah. The giddiness. He felt crazy with it. Crazy for it. Crazy for Jennifer.

He was falling for her, he realized in the next instant. Falling harder every day. Somehow, their talks and late-night laughs and trips to his favorite seaside spots had *done* something to him . . . something he hadn't expected or even known he wanted. It was incredible. Unlikely. And yet . . .

But then Jennifer was kissing him again, her hand shoved in his hair with passion, and Gavin just gave in. There was nothing cautious about the way he kissed her back, nothing aloof in the way he smiled at her as they parted again. He'd never seen a woman more beautiful. More necessary. He pulled her down and kissed her once more, and as the heat rose between them, as he began to consider where this might be taking them, Gavin knew he had some decisions to make.

"You want to help me shower off this stuff before?" he asked, sliding his hands to Jennifer's hips, "or after?"

"Before or after what?" Breathlessly.

"Before or after we make the sofa spontaneously combust."

She grinned, tendrils of hair clinging to her flushed face. "Let's just go with the flow. I hear that's a good method."

"It's excellent." Another kiss. "Highly recommended."

Murmuring her agreement, she levered upward in his lap, trailing her finger through his mocha masque like a baker sampling a cake batter—and finding it delicious. Her fingertip hooked at the waist of his boardshorts, tickling him.

Gavin nearly shot off the sofa.

A few inches lower, and he'd quit making sense altogether.

"I've wanted you for a long time now," Jennifer mused. "But I guess you knew that, didn't you?"

She'd wanted *him*? Unreal.

"And now here you are. I can't believe it."

"Believe it. Oh Jen . . . believe it."

Ridiculously thrilled, Gavin hauled her downward for another kiss. It was tricky to pucker with part of his face all covered in coffee-and-cocoa masque, but he felt motivated. So, apparently, did Jennifer. She moaned and clung to him.

This was incredible. Even better than he'd dreamed. Exhilarated, Gavin kissed her more deeply, rapidly calculating the odds of his being able to walk to her bedroom with a raging hard-on. Given his boardshorts' loose fit, he just might—

The front door whooshed open.

Caught by surprise, Jennifer and Gavin broke apart. The whole sofa shuddered as they bolted to opposite corners. They gawked at Nyla, who stood in the foyer wearing an expression of amazement. A Jamba Juice cup dangled from her hand. A brown paper shopping bag from Ralph's crumpled at her opposite elbow.

"Ahhh." She nodded, a tentative grin quirking the side of her mouth. "So *this* is how it is between you two, huh? I guess I should have known."

"No!" Jennifer blurted. Her gaze whisked over Gavin, seeking his cooperation. "This isn't what it looks like. We were just, uhhh . . ." She gestured lamely.

"Checking the want ads," Gavin finished for her.

Gratefully, Jennifer nodded. "Yeah, the want ads. Scoping out job opportunities for Gavin."

Nyla's attention focused on Jennifer's face. His sister peered closer. Then her grin widened. When she turned away to put down her Ralph's bag, Gavin examined Jennifer too.

A telltale brown ring smudged her mouth, looking grainy and sweet and awfully familiar. Great. He probably sported a matching one, both of them cocoa- and coffee-flavored.

They'd just have to wing it. "Jennifer's been *totally* helpful while I've been here," he said seriously. "We're heading out to Kinko's later to make copies of my résumé."

"Mmm-hmmm." Contemplatively, Nyla sipped some Jamba Juice. "Well, before you go, there's just one thing I have to know." She picked up her notepad. "For the sake of journalistic integrity—since I *do* have a spa article to write on that stuff—exactly how good *does* Coca-Mocha Madness masque taste?"

Realizing how he felt about Jennifer—realizing how *she* felt about *him*!—changed everything for Gavin.

He still sat on the sofa picking out tunes on his steel-stringed Gibson while she got ready for her dates. But he appreciated Yoga Jennifer, Sporty Tomboy Jennifer, and even Junior Dominatrix Jennifer on a whole new level. He still waited for her to come home for their regular postdate playback sessions. But now he paced, eager and impatient for her return, more than he ever had. He still kissed her, during stolen moments when Nyla stepped out and Jennifer stepped in. But now every moment meant more, more, *more* to him.

He was officially a wimp. A fool for love.

For Jennifer's sake, Gavin dived full-on into life in an all-girl apartment. He endured Diet Coke avalanches and razor-obliterating makeup clutter and throw pillows and sappy chick-flick movie marathons. He ate fat-free potato chips and skipped *SportsCenter*. He even put away his surfwax. But he knew it would all be worth it. When Jennifer realized what they could have together if they just gave it a shot. . . .

Except she didn't.

She just went on with her loser datathon, spending most of her time with guys who didn't really know her and never would. It drove Gavin crazy. They could be so good together.

If he would just take a number.

Screw that. He wanted her. She wanted him. It ought to be that simple. End of story.

"So, what do you think?" Jennifer asked.

She stopped in front of him the way she always did, cell phone in hand, wearing a curve-skimming dress made of some kind of crinkly blue fabric. Peppermint wafted from the Altoid she sucked on, and a bright flush lit her face. Her hair hung down her back, painstakingly and expertly straightened. It made him sad. Nobody should have to *iron* their hair, for Christ's sake.

"Why don't you just be yourself?"

Jennifer looked stricken. "Because I'm dating a high-tech entrepreneur, and this is my Techno Jen look."

"What happened to just letting things flow?"

Her expression of empathy nearly wrecked him.

"I have to do this, Gavin. I have to find the real me." With a sigh, she sat beside him, letting her blind-date perfume—probably Geek Magnet Number Five—waft closer. "I know you don't get it, but I feel as if life has just been *happening* to me. I want a hand in it. I want to decide things on my own."

He *didn't* get it. "The 'real' you is right there," Gavin insisted stubbornly. "Right in front of me. And she's unique and determined and honest—"

"Gavin—"

"And she goes crazy for puppies and shoe sales and Fat Tire Ale. And she's a good friend and a good stylist—"

"You can't *give* this to me," Jennifer interrupted, her gaze soft. She put her hand on his thigh, making all his nerve endings stand at attention. "I have to get it for myself."

Frustrated, Gavin met her gaze. He cared about her too much—as a friend and more—to push her. But damn, this was hard.

He squeezed her hand. "Okay. Do what you have to do."

Wordlessly, he fisted his guitar, carrying it toward the patio doors. He needed some fresh air. Some sea breeze.

Maybe some perspective too.

Jennifer's voice trailed him. "Gavin!"

In the semidarkness, he paused.

"Don't worry, I'll be here when you get back." *As usual.* Gavin held up his hand in farewell, wanting to reassure her as best he could. A full-fledged smile was more than he could manage though. He was a man, not a freaking game-show host. "Have fun."

Jennifer watched Gavin walk away, his back straight and his gait steady. An instant later, he disappeared through the patio doors to the accompaniment of the nearby surf. The roar of it still hung in the air, rhythmically pounding against the beach.

Jennifer sighed. There was a certain irony in Gavin's parting "hang ten" sign—not the least because hanging ten was one of longboard surfing's most tricky maneuvers. Getting through the next week's worth of blind dates was going to be tricky indeed. And it was going to require all the discipline and finesse she could muster too.

But what else could she do? If she didn't learn who she really was, how could she commit herself to someone else? To Gavin?

If she just gave up now, Jennifer reminded herself, it would be the same thing as admitting her search for self-discovery was as silly and doomed as everyone said it was.

Now more than ever, Jennifer refused to do that.

She owed it to herself to finish, and that was exactly what she planned to do. No matter how much she wanted to chase after Gavin instead . . . and grab him before he surfed away for good.

Chapter 5

Uh-oh. Watch out for razor burn! Unfortunately, there's no remedy for painful surprises. We recommend avoiding them whenever possible.
    —Tips courtesy of "The Girls' Guide to Getting Smooth" (Goddess Razors, Inc.)

"So, how are the blind dates going?" Nyla asked.

She popped a few edamame in her mouth and chewed, waiting interestedly for Jennifer's reply. Stephanie sat beside her, waiting for the plate of tuna tartare with wasabi sauce she'd ordered. Jennifer wasn't eating. Three-and-a-half-weeks' worth of coffee breaks and restaurant meals had taken their toll on her. At this point all she wanted was a nice PBJ sandwich.

"They're going okay, I guess." She slumped at their table, exhausted from nonstop meeting, munching, and chitchatting. "I haven't missed a single date in twenty-five days, and number 26 is coming up later tonight. So I guess that's progress, right?"

"Definitely. That sounds encouraging." Stephanie eyeballed the edamame. "You're awesomely disciplined, Jen."

Nyla snorted with laughter.

"Go on," Jennifer deadpanned. "Make soybeans come out

your nose." She rolled her eyes at her friend. "I'm not *that* bad."

"If you say so." Straight-faced, Nyla zipped open another pod. She'd been unusually quiet all night.

"The weird thing is," Jennifer went on, "all of a sudden it's as if something's been interfering with my dates."

"Yeah," Stephanie sympathized. "PMS can be like that."

"No, not that." A grin. "But lately I've had messages gone missing, phone calls that weren't returned . . . people have been telling me their blind-date suggestions weren't passed on. Also, a flower delivery went astray yesterday, and one of my dates even told me he was almost 'deterred' from picking me up!"

" 'Deterred'?" Stephanie frowned. "What does that mean?"

Nyla merely sampled more edamame and listened.

"He said there was 'intimidating looming' involved. I don't know." Jennifer shook her head. "I'm not sure how seriously I can take him though. The guy was the size of a seventh grader. I could have tucked him under my armpit."

Her friends murmured in commiseration. Short men were the worst. Not because they were tiny, but because so many of them seemed to have a complex about their size.

"He practically needed a booster seat at the restaurant."

Stephanie sighed. "Shorties are cute. They should lighten up a little. Be more like Muffin." Muffin was Stephanie's toy poodle. "She's convinced she's really a Great Dane, and I swear it works for her. It really does." She beamed.

Stephanie's tuna arrived, and so did another cocktail for Nyla. She pushed aside the bowl of edamame and went to work on her Saketini, smacking her lips with pleasure after the first sip. She didn't comment on the shorties discussion.

"Ooh, ooh!" Stephanie cried after she'd forked up some tartare. "How did it go last night? With the opera guy?"

Jennifer groaned. "Dollar Bill Dennis?"

Nyla quirked her brow. Stephanie nodded eagerly.

"Let's just say that his nickname is no longer a mystery. I'm happy to go Dutch on a date, but fronting the check for a swanky dinner in La Jolla, two bouts of twelve-dollar parking—downtown space *and* valet—plus buying a dress appropriate for Opera Jennifer does *not* constitute a good time in my book."

Her friends sighed understandingly.

"Dennis got the opera tickets for free because his boss has the flu," Jennifer explained, "But he claimed he 'forgot' his wallet and only had a few dollars on him. Which left me holding the bag. He said it was very 'egalitarian' of me to help out, but sheesh! I had to bankrupt my new-jeans budget and my whole cache of latte money just to keep the date afloat. You know, to give Opera Jennifer a fair shot."

She frowned, already missing all the foamy espresso drinks she could no longer afford. Fortunately, though, not all of her dates had been wipeouts like Dennis. In fact, several of them had been real contenders, men she might have continued seeing under other circumstances. But now, with her and Gavin becoming so close, getting to know each other again . . .

Jennifer rested her chin in her hand, reliving the coffee-and-cocoa kiss they'd shared. She hadn't exactly planned on jumping him like that, but it had been worth it.

Wow, had it been worth it.

Being with Gavin was amazing. He was funny and smart and generous, and he was man enough to let her help him research job opportunities too. It took strength to do that. Strength most men, surfers or not, didn't possess. But then Gavin was special in lots of ways. What other man would have respected her need to find herself so much that he'd support her seeing other men?

Nobody, that's who.

Besides, they liked so many of the same things. The ocean. Farrelly brothers movies. Yoo-hoo. Modern art. Bowling. Before, her crush had been a mere blast-from-the-past infatuation. Now it had morphed into something real.

Something intoxicating and deep and impossibly *easy*.

"So?" Stephanie prodded, breaking into her reverie. "*Are*

you Opera Jennifer? Or what? You've been doing this for *weeks*. You must have learned something, right?"

"Sure," Jennifer agreed, nodding. Reluctantly, she ended her mental Gavinologue. "Let's see . . . I've learned that I don't find aggressive driving, lots of tattoos, or extreme frugality appealing. I don't enjoy baseball games, indie movies with subtitles, or Sasquatch-style body hair. Also, sad to say, if you want to dress yourself as a Trekker or me as a medieval wench—or if your idea of a good time involves paint guns or laser tag—I'm definitely not your gal."

Nyla grinned. "Picky, picky."

"There is an upside though. All this dating has clarified a few things for me too." Jennifer listed a few of them. "For example, yes to rock-climbing lessons, no to deep-sea fishing. Yes to cute skirts, no to faux nose piercings. See? All in all, it's been interesting. And kind of empowering too, because of all the new things I've tried."

Her friends gazed at her, nodding. All around them, the restaurant filled with noisy clumps of diners: singles on dates, groups of women, a few older couples. The place was trendy but casual, with a combination of surf-side elements. It wasn't one of Nyla's hot new finds, but it was in their neighborhood.

"Then you've found the real you?" Stephanie asked.

"Well . . ." Jennifer hesitated, trying to decide. "I've found a lot more of the real *not* me," she admitted, "than the real me. Most of the things I've tried don't exactly feel like a perfect fit. But hey, I've got five more dates to go, right? So maybe my authentic self is still out there somewhere"—she gestured grandly toward the restaurant's doorway—"just waiting for me to put on the right man-cessories."

Automatically, they all glanced to the doorway, as though expecting Jennifer's genuine self to come gallivanting through—possibly outfitted in a new pair of Sevens with a promotion to tease's head stylist in her pocket.

"Hey," Stephanie blurted, "isn't that Gavin?"

Jennifer peered toward the bustling foyer. It was! Instantly,

even in profile, she recognized his sun-bleached hair, his ambling gait, his broad shoulders.

He smiled and held up his hand to someone at the bar.

Oh God. Was Gavin here on a *date*?

The idea made Jennifer's insides flip. Her heart stuttered to
a near stop as she watched the man she'd kissed this very
morning—clandestinely, over donuts and Chai tea they'd carried out over the water at Crystal Pier—make his way through
the crowd. His eyes sparkled. His body, clad in a loose shirt
and artistically ripped jeans, looked capable of . . . well, anything.

So long as *anything* was athletic, erotic, and thoroughly enjoyable. Damn it. Why hadn't she tied him up at home?

The idea called to mind several intriguing possibilities, a
few of them worthy of a night-school course in sailor's knots.
But Jennifer could hardly contemplate them in public—especially while he was here with another woman. Another
woman!

Sure, technically, Gavin was free to date other people. They
were hardly exclusive. But . . . still.

Jennifer wanted him for herself, she realized at that moment. She wanted him completely.

"It's my brother, all right," Nyla confirmed with a frown.
She gulped the rest of her Saketini and signaled for another.
"And it looks as if he's on the prowl too."

"Hey, it's a good thing you waved for that drink," Gavin
told his sister, nodding to her cocktail. He gave Nyla a grin.
"Otherwise I would have totally missed you guys. This place is
dark. And noisy. Whoa!"

He ducked as a nearby brunette plucked the tiki umbrella
from her drink and flung it over her shoulder with a whoop.
Good-naturedly, Gavin straightened again. He liked a lively
place. Especially if Jennifer was in it.

"Yeah." Nyla smiled tightly. "Really good."

"It's fine by me." Stephanie snuggled closer to Bobby, who'd come out to meet Gavin tonight. She gave him a flirtatious look. "I like meeting new people."

Bobby reddened. "Me too," he said roughly.

There. Introductions accomplished. Happily, Gavin slung his arm over the booth. He nudged Jennifer closer, his fingers sliding over her bare shoulder. Her skin felt warm and soft and incredible enough to make him want the whole place to disappear—wasabi sauce, Asahi Dark beer, and all.

"But I promised the boss, here," Bobby said, turning away from Stephanie to nod toward Gavin, "that I'd give him an update on the business end of—"

"It's okay, Bobby," Gavin interrupted. "We'll do it later."

Beside him, Jennifer gave a questioning look.

"Nickname. The whole 'boss' thing," Gavin muttered to her, then gulped his beer. Damn. He hated not being straight with people. But for this . . . It was a necessity. He tried another smile. "What, no hot date tonight?"

That distracted her. "Actually, yes. I'm meeting date number 26 for an evening harbor cruise." Jennifer touched his dangling hand, twining her fingers with his. "But I've got a few minutes before I have to leave."

Gavin smiled at her. He'd take whatever he could get. A few minutes, a few hours . . . a whole night of hot, amazing—

"Sadly, *I* don't." Abruptly, Nyla stood. She swept the table with a bewilderingly irate look, then grabbed her purse. "I've got to start packing for my trip to Monterey."

"But that's three days from now," Jennifer protested.

Gavin watched in confusion. He only saw his sister disconcerted like this once in a while, and it usually meant—

"Can't hurt to plan." Nyla waved. " 'Night, all."

They all stared after her, foreheads puckered.

Bobby hooked his thumb toward Nyla's parting figure. "Geez, was it something I said? What's the matter with her?"

Stephanie only bit her lip and shook her head.

But Jennifer seemed more enlightened. And a lot more concerned. "I think I know," she said, looking worried. "The trouble is . . . I'm not sure what to do about it."

The good thing about meeting someone at a bookstore, Jennifer decided later that week as she browsed the shelves at the Borders in Gaslamp Quarter, was that the surroundings provided plenty of distraction. Books, magazines, café snacks—they were all good. The bad thing was the couples. The whole place seemed packed with intimate twosomes. They whispered in quiet corners and canoodled on the cushy loveseats, poring over home-décor books or bridal magazines and shooting each other affectionate, goo-goo-eyed looks.

If she had to witness another hand-holding couple meandering toward the checkout with a copy of *The Ultimate Wedding Planner* she was going to scream. Not because she was dying for a pouffy white dress and a gazillion-layer cake that cost as much as her rent did (because she wasn't), but because her latest blind date—a mystery novelist from Carlsbad—was late.

It was too bad, because Literary Jennifer was a real babe. Even if Jennifer did say so herself. She glanced down at her tweed pencil skirt, silk blouse, and sexy pumps, then put her hand to her messy updo—haphazardly anchored with a pencil for that "I just finished jotting down a masterpiece" look. When Mitch got here, he would be blown away for sure.

But until then . . .

She'd been lingering in the mystery-and-thriller aisle for the past half hour. While several of the books looked good, there was only so much murder and mayhem a girl could handle on a Friday night. Biting her lip, Jennifer glanced at the store's entrance. No sign of her erstwhile twenty-ninth blind date.

Well, until Mitch got here, there was nothing wrong with amusing herself . . . in the celebrity-gossip section of the magazine racks. Jennifer headed in that direction, reminding herself that picking up *Us Weekly* practically qualified as career development for her. She had to stay in touch with which celebrity-inspired hairstyles her clients were likely to want next, didn't she?

Four glossy weeklies, two lattes, and a chocolate-covered graham cracker later—plus the requisite sixteen Altoids—Jennifer finally realized the truth. Her date wasn't coming . . . ever.

Dispiritedly, Jennifer kicked the door shut behind her. Her apartment's warmth and colorful coziness closed in around her, letting her breathe easily for the first time in almost two hours. After slinking out of the bookstore, battling traffic, and navigating the walk home in her killer pumps, she felt more drained than ever.

She slung her purse on a chair. Her Borders shopping bag followed, clunking with its emergency purchase of two discounted hardcovers by authors she'd never read before. After spending the equivalent of a hair-color retouch, trim, and blow-out in the store, she hadn't had the heart to leave empty-handed.

Her shoes came next, kicked off with a grunt of relief. Toes weren't meant to be squished in that position. Hobbling to the kitchen, Jennifer listened for sounds of anyone at home.

Nada. But that wasn't surprising. Nyla was off on her spa-scouting trip to Monterey, and Gavin was off . . . doing whatever he did while she went on blind dates. It felt weird to be home alone, especially after all the time she'd spent with him lately. She opened the fridge, then hesitated with her hand almost closed on a bottle of beer.

Later, she decided, and headed for the patio. There, the sounds of the surf filled the night, punctuated by squeals of laughter from some teenaged tourists running in and out of the tide. A few locals hung out at the boardwalk. Jennifer waved to her elderly neighbor, Sally, who was out walking her beagle. They paused briefly beneath one of the lights, then moved on.

The jangle of keys caught her attention, starting someplace

around the other side of her duplex apartment and coming closer. Footsteps moved nearer, steady and sure. Then, whistling.

She recognized that whistling.

The front door opened, then shut. *Gavin.*

His footsteps continued through the apartment, then paused in the kitchen. Jennifer sensed his presence—and probably his confusion—as he spotted her huddled in the semi-darkness.

"Jen?"

"Out here." She waved him onto the patio.

At the sight of him she nearly sobbed, desperate for commiseration. He probably wouldn't understand. But he was there, and that counted for something. Besides, he looked sure. Carefree. Wonderful. She'd bet *Gavin* had never stood up a girl after she'd gotten three paper cuts waiting for him.

With a nod for hello, he hunkered in front of her chair, gazing up at her. Wherever he'd been, it hadn't been a date.

He wore his oldest pair of boardshorts and a threadbare Billabong T-shirt, and there was a smudge of something black on his forearm. His hair was all messy too, as though he'd shoved it out of the way repeatedly. But his eyes were bright and caring, and his palm on her thigh was gentle, and before she knew it, Jennifer really *was* sobbing.

"Hey, hey." Gavin rubbed her thigh, his concern evident. "Whatever it is, it can't be that bad. You'll get through it."

"No I won't." She sniffed. "That lipstick ad? It's going to get the better of me after all. I mean, my plan hasn't been all *that* brilliant so far, I'll admit. But now it's *ruined.*"

"Are you kidding me? *Nothing's* getting the better of you." More gentle rubbing. "Not the Jennifer I know. You'll just keep going until you make it happen, right?"

She shook her head. "Not all by myself, I won't."

He squeezed her thigh. "You're not all by yourself. You've got me. I'm not going anywhere."

Jennifer believed him. Unless . . . "You don't write books on the side, do you?" She blinked. Heavily. Her mascara must be a mess. "Because apparently I'm not appealing to literary types."

Gavin made reassuring sounds, his very presence solid and comforting. Twisting sideways, he handed her a tissue.

She accepted it gratefully, too downhearted to care if she was grossing him out by blowing her nose. She sucked in a shuddering breath. "I got stood up tonight."

Silence fell. Gavin's hand stilled on her leg. It occurred to her, belatedly, that he was probably glad Mitch had been a no-show. Gavin supported her finding-herself plan, but he did it grudgingly, she knew. Only because she wanted him to.

But all he said was, "Then somebody's missing out right now, big time." With his free hand, he nudged up her chin. "Any guy who would stand you up doesn't deserve you. Period."

She gazed into his eyes, nearly lulled into accepting his reasoning. It sounded so good. So absolving.

"That's nice of you, Gavin, but . . ." Jennifer hauled in a deep breath, trying to articulate the problems this caused. "What if Literary Jennifer really *was* me?" she wailed. "What if now I'll never know?"

He shrugged, typically accepting of . . . everything.

"What if you don't need to know?" he asked.

Desperately, she fisted her tissue. "You don't get it! What if I just keep on drifting through life, exactly like I have been, never knowing who I am or who I'm supposed to become? What if I just keep making one autopilot choice after another until I'm old and decrepit and gray?"

She stared at him, her eyes still watery, demanding an answer. But all Gavin did was quirk his eyebrow.

Don't you think everyone feels that way? she expected to hear. But instead . . .

"Gray? Be real." He shook his head, his gaze kind and his touch encouraging. "You, among many other amazing things, are a dead-on, crack hairstylist. You'll *never* go gray."

Jennifer gawked. He didn't take anything seriously! Why

hadn't she chosen someone more commiserating? More thoughtful? More inclined to wallow in self-pity with her?

Then she realized . . . he was right. Damn him.

"Okay," she admitted. "So long as there's Miss Clairol Spring Honey 27G, you've got a point."

Gavin grinned. "See? It's all good. No worries."

But despite his encouragement, despite everything, Jennifer stared despondently out to sea. She needed . . . more. She needed for all her blind dating not to have been for nothing.

She needed to understand all the options available to her, including blind date number 29. Otherwise, how could she relax and be happy with her decisions . . . about anything?

"Go on," Gavin urged quietly. "I'm still here."

Jennifer cast him a dubious look. Then, even though she'd never meant for such a thing to happen, she suddenly found herself pouring out *everything* to him. How she feared missing out on things. How she yearned to have a purpose to her life, a sense that she was doing okay. How she wanted to know—through blind dating, if necessary—what she was really all about.

How she'd eaten six of those yummy chocolate-covered graham crackers at Borders, even though she'd told the café checkout girl they were for her imaginary niece's preschool snack time.

"I mean, I love my job. I really do. But what if being a stylist isn't my destiny? What if it's just the thing that's easiest for me? What if I'm blowing it?" she asked intently. "I feel like there should be . . . *more* to my life somehow."

Through it all, Gavin listened. He handed her tissues, he nodded and talked and listened some more. And the more he stayed, the more he listened and tried to help her, the more Jennifer felt he would stay through anything—would stick with her, through high tide and low.

"Maybe the easy things are only easy because you love them," he said. "Maybe your destiny found *you*. Already."

"No." She shook her head. "It can't be that simple."

His eyes gleamed, filled with good humor. "It can't?"
"Nope."

At her continued skepticism, Gavin shrugged, possessed with a certain bohemian wisdom she hadn't quite appreciated before.

"I think it can . . . if you want it to be. It can be easy."

Jennifer knew he was wrong. "But *nothing* is—"

He cut her off with a kiss. "Easy," he repeated, his voice a seductive murmur. "Easy, easy, easy. Just like the way I feel about you. Easy."

Gavin cupped her face in his hands, his whole attention focused on her. He smiled, then kissed her again. "You're all you need to be. And if that's not enough . . ."

His palms felt warm against her cheeks, his jaw vaguely scratchy and sexy and masculine. His reassurance tugged at her, making her feel all cozy and cared-for. Significant.

"If that's not enough," Gavin continued, "then I haven't made myself clear yet." He linked his fingers with hers, his gaze steady and intent. "I'm here for you, Jen. I didn't think it would come to this, believe me. Wanting more, needing more." He offered a wobbly, not entirely credible shrug. "But if the best I can do is be here for you, then that's what I'll do."

He meant supporting her blind-dating plan. He had to. But at that moment, Jennifer would have traded a thousand blind dates for five more minutes with Gavin. For six more of his smiles or a few more of those gorgeous, undressing-her-with-his-eyes kinds of looks he kept giving her. If those looks meant what she thought they did . . .

"I'm glad you've been here for me."

Finally giving in, she kissed him back. Jennifer leaned nearer, inhaling the mingled scents of ocean and man, enjoying the lazy slide of Gavin's mouth over hers.

He kissed her as though he had all night to do it, touched her as though he couldn't enjoy it long enough, and being with him made her think of lazy poolside afternoons and sugary drinks and the tang of chlorine on a wet bathing suit. How many days had she spent at the Collaro household, sneaking glimpses of Gavin while she and Nyla hung out? How many times had she, in her daydreams, put herself in exactly this place?

None of those times compared with reality. Reality was Gavin's mouth slanting over hers, his broad hands on her shoulders, his deep, throaty murmurs as he went on kissing her. Reality was here, it was now, and it was more familiar and right and perfect than she'd ever thought it could be.

Breathlessly, Jennifer broke off. "Gavin, we should—"

"Oh hell. I know. I'm sorry." He lifted his hands from her shoulders, then held them in the air in an automatic pose of surrender. "I got carried away. The last thing you need right now is me all over you."

She examined his serious gaze, his determined stance, his air of contrition. Gavin was honest. He was real. He was right. She loved those things about him.

She loved . . . *him*. Crazily, implausibly, awesomely.

"Go on." He gestured earnestly, his attention fixed on her face. His chest rose and fell on a few leftover passionate breaths, but he actually seemed ready for a good, long, heart-to-heart. "Talk all you want. I'm listening. Still here."

He said it as though it was a mighty sacrifice, but one he was more than willing to make. Because of that, Jennifer couldn't help but smile.

"That's not what I meant. I'm done talking."

He was clearly skeptical. "No woman is *ever* done talking."

"Spoken like a man with a sister." Jennifer felt her grin widen. She grabbed his hand and squeezed. "But *I* am done. For now. What I really need, what I really want . . ."

His interest sharpened. She felt the tension rising in the flexing muscles of his hand, his wrist. Gavin waited.

"Is you," she finished. "All over me."

His eyebrows dipped. "You mean . . . ?"

"Yeah. You. Me. My bedroom. Last one there is—"

Gavin hauled her to her feet in a rush. "*Not* going to be me. Let's go."

It took them a while to get there. There was the detour on the patio, when Jennifer had finally convinced Gavin she meant what she'd said and they needed a kiss to celebrate. There was the stopover just inside the patio doors, leaning against the chilly refrigerator, when they needed a kiss to officially get started. There was the layover on the edge of the sofa, the seductive holdup in the hallway, and finally, *finally* the meet-up on her messy bed.

"You're a tricky woman to get into bed." Gavin murmured the complaint as he kissed her atop the comforter, both of them balanced on their knees. He smoothed his hands over her silky blouse and smiled in appreciation. "If I didn't know better, I'd swear you were only teasing."

"With you? Never." And Jennifer realized it was true. With other men, she'd been playing a role—trying on a persona. But with Gavin . . . with Gavin, she could be herself. "Besides, *you're* the one who couldn't wait to get past the kitchen."

"Guilty." His eyes darkened as he looked at her—probably remembering the squirming, arching kisses they'd shared against the Frigidaire. "But this has been a long time coming. You can't blame a guy for being into the moment."

Into the moment pretty much defined Gavin, Jennifer learned that night. When he kissed her, he did it with all his heart and soul. When he unbuttoned her blouse and pushed it over her shoulders, he did it with awe and focus and a series of caresses that drove her wild. When he held her close, when he helped her squirm out of her too-tight puzzle of a pencil skirt, when he pulled the *actual* pencil from her updo and smiled at it quizzically, he did so with caring and tenderness and love.

Jennifer couldn't imagine why she'd resisted this for so long. What could be wrong with savoring the crazy, swept-up-in-the-moment feeling of being with Gavin? With enjoying the sweet words they shared? With pushing him down on her comforter, dragging off his clothes, and finally feeling all those hot, hard muscles pressed against her?

Nothing, that's what.

Giggling, giddy, Jennifer just let loose. Her reservations vanished beneath the safe and familiar and thrilling togetherness she and Gavin shared, and by the time he balanced over her, naked and needy and raw, by the time she urged him closer, breathless and bare and open, there wasn't a single secret left between them.

She knew it in her heart. She glimpsed it in Gavin's eyes. She felt it as they collapsed together afterward, arms and legs and feelings entwined. This was different. It was special.

It was *real*. It was love. And from here on out, it was going to be amazing.

Chapter 6

Buh-bye nicks and cuts! With practice, you'll find even awkward maneuvers become easier. For the most comfortable results in the future, take note of which grips work best for you. And don't forget to slather on a generous quantity of body cream (we suggest tasty vanilla-bergamot body whip) for a finish you and your man will both enjoy!

—Tips courtesy of "The Girls' Guide to Getting Smooth" (Goddess Razors, Inc.)

The sound of the surf awakened Gavin first, whooshing in on a sliver of breeze through Jennifer's partly opened window. Ordinarily, he'd have grabbed his board and headed out. But the sight of her sleeping beside him, all rumpled and warm in the daylight, kept him cozy in bed instead of out on the beach.

He'd never been a morning person. But if waking up early treated him to sights like this one from now on, Gavin figured he just might become one. Jennifer's arm lay flung overhead with drowsy abandon, her hair wild and kinked. Her makeup smudged below her closed eyelids, reminding him of seductive nights and slinky dresses. Her jaw was slack and her mouth gaped open and he was pretty sure a woman's long-wearing lipstick wasn't supposed to perform its magic all graffiti-style on her cheek like that.

She looked beautiful to him.

Jennifer's fingers curled on his chest, her palm upward-facing and empty. With a feeling of ridiculous tenderness, Gavin blinked groggily. Carefully, he slipped his hand in hers. She snuffled in her sleep, but didn't awaken. She was, hands down, the most adorable sleeper he'd ever seen in his life.

He could have spent hours that way. Days. Just watching her sleep, knowing they were together, remembering everything they'd shared. It had killed him to know she'd been hurt last night. Even though he'd only stopped by the apartment to pick up something he'd forgotten, even though he'd probably live to regret the risk, Gavin hadn't been able to resist staying.

Because somewhere between trying to help and feeling Jennifer peel off his boardshorts with clear enthusiasm, he'd fallen more in love with her. From here, there was no way out.

Not that Gavin wanted one. Because looking at her, thinking of her, he realized what the *something more* he'd been yearning for really was. It was Jennifer.

They could spend the whole day together, he decided cheerfully. Once he'd taken care of a few details from last night, he could wake her with kisses, or maybe try making her breakfast. He hoped donuts counted. He wasn't sure. He only knew he wanted to make Jennifer happy, and she had a major soft spot for those devil's food donuts with vanilla glaze.

Rolling over, Gavin propped his head in his hand and watched Jennifer a little longer. Hell, he could even tell her he loved her. Out loud. There was no reason not to.

But first . . . he had a few things to deal with.

Jennifer awakened with a headful of postupdo hairsprayed curls, a serious case of chocolate-graham breath, and a feeling of utter contentment. Drowsily, she untangled her hand from her hair and tried to remember why she felt so happy.

Zipped her smallest jeans?

Found the perfect shade of lipstick?

Gave a client the hairstyle of her dreams?

Nope. Nope. And not this week.

Then what was it? Thinking some more, Jennifer shuffled around with her eyes closed, getting comfy. Her pillow smelled like ocean and surfwax. The coconut kind, like Gavin used.

Gavin. Oh yeah. Joyfully, Jennifer grinned. She stretched her arms, thumping the headboard unconcernedly, then rolled sideways. She'd bet he liked being awakened with a little snuggling. Who didn't? With a body like his, Gavin probably had a lot to offer in the AM entertainment department.

The sheets were cold. She opened her eyes.

Her bedroom stood awash in sunlight. The distant sound of surf reached her, and then . . . nothing. It was quiet.

Too quiet. A chill swept over her, making her grab for the comforter. Huddled beneath it, she tried to shake off the weird sensation that something was wrong. With Nyla out of town till tomorrow, Jennifer and Gavin were alone in the apartment, so it *should* be quiet, she reasoned.

Except Gavin always made noise. Talking, whistling, singing, humming, playing his guitar. With him, thoughts emerged in tone and rhythm. So, she remembered wickedly, did other, more pleasurable things. Mmmm . . .

The sound of the front door closing very, very softly cut short her musings. Sitting upright in bed, Jennifer clutched the sheet and listened. Footsteps. Keys quietly jangling. Something, maybe a paper sack, sliding onto the countertop.

Gavin must have gone to get breakfast, she realized. They both loved the donut place down the block. Although usually she could hear his ramshackle, beach-ready van—big enough to hold all his surfboards and a wetsuit, and battered enough that a little sand and surfwax on the seats didn't matter—coming from a mile away. This time she hadn't heard a thing. That was strange.

Oh well. He was here, she was here, and they had the

whole day to spend together. Jennifer figured she couldn't ask for much more. She'd sneak out and surprise him and make a big deal out of his breakfast plans. She hoped he'd gotten devil's food donuts. Then she'd sit across from him on the patio and they'd talk and eat and cuddle. It would be perfect, the ideal start to whatever was destined to happen between them.

Stopping in the midst of untangling her hair and yanking on a robe, Jennifer marveled at herself. *Destined?* Things were different already! Maybe being with Gavin had been the key to uncovering her true self all along. And she'd almost missed it.

Alight with satisfaction, she sashayed toward the living room. She could picture Gavin already—nervously arranging the donuts, awkwardly making coffee, his hair sticking up in that endearing, carefree way of his and his eyes all sparkling like—

"Message deleted," declared her answering machine in a flat computerized voice. A beep followed. "Message deleted."

Confused, Jennifer stopped in the doorway. Gavin hunched at the side table near the phone, evidently having just deleted two messages from the machine. While she watched, he picked up her blind-date-designated cell phone. He studied it, his face in profile. He pressed a few buttons.

The phone issued an instantly recognizable tone. Her unread incoming text messages had just been erased.

Carefully, Gavin set down her phone. He turned away, his posture tense as he swept his gaze over the kitchen peninsula.

Jennifer did the same. She saw two placemats with napkins and plates. A take-out donut bag. A water glass with two daisies propped in it. Matching coffee cups.

It all looked so very, very perfect.

And so completely, utterly wrong.

"Okay, all set," Gavin said under his breath.

He turned. His cheerful expression, so open and hopeful,

almost broke Jennifer's heart . . . but not as much as the guilt that transformed his features the moment he spotted her.

That was when it all hit her with sudden, unwanted clarity.

"*You're* the one," she said, trembling. She crossed her arms over herself, moving closer. "You're the one who's been sabotaging my blind dates! I thought it was Nyla."

She could hardly believe it. But he didn't deny it.

"Wait. Just hang on." Gavin held out his hands, palms up. His usual smile wobbled, then vanished. "I can explain everything, if you'll just—"

"It was all a big joke to you, wasn't it?" Unexpected tears scratched at her throat, making the words come out unevenly. No, no, no. She wasn't going to cry. "My self-discovery plan. You didn't care about it at all, did you?"

"Yes. No. I—what I care about is *you*. It's always been you. I—Jesus, Jen." Awkwardly, Gavin ran his hand through his hair, seemingly at a loss for words. His gaze shifted to the answering machine, then darkened. "Do you know how hard it was to see you go on date after date after—"

"Obviously, today wasn't going to be quite that tough for you." Feeling wounded, Jennifer glanced at the answering machine too. How many messages had he erased? How many opportunities had he cost her? "Was it?"

"That? The machine? It was just today. I thought—"

"Do you honestly expect me to believe that?"

Gavin's mouth tightened. "Would you *listen* to me, damn it? I'm trying to tell you that—"

"And I'm trying to tell *you* that you betrayed me!" Jennifer flung her hands in the air, striding toward him with a need to move, to vent, to do *something*. "How could you sabotage me like this, Gavin? How? I thought you knew me." She sucked in a deep, quavering breath. "I thought you knew how much this meant to me."

Silence. Gavin looked at her, taking in her bare feet, her hastily wrapped robe, her rampant bed-head hair. Something in his expression softened for an instant, but frustration quickly overrode everything else. His hands fisted.

"If you'd let me finish," he said slowly, keeping his gaze fixed staunchly on her, "I'd—"

But Jennifer had had enough. She couldn't just stand there, letting him lie to her. Letting him make a mockery out of her blind-dating plan—out of *her*.

"This was a mistake," she said, turning away. "I have someplace to be."

"Where?" Gavin demanded. "Damn it, Jen, don't just—"

She shut the bedroom door on whatever else he said. By the time Jennifer emerged again, wearing jeans and flip-flops and her old Sebastian International sweatshirt, the whole apartment was quiet. Had Gavin left? Feeling raw and exposed and defiant, she stormed down the hallway to find out.

Nope. He glanced up wearily from the sofa as she entered the living room. "Ready to talk yet?"

"Geez, more talking? Be a man, why don't you?"

She hadn't meant to say it so harshly—or at all. But the words found their mark, all the same. Gavin's face hardened.

"I *am* a man. A man who cares about you. And if you weren't so busy running around playing dress up—"

"Dress up? How *dare* you?"

"You might realize that. But you're so wrapped up in your 'plan,' you can't see what's right in front of you."

"Oh no." Jennifer advanced on him, her voice shaking. "You're not starting that up again. You can just keep your stupid surf wisdom to yourself. Because I'm sick of—"

"Maybe if you listened," Gavin said quietly, "I would."

How could he be so calm? So quiet? All the things she'd loved about him—his easygoing nature, his cheerfulness, his openness—suddenly seemed to mock her. To patronize her.

Jennifer shook her head. "I'm leaving."

Gavin's voice followed her to the door. "Maybe you should ask your friends to pick an exit strategy first. It might be tough on you to think for yourself."

Shocked, Jennifer stopped with her hand on the doorknob. That was a low blow. An obvious reference to her blind-dating plan—and the fact that her friends and coworkers had made suggestions for it. She couldn't believe he'd say such a thing.

But then, she couldn't believe he'd sabotage her either.

Obviously, when it came to Gavin, all her thought processes shut down completely. She couldn't be trusted with herself.

"Just think of this as me finally learning to go with the flow," she said, and opened the door. " 'Bye, Gavin."

Gavin listened to the apartment door whoosh open, hardly able to believe Jennifer was leaving. Now . . . after all they'd shared together. Feeling wrecked and empty, he stuck his head in his hands and scrubbed his face, trying to get a hold of himself.

It figured, he thought with unaccustomed bitterness. The one time he seized control of his destiny—of his destiny with the woman he'd been crazy about for years—and it came back to bite him in the ass. Hard. Life just wasn't fair.

"Hey, be careful!" came a familiar feminine voice from the doorway. "You almost bulldozed me."

Nyla. She laughed at Jennifer and pushed past her to get inside, forcing Jennifer to sidestep the huge burden of suitcases she carried. His sister didn't know the meaning of traveling light. Her tendency to pack for every possible contingency showed in the multiple bags she humped into the foyer, then dropped beside his waiting surfboards.

She brushed off her palms, then surveyed them both. Her sunny expression drooped. "What's going on?"

"We could ask you the same thing." Jennifer shot Gavin a wary look, then focused on Nyla. With apparent difficulty, she mustered a breezy tone. "Ummm, what happened to Monterey?"

"Allergic reaction to the strawberry-martini moisturizing body wrap." Nyla lifted her shirt, baring the vivid rash on her middle. "I decided to call it a day and come home for some calamine lotion."

"Ouch," Gavin and Jennifer said in unison, wincing.

"Yeah. All these food-based spa products definitely have their downside. But on the plus side, the spa comped my whole visit, so that's definitely going into my report." Nyla kicked the door shut, effectively—and obliviously—trapping Jennifer inside for at least another twenty seconds. "So . . . out with it, you two. What's going on here?"

Stubbornly, Gavin remained mute. So did Jennifer.

His sister eyeballed their jointly mulish expressions, then sighed. "If I didn't already think you two were perfect for each other, this display of idiot childishness would clinch it for sure. I guess this means you slept together, right?"

Jennifer stared out the window, tugging her sweatshirt.

Gavin kicked the coffee table, deliberately not thinking about last night. He wished he had a donut, but he refused to cave in to hunger first. If Jennifer could resist her favorite devil's food with vanilla glaze, so could he. Besides, he'd been too twisted in knots to eat anything.

Jennifer hefted her purse. "I'm leaving. 'Bye, Nyla."

"Oh no you don't." His sister slammed her hand on the door, keeping it closed. "Not until you tell me everything."

Then, to Gavin's dismay, Jennifer did. At length. With gusto and hand gestures and an alarming quantity of detail. She started with last night, detoured around the romantic parts in a way he felt profoundly grateful for—given who their audience was—and wrapped up with an accusatory, completely unrealistic retelling of the debacle this morning.

Afterward, Nyla crossed her arms, looking disappointed. Clearly, the women had banded together against him.

"Gavin, you should know better."

"It was only the one time!" He held up his hands, grumpily unprepared to be knocked around by his big sister *and* the woman he loved (and was losing), both in the same day. "Just today. I thought if I could clear Jen's schedule and have her all to myself, just this once, we could—"

"Well, *I* know *that*!" Nyla interrupted.

He gritted his teeth. "If I could just finish a damned sentence for a change—"

"Wait a minute," Jennifer butted in. "You *do?*"

"Of course." Nyla shooed away Jennifer's surprise—and Gavin's. "Who do you think was 'looming intimidatingly' over your shortie date, trying to discourage him? Who do you think was *not* passing on all those messages? All those flowers? Sheesh, Jen. Catch up, why don't you?"

Jennifer blinked, seeming discombobulated.

"You might remember," Nyla went on reasonably, "that I was never all that on board with your blind-date plan to begin with. It's not healthy to base your identity on a few outfits and a bunch of fix-ups. Besides, if you kept on dating all those guys, who knew how long it would take you to notice my brother?"

Gavin felt vindicated, if a little confused. He seized on the part he understood. "See? I wasn't sabotaging you, I—"

He was stopped by a wallop upside the head—from his sister, who rounded on him next.

"And *you!*" Nyla declared. "What's the matter with you?" She smacked him again for good measure, big-sister style. "Why didn't you just take Jennifer *out* someplace, away from the answering machine and the cell phone and the blind-dating thing, and have her all to yourself that way? I swear, for a nice guy and a good brother, sometimes you're really dense."

Gavin shot her an irritated look. "Because I had one of my Sunshine Pool Cleaning trucks with me," he muttered grudgingly, "instead of my van. That's why. It's parked around the corner. I just moved it out of sight this morning."

Jennifer stood by, obviously trying to keep up. "You had one of your whats?"

"Your *work* truck?" Nyla blurted. "Why did you have your work truck, when you just got downsized from your job?"

"Actually I . . . " *Oh hell.* Gavin *really* didn't want to go into this now. But everything else was falling apart, so he guessed he didn't have much more to lose. "I bought the company a while ago. I'd saved up some money with an eye toward Brett's retirement, and he was in favor of the idea, seeing as how I'd worked there so long and knew all the customers, and I figured, why not? I can't be a surf bum all my life." Defensively, he jutted his chin. "I've got a twenty-two-truck fleet, all over So Cal. I was going to tell you."

"You were going to tell me," Nyla repeated, in disbelief.

"Yeah, after . . . " He gestured futilely toward Jennifer. "After I could explain it all. I needed an excuse to stay here, because of—" *Because of Jennifer.* He broke off with a biting obscenity. "Never mind, there's no point in explaining."

"That's why I didn't hear your van," Jennifer marveled. "That's why you weren't worried about finding a new job!" Her eyes narrowed. "That's why it was so easy for you to tell me to take things as they came. Everything was going *right* for you!" She hesitated. "And to think I felt sorry for you."

He saw everything flash through her mind. Bobby calling him "boss" at the restaurant. His old clothes, smelling of chlorine and worn last night because he'd been working on a pool-cleaning job after hours. All the time he'd had for surfing and guitar playing and spending afternoons with her.

"It took some juggling," Gavin protested. "It wasn't easy. Keeping everything together, keeping everything a secret—"

"Yeah," Jennifer scoffed, looking hurt, "I'll bet that was *really* tough for you."

Gavin gave her a long look. He was a patient guy, but this was more than he could stand. It didn't take a genius to see that things had wound up pretty lopsided—and not in his favor either.

"It *was* tough," he said honestly. "I thought it would be worth it. But now . . . I'm done."

He stood, then stopped in front of Jennifer. She wrinkled her nose, looking bewildered, gobsmacked . . . and beautiful. Looking like everything he'd ever wanted and couldn't have.

"Wait," she said. "I'm still trying to figure out—"

Gavin shook his head. "If you decide one man is better than thirty, you know where to find me."

Four steps later, he was out the door.

For the next few days, all Jennifer wanted to do was wallow in misery. Despite everything, she missed Gavin. That was the plain truth. She missed nightly beer-and-talking dates with him. She missed hearing him playing his guitar whenever she was at home. And even though he'd hurt her, she couldn't get over how empty everything felt without him.

The sofa seemed freakishly sleek and smooth without Gavin to rumple it. The foyer seemed ridiculously empty without Gavin to prop his surfboards in it. The skies seemed dark and the nights seemed long, and her final two blind dates loomed on the horizon with depressingly little hope of self-revelation to offer—especially without Gavin there to help her analyze them.

And—let's face it—to offer perspective too.

"I'm really sorry," Nyla said while Jennifer prepped for a rerun date with Mitch—who, it turned out, had tried to meet her at the wrong Borders. "I had the best of intentions all along, I swear. I didn't mean for things to get so out of hand. I didn't know you were so serious about everything!"

Jennifer *had* been serious. About Gavin, most of all.

"It's all right." After several long talks, she and Nyla had come to an understanding, thanks to long friendship and a commiserating shopathon. "You were kind of stuck in the middle, after all. None of us thought things would turn out this way."

Stephanie handed her a tube of Lancôme lip gloss in vivid, shiny pink. She'd been called in for emergency girlfriend-in-trouble duty, and had stayed loyally nearby all day.

"You could just give up on the blind-dating thing," she suggested with concern, "if it's making you so miserable."

Jennifer sucked in a breath. "No. I can't. I owe it to Mitch to show up." She thought about it some more, then realized something even more important. "I owe it to *myself* to show up—to see this thing through, the way I said I would."

Nyla frowned. "It's not exactly helping you 'find yourself,' " she pointed out. "You told us the other day that it's been more about learning what *isn't* you than what *is*."

"Yeah," Stephanie agreed. "The best decisions aren't always the most researched ones, you know." She handed over a gleaming compact of Nars Orgasm blush. "There's a lot to be said for the power of intuition. For doing what *feels* right."

Jennifer stared at the blush. That might be as close as she got to a "good time" for quite a while, if she didn't . . . No, she refused to go there. No matter how right and wonderful being with Gavin had felt, she was moving on. Starting now.

She only wished she could move on *with* him.

"Nope. I've only got two more dates to go, and I'm finishing them," she said. "Don't wait up."

"You're going to lose her," Nyla prodded, unexpectedly showing up to haunt Gavin for the second day in a row. "She's not waiting around, moping, like you are."

He shrugged irritably, dragging on his thickest Baja-style pullover in an attempt to warm up. All around him, the oceanside park was green and sunny and picturesquely dotted with quirky Torrey pine trees. It was also blissfully quiet, except for his sister's nonstop yammering.

"Tell me again. Did I ask you to come out here?"

"No. And it was a bitch to find you, believe me." Nyla poked him. "Since when do you surf all the way out here?"

He stared over the cliffs. Surf spray splashed, almost reaching the sun bleached fence they leaned on. "I always surf Sunset Cliffs. The waves are good here."

"Not lately, you don't. You're avoiding Jennifer."

Gavin gazed out to sea and offered a choice expletive.

Nyla smacked his arm. "Don't talk to your sister that way! I'm trying to help."

"Then leave me alone."

"I can't. You'll be miserable without Jennifer."

He heaved a sigh. "I'll be fine."

Although, given the way he'd been feeling lately, he doubted it. Usually, whenever he had problems in his life, Gavin could always paddle out and forget everything. Surfing had always been there for him in a way he couldn't explain. But now . . . now even the demands of surfing weren't enough. He still wanted Jennifer, and he couldn't forget *her*.

"Come back," Nyla urged. "Make a stand! I'm telling you, one of those stupid blind dates is going to steal her away."

"Nyla—"

"Date number 30 owns a nightclub downtown." His sister named the place, recently opened and wildly successful. She spilled all the details. "Jason will be tough competition. You should definitely get to Jennifer beforehand."

Closing his eyes against the brisk offshore wind, Gavin considered it. He imagined himself . . . Jennifer . . . The two of them, happy and together again.

It was what he wanted more than anything. Almost.

He opened his eyes. Shook his head. "No."

His sister stared at him. The breeze, chilly despite the sunshine, tousled her hair. Her teeth chattered.

Gavin hauled off his pullover. "Take this. You're cold."

Nyla rolled her eyes. Then, wordlessly, she grabbed it. The handwoven knit hung past her wrists and down to her hips, but within moments, she'd quit shivering. Gavin nodded, satisfied. They leaned on the fence together, side by side, watching the waves. Salt spray tickled their cheeks.

"Why can't she just give it up?" Gavin heard himself ask. Bone-deep despair welled inside him, untouchable but real. "Why can't Jennifer just quit going on those dates and accept that she is who she is? Period?"

Nyla gazed steadily at him. "Why can't you quit surfing?"

Her question gnawed. "That's not the same thing."

"It's not? Really?" A pause. "How, exactly?"

Exasperated and pained, Gavin frowned. The last thing he

needed right now was a smart-ass big sister. Nyla had been wrong about that whole "Your face will freeze that way" thing when they were kids, and she'd been wrong about the likelihood of his being caught ditching school to beat the high score on Galaxian in seventh grade, and she was wrong about this too.

"Nobody likes a know-it-all," he muttered.

"Oh yeah?" Nyla poked him. "Tell it to Jennifer."

"Fine!" Gavin yelled. He gestured out to sea, his whole body striving to explain himself. "Surfing is about being free. It's about proving you can handle whatever the ocean throws at you. It's about challenging yourself."

"Yeah?" Nyla raised her eyebrows. Aggravatingly.

"It's about finding out what you're made of," he explained in a ragged voice, "and it's damned important."

Gavin thought that was a pretty triumphant finale, an excellent summation of the appeal of surfing. But his sister only nodded indifferently. Then she turned away again, resting her forearms on the splintery fence.

A minute passed. Silently, accusatorially.

"What is the *matter* with you?" he groused.

"Me?" Nyla shrugged. "Nothing. You're the one who's denying reality, *brah*." Deliberately, she nudged him. "Want the address of the nightclub? It's at the corner of—"

"No, I don't want the address. Haven't you heard a word I've been—" Abruptly, Gavin broke off. Something echoed at the back of his mind, something meaningful and necessary. Something crucial. Something *parallel*. "Holy shit."

"Yeah," Nyla said. "You've got some decisions to make."

Then she left him alone, finally, to make them.

By the time Jennifer's thirtieth blind date rolled around, she'd expected to feel accomplished. Satisfied. Filled with new-found self-knowledge and possessed of a clever answer to that goading question: *Who do you want to be today?*

Instead, as she hurried along Fifth Avenue—past bustling restaurants with trendy interiors and Gaslamp Quarter façades—she merely felt confused, and discouraged. Despite all her efforts, she wasn't much closer to understanding who she really was. She'd dated, she'd sampled, she'd tried on. But all she'd emerged with were a few crazy memories, one unforgettable fling, and a broken heart. Not exactly what she'd had in mind.

Shaking her hair away from her face, Jennifer peered past the crowd up the dark, neon-spangled street, girding her resolve for the evening to come. Jason's nightclub, Luxe, was on the next corner, and he'd promised to meet her outside. She was still too far away to make him out though. There were too many people waiting outside the much-profiled, cozy-chic space.

A few steps took her closer. Then, amid the bent heads and shuffling bodies, she glimpsed a grinning man with blond hair.

Gavin? Jennifer stopped cold, letting the crowd on the sidewalk surge past her. She squinted intently, feeling her heart kick into high gear. If he was here . . .

Adrenaline pumped through her with abandon, setting her in motion again. A smile pushed its way onto her face, despite her best efforts to stay calm. If Gavin was here . . .

But he wasn't. The man turned just as she reached him, revealing a different set of features and a broad smile. He wasn't Gavin, but he *was* almost equally gorgeous, outfitted in what had to be the latest in Urban Hunk from Milan.

Confusingly he held out his hand. "Jennifer! I knew that must be you. I'm Jason."

Jennifer and Jason. They were practically preordained via popular baby-naming books and Hallmark cards. Or something.

He enveloped her hand warmly in both of his, leading her into Luxe. Heads turned as they entered, then followed them to a special table he'd doubtless set aside. Jason ushered her into a chair, his smile warm and his hand courteous on her back.

"I'm so glad you came." He settled in the chair opposite her, then regarded her with a sincere—and wildly flattering—expression of interest. "What would you like to drink?"

In short order, Jennifer found herself with a caramel apple-tini, swept up in an intimate, funny conversation with a man who couldn't get enough of talking to her. Jason clearly commanded respect from his staff and camaraderie from his friends and patrons, but he didn't seem caught up in the flurry of activity and decisions and local hipsters "just dropping by." He seemed interested only in getting to know *her*, and the sensation was amazingly gratifying.

Or would have been, had Jennifer had any enthusiasm for being there. But her heart had sunk the moment she'd realized Jason wasn't Gavin, and recovering from that proved tricky.

Trying her best, she toyed with the toothpick-anchored, caramel-and-green apple garnish on her martini. She asked Jason questions and answered his inquiries with as much aplomb as she could muster. She even managed a few smiles. But through it all, Jennifer felt increasingly dispirited.

This—however perfect it seemed—wasn't what she wanted.

It was, however, what she'd promised to do, she reminded herself with staunch resolve. Thirty men in thirty days. End of story. If nothing else, by the end of the night she'd see her project through. Because *she*, despite her faults, was a woman who finished what she started.

The thought stopped her cold, her appletini halfway to her lips. She *was* a woman who finished what she started, Jennifer realized with a surge of pride.

She put down her drink, sideswiped by the realization.

In addition to that, she was a person who made decisions. A person who laughed and cried and sometimes ate vending-machine peanut butter crackers for dinner. She was a person who liked to cut hair, to give highlights, to see a client's face light up when she saw her new 'do for the first time.

Jason went on talking. He went on smiling and touching her hand, but suddenly his voice was indistinct and his face was as blurry as the garbled background of an experimental indie movie. Because Jennifer was caught up in a series of revelations she couldn't quite stop and didn't really want to.

She was a person who cherished her job and her friends (but not in that order), she realized. She was a person who licked off the Oreo filling but skipped the cookies, who indulged in nice sheets but bought cute knockoff shoes at half price, who believed in honesty but not in gossip. She was a person who had never, for a single moment, been afraid to try something new.

She was *all* those things. And more. Much more.

She might not discover all of herself right now. Or next week. Or even—especially—on some arbitrary, quarter-life-crisis-busting schedule, dictated by a stupid lipstick ad.

But she would do it eventually.

And for now, Jennifer decided, maybe that was enough.

" . . . which is an *incredible* coincidence," Jason was saying. He gave her a kind, fascinated look. "What do you think?"

"I'm sorry." With her first genuine smile of the night, Jennifer put her hand on his wrist. It felt nice and manly and definitely well-groomed—and his fancy watch was impressive too—but she just didn't care. Jason was another in a long line of *not*-the-real-her encounters, and not only because her nightclub-appropriate shoes were already giving her blisters. "I just remembered. I have someplace else I have to be tonight. I'm really very sorry. You seem like a very nice man."

Then she shot back the rest of her appletini—for courage—threw a twenty on the table, and bolted outside for her car.

Wet and cold and worried, Gavin paced along the boardwalk outside Nyla and Jennifer's apartment. He'd abandoned his surfboard a half hour ago, after a disastrous attempt to catch a head-clearing wave had ended in a bone-jarring wipeout instead, letting him know for sure that his wrecked state of mind was not an illusion.

He really *was* a gigantic mess.

He missed Jennifer. It was as simple as that. He missed her smiles and her laughter and her crazy backward way of doing things. He missed her touch. He missed her Chips Ahoy! stash and her marathon sessions of *The O.C.* He missed her weird decorating. He missed *her*. End of story.

Gavin stopped, squinted down the boardwalk, then paced some more. No sign of Jennifer yet. To hear Nyla tell it, this guy Jason—her nightclub owner turned blind date number 30—was like a gazillionaire playboy with morals and manners. Like a chick flick Mr. Perfect and a sweet, down-home guy, all rolled into (as a certain *Union-Tribune* profile had put it) one "drool-worthy entrepreneurial package."

"Jason is, like, absolutely breathtaking," Nyla had gushed.

Given that his sister actually used the word *breathtaking* without irony, Gavin knew there was no way in hell he could seriously compete.

Not because this Jason person was loaded, idiotically handsome, and freak-of-nature nice. But because if Jennifer wanted breathtaking, if *breathtaking* would make her happy, then she deserved a shot at it. And Gavin intended to give her that, without interference. Even though his heart might crack in two in the process.

Because in the end, he'd realized, surfing and blind dating were both about the same thing: taking a chance. And if he couldn't give Jennifer the same freedom *he* needed, the same freedom *he* enjoyed, then they didn't have the future together that Gavin hoped they did. That was all there was to it.

Although he'd still rather eat surfwax than set foot in a frou-frou place like Luxe. A man like him didn't need the aggravation, the overpriced drinks, the dress code.

Unless Jennifer wanted to go, Gavin amended. Then he'd do it. He'd probably even wear a suit, if she wanted. With a tie.

Christ. He really had it bad.

He hoped like hell she got here before he was forced to consider real shoes instead of flip-flops.

The walk to Jennifer's car took eons. The drive home, through twisty, tourist-packed San Diego streets, took even longer. But the whole way, Nyla's parting words rang in her ears, offering more hope than Jennifer probably had a right to.

Oh . . . and Gavin might be dropping by later, her roommate had casually said, offering a grin. *You know. To see how your final blind date went.*

At the time, Jennifer hadn't been ready to consider what that meant. But now . . . now she hoped, and she clutched her steering wheel in a finger-tingling grasp as she veered into a hard-won parking space on a side street. She vaulted out of the car and followed the sound of the ocean, catching glimpses of the surf between close-cramped houses and pastel apartments.

She refused to consider that she might be too late. She was a person who valued punctuality, Jennifer recognized about herself, still clip-clopping toward the boardwalk. And she would never be late to something this crucial.

Hey, that was something else she'd learned, she realized. She was introspective, with more varied and identifiable "real her" qualities than she'd ever dreamed.

All she'd needed to do was appreciate them.

Waves crashed, all but daring her to come closer. To finish what she'd started—for real, this time. If she was lucky, Gavin would be waiting for her. Sucking in a breath, Jennifer shuffled off her high heels and carried them instead.

She broke into a run, her heart pounding in a way spinning class had never accomplished.

Then she saw him. Gavin stood at the seawall with his hair wild and his shoulders straight, his whole body emanating hope and worry and a macho effort to cover up both, all at the same time. Remarkably, he wasn't looking at the waves.

He was looking at her.

His smile, broad and sudden and disbelieving, urged her to go faster. So did her heart. What Jennifer hadn't counted on—what she *should* have counted on—was that Gavin met her halfway.

"I'm a person who loves the ocean," she blurted as she

stopped, dropping her shoes and catching hold of his shirt-front for balance. "I just realized it, just this minute. I love the ocean, and the color fuchsia, and those little cherries they put on the sundaes at the Ghirardelli shop downtown."

"Maraschino cherries," Gavin supplied gravely.

He looked at her as though seeing her for the first time. Somehow, Jennifer thought, she *felt* brand-new too.

"Maraschino cherries. Yes! Those," she agreed, too excited and relieved and happy to stop now. Geez, he felt good and warm beneath her hands. "And I love stupid dance songs, and putting on my fuzzy slippers after a long day of styling hair, and seeing my mom smile when she talks about her disastrous honeymoon with my dad in Napa."

"Fuzzy slippers, huh?" Gavin echoed. "Sexy."

Somehow, Jennifer thought, he made the idea sound believable. Maybe Gavin *would* find her sexy in pink poly-fuzz.

Maybe they would find out.

"Mmmm-hmmm," she agreed, bedazzled.

They gazed at each other, with the surf pounding and the seagulls squawking and the tourists running in and out of the tide. It felt as if they were alone, though, and it felt pretty damned phenomenal too.

"Are you ever going to kiss me?" Jennifer asked.

It seemed pretty obvious to her what she was there for.

"I don't know. Would it violate your sense of freedom and adventure?" Gavin took a single step closer, his gaze traveling down their bodies to the place where their arms nearly touched. He caught her hand in his. "Because I've been damn near killing myself to make sure you get what you need—Mr. Perfect McMoneypants included—and there's no way I'm blowing it now."

Huh? *Mr. Perfect McM*— Ahhh . . . Jason.

Jennifer almost guffawed at the idea of herself choosing anyone except the man in front of her. But Gavin looked so serious, so scared and determined and wonderful, that she just couldn't do it to him.

Solemnly, she squeezed his hand instead. "Why would I want him? You're *breathtaking*."

Gavin tried to look suspicious. Even skeptical. Which, given what she'd said, didn't make much sense at all.

But his broad smile and aw-shucks look completely destroyed the whole effect. "Breathtaking?"

Jennifer nodded. "Every minute of every day. I'm sorry it took me so long to realize it."

"I'm sorry I messed with your plan," Gavin said. "I swear I never meant to hurt you."

She leaned upward and kissed him. "All's forgiven."

But Gavin resisted, and their kiss was short. "So in the interest of full disclosure," he said, "I've got to tell you . . ."

"What? Your superserious expression is freaking me out."

When he hesitated, Jennifer gazed at him worriedly. Was he a surfing addict? A closet workaholic? A chronic hair-gel user?

"I really *hate* those maraschino cherries."

Relief flooded through her. "Good. More for me."

"You know I'll share," Gavin promised.

And this time, their kiss was real, thorough and magical and filled with the possibility of more. More love, more togetherness, more discovery. Just more. And it reminded Jennifer of something else—something important.

"I love you, Gavin. I really, really do."

He cupped her face in his hands, his newfound solemnity vanishing beneath a happiness that must have felt exactly like hers. The two of them were probably insufferable to innocent passers-by who *weren't* head-over-heels in love, but Jennifer didn't care. Their turns would come—she believed it.

"I love you too." Gavin nodded. "Enough to wear a tie."

His next kiss delayed her inevitable neckwear question, and Jennifer dizzily decided she'd find out later what he meant. For now, being with him was enough. That, and strolling along the boardwalk hand in hand—Gavin chivalrously carrying her shoes—like a pair of those gushy Borders wedding-book buyers.

She was definitely introducing Gavin to those chocolate-covered graham crackers sometime soon.

Moments later, they paused beside Gavin's surfboard, instantly recognizable to Jennifer and obviously abandoned for her sake. She gave it a mischievous grin, struck with an idea.

"Hmmm," she mused, tugging Gavin nearer. "A surfboard."

"Uh-oh," he said. "I smell another plan brewing."

Jennifer shrugged. "This one's *really* good."

"Mmmm-hmmm." His smile said it all. He'd stick by her, whatever it was—and however crazy it happened to be.

"You know, I've spent all this time hanging out with surfers," she continued, "and I've never actually learned to ride the waves myself. Can you believe that?"

Gavin's grin broke wider. "I guess somebody's going to have to teach you how. Somebody like me."

Jennifer agreed, nodding happily.

Then they bypassed his board and sat on the seawall to watch the stars, talking until they laughed themselves silly. Because with a future like theirs waiting . . . they had all the time in the world to savor the journey.